MW01146894

Amish Weddings
Collection

Contains ALL 6 books

Copyright © 2017 by Samantha Bayarr

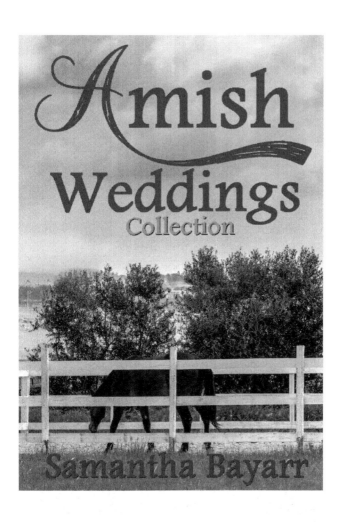

Contains ALL 6 Books

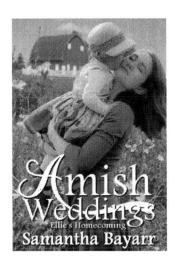

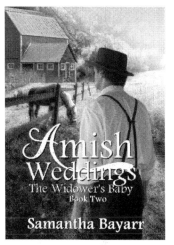

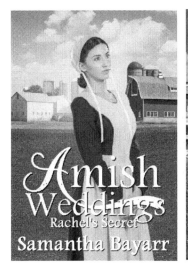

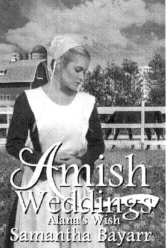

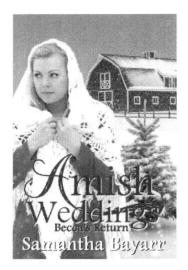

Amish Weddings
Becca's Return
Samantha Bayarr

Amish Weddings
A Christmas Wedding
Samantha Bayarr

Amish Weddings

Ellie's Homecoming
Book One

Samantha Bayarr

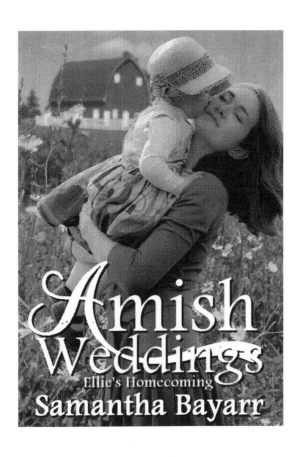

Amish
Weddings
Ellie's Homecoming
Samantha Bayarr

Chapter 1

Ellie bounced little Katie lightly in her arms, trying to coax her back to sleep, while staring at the wedding invitation in her hand. Why had her *mamm* sent it when she knew Jonas had been her first and only love? Her *mamm* knew the history; knew that he'd made his choice to marry Hannah instead. It had broken Ellie's heart, but the real damage had already been done, and she hadn't realized it until weeks after she'd left the community. That afternoon she'd spent in the hayloft with Jonas trying to convince him to change his mind and leave the community with her had only resulted in the *boppli* she now held in her arms. But it had left her with more than that. She'd suffered heartache and shame, and in the end, made the difficult decision to raise the child on her own.

She thought Jonas would have married Hannah that very next month after she'd left, but instead had made her wait more than two years. Ellie had to wonder if he'd waited for her to return all that time, and when she hadn't, she supposed he'd given up on her.

Knowing Jonas had a right to know he had a daughter, this trip home was not going to be easy, but she was not going to break up his marriage if he was truly happy with Hannah.

Since she'd managed to keep little Katie a secret even from her *mamm,* as time went by, it became easier to keep it from her. She didn't expect that Jonas knew, or he'd likely have come looking for her. If *daed* were still alive, she'd not have dared to step foot back on the homestead, but *mamm* had been all alone after she'd left the community. Her twin brother, Eli and his wife, Lydia, who had married just before she'd left, were nearly ready to have their first child. *Mamm* had written her about her excitement over being a *grossmammi* in one of the many letters of correspondence to her in the time that she'd been away. She'd wished more than anything that she'd had the nerve to write in her return letter about little Katie, but she lost her nerve every time she began that letter. Now, as she sat at the train station waiting for the cab to take her home, she wished she'd said something—anything that would prepare her *mamm* for the shock that could hurt Katie.

Would *mamm* welcome another grandchild? Would her own brother refuse to allow little Katie to grow up alongside her new cousin? They were all questions that put fearful butterflies in the pit of her stomach. Not the happy fluttery kind she used to get when Jonas would kiss her. These were the ones that made her shake and shiver at the slightest autumn breeze that cooled the perspiration from her cheeks.

The bigger question on the forefront of her mind at the moment; the one that caused her much more anxiety than coming home with a *boppli* in her arms, was the wedding invitation. Hannah was her best friend, and Jonas had been the love of her life ever since they were old enough to walk and talk. But her decision to spend her *rumspringa* among the *Englischers* had been what had caused her to lose her best friend and her would-be husband forever.

Why couldn't Jonas have gone with her the way she'd begged him to? He'd threatened he would marry Hannah if she left, and she'd foolishly challenged him, hoping in the back of her mind he would follow her, run after her, and beg her to come back, or at the very least, wait for her.

He hadn't done anything but choose to marry Hannah just as he'd threatened, and it had broken her heart. Now, as she looked at his wedding invitation, she felt fresh hurt writhing in her gut, rolling around like hot coals in her *mamm's* old cook-stove.

Little Katie's breath hitched from crying so much; she hadn't liked the train ride, and it had upset her stomach so much she drooled a bit of milk on Ellie's shoulder. Her Mennonite cousin, Esther, had cried when they'd left the city. She'd taken Ellie into her home when she first realized she was pregnant. Esther had advised her to go home and tell Jonas about the baby then, but she was too concerned with being shunned by her strict Amish *familye*.

She wished she'd taken that advice.

Ellie closed her eyes against the warm, afternoon sun, remembering the last day she'd seen Jonas. Over the past couple of years, she'd tried to put that rainy afternoon in the barn out of her mind. She'd struggled to forget it, but every gurgle from little Katie brought that day fresh in her mind as if it was only yesterday. Never would she have dreamed things would go that far with her and Jonas. Afterward, it had been awkward. With the passion between them spent, Jonas quickly realized what a mistake it had been, and tried to make excuses for losing control of his emotions the way he had. Ellie had certainly taken it personally, believing he wished it had not happened.

She cuddled her daughter, knowing because of Katie, she could never regret that day. Her only regret had been in leaving the community, and it was too late to take it back now.

A taxi pulled up in front of the bench she rested on in front of the train station. His brakes squeaked as he came to a complete stop, and the tailpipe rattled and sputtered as if it might just fall off if he hit a bump in the road. Thick smoke trailed from the pipe, causing Ellie to rise from the bench and cough at the smell of exhaust. She covered little Katie's face with her blanket to shield her from the smell, as she motioned to the driver to get her bags that lay on the bench where she'd been sitting.

He snuffed out the butt of a cigar with a clunky brown shoe, and grunted as he bent down and grabbed for her bags. His button-down, short-sleeved Hawaiian shirt puckered at every button over the girth of his belly that protruded over the waist of his Bermuda shorts.

"You travel pretty light with that baby, Miss," he said as he picked up her bags. "You must not be planning on visiting long."

She nodded and forced a smile.

She hadn't thought about how long she would stay; she'd only thought about whether or not she'd be welcome. Fresh anxiety filled her as she watched the driver pick up the car seat and buckle it into the back seat as if he'd done it a thousand times for the passengers before her. Katie didn't even wake up as she strapped her in, and then tugged on the seat to make sure it was secure. Katie was oblivious to the trouble they could be walking into, and Ellie suddenly wondered why she was putting herself through all of this.

She kissed little Katie's soft cheek and buckled herself in next to the child, reminding herself she had to put away her own fears for the sake of her daughter. She and her father had a right to know one another, even if that meant Ellie, herself, had to endure a little pain to make it happen for them. Her life was no longer her own, and for that reason, she would do anything for her daughter.

Chapter 2

Before she was ready to face it, the taxi pulled into the driveway Ellie hadn't seen in over two years. She paused before getting out of the cab, looking out at the house she hadn't stepped foot in for the same amount of time. Maybe she was being silly, but the trees seemed to have grown several feet, and the grass seemed a little thicker, perhaps because her brother hadn't cut it as often as he should.

The cherry tree on the side yard that her *daed* always carefully pruned and babied had grown a little out of control. The cherries had been picked from the lower branches, indicating her *mamm* had likely used them for a few pies, or perhaps a few jars of preserves, but the rest remained on the top limbs of the large tree, where birds fought over the fruit. Her *daed* would have never let the tree get to that condition if he were still alive, but she supposed her *mamm* had done the best she could.

All was quiet, except the familiar squeak of the windmill near the barn. She listened to the constant click, click, click, as it turned in the slight breeze. Her *daed* had promised to fix it just before he'd died, and afterward, her *mamm* would not let her brother repair it. She knew it reminded her mother of her father, and she'd stated more than once that every time she heard it, she could hear his voice right along with it promising her he'd fix it just as soon as he had the time. With him growing weaker from the cancer that had consumed his liver, fixing the windmill had been the last thing on his mind. And now, as Ellie listened to it, the sound almost brought her the same comfort.

She lifted little Katie from her car seat and stepped out of the vehicle, closing the bulky door a little hard. The noise startled the birds, causing them to scatter from the cherry tree and squawk their annoyance with her. She giggled slightly remembering the day her *daed* had offered to pay her a whole dollar to be a scarecrow under the tree. She was only ten years old, and had wanted some candy at the store in town so badly; she'd stayed out there *cawing* almost all day, despite her brother making fun of her. The following day, she was so sore from flapping her arms to shoo away the birds, she told her *daed* she didn't want to be a scarecrow anymore, but he'd given her the dollar just as he'd promised.

After that, she decided it was easier to stick to gathering the eggs for the morning meal. From the time she'd been big enough to walk, *mamm* had trusted her with the chore; the chickens being her responsibility. But from that day on, she stuck to taking the extra eggs to their *Englisch* neighbors for the quarter they'd *tip* her for walking them over.

Ellie took in a deep breath and swallowed the lump in her throat. Now was not the time for remembering her *daed;* she needed to prepare herself for the possibility her *mamm* would not welcome her home.

The taxi driver had set her bags and Katie's car seat in the grassy area beside the gravel driveway. She handed him the money for the fare and asked him not to leave—just in case she wouldn't be staying.

Lifting her eyes toward the house, she noted the front porch was in need of sweeping, and the windows in need of washing. Had her *mamm* let things go to such an extent that she didn't even keep up with her regular chores anymore? Or perhaps her mother was ill and had not mentioned it in any of her letters. She knew her mother had still been slightly depressed when Ellie had decided to leave for her *rumspringa*, but the heartbroken woman had urged her to go anyway.

Her *mamm* had missed out on her own *rumspringa* because she had married her father at such a young age. She'd never regretted the decision. However, she'd still urged Ellie to explore the world a little before getting married to Jonas. Ellie sighed, wondering if she could use that as an argument in case her mother rejected little Katie. She knew it wasn't her mother's fault that she'd gotten pregnant, because it had happened before she'd left for her *rumspringa*.

Had Ellie known at the time she left that she was with child, she likely would not have gone. But after three months had passed, she found out the news. At that point, she worried about coming back to the community and finding Jonas had married Hannah, and knew it would break her heart that much more. And so she stayed away, and never said a word about it to her mother. Weeks had turned into months, and the months somehow got away from her, turning into years.

Jonas's wedding invitation was the first mention of him since she'd left. She'd made her *mamm* promise she would not discuss him in order to give Ellie the time she needed for her *rumspringa* without feeling guilty that she'd left him behind.

Not only that, her mother had reminded her of his threat, and told her that if he followed through with that threat he wasn't worth wasting any tears on. She told her daughter just before she left *"Don't shed any tears over anyone who wouldn't shed any for you."*

Her *mamm* was always wise like that, and full of advice for her, but taking her *rumspringa* was one bit of advice she wished she would've ignored.

It was too late for all of that now; the damage was done, and could not be undone.

Leaving her bags near the driveway, Ellie put Katie over her shoulder and walked up onto the wraparound porch of her childhood home. She sighed, pulling in a ragged breath as she lifted her hand to knock on the door. Before her knuckles met with the heavy wooden door, it flew open unexpectedly; her *mamm* standing before her with a surprised expression.

Ellie stood there staring at the woman, whose tired eyes darted between her and the little girl in her arms, and then back again to look at her straight on. Though her *mamm* had aged, the familiar look of *home* in her eyes was enough to bring tears to her eyes.

Her *mamm* stepped back after a moment's pause, as if to invite Ellie inside the house, but couldn't find her voice.

"You must be tired from the long journey from Ohio," the woman finally said, stumbling over her words.

She smiled nervously, avoiding asking about the baby.

Ellie stepped inside the house feeling suddenly very out of sorts in the place she used to call home.

Maybe this was a bad idea, she thought to herself. *But it's too late to turn back now, she's already seen her.*

Little Katie hiccupped and then began to cry, likely sensing her mother's nervousness. Ellie's *mamm* looked at her, and then held her arms out awkwardly toward the *boppli*. Ellie relinquished Katie into her *mamm's* arms, but still the woman had said nothing about her.

Ellie watched as her *mamm* cradled her daughter, jostling her slightly and cooing to her. She immediately stopped crying and she raised her gaze toward her own daughter.

Feeling terrified to even breathe, Ellie stood in front of her *mamm* paralyzed, feeling as if she'd just gotten caught stealing an extra cookie when she was five years old.

Her *mamm* looked back down into little Katie's face, her eyes wide open and looking at the woman. "If I'm not mistaken," she said to little Katie. "I think I'm your *grossmammi*."

Ellie let out the breath she been holding in as if she'd never breathe again, blowing out a sigh of relief.

"*Jah*," she said awkwardly. "She is *mei dochder*."

Her *mamm* rolled her eyes upward, narrowing them as if she were thinking. "And I'm guessing by her age, she's Jonas's *dochder* as well."

"Jah, Mamm, she is," Ellie said.

"What do you plan to do about it?" her *mamm* asked in her matter-of-fact way.

"I wish I knew," Ellie said. "But I think my biggest worry right at the moment," she admitted, "is whether or not I should get my bags off the front lawn and bring them in."

Her *mamm* smiled, tears welling up in her eyes. She held her arms out to her daughter and pulled her close, kissing her hair. "*Wilkum* home, *dochder,*" she said. "*Wilkum* home."

Chapter 3

Jonas finished shaving, and then took a good hard look at himself in the small mirror in his bathroom. If something didn't change for him soon, if God didn't answer his prayer, this might be one of the last times he would ever shave his face in full again.

He'd thought many times about backing out of his pact with Hannah, but he most certainly didn't want to grow too old without the opportunity to start a family and be married. He couldn't help but feel that marrying her was not the right thing to do. Not when he still carried so much love for Ellie. They were supposed to be married and have a family—and grow old together. That was the plan his entire life. They likely would have celebrated an anniversary, and possibly the birth of a child by now if she hadn't left.

When she left, everything changed for him.

His future was about as unstable as a person's life could get. He was about to marry a woman he didn't love, and have a family with her. What had he been thinking when he'd agreed to such a thing?

He'd been grieving, that was for certain.

Grieving for the loss of the love of his life, and he'd agreed to such a plan hoping it would ease the pain, but it hadn't. It had only brought him new grief.

Was it fair to Hannah to keep it from her that he had sent for Ellie? He'd hoped that seeing her again would either give him the closure he desperately needed, or he would know once and for all that his love for her was still so genuine he couldn't live without her.

But what if she didn't come to see him? What if she decided to ignore the invitation and let him marry Hannah?

He dried his face and took one last look at his clean-shaven face.

At least then, I'll know for sure.

He went out to the kitchen of the house he'd built hoping his Ellie would return to him and marry him, suddenly realizing Hannah would soon be making this kitchen her own.

Pouring himself a cup of coffee, he stood at the window and stared out at the spot where he'd started a kitchen garden for Ellie, and the chickens that roamed the yard that she'd been so eager to raise. Everything about this house had been made with Ellic in mind, and now, another woman was about to invade those future dreams they'd shared so long ago.

Though Ellie had never spent a single minute at this house, there wasn't one part of it that didn't remind him of her. He'd laid awake many a night in the room he'd hoped to share with her, thinking about what their children would look like, and how many grandchildren would eventually fill the house with an equal amount of noise.

He felt sad as he thought about not having a little Ellie running around this house. He supposed he and Hannah might eventually grow their relationship enough to include a few children. But what if they didn't? He wasn't even certain if he was going to sleep in his own bed after the wedding. He knew the right thing to do would be to offer to sleep in one of the many rooms in the house until they got to know one another better, but he wasn't exactly eager to make the offer. She'd expect to be able to use the master bedroom. It would be her right to do so, but it hardly seemed fair to him. After all, it was *his* home that she was invading.

I suppose it will be her home too once we get married.

Lord, I'm not sure I'm ready for this. I pray you'll intervene and show me the right thing to do. I don't want to hurt Hannah, but you know my heart, Lord. You know I'll never be able to love Hannah the way I love Ellie.

An unexpected tear streamed down his cheek and he swiped at it angrily. Before the day was through, he had to tell Hannah the truth, whether Ellie returned or not.

He just wasn't ready to put away his feelings and marry another woman, no matter how practical it seemed.

His heart just wasn't in it.

Chapter 4

Fifteen-year-old Rachel went running into the house, yelling for her sister. She ran up the stairs calling for her, when the sound of her mother's voice stopped her.

"Don't run in the haus!" her *mamm's* memory scolded her.

Rachel ignored her mother's haunting voice that came from deep within her grieving heart, continuing to run up the remainder of the stairs until she found her sister. She paused to watch Hannah making the beds with the fresh linens from the clothesline. Her sister looked so much like their *mamm* she could almost trick her mind into believing the woman had not recently gone to Heaven, but she had, and Hannah had tried to fill the gap for her as best she could.

She ignored the thought of her *mamm* the same as she had for close to two years since she'd been gone.

"You'll never guess who's back!" she said, gasping for breath.

Hannah waited impatiently just the way her *mamm* would have, waiting for her little sister to catch her breath before answering.

"Our cousins just told me your old friend, Ellie, is here visiting her *mamm,* and she's brought a *boppli* with her!"

Hannah dropped the pillow onto the bed and grabbed her sister by her shoulders, forcing her to look her in the eye. "Tell me everything!" she demanded, sitting on the partially-made bed. "How old is the *boppli*? Is it a boy or a girl? Who is she married to? Did she bring her husband with her?"

"Wait a minute; that's too many questions! They said she was here by herself," Rachel said. "They don't think she's married, and she has a little girl about eighteen months old. Almost certain it's her *boppli*. They did say she looks like an *Englischer*."

Hannah stood up and went over to the second-floor window and stared out as she did the math in her head. The timing of Ellie's absence from the community suggested she'd gotten pregnant just before leaving, or perhaps within days after arriving in Ohio. If before, was there a chance her Jonas was the *vadder?* If not, that could only mean she'd been untrue to Jonas and had someone waiting for her in Ohio.

Hannah sucked in her breath and swallowed hard at the realization. It was gossip, she knew, but she *had* to know more.

"Why is she here?" she asked, picking up the quilt and smoothing it over the bed.

Rachel picked up the other end and helped her finish making their parent's bed. "They said her *mamm* sent her an invitation to your wedding. Rumor has it that Jonas gave it to her to send!"

"He never said anything to me about inviting her! Why would she want to come to my wedding when she hasn't spoken one word to me in more than two years?"

"To see Jonas! Do you suppose she's here to get him back?" Rachel asked.

Hannah tossed the pillows onto the bed, and Rachel straightened them.

"I don't think I want to wait around to find out!" she said, crossing to the bedroom window and looking out at the neighboring farm where her friend used to live, and was now visiting.

There used to be a time when she and Ellie would meet each other halfway in the cornfield. They would run around in the maze of rows for hours, catching fireflies and giggling. They didn't have a care in the world then.

Now, she'd invested two years of her life into Jonas, waiting for him to propose.

If Jonas was the father of Ellie's baby, he would call off the wedding for sure and for certain. She had to go over there and confront her friend. She had to know the truth, even if it ruined her life.

Hannah marched up the steps to the Yoder house and knocked on the door boldly, intending to put a stop to the gossip before it started. The Widow Yoder answered the door; a little girl dressed in *Englisch* clothing in her arms.

"Hannah," she greeted her daughter's friend. "*Wie ghetts?* I haven't seen you for a long time. Would you like to come in?"

Hannah looked deeply into the child's little face noting the same features of her betrothed. Her heart sank at the thought of such a beautiful little gift from *Gott* could cause the destruction of her marriage.

"I came to see Ellie," she said, unable to take her eyes off the *boppli.* "Is she here?"

"I sent her in town to run a few errands for me," Widow Yoder said. "You're *wilkum* to stay and wait for her if you'd like.

She'd seen all she'd needed to see, but it wouldn't seem polite to turn down an invitation from a neighbor. She had truly missed sitting in *Frau* Yoder's kitchen eating cookies with her friend. But those days were gone. Things had changed; and not for the better. She shook inside as she walked into the home she hadn't been in for more than a handful of times since Ellie's departure. There was a time when her own ma'am could not pry her away, but now she would do almost anything to get out of having to go inside and face what was before her. How was it that she'd become part of a triangle with her own best friend?

Had Jonas used her all this time to get over Ellie? She was about to be dumped, and for a fleeting moment, she wasn't sure if she truly cared. It was almost more of a relief to her. She'd been stricken with so much guilt for having taken Ellie's place in Jonas's life all this time. She had known all along that his heart truly remained with Ellie, and that she had been his second choice.

She sat down on the settee very methodically. Before she realized, Frau Yoder had begun to fuss about something and she hadn't been paying attention. Lost in her own world, Hannah was suddenly holding Ellie's child.

"I'll just be a minute," *Frau* Yoder called over her shoulder to Hannah. I don't want my cookies to burn.

Hannah focused on the little girl sitting happily on her lap. The little girl smiled, putting a lump in Hannah's throat.

"What is your name, little one?" Hannah asked.

Frau Yoder overheard her. "Her name is Katie," she said from the kitchen.

"She looks so much like Ellie when we were younger," Hannah said loud enough for the widow Yoder to hear her.

"She certainly was a surprise," the woman said. "Did Ellie write you about her?"

"*Nee*," Hannah said. "I haven't gotten a single letter from Ellie since she left for her *rumspringa*. I'll bet her father is very proud of her," Hannah said, fishing for information. "Did Ellie bring her husband along on this trip?"

"I'm sure when Ellie returns from town, the two of you can catch up and she'll tell you all about it," *Frau* Yoder answered, bringing a plate of warm cookies from the kitchen on a tray with two teacups and a ceramic pot of tea.

Hannah knew better than to continue to pry, but she had to admit she was eager for Ellie to return so she could get the truth even though she knew it already. Mostly in the way *Frau* Yoder was avoiding answers that were easy. It was all in what she *wasn't* saying that made Hannah realize she was trying very hard to keep the truth from her.

It was obvious to Hannah that Jonas was this child's father; she looked just like him and had his eyes. But the two of them had vowed to save themselves for their wedding night; had she been alone in that vow?

Katie leaned against Hannah's unyielding frame and yawned, looking up at her with a pair of blue eyes that mirrored Jonas's. She'd anticipated having *kinner* with him, and had often wondered what his offspring would look like.

Now she knew.

Hannah felt the weight of the *boppli* shift as she slumped against her, falling into a deep sleep. She cradled the child, leaning down and smelling her hair. She still had that *baby smell.*

The child trusted her enough to fall asleep in her arms, and it made her regret some of the things she was already feeling. They were selfish feelings; feelings that would only benefit her, when she should be thinking of the child.

Jonas will be able to see this child if she was his, even if he married her instead of Ellie. Hannah would make sure of it. She cared enough about Jonas to let him do his own choosing. It was true, she had not allowed herself to love him the way that a wife should, but she hadn't dared give him her whole heart, for fear Ellie would come back and her heart would be broken.

Now, it would seem that time had come.

Chapter 5

Ellie stood in front of the shops on Main Street, her *mamm's* quilt in her arms. She'd asked her to take it into the shop for a customer who was waiting on it, but Ellie knew it was so her mother could spend some time with Katie. She didn't mind running her *mamm's* errands, and she was happy that she wanted to spend time with little Katie. She hoped they would bond so her child could have a grandmother.

She walked into the shop, anticipating a welcome from Mary, the shop owner, but instead, ran into Jonas. With the quilt in front of her face, she was unable to see where she was going, and ran smack into him!

Dropping her *mamm's* quilt, she bent to pick it up, and bumped heads with Jonas. Was this a cruel joke?

"I'm sorry," he said, staring.

She placed her hand on her forehead and bent over to pick up the quilt, watching to be sure he didn't bend a second time and bump her again.

"I'm so glad I ran into you," he said, rubbing his head. "Not literally, but you know what I meant."

She forced a weak smile, and he flashed her the same swaggering smile that used to make her melt at the sight of it. She wasn't surprised that it had the same effect on her even now. It unnerved her that his smile could still make her swoon.

"Did you get the invitation?" he asked awkwardly.

She pulled the wadded quilt close to her and blew at the hair that hung over her face so she could look him in the eye.

She was too stunned to answer.

"I took an invitation to your *mamm* so she could forward it to you since I didn't have an address for you," he said with confidence.

"Why would you want *me* at your wedding to Hannah?"

His look softened, and he fumbled with the spools of white and blue thread in his hand. "I was hoping to see you once more before I…"

His voice trailed off, and anger set in her.

"So you could what?" she asked, trying to be quiet, despite her temper flaring. "So you could break my heart one last time before you marry my best friend?"

"It's not like that, Ellie," he said softly.

"You told me you were going to marry her when I left here more than two years ago, and now you've made her wait all this time, and you're still not sure?"

"It's not like that, Ellie," he said a little louder. "I promise you it isn't. Hannah doesn't love me any more than I love her!"

Ellie nearly dropped the quilt. Did this change anything, or did it only complicate things?

"How do you know she doesn't love you?"

She wished she hadn't asked. She wished she could walk away. Lord help her, she still loved him, and if there was even a semblance of a chance she could have him back in her life, she would listen to what he had to say.

"Neither of us is getting any younger, and we've talked about this. We're *gut* friends, but we don't love each other like—well, not with the sort of love and passion you and I had."

Ellie had silently paid for that *passion,* and now her daughter would too if she didn't at least give her father a chance to know her. But she would not get between Jonas and Hannah no matter how much she wanted to be a family with Jonas.

"What if you're wrong about Hannah? You can't break her heart."

"From the talks we've had, I don't think her heart would be broken if I didn't marry her. You know I've always loved you, Ellie, and thought you and I would get married."

Ellie walked toward the counter when she noticed the store owner go to the back room. She set the quilt on the counter and turned around, realizing Jonas was on her heels.

"You made up my mind when you threatened to marry my best friend simply because I wanted to enjoy my *rumspringa!*"

"I only said that because I was hoping it would make you stay. Then when you told me to go ahead and marry her, I thought you didn't love me anymore."

Mary came back to the counter, her eyes lighting up when she saw Ellie. The older woman pulled her into a hug. "I'm so glad to see you, Ellie. You're so grown up!"

Ellie smiled, realizing Jonas had walked back to get the notions he'd set down.

"Your mother told me you were coming for a visit."

Her *mamm* had been friends with the *Englisch* woman for as long as Ellie could remember, and had been bringing her quilts to sell ever since *daed* had died. She'd needed the income, and the older woman who owned the shop had been very helpful in helping her *mamm* make enough money to live off.

She picked up the quilt. "My customer is going to love this new quilt. It turned out better than I thought it would. She'd brought me a hand-drawn design, and I wasn't sure how your mother was going to pull it off, but she did a beautiful job!"

"Thank you, I'll be sure to pass that on to her."

The woman handed her a receipt for the quilt, and Ellie walked toward the door, intending to end the conversation between herself and Jonas, but he caught her gently by the arm and stopped her.

"Let me pay for *mei mamm's* things and give me a few minutes, please? I'd like to finish our talk."

Ellie reluctantly nodded, though she thought they'd said all there was to say. He was marrying her best friend, and nothing would ever be the same again.

Seconds ticked by in her head as she waited for him, though they seemed like hours. She didn't want to be there; it made her feel uncomfortable. Almost as if she worried the old woman would tattle on her to her mother like she was a child in trouble. Why had being back home suddenly made her feel like a child again? She was a grown woman with a child of her own, and here she was shaking in her shoes.

It was too late for the two of them to talk, wasn't it? Her heart felt heavy, and her throat constricted. She would not cry over him again. She had steeled her emotions against this, and it had been a hard lesson. Why, then, was she so willing to go back to that place in her life where he could hurt her? Being in his presence made her feel vulnerable, and she'd worked hard to be strong for little Katie's sake.

Ah, Katie.

That's who she would endure this for. Even if he rejected her all over again, Ellie would give him a chance—for her daughter's sake.

Chapter 6

Ellie stood outside the quilt shop, lifting her face to the sky and breathing a simple prayer.

Lord, please show me if I'm doing the right thing by speaking with Jonas. I still love him. He's the love of my life and the man I believed you had for me. Remove the guilt from my heart, Lord, if it is not a warning from you, but a trick from the enemy. If I am not to have him in my life, please remove the love in my heart that I have for him. Help me not to be selfish, but to put the needs of my friend, Hannah, before my own. If it is your will, please bring Jonas back to me if he's truly in love with me, not just for my daughter's sake.

No sooner had she finished speaking her prayer in her mind and in her heart, than Jonas exited the quilt shop and stood quietly beside her.

~~~~

"Hey, Rachel, isn't that Jonas with that *Englisch* woman over there in front of the quilt shop?"

Rachel pulled her cousin, Lydia, behind a row of cars parked in front of the meters downtown. "Let's spy on him for *mei schweschder!*"

Both girls giggled, and followed as the pair walked the opposite direction toward the park.

"What do you suppose he's up to?" Lydia asked quietly, as they ducked behind another car when the woman turned around.

"Wait a minute!" Rachel said, entirely too loud. "That looks like Ellie! What is he doing with her? Wait till Hannah finds out!"

~~~~

Ellie and Jonas stood in front of the fountain they'd spent many hours near when they courted, talking over future plans, and sharing too many kisses to count. It seemed only natural they would migrate there now.

"You know I didn't want things to be this way"' he said. "I hoped we'd be married and maybe with a *boppli* on the way."

Ellie's face turned red for two reasons; first, because she was keeping the baby a secret from him, and two, it brought to mind that steamy afternoon they'd had in the barn with wild abandon.

"*Ach,* I didn't mean to speak in such a forward manner," he said.

Ellie drew her hands up to her warm cheeks. Had he noticed the redness?

She struggled to speak, wanting to tell him everything about Katie, but for some reason she couldn't find her voice. Not only was she unable to speak the words he needed to hear, she had suddenly realized it may not be the right time. She did not want him coming back to her simply for little Katie. His relationship with his daughter would have to be completely separate, but if he was to return to her and be one with her, he needed to do it without knowing about Katie first. The last thing she wanted was for him to ask to marry her out of obligation. She still loved him as much as she ever did, if not more now because of Katie, and she needed to be sure his love for her was genuine.

"I only meant," he continued. "That I had hope for a future with you. Until you left, I always thought we'd be married."

"Why didn't you come after me?" She asked

"When you left, I thought you didn't love me anymore, because when I told you I would marry Hannah, you told me to go ahead and marry her. I don't think you understand how much that hurt me."

"I didn't think you'd go through with such a thing. I was young and stupid and angry," she said. "I was so hurt by your threat that I thought, if you were capable of doing it, then I didn't want anything to do with you. I thought you no longer loved me."

He chuckled lightheartedly, trying to make light of an awkward situation. "It sounds as if we both had the wrong idea about each other. But the fact still remains, I still love you, and if you love me, I don't want to marry Hannah simply to be married. I have a promise to marry her, that's all. We made a promise that if neither of us was married in two years, we would marry each other and start a *familye*. But that's not what I want. I want to have a *familye* with you. I love you. I've always loved you. I could never love anyone but you."

Ellie was tempted to throw her arms around his neck and pick up just where they'd left off, but she had her child to think about now. What if he changed his mind once he saw Katie? She would be devastated, to say the least. How could she tell him now in this moment? She'd waited this long. A few more days couldn't possibly hurt anything.

"When do the two years expire?"

Jonas looked down at his feet, unable to look her in the eye. "On the eve of our wedding. Two days from now."

Ellie thought back to the wedding invitation she received. They were to be married on Thursday, a traditional Amish wedding day. Her heart sank at the realization that Jonas must have already taken the baptism. She had not. He would not be able to marry her without being shunned, and knowing Jonas, he would not be able to live with that. Neither would she.

Ellie collapsed onto the park bench and stared into the water shower the fountain was making. How could she agreed to marry him now when it would ruin his standing in the community?

He sat beside her, and stared equally at the fountain, unsure of what to say to her. How could he convince her of his love after what he just confessed to her? Really, he wouldn't blame her if she never wanted to speak to him again. He knew he'd hurt her not once, but twice. He'd avoided taking the baptism until the last minute, knowing he would have to confess his love for Ellie. Was he hoping Ellie would get him out of this jam?

Certainly, he didn't want to have to confess his sin of passion with Ellie to the bishop, but that was no reason not to marry Hannah. He fully intended to make good on his commitment to Hannah if it was Ellie's wish that he do so, but he prayed heavily that was not the case. The confession, he knew, was merely an excuse. He loved Ellie so much his heart ached just sitting next to her. It took every ounce of his strength not to pull her into his arms and beg her to marry him. But he would not put pressure on her, nor would he try to influence her decision in anyway. He stated the facts to her, and that's all he could do. The rest was up to her.

Ellie rested her head on Jonas's shoulder, feelings of helplessness overtaking her. He wrapped his arm around her and cradled her, making her feel like that same young girl who fell in love with him an entire lifetime ago. Had things really changed that much for them? They had a bond, it seemed, that was unbreakable no matter what the circumstances. But was it really? Jonas was days away from marrying another woman, and he had no idea he and Ellie had a child together. Had she made a mistake in coming home?

"I'm afraid it might be too late for us," she finally said.

She stood up, not wanting to leave him, but she promised her *mamm* she wouldn't be long.

"I have to go," she said abruptly.

She knew if she didn't leave now, she would never be able to leave his side. She would not be the one to make this decision; she could not make it no matter how much she wanted to. She had a million things rolling in her head at the moment, her head swimming with emotion. But she knew that to allow her emotions to make her decision could cause a lot of unnecessary hurt. How funny it was to her that she longed to hear those words from him for so long, but now that he'd said them, she wasn't sure if she could accept them. Had she grown up a little too fast? She knew time was short, as the wedding was only a few days away, but that was no reason to make a hasty decision that could hurt her friend. Did she have a right to be so selfish as to take away Hannah's betrothed?

Jonas stood up, pulling her hands into his. "Please don't go," he begged her.

She looked into his eyes, knowing that all she wanted was to be able to look into them for the rest of her life. If he kissed her now, she knew there would be no turning back.

Before she could break free from him, he pulled her into a passionate embrace, pressing his lips to hers, his love for her all too evident. Her eyes drifted closed as she felt his lips on hers, sweeping across them with the passion she longed to feel once again. She deepened the kiss, unable to hold back her love for him. Concern for Hannah had left her; all her thoughts were now consumed by the passion of Jonas's embrace.

She was not ready to let him go. God help her, she loved this man with every fiber of her being. He was a part of her. He always would be. Even despite their separation, she'd felt his presence across the vast miles that had separated them for more than two years. Time and distance had not separated them; it had not destroyed the love they had for one another.

Nothing, not even Hannah, could ever get between them.

Chapter 7

Ellie straightened up on the buggy seat, inching away from Jonas's embrace as they entered the long driveway that led to her childhood home. She had good news for her mother about Jonas's proposal, but she would not present him in an inappropriate light. She knew her *mamm* already had misgivings about him because of the child she'd brought home with her, and if she could help it, she would make Jonas look like a shiny new penny in order to sell her *mamm* on the idea things would be alright with them.

Her biggest worry now was to get through introducing Jonas to his daughter, and hope they took to one another. Little Katie had been a good baby, and had taken to her *mamm* quite easily, but she'd not been around any men except Cousin Henry, and she cried whenever he spoke in his deep voice.

Ellie knew there would be no preparing him to meet little Katie, and so she hadn't said a word the entire trip back home. She'd simply enjoyed having his arm around her and the security that came with it. She hadn't even thought about what she was going to say to him, but merely assumed the situation would take care of itself. Knowing what a kindhearted man he was, and how much he had just told her he wanted children with her, she almost couldn't wait for him to see the child they already had.

Jonas parked the buggy near the porch, and hopped out to help her down. Putting his hands around her waist, Jonas looked as though he would kiss her, but Ellie backed away. "Not in front of the *haus*," she warned him. "I don't want *Mamm* to get the wrong impression."

He smiled that same smile that always melted her heart. "I understand. Let's give her the good news first."

"What exactly is that news?" She asked curiously.

His expression fell. "Was I wrong, or did you agree to marry me back there in the park? I hope that kiss meant more to you than just a casual flirtation."

"Of course it did, but I suppose I hadn't realized that you'd officially asked me," she admitted. "I didn't want to assume anything."

He raised an eyebrow over his blue eyes. "I thought that kiss said it all, didn't it?"

She smiled happily, feeling even more giddy than ever.

"I believe it did."

They headed up the steps of the porch when the front door flung open. Hannah stood in the doorway, anger clouding her expression. Ellie looked around her for any sign of her *mamm* and little Katie, but Hannah was the only one there.

"Ellie, it's so nice to see you again," Hannah said.

Ellie wasn't convinced she was all that happy to see her, and fear entered her mind. Surely if Hannah was visiting with her *mamm*, then she also knew about little Katie. Would she open her mouth before she had a chance to introduce the child to Jonas? By the look on her face, she could tell she knew. Ellie walked up the remaining steps toward her friend, pulling her into an awkward embrace.

"I've missed you so much!" Ellie said to her.

Hannah looked between Ellie and Jonas, her jaw clenching from the tension between the three of them.

"I'd love to stay and visit, but I've been here waiting for so long, I just don't have any more time to spare; we'll have to *catch up* later. Please take me home, Jonas," Hannah said suddenly, slipping her arm in the crook of his elbow. "I have a lot to prepare for our wedding." She turned to Ellie. "You'll be there, won't you? At our wedding?"

Ellie couldn't mutter a word, but forced a smile. It was better coming from Jonas; it was his mess, and he'd have to get himself out of it. She could see by Hannah's mannerisms that she was not happy to see the two of them together, and she didn't want to be in the middle of it.

"Hannah, we need to talk," Jonas said grabbing her hand. He walked down the steps of the porch hand-in-hand with Hannah, but looked over his shoulder to flash Ellie a sorrowful look.

Ellie stood on the porch of her childhood home watching the love of her life walk away with her best friend. Hadn't he just proposed marriage to her? Yet here he was leaving with Hannah. She watched him assist Hannah into his buggy, looking up one last time in her direction before driving away.

What had just happened? Her world felt suddenly very small; her worry growing by leaps and bounds. No matter how much she tried to convince herself Jonas was going to let Hannah down easily, she just wasn't able to.

She walked into the house, determined that she would drown her sorrows in hugs from the child they shared, and wait for Jonas to come back. She hadn't even had a chance to introduce him to his daughter, and now he was gone. They were also going to break the news to her *mamm,* but now, she feared saying a word to her mother for fear it would not come to pass.

What if he never returned? Would she be any worse off than she was now? She'd thought Hannah and Jonas had been married all this time, and had shouldered the responsibility of little Katie alone.

Then her mind drifted to the passionate kiss they'd shared out in public in the park, without any reservations about anyone seeing them. It was that same passion that had brought Katie into this world, and now, it could be the last thing she remembered about him. It would stick with her in the same manner as the pregnancy had. Even little Katie was a constant reminder of the loss she'd experienced.

Ellie hadn't missed the look of guilt on Jonas's face as he drove off with Hannah. If he chose her friend a second time, it would crush her. What had she been thinking, getting involved in such a triangle of passion with Jonas a second time? Hadn't she learned her lesson the first time?

Walking into her childhood room, she went to her daughter, who slept peacefully in the same crib she'd slept in as a child. Her *mamm* must have dragged it in from the spare room where it had always been waiting for the grandchildren her parents had talked about so eagerly before her father's untimely death.

She smoothed her hand over Katie's blonde curls that reminded her of Jonas's.

Apparently, she hadn't learned her lesson at all.

Chapter 8

Jonas steered his buggy into the neighboring driveway, gathering his thoughts to prepare Hannah for a gentle let-down. He didn't want to hurt her; she'd become very close to him, and he considered her a cherished friend. But after seeing Ellie again, and the kiss they shared, all he had on his mind was marrying her before she had a chance to get away from him again. He'd been a fool to let her go, and he'd been an even bigger fool to think he could forget her if he married Hannah.

He was both angry and annoyed with Hannah for interrupting what could have turned out to be his engagement dinner with Ellie. But he supposed he shouldn't have that yet until he was no longer engaged to Hannah.

Hannah sighed as he pulled the buggy up to the barn behind her house. She knew what was coming; she knew Jonas was quiet the five minutes it took for him to get her home because he had breaking up with her on his mind, and didn't quite know how he intended to word it. But why should she suffer just because Ellie was back? Ellie didn't have any claim on Jonas any longer. He was *her* betrothed; Ellie had given up any claim she had on him the day she left the community and told him to marry her instead. Now, after all this time, did she really have that kind of power to ruin Hannah's life? It was true, she didn't love Jonas the way Ellie most likely did, but she still had a strong bond with the man; she wouldn't have agreed to marry him if she didn't. Most of all, she had his word he'd marry her; Ellie didn't have that.

"I think you have the right to know that I had a long talk with Ellie, and it seems maybe our business with one another isn't exactly finished, and I made the mistake once before thinking it was. I don't want to hurt you, but I've made this mistake once already. I don't intend to make the same mistake twice. I really care about you, Hannah, honest I do, but I think we should wait to marry until I've sorted all this out. I pray that you will understand, because the last thing I want to do is hurt you, especially if I decide not to marry you at all."

"If you intend to marry Ellie," Hannah said. "Please tell me now, and spare me the details."

"If honesty is what you seek," Jonas said. "Then I will be honest with you and tell you that I've asked Ellie to marry me once again."

"You asked Ellie to marry you when you were still betrothed to me? How could you humiliate me like that? Before the end of the day, the entire community will know what you've done!"

Jonas was distraught. He didn't know how to handle the hysterical woman, and he wasn't liking it one bit. If she didn't calm down, her dad would be out in the yard removing him from his property before he had a chance to fully explain things to Hannah. He was trying not to hurt her, but he wasn't doing a very good job of it.

"If you're marrying Ellie only for the *boppli*, we can have *kinner* of our own soon," Hannah tried bargaining with him.

Jonas looked shocked.

Didn't he know? If Ellie hadn't told him about Katie, perhaps she was not his biological child after all. In which case, she may just be in the market for a father for her child.

If Hannah had any say in the matter, that was not going to happen.

"Ellie has a *boppli*?" He uttered the word in almost a whisper, and his eyes had a far-off look in them.

"She didn't tell you she has a *boppli*?"

Jonas shook his head, his expression still blank.

"Are you sure you want to get mixed up with Ellie again; especially if she's keeping such a big secret from you? It seems to me she's only seeking a *vadder* for her *boppli*, and you're her target!"

Was this all a cruel joke at his expense? Why hadn't she told him about the child? Was she going to wait until after they were married and then spring it on him? Surely she was not that kind of woman! But then again, if she had a child, perhaps she was already married once before, or perhaps she was still married. Worse than that, did Ellie have a child out of wedlock? If she did, then perhaps their time of intimacy before she left the community must not have been the only time. Was she that kind of girl? He would have never thought so, but if she truly had a child of her own, what else was she capable of? By his definition, keeping such a thing from him was just as bad as lying to him. He had to know the truth, no matter how bad it was.

"Hannah, I'm sorry," he said. "But I have to go talk to Ellie and find out if what you say is true."

Hannah began to cry. To think all this time, she thought Jonas was an honorable man. She was obviously wrong about him, that he could be so fickle that he would go back to Ellie after all she'd done to both of them. She'd broken both their hearts when she left the community, and now it would seem she had returned to do more of the same.

"Hannah, please don't cry. I still cared deeply for you, but I have to know that you and I are not making a big mistake by marrying one another just for convenience."

Convenience was the exact reason she was marrying him, and she'd come to terms with that, and was okay with it. She knew what her prospects were at her age, and in the community in which they resided, and they were next to none if not none altogether. She'd accepted it. She'd come to terms with it. And now, he was taking even that away from her. Ellie had a child by whatever means that child came into this world, but Hannah, it would seem, would never have any. She'd been foolish to trust Jonas, especially since she knew he was on the rebound from Ellie. She knew he would never love her as much as he loved Ellie, and she accepted that.

Why had she let Jonas make such a fool of her?

"I'm sorry Jonas," she said, gritting her teeth. "But you made a vow to marry me, and I expect you to honor that vow. If you don't, you leave me no other choice but to have *mei daed* go to the bishop."

Sadly, she knew she didn't have a leg to stand on with the bishop since Jonas had not taken the baptism yet, but she was not above making the threat. She, herself, felt threatened at the moment, and desperation had taken hold of her.

He assisted her out of his buggy. I'm sorry it has to be this way, Hannah" he said. "I understand you feel the need to do what you said, but I have to do what I have to do as well. Perhaps when this is over, we can still be friends, no matter what the outcome."

Hannah wiped her tears and sniffled. "Somehow, I find that hard to believe."

Jonas hopped back in his buggy, guilt tearing at him. He hated to leave Hannah in the condition she was in, but the only thing he had on his mind was finding out about Ellie's baby.

Chapter 9

Hannah walked over to Ellie's house, knowing she was taking a risk, but she felt she couldn't just stand around and wait for her life to crumble around her. Though the sun was still low in the sky, it was already promising to be a very hot day. Birds chirped and squirrels skittered around the trees in her path, but she couldn't find her usual joy in any of it. Her heart felt heavy, and she was torn between doing what was right, and doing what was right for *her*.

Since she hadn't heard back from Jonas, she could only assume that he'd had a talk with Ellie last night after he left her, and the two of them had made plans to marry. She knew that if his plans were already made, there would be little that she could do to stop them, however, she knew she would regret it if she didn't at least try.

She stepped up cautiously on to Ellie's porch, where she was playing with her daughter.

Ellie forced a smile, wondering why Hannah was back. "Good morning," she said.

"I'm sure I'm the last person you want to see right now," Hannah said. "But I need to know what happened between you and Jonas when he came back here last night."

"He was here, but I was asleep," she said. "My *mamm* told me he was here but she didn't want to disturb me, since I was overtired from my trip here. After the two of you left yesterday, I went upstairs to take Katie for a little nap, and I fell asleep with her. I think it was a good thing I was asleep when he showed up, because it gave me more time to think about the situation."

"Ellie, if you're here to break up my wedding so that you can get Jonas back, and make him the *vadder* of your *boppli*, I'm asking you to turn around and go back to your cousin's house in Ohio!"

Ellie's heart jumped behind her rib cage at her friend's comment. Either Hannah felt extremely threatened by her presence there, or it was time she faced the reality that she and Hannah were just not friends anymore. She had not yet had the opportunity to speak with Jonas and tell him about Katie, and so she kept her mouth shut about the subject. Besides, she knew Hannah would never understand her dilemma, and even if she did, it didn't seem that she would care. Their friendship had obviously come to an end a long time ago without her realizing it.

It would seem Ellie had outgrown her.

"I don't owe you an explanation," Ellie said, defending herself. "And I would appreciate it if you would stay out of my personal business. You have no business and no right to come here talking with my mother trying to get information from her while I was gone yesterday."

"That's not how it started out," Hannah said. "I came over here because I heard you were in Town. That's all."

Ellie shook her head. "Your cousins saw me get off the train. They had a clear view to see that I had a child with me. After seeing me, they ran back and told you everything, and that's when you decided you needed to come and see for yourself."

"I didn't have to see for myself the kiss between you and *my betrothed* to know that it really happened—and in public!"

"I remember how things work around here. And I know you, Hannah. You couldn't wait to get information that would be the top gossip in the community. You and your cousins always did talk about anything and everything, and what you didn't know for fact, you would make up the details."

"Are you accusing me of being a gossip?" Hannah asked with a huff.

Ellie pursed her lips, and cast her eyes downward. It was obvious someone had seen her and Jonas in the park, and the steamy kisses they'd shared. But she was not going to let her friend suck her into the drama of the community. It had been one of the reasons she had wanted to venture out on her own. She needed to see if people outside of the community were the same, or if there were differences. Unfortunately, she'd discovered that they could sometimes be even more harsh.

Hannah watched Ellie play with her child, and couldn't help but feel a twinge of envy. If Ellie was successful in taking away her only chance to marry, then she would be childless. She was angry, and rightly so. She and Ellie had been friends for many years, but she'd always envied her. Things seemed to come easily for Ellie, whereas Hannah always seemed to struggle with everything.

Frau Yoder walked out onto the porch with a pitcher filled with lemonade and a couple of glasses, along with a plate of whoopie pies on a tray. She set the tray on the little table between the two friends, and picked up Katie, walking into the house with her without saying a word to either of them. It was obvious that her mother did not approve of their heated conversation out on the porch, but surely she had to know that the two of them needed to iron out their differences once and for all.

Ellie felt discouraged as she poured two glasses of lemonade, handing one to Hannah. She offered her a whoopie pie, but she shook her head without even looking at her. Putting the plate back on the tray, Ellie sighed, wondering if the two of them would ever see eye to cyc on anything ever again.

"This bickering is getting us nowhere," Ellie said. "If Jonas is truly happy with you, and truly wants to marry you, then I wish you both the best. However, I came here to speak my piece to Jonas, and I intend to do just that. If he decides otherwise after hearing what I have to say, then that is up to him and not either of us."

Hannah slammed down her glass of lemonade onto the tray and furrowed her brow. "If you intend to pass that child off as belonging to Jonas, I'm going to have a say in it!"

Ellie stood up, placing her glass onto the tray, and turned to her friend. "I believe our conversation here is done. In fact, I think all future conversations between us are over as well. I thought we could pick up where we left off with our friendship, but I was wrong. I think our circumstances have caused us to outgrow each other."

Hannah stood, determined to have the last word. "If you think I'm going to stand by helplessly while you destroy my life, I'm afraid I can't do that. Jonas made a promise to me, and I intend to make him keep his commitment to me, and that includes marrying me—not you!"

Ellie turned toward the door intending to leave it at that, but changed her mind. She was not going to let Hannah bully her into letting go of Jonas. She'd come this far to offer him his child, and that's just what she intended to do. "I will leave that decision up to Jonas!"

Hannah turned back. "There's nothing more for him to decide. He asked me to marry him, and we will be married in two days."

"He asked me too!" she shot back.

Ellie walked into the house and shut the door before Hannah could say another word.

Chapter 10

Hannah walked back home, feeling anger and resentment rise up in her. Was she destined to remain merely the midwife for the community since her *mamm* had passed away? There had been no one else in the community with the amount of experience she had since she'd always gone with her *mamm* to assist, and with her gone, Hannah had naturally taken over the position. She was always delivering others' *bopplin,* and now, it would seem she would never be able to have a *boppli* of her own.

She refused to accept that was to be her destiny. It wasn't what she'd prayed for. Jonas had been the answer to those prayers, hadn't he?

She kicked at a stone on the gravel, country road. Since she'd walked straight out from Ellie's house and down the driveway without thinking, she was now on the road, having to go around. With the fence along the road, there would be no cutting through the way she usually did. She'd gotten over there by cutting through the field, and now out on the road, it would be a long walk home. Wishing she'd worn her black, over-bonnet to shield her eyes from the sun, she lifted a hand, holding it there for a minute, as she squinted to see a bird's nest. Even the birds, it seemed, had wee ones of their own.

Was that the only reason she had agreed to marry Jonas?

She'd spent the last year forcing a courtship with him, knowing she had feelings that amounted to little more than friendship for him, and he likely had the same for her. She'd even taken the baptism a year ago, hoping it would prompt Jonas to take it and marry her, but he hadn't. He'd dragged his heels for the past year, and now his baptism was to take place tomorrow, and she didn't believe he intended to take it. If he didn't, he would not be able to marry her without her being shunned.

It was obvious Ellie had not taken the baptism either, and the two of them could be married immediately with no complications or repercussions to either of them within the community. They would not be able to be an active part of the community, but they would not be shunned from communication with other members. Knowing this did not help matters in her mind.

Was it right for her to stand in the way of her friend's happiness? Knowing how much Ellie loved

Jonas, how could she? But what about her life, and her dreams, and her happiness?

"*Gott*, am I being selfish?"

Hannah had gotten so caught up with the idea of being married and having a *boppli* of her own, that she'd lost sight of what was right and wrong. Was she determined to have Jonas for her husband no matter what it cost her? Was she really willing to lose her friendship with Ellie?

At last, she reached her own driveway and dragged her feet up the grassy path. She didn't like walking in the dirt where the buggy wheels had worn off the grass, as she often twisted her ankles in the ruts in the path. But the grassy area did not come without obstacles that the horses had left behind, requiring her utmost attention along the way.

Lost in thought, she stepped with both feet into a large pile of fresh manure. Looking down at her soiled feet, she began to cry. She stomped her feet in the dirt, wiping them and scraping them to no avail. She stomped angrily all the way up to the porch of her house. Slipping out of her shoes, she stomped up the wooden steps of the porch, walked through the door, slamming it behind her.

Hannah ran up the stairs and into her room, letting the door slam behind her, and then flung herself across her bed, sobbing. Too many thoughts rolled around in her head. She had missed Ellie all this time, and would have wanted to share her wedding plans with her. But the fact of the matter was, she couldn't share them with her, because she was taking away the man whom her friend loved. All that time she'd spent grooming Jonas to be her husband had all been in vain. If she'd paid better attention, she would have noticed he didn't love her enough to marry her, but was simply going through the motions just as she was.

Was it right for the two of them to force a marriage where there was no love? A marriage of convenience could only end up in disaster, especially when they both loved Ellie so much. She'd lost her friend and her betrothed long before today, and it hurt her to realize the truth.

She turned her head from her pillow where she'd had it buried, and noticed her wedding dress hung over the chair in the corner of her room. She pushed herself from her bed and walked over to the dress, lifting it from the chair and pulling it to her cheek. She'd sewn that dress with so much care and so much hope, and now all that hope was gone. She clenched the dress in her fists, and in a rage of anger, tore the dress in two.

Shocked, and realizing what she'd done, she tossed the dress on the floor and flung herself back across her bed, sobbing even harder.

After several minutes, she wiped her eyes and began to pray.

Lord, please bless me with a peace in my heart if I'm to let Jonas go. If Katie is his kinner, take away the selfish thoughts I have of keeping that boppli away from her daed. Take away the fear I feel that I'll never have a husband or a boppli of my own, and replace it with a peace and trust that you'll work everything out with your plan for my life, and not my own. Restore my friendship with Ellie, and help me not to be bitter or envious. Put happiness in my heart for my two friends, deliver me from this anger and disappointment. Give me the patience to wait on you to provide a husband for me—the husband You would have for me. Please forgive me for trying to rule my own life when I know You are the ruler of my life and the universe. Danki, Lord, for all your many blessings, and bless Ellie with the courage to do what she needs to do for her familye. Give Jonas the courage to let me go and do what's right by his kinner. Give me strength, Gott, to let them be a familye. Give me strength, Gott, to let Your will be done in my life.

When she was finished, she felt a peace wash over her, and she knew it was time for her to step back and let it go. She would let God find her the husband he would have for her, and she would wait patiently for him.

Chapter 11

Jonas paced the barn floor, rehearsing what he would say to the two women he was now betrothed to. Hannah would likely never forgive him for changing his mind at the last minute, but he had to try with Ellie, even if it didn't work out in the end.

He would at least try.

As for the child she brought with her, he had thought deeply about that, and determined it didn't matter if all she needed was a father for her child. It was Ellie's flesh and blood, and he would help her raise her, and would gladly treat her like his own. Katie was a part of Ellie, so of course he would love her.

He stopped pacing for a moment, and faced the loft of the barn, leaning up against the post and reminiscing about that steamy afternoon before Ellie left the community. Was it possible that a child had resulted from that union? If so, why had she waited so long to return? Had she denied him the right to his own child this whole time? Hannah hadn't mentioned the age of the child, only that it was a girl and her name was Katie, but she had referred to her as a *boppli*. He did the math in his head, realizing that if he had fathered Katie, she would be approximately eighteen months old by now.

Suddenly, he was more eager than ever to find out the truth; he had to know if Katie belonged to him.

Removing his horse from his stall, Jonas harnessed him and then hitched him to the buggy. He still had plenty of chores to do, but he couldn't wait until later to speak with Ellie. After a failed attempt to talk to her last night, he realized it was a blessing in disguise, because it had given him time to think things through thoroughly.

He hopped in his buggy confident that a talk between him and Ellie was long overdue.

Driving down the lane, he contemplated whether or not he should finalize things with Hannah before he went to Ellie, but instead he said a little prayer for guidance.

Lord, I'm feeling confused, and angry, and betrayed. Help me to forgive Ellie for keeping Katie from me all this time if she is my kinner, and help me to understand her reasons. Help me to find my way through this mess without hurting anyone. Grant me

*peace about my decision to honor my commitment to
Katie if she's my kinner and to Ellie, and forgive me
for breaking the commitment with Hannah. Put
forgiveness in Hannah's heart for me and help her to
realize we are not the right match. Forgive me, Lord,
for leading her to believe we should be married when
we're not equally yoked. Bless me with favor in
Ellie's eyes; Open the floodgates of love between us
if it is your will. Amen.*

By the time he finished his prayer, he was
steering his buggy into the lane of Ellie's family
home. As he neared the house, he could see Ellie
sitting on the porch with the child on her lap. From
what he could see, the little girl, with her blonde curls
that matched his own, was approximately the age
he'd guessed. Feelings of giddiness and nervousness
mixed in his stomach, making him feel as if he
wanted to run to the child, but yet turn away at the
same time for fear it wouldn't be true. Was he ready
for this?

He parked his buggy, unable to take his eyes
from the child. Her blue eyes that mirrored his own
sparkled in the late afternoon sun, and her little smile
was almost intoxicating. A warm feeling in his heart
traveled to the lump in his throat bringing tears to his
eyes. He hopped down from the buggy and stood
there for a moment just to take her into his heart.
Even from that distance, he could see that Katie was
his flesh and blood.

He walked swiftly to the porch steps and Ellie put the child down from her lap. He flashed a quick glance to Ellie as he reached the top step, and she released her grip on the child. Little Katie ran to greet Jonas, and he scooped her up in his arms, holding her close, tears flowing from his eyes. His lower lip quivered, despite the smile he could not wipe from his lips.

"Without a doubt, this has to be the best feeling in the world," he said.

He twirled the child around happily, and she giggled. "That's my girl," he said. "That's my girl."

Nothing else mattered to him at this moment, only the love he had for his child. There was a bond there that no amount of time or distance could steal away from him. He would never let anything stand between the two of them again. Not pride, which had kept him from going after Ellie when he should have. Not his standing in the community, which had torn him away from Ellie in the first place. But most assuredly, not his empty commitment to Hannah. His only commitment now would be to his child and her mother whom he loved dearly.

"*Danki,* Lord, for opening my eyes to the truth."

Jonas looked at Ellie, who waited patiently for him to come to terms. He adjusted little Katie in one arm, and extended his other to the woman he loved. She went to him easily without saying a word, and he pulled her close, tilting his head affectionately against hers.

All at once he realized he had everything he wanted and needed right there in his arms, and nothing else mattered. He would love them, and shelter them, and take care of them for as long as he lived. In doing this, he would fulfill the only commitment that mattered, and that was the one to his family and to God.

Chapter 12

The familiar sound of clip-clops and grinding wheels in the gravel driveway alerted Jonas to a buggy coming up behind him. He turned, keeping hold of his new family, his heart skipping a beat when he saw it was Hannah.

It was time to take care of the mess he'd created, and try to fix whatever he could, and let go of what he couldn't. He could do no more or no less.

Ellie tensed in his arms, and then lifted her head from his shoulder. "I'm not sure I'm ready for this visit."

"Let me take care of it," he whispered into her hair.

She would gladly let him handle his own dispute with Hannah, but she was her friend too, and Ellie didn't like being at odds with her. Truth was, she'd missed Hannah, and had often wished she could talk to her over the past couple of years since she'd been gone. They'd always confided everything in each other, and she'd kept so much bottled inside all this time, she felt deprived of the closeness they once shared. She'd confided some in her cousin while she was living there, but they weren't close enough that Ellie felt free to burden her with everything.

Hannah had always been such a good listener, that Ellie would often go on for hours about things she wanted to do when they grew up. She'd talked her ear off about her future plans, and how smooth her life was going to be once she was old enough to be on her own—and now look at her. Here she was, shaking in her shoes on the porch of her parent's home, and trying not to lose her temper over Hannah's unannounced invasion. Granted, her own sins had gotten her into the mess she was in, but now, she needed to rely on Jonas to stand strong with her while she worked her way out of it.

Hannah remained in the buggy, observing Jonas holding Katie. Seeing the two of them together, there was no doubt in her mind she was his flesh and blood. She took in a deep breath and released if slowly, as if letting go. Peace filled her heart, and she knew at that moment Jonas was exactly where he was meant to be, and God had something else in store for her future. But for the time-being, she had two friends waiting for her on the porch of the Yoder farm, and she was not going to let anything separate them again if she could help it.

Ellie had made her an *aenti,* even though they weren't related, they'd always been as close as two sisters could be, and they'd promised each other long before Katie was even a glint in Ellie's eye that they would always be *familye.*

They'd always planned to be married at the same time and they were going to raise their *kinner* together. They had done everything from pick out the names of their children, to deciding how many of each they would have. Always in that picture, Ellie was the one to marry Jonas—not Hannah.

Lord, bless me with renewed strength to put aside the envy I feel and step aside so that Ellie and Jonas can raise Katie together and be a familye. Put joy in my heart for the two of them, and bless me with the strength to support their future in any way I can.

Bless me, Lord, with a Jonas of my own...

Her thoughtful prayer trailed off as she felt in her heart that God was telling her to be patient and wait for the reward He had for her to repay her for the unselfish act she was about to perform. She felt at peace as she exited the buggy, fully intending to release Jonas from his commitment to her.

Jonas and Ellie walked down the steps and toward the buggy with welcoming smiles. Hannah ran to her friend, pulling her close.

"I'm so sorry for getting in the way of your rightful future with Jonas," she said to Ellie. "I've not been a *gut* friend, but I pray you'll still let me be Katie's *aenti.*"

Jonas and Ellie looked at each other, Hannah's comments taking them both by surprise. But they were of one mind where their friend, Hannah, was concerned.

"*Jah,*" Ellie said. "You'll always be *mei schweschder*—and Katie's *aenti.*"

"I've missed you so much, Ellie," Hannah said, tears filling her eyes, but her mouth formed a smile so wide, her heart overflowed with happiness for her friend and sister. "I wasn't sure if you'd ever be happy enough to want to come back home."

Ellie gave her a squeeze. "I am now!"

"*Wilkum* home."

Chapter 13

Hannah slipped inside the front door with *Frau* Yoder, allowing Ellie and Jonas a little quiet time alone. Once inside the house, *Frau* Yoder put her arm around Hannah and hugged her tight. "Are you all right?"

"*Jah*, I'm all right. It wasn't meant to be with me and Jonas. It wasn't part of *Gott's* plan for my life, and I know that now."

"I'm certain that *Gott* has another husband for you out there somewhere," *Frau* Yoder said. "I'm sure glad that you made up with Ellie. I've missed you. What do you say we go into the kitchen and finish the *familye* dinner?"

"But I don't want to interrupt your *familye* dinner. This is Ellie's homecoming, and I'm guessing it will be her engagement dinner as well."

"Don't you know by now that you're *familye* too, Hannah?"

"*Danki*. I have really missed working in this kitchen with you."

Hannah smiled. She certainly missed spending time in the kitchen with Ellie's mother. After Ellie left the community, Hannah had spent a lot of time with her mother. She missed having a mother around, and Ellie's mother had filled a void for her. When she began pursuing Jonas, she'd stopped visiting with the woman. She'd felt guilty for going over there while she was pursuing the woman's daughter's betrothed. She was certain the woman knew what she was up to anyway, which made it more difficult for her to face her.

To Hannah it was easier to stay away than to face the truth about what she was doing. Realistically, she was betraying her friend by showing interest in her betrothed. She would no longer have to be ashamed for what she did since she stepped aside and did the right thing by Ellie and Jonas, and even little Katie.

Though her wedding day was to be in two days, Hannah felt a sense of peace despite the fact she was no longer getting married. The peace that she now found would serve as a reminder that God was answering her prayer, and would bring her the right man to be her husband.

She washed her hands and set to work rolling up dough-balls to make rolls. She listened to Ellie's mother humming happily, and mentally went over the eligible man in the community. There were only two men, one was way too young for her, and the other was way too old. What was she to do? Perhaps her dad would agree to send her to another community to reside with one of her cousins where there might be some eligible men there. It was likely her only chance to find a husband. She would certainly pray about it, but already, she'd nearly made up her mind. There was nothing more for her here. Though she was happy that she'd made amends with Ellie, she didn't believe she could easily stay around and watch her friend have a life with the man she was supposed to marry. She wanted very much to put the bitterness behind her, and she wasn't sure she would be able to do that if she stayed too close to home.

Hannah and Ellie's *mamm* worked side-by-side in silence in the kitchen just like they always did. Occasionally, her *mamm* would tell her funny little stories about when Ellie was little, or Hannah would talk to her about missing her friend, but other than that, not much was ever said. They seemed to have an unspoken bond that didn't require a lot of conversation, and that usually suited Hannah just fine. It gave her a chance to have a bond with a motherly figure, without making a commitment or betraying her *mamm's* memory.

Before long, Hannah could hear Jonas and Ellie entering the house and it seemed Lydia and Eli were with them. The noise in the house had suddenly increased and *Frau* Yoder wiped her hands hastily on her apron and smiled excitedly.

"Everyone is here, Hannah," she said. "Let's go greet everyone."

"*Nee,*" Hannah said, shaking her head. "I'll finish up in here; you go and greet your son and his *fraa.*"

Before long, Lydia entered the kitchen and smiled at Hannah. She placed her hand over her enlarged abdomen.

"It won't be long before you're helping me bring this wee one into the world," she said with a smile.

Hannah had forgotten that she had agreed to deliver Lydia's baby. She wasn't due for a least three more weeks, and Hannah had no idea how she would be able to stand staying here that long. She had already decided that she would stay with her cousins and leave immediately after Jonas married Ellie. Surely she could be gracious enough to stay for their wedding, but she could not stand by and watch them live a life that she was supposed to live. It would do well to help rid herself of the anger and the bitterness, and give her the peace she sought after.

Lydia put a hand on Hannah's shoulder. "I know this probably isn't the best time," she said. "But in light of your circumstances, I'd like to know if you'll agree to stay with me for the next few weeks until I deliver my *boppli.*"

She hadn't given such a thing much thought, but she supposed it would allow her to stay away from the rest of the community. Lydia's home was on the outskirts of the community, making it an easy place to hide out.

"Eli will set up the room across the hall for you, and I think being away for a couple of weeks might do you some *gut.* I could certainly use the help, and will pay you wages, as I have a feeling you intend to go visiting *familye* outside the community, am I correct in saying so?"

"*Jah,*" she said, forcing a smile. "If you need me to stay, then I'll stay until you deliver."

Lydia threw her arms around Hannah excitedly. "*Danki*, Hannah. I promise I will pay you well, and after I deliver, you can go wherever your heart leads you, but I have a feeling you're going to be all right."

Hannah prayed that her decision to stay with Lydia was God's will. If not, she had just agreed to do something else without consulting God first.

It would seem that listening to God and waiting on Him was going to be a hard lesson for Hannah to learn.

Chapter 14

Hannah tried her best to focus on conversation during dinner, and not allow the looks between Jonas and Ellie to bother her. She stuffed a bite of roast chicken in her mouth hoping it would divert her attention away from them and give her a moment to think without having to speak. She reminded herself that God had something else in store for her and silently begged God once again to take away any apprehension she had of her decision.

Would it always be this way? Or would she get to a point where it never bothered her again? At the moment, she didn't think so, but she supposed with time, like all wounds, it would heal.

There was no talk of the wedding, and Hannah thought that it was probably awkward for Jonas and Ellie to be around her right now. She suddenly wished that she hadn't accepted the invitation to dinner, knowing that she was keeping them from making their plans. She had to assume that they wanted to marry as soon as possible before Lydia gave birth so that she would not be still recovering after the pregnancy and unable to attend.

At the conclusion of the meal, Hannah began to clear the table. She just couldn't sit there any longer, and she didn't know what to do with herself. Keeping her hands busy was all she could do, and clearing the table would keep her mind busy too.

Ellie followed her into the kitchen, setting down the single plate she'd grabbed as an excuse to tag along behind her. She set the plate down and turned to Hannah, trying not to let discouragement set in.

From the other room, Hannah could hear little Katie giggling where she sat bouncing on Jonas's lap. Her focus turned back to Ellie, who was standing before her looking as though she wanted to say something.

"I'm sorry if this is hard for you," Ellie said. "The last thing I would ever want to do would be to make you feel uncomfortable."

Hannah turned on the water in the sink and squirted some soap in to start some dishwater. With her back to Ellie, she took a deep breath and pushed it out slowly to keep her tone cheery. "I'm not sure it can be helped. The situation sort of calls for it, don't you think?"

Ellie put the plate into the dishwater and then leaned her back against the counter. "I suppose you've got me there. But our friendship means so much to me and I want so much to include you in our plans."

"*Ach*, you don't want me tagging along. I'd be a third wheel. Besides, I was courting Jonas, so why would you want me to attend your wedding?"

"Because you're my friend above anything else!"

Hannah scoffed. "How does Jonas feel about that? I'm certain he doesn't want to be reminded that I nearly talked him into marrying me so easily."

She'd lost that quest, and she fought hard to push back envy for her friend. She reminded herself that she would have faith that God would bring her the right man to marry, and that Jonas was not that man for many reasons, little Katie being the biggest one.

"He doesn't hold anything against you," Ellie said. "If that's what you mean."

Hannah sighed heavily as she stared out the kitchen window, washing a plate mindlessly. Winter would be here soon enough, and another Christmas would pass her by without a husband. She had hoped that this would be the year that she would not go through another set of holidays alone. Granted, she had her sister, Rachel, but her dad had been too quiet since their *mamm* had died almost two years ago. Ellie hadn't even been here for her for that.

Instead, Jonas had been the one to get her through those hard times. And for that she would always be grateful for his friendship. But looking back on it, that's all it had ever been between the two of them. They hadn't even shared a kiss, making the excuse to one another that they would wait until their wedding. She had fooled herself into thinking that day would ever come.

As if she knew what Hannah was thinking, Ellie placed a hand on her shoulder thoughtfully. "I wanted to tell you how sorry I was to hear about your *mamm*. But I'm glad that Jonas was there for you."

"How did you know I was thinking about her just now?"

Ellie looked at Hannah seriously. "Because we're friends and we've always been connected that way."

Hannah smiled. "You always did seem to be able to look right through my soul."

"Maybe because you've always been so transparent. I knew when I saw you yesterday that you weren't really in love with Jonas so much as the idea of being married. It was all you ever talked about when we were younger. You were the one that wanted to be married more than I ever did. And here I am the one taking that leap of faith. But don't worry, because I know *Gott* has a wonderful husband in store for you, one that will love you and cherish you for the rest of your days. And you'll have lots and lots of *kinner*."

Hannah's face brightened. "Do you really think so, Ellie?"

"Of course I do, and to show you just how confident I am about that, I'd like it if you'd stand with me at my wedding," Ellie said. "I'll be married in the Mennonite church since we won't be able to be married by the bishop. Since neither of us has taken the baptism, being married in the Mennonite church is the only logical solution for us right now. But I'd really like you to stand with me when I get married."

"You mean like a maid of honor at an *Englisch* wedding?"

"Yes, exactly like that."

Hannah paused for just a moment, and there it was; the peace that she'd been asking God for.

She smiled. "*Jah*, I'd like that very much."

Chapter 15

Eli hugged his twin sister tightly. "I'm proud of you, Ellie, for enduring what you had to in order to bring little Katie into this world. I only wish you would have brought her home sooner than this so we could've gotten to know her a little better. Seeing her makes me even more eager to be a *vadder*."

A lump formed in Ellie's throat, guilt threatening to overtake her. She hadn't wanted to be so secretive where little Katie was concerned, but she just hadn't been certain what would be waiting for her back home when others found out she was an unwed mother. It helped to ease her fears knowing that her family was so close with her and supported all the surprising changes that had taken place since she got home. She hadn't expected the kind of support they were giving her, or even the drastic change with her relationship with Jonas. All she knew was that she would no longer have to be shameful, for she would no longer be an unwed mother.

"Thank you, Eli, it means a lot to me that you support me and Jonas."

He smiled. "All too soon, me and Lydia will have a *boppli* of our own, and Katie will have a new cousin."

"Did you want me to come over and help with the delivery?" Ellie asked.

"*Nee*, Lydia has made arrangements with Hannah to stay with us for the remaining days until the birth. And since she's taken over being the midwife for her *mamm*, we have every confidence in her. But we would love for you to be there too. We're nervous, and we can use all the support we can get."

It surprised her that Hannah would agree to such a thing, but she supposed now that her plans with Jonas had abruptly ended, she needed a distraction, and staying so far out of the community would probably be good for Hannah right now. She'd left quietly more than a half-hour ago, or Ellie would have gone to her and made sure that she was all right with this. She supposed it would be a while before she could totally mend fences with Hannah, and things might be strange and awkward for a while, but she hoped it wouldn't be for long.

"Of course we'll be there," Ellie promised. "We'll check in with you as often as we can over the next few days. And if things happen sooner, please send word so that we can be there."

The two of them hugged tightly as Lydia exited the house with their *mamm*. Eli gave his *mamm* a good strong hug, and then wrapped his arm around his wife and held her hand as he assisted her down the stairs and into their buggy. Once he had his wife situated, he turned to wave, and then turned his buggy around so they could go home.

Jonas, who was carrying Katie on his hip, caught up with Ellie on the porch just in time to wave goodbye to his soon-to-be brother and sister-in-law. He handed Katie over to Ellie's *mamm* so the two of them could have some quiet time on the porch and watch the sunset together. He placed a hand at the small of Ellie's back, guiding her to the porch swing at the end of the porch.

"Do you want to take the baptism?" He asked.

She shrugged. "I thought a lot about it, but I would have to take the classes, and that would delay our wedding. Did you still intend to take the baptism tomorrow?"

He shook his head. "I've been dragging my heels all this time, not wanting to take the baptism unless you did. If I took the baptism, you and I would be unequally yoked. I want to be married first, so we don't delay our being a *familye* any longer. We can discuss the baptism later, unless you're determined to take it beforehand."

She shook her head as well. "I won't take it unless you do. But we can discuss that later, I suppose. Right now, all I want to do is be married to you and be a *familye* with Katie. I believe the rest will take care of itself. I've talked to *mei familye* about it, and they're not requiring it of me at this point. And since we won't be under the rules of our community, we won't be shunned."

"I agree," she said with a smile.

"Then it's settled," he said. "I'll make arrangements with the Mennonite preacher."

"*Jah*, I can't wait to be married to you."

He smiled, feeling happier and more at peace than he'd been in a couple of years. "I love you, Ellie."

Warmth filled her from the top of her head all the way down to her toes, making her feel as giddy as she had when they were younger and so much in love. She knew that her love for him had never wavered. Now, nothing would stand in the way of their happiness and their future together as a family.

"I love you too, Jonas."

He pulled her close, love and renewed passion filling him so much, that he couldn't help but press his lips to hers. He swept his lips across hers, and over to her cheek, then, down her neck, following the trail back up to her ear where he whispered to her how much he loved her. She closed her eyes, enjoying the closeness with him so much she hadn't realized a buggy had approached in the driveway.

Before either of them realized, and angry male voice was interrupting they're passionate kisses.

Jonas pulled away from Ellie, and stood up to greet Hannah's father.

"Why have you dishonored my *dochder* by kissing Ellie when you're betrothed to my Hannah?"

Jonas cleared his throat, and took a deep breath to calm his racing heart. His hands shook, and a bead of sweat formed on his forehead. He hadn't put much thought into having to give an explanation to her father, but he supposed it was the right thing, and he should've done it long before now.

"I'm no longer betrothed to Hannah," he said cautiously. "I'm going to marry Ellie."

"When she tried telling me that you had called off the wedding, I had to come and see for myself. I had no idea this is what I would find—you kissing her best friend. You have shamed my daughter, and now she will be a spinster because of you."

Jonas felt guilty enough for the way he'd handled the situation with Hannah, but the words of her father stung.

The angry man turned his attention to Ellie, who had remained on the porch-swing with her eyes cast downward. "And you, Ellie, you're supposed to be her friend. How could you betray her in this way?"

Ellie's heart skipped a beat. Had Hannah gone home and embellished the situation with her father in order to save-face with him? Surely she would have had to explain things differently to her strict father who wouldn't have understood the way Hannah claimed she had. Or perhaps Hannah had been hurt far more than either of them had noticed. Had they been caught up so far in their own desires that they had lost sight of the hurt they'd caused Hannah?

"It was never my intention to break up the wedding between Jonas and Hannah, but Jonas and I have a child together, and because of that we intend to marry."

His jaw clenched and his eyes narrowed. "My Hannah told me that the two of you have a *boppli*, and I think it's a shame to the community what you have done. I don't want you to have anything more to do with my *dochder*. As far as I'm concerned you're no longer a part of her life, and you are no longer friends because you've not acted like one."

"I mean no disrespect," Jonas said. "But we will always be friends with Hannah."

"*Nee*," he said. "You may not be shunned as far as the bishop is concerned, but as for *mei haus* and *mei familye*, you're shunned."

He walked down the steps of the porch and jumped in his buggy, driving off before either of them could gather their wits about them enough to say another word. It was probably for the best right now, that they allow him time to adjust and calm down. They had both been raised not to argue with their elders, and for now, Jonas would let the matter drop.

Ellie began to cry. "I want Hannah to be at our wedding," she sobbed. "She promised me she would stand with me as a maid of honor."

Jonas pulled her close. "I'm sorry, my dear Ellie, but we might be on our own for a while. I'm sure our decision and the news of Katie will shock the entire community. It might be a while before we have their support, and it's possible, that we may never have it."

Ellie sobbed even harder. She had thought by marrying Jonas that everything in her life would fall into the proper places, but it was apparent that they had not. Hannah's father was an important and respected man in the community, and his anger could change everything for them. She didn't want their decision and their mistakes to cause her family to be shunned because of it, and Hannah's father had that power.

Chapter 16

Ellie paced the length of the room off the side of the little Mennonite chapel where she was readying herself to meet Jonas at the altar.

Lord, Hannah promised she'd be here to stand up with me. Please allow her safe passage to be here. I don't want to be married without my best friend here.

A quiet knock sounded at the door, and Ellie rushed to open it.

"Ach, it's only you!" she said to her twin brother.

"Danki for the warm *wilkum,"* Eli complained.

She pulled him into a hug. "I'm sorry; I was hoping you were Hannah."

"Did I hear my name?"

Ellie's face lit up as her friend walked in the room. She threw her arms around her and began to cry. "I'm so happy you're here! I didn't want to get married without you here."

"*Ach,* I wouldn't have made it if it weren't for the fact *mei daed* had agreed to let me move in with your *bruder* and his *fraa* today. *Danki* for arranging that for me, by the way," she said, directing the last part to Eli.

"I'm glad I could help in any way," he said. "Besides, Lydia is eager for you to be there. She's been anxious; worrying you wouldn't be there on time to deliver the wee one."

Hannah giggled. "Every woman goes through that in their last few days," she assured him. "It's nothing to be alarmed about. I'm all packed, so after the wedding, I can take my things to your *haus.*"

"Lydia will be pleased to know that," he said.

"I saw her out in the hall before I came in here, and told her the news already, so she's breathing a little more calmly now."

Hannah began to fuss with the collar on Ellie's dress to smooth out the crisp, white linen, which was a nice compliment to the traditional blue of her dress. It seemed odd to her that Ellie would choose the color even though she wasn't being married by the bishop, but she didn't pry. She could only assume the two of them intended on taking the baptism after they were married. She would have to remember to ask her about it later, but for now, it was time to get her ready to walk down that aisle to meet Jonas.

Hannah took one last look at her. "You're a beautiful bride, Ellie."

"*Danki,* Hannah, but you know you're next!"

Hannah scoffed at her. "I'm not so sure about that."

Eli kissed her forehead. "I agree with *mei schweschder,* Hannah. You're a beautiful person, and any *mann* will consider himself lucky to have you as his *fraa.*"

His comment and affection surprised Hannah, but they'd all known each other their entire lives, and she and Eli used to kiss behind the barn; there had been a time when they were much younger that Hannah had thought she would marry her best friend's twin brother so they could be sisters, but it hadn't worked out that way.

Lydia had come to the community to live with her grandmother and take care of her in her last days, and Eli had become smitten with her from the moment he met her.

After that day, their childhood crush ended.

Hannah thought it funny how naïve they had been when they were younger, and she suddenly wished for those days back, but they were all grown up now. Maybe, just maybe, they were a little too grown up.

Chapter 17

Hannah watched Jonas kissing his new bride, and couldn't help but wonder what it would have been like to be standing right where Ellie was right now. She glanced back at Eli and Lydia and wondered the same thing. She'd passed up two opportunities to be married, and now she was going to be residing in the home of one of them. It was tough not to be envious, but she had to remind herself for the millionth time today that God had another plan for her future. She would likely be spending a lot of time in prayer and reminding herself of his plan for her life over the next several weeks. She had determined to leave the community to go stay with her cousins after the birth of Lydia's baby. There was just too much history here in this community and it was all too close to home. She needed to be free from the past in order to move forward in her future.

No matter how many times she tried to tell herself that it was a temporary situation, she couldn't shake the feeling it was going to turn into a permanent one. No matter how many times she put it out of her head, she just couldn't see a life outside of this community, no matter how much she tried to envision it and plan for it. Regardless of whatever it was that was in her way, she would continue to believe it was the right plan even though God always seemed to have a way of changing her plans on her.

Once outside the church, Hannah walked toward her buggy, but Ellie called after her. She stopped and waited for Ellie to catch up to her even though she couldn't get away from the scene fast enough. Although she wasn't eager to be settling into Eli's house with him and his wife, it was the best solution all-around.

"I wanted to thank you for being with me today, Hannah," she said a little out of breath. "Even though I know how tough it must've been for you. I appreciate the sacrifice more than you know."

"I was happy to do it. But I'm afraid I must go and get myself settled into your *bruder's haus*. I'll come back after unpacking so I can help your *mamm* serve your guests."

Ellie pulled Hannah into a hug, thinking how sorry she was for putting her through all of this. She's been a gracious friend to endure all of this, and she said a little prayer that God would bring her a husband of her own very soon.

Ellie released her friend, and Hannah knew she'd been praying for her. Not only could she feel the blessings pouring down, but she knew by her friend's silence that she was deep in prayer.

They parted ways, and Hannah knew without a doubt that everything was going to work out just the way God planned it.

As she drove away from the church, she resisted the temptation to look back. Her future was not there, it was somewhere out in front of her, and she was more than ready to get there and settle into it—in God's timing.

Chapter 18

After the last wedding guest had left, Jonas turned to his bride and whispered in her ear. "Are you ready to go home?"

She had been so caught up in everything that she hadn't really given it a thought, but she was eager to see the home she would be living in with her new husband. He'd casually mentioned he had a place of his own, and she was certainly ready to begin her life with him.

They packed up Katie, despite her *mamm's* offer to keep her for the night. As parents, they knew it would be best to get her settled into her new home as quickly as possible to avoid adding anymore uncertainty to the already stressful changes that the child had endured. She'd been very content with the move so far, and they hoped the transition to their final home would be an easy one for her.

Ellie had already packed their things, and Jonas had gotten the crib his *daed* had made for him and placed it in the room across the hall from the master bedroom. He'd thought of everything, and it had given Ellie a chance to concentrate only on the wedding itself.

As they pulled into a long driveway almost directly behind her family farm, Ellie was happy to know that she would be living so close to her *mamm,* whom she'd mentioned to Jonas she'd needed to keep an eye on. He'd agreed, and had assured her his farm was very close; she hadn't realized it would be this close, and she was pleased.

As they neared the house, Ellie looked at a large, two-story farmhouse with a wraparound porch against the backdrop of a large pond. The moon shone on the water, lighting up the heavily-wooded property. Her breath caught in her throat at the beauty of her new home. When Jonas pulled the buggy in front of the porch, happy tears filled her eyes. It was just as they'd talked about; the home they would build when they married.

Jonas noticed Ellie being so emotional.

"I built the *haus* from memory; I hope I got everything just the way you wanted."

She giggled, letting out a joyful cry. "It's perfect!"

"It should be," he said, leaning in and kissing her damp cheek. "I built it just for you."

Ellie pushed the thought from her mind that her own stubbornness had almost caused another woman—Hannah, to live in the home that Jonas had built for her.

None of that mattered now. They had both grown up today, and done the right thing—by each other and their daughter.

He assisted her out of the buggy; Katie was sleeping soundly in her arms.

Once on the porch, Jonas scooped both of them up in his arms and carried them into the house. He let her down easily, so as not to wake his daughter.

He kissed Ellie and smiled. "*Wilkum* home!"

She giggled as she looked around the house he'd built with love, feeling that she had finally found her way back home.

THE END

Amish Weddings
The Widower's Baby
Book Two

Samantha Bayarr

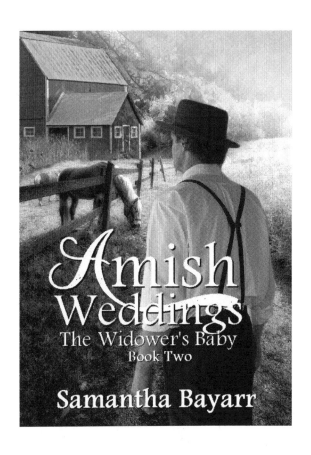

Amish
Weddings
The Widower's Baby
Book Two

Samantha Bayarr

A note from the Author:

While this novel is set against the backdrop of an Amish community, the characters and the names of the community are fictional. There is no intended resemblance between the characters in this book or the setting, and any real members of any Amish or Mennonite community. As with any work of fiction, I've taken license in some areas of research as a means of creating the necessary circumstances for my characters and setting. It is completely impossible to be accurate in details and descriptions, since every community differs, and such a setting would destroy the fictional quality of entertainment this book serves to present. Any inaccuracies in the Amish and Mennonite lifestyles portrayed in this book are completely due to fictional license. Please keep in mind that this book is meant for fictional, entertainment purposes only, and is not written as a text book on the Amish.

Happy Reading

Chapter 1

Lydia's tormented screams reached Eli all the way to the barn, filling him with a fear he'd never known before. Hannah had urged him to call for the doctor, explaining it was too much of a gamble for a midwife alone.

Was she as fearful as he was?

His beautiful wife had tried to insist she didn't need or want the doctor, but Eli had gone against her wishes, worry forcing a decision out of him.

Desperation motivated him as he dialed the number with a shaky hand. He'd had the phone installed in the barn for this exact kind of emergency, and he prayed now that the doctor would answer.

He paced impatiently on the floor of the barn, crushing the fresh hay beneath his feet, while he waited through four rings. When the voicemail began, he hung up, saying another hasty prayer asking for guidance.

Hannah had used the term *breech,* and he'd lost a foal recently for the same reason, and he was terrified of the same fate for his child.

Another chilling scream rent the air, startling him out of the stupor of his prayer. He focused on the phone and dialed the emergency line, begging for an ambulance with one long, ragged breath. Tears pooled in his eyes as he answered several questions that indicated the person on the other end of the line was just as afraid for the safety of his wife and child.

"Please hurry," Eli pleaded with the man. "I have to get back to *mei fraa.* She needs me."

He set the phone down, the man still trying to get him to answer, but Eli was not thinking straight. Stumbling back to the house, he pleaded with God to save his family, each heavy step bringing more anxiety as he made his way back to them.

Once inside, Lydia's screams made him cringe, but there was something different about them now. As he made his way up the stairs to their room, he realized they had become weak and faint.

Forcing his feet to take him to her bedside, he avoided the scene at the foot of the bed where

Hannah mopped up blood from the sheets. The sight of it made his heart race, but he wouldn't let either of them know how terrified he was.

He collapsed onto his knees and buried his face in his wife's neck, kissing her and whispering in her ear.

"I'm here, Lydia. Be strong."

She let out another weak cry, and then he heard the squeal from his child. He looked back at the infant, feeling his wife's grip on his hand loosen.

He watched with unseeing eyes as Hannah placed the *boppli* in Lydia's waiting arms, her smile weak, but proud.

"She has your blue eyes," Lydia whispered to her husband. "And blond, curly hair like her *mamm.*"

Eli watched his wife coo to her new daughter, and look up into his eyes. Her eyes were cloudy and dull, and her face seemed weighted down with a sadness.

"I want *mei dochder* to have a *mamm,*" she said with great effort.

"She has a *mamm,* Lydia. She has you." He didn't like the labored sound of her voice, nor did he like the words she was speaking.

"Nee, I don't think I'm going to make it."

"Shh," he begged his wife, his lower lip quivering. "Please don't talk like that. I called an ambulance, and they're going to take you to the hospital, and everything is going to be just fine, ain't so, Hannah?"

He looked up at the young woman who was working desperately and frantically mopping up blood his wife was losing. She glanced at him only for a flicker of a moment, and then nodded as she focused her attention back to the emergency that his wife's condition presented.

Lydia kissed the baby's face and smiled.

"Name her Mira, after *mei mamm,*" she said, and then motioned weakly for Hannah to come nearer.

She reluctantly left her task, knowing it wasn't making much difference.

"Hannah," Lydia whispered. "I want you to be her *mamm.*"

"*Nee,* you're her *mamm,* Lydia," she said, forcing a smile around the tears in her eyes. "You're going to be chasing after her for many years to come."

She placed a hand on Lydia's arm, and then went back to the task of cleaning, but she knew if the ambulance didn't hurry, they were going to lose her.

Eli held her close, rocking her back and forth, willing her to live, but it was all in vain, and his heart sank at the reality. *"Gott,* please!" he whispered into her hair.

In the distance, he could hear the faint sound of sirens from the nearing ambulance.

Lydia smiled at her husband. "Promise me you'll marry Hannah so our *dochder* will have a *mamm."*

He hesitated, not wanting to commit to such a foolish thing.

"Promise me," she said weakly.

"I promise," he whispered, glancing briefly at Hannah, hoping she hadn't heard his promise, but she had.

Lydia exhaled weakly, and didn't draw another breath. He pulled her away from him and jostled her.

"Gott, please don't take her from me," he sobbed.

He could hear the ambulance pulling into the driveway of their home, but Eli knew it was too late. She'd already drawn her last breath, and there would not be another.

Chapter 2

Eli watched methodically as Hannah wept quietly while she prepared Lydia's body to be taken by the mortician, where she would be further prepared for burial, and then brought back for the funeral.

Nothing seemed real to him anymore.

His sister and *mamm* had gathered in the corner of the room quietly to watch the doctor check over his child.

He could hear her crying, but he couldn't go to her.

His *boppli.*

He hadn't even really looked at her, except when Lydia had pointed out the blond curls that matched her own.

It didn't matter now. The child belonged to Hannah. His wife had given her the child, and he would honor her wishes. He didn't know what to do with the child. He wasn't her *mamm,* and he had no idea how to be. A girl would need a woman's care more than she would need him, and he hadn't even been able to bring himself to looking at her a second time. He feared it would cause him to break down if he saw too much of his wife in the child.

Ellie stood next to her twin brother, trying to urge him away from the morbid scene in front of him. He held fast to Lydia's hand, staring blankly, but unmovable. She had to wonder if he even heard her or knew she was there. She prayed silently that her brother's mourning would not consume him.

It wasn't that she didn't feel he had a right to grieve, but he had a new daughter who would need him to be strong. She felt sorry for Hannah, who had confided in her about Lydia's last moment before she passed on, knowing what a burden such a promise could be. She tried to reassure Hannah that everything would be alright in a day or so. They would get through the funeral, but she agreed Eli would need some help with the *boppli.* Ellie had encouraged her to stay on for an extra week to help her brother with the transition. Not exactly knowing how to react to the dying wish of her sister-in-law, whom she barely knew, Ellie tried to assure Hannah that it would likely be forgotten in a few days.

Seeing her brother now, Ellie had to wonder if she believed that herself.

Eli's attention turned to Hannah as she cleaned the baby and wrapped her in a blanket. He could hear her soft breath as she presented the child to him. His arms would not reach out to her. He stared blankly at the bundle in front of him, but could not look at her face. Little gurgles and squeaks reverberated from the folds of the blankets, and the child seemed content where she was.

He shook his head, and put up a hand.

"*Nee,*" he said firmly, keeping his lower jaw clenched to keep it from quivering with sorrow. "She needs a *mamm.* You are her *mamm* now, Hannah."

Hannah's breath hitched. She pulled the infant close to her, feeling elation and sorrow swirling inside her. She'd overheard the promise Lydia had prompted from Eli, knowing he'd only accepted to appease his wife. Surely he didn't mean to give away his child. As much as she wanted to have a child of her own, she could not accept such a burden, for Eli would take her back when he was finished grieving, and she would mourn the child forever.

Ellie hadn't missed the look on Hannah's face, and it caused her to worry. She knew the deep desire her friend had for wanting a baby of her own, and it wasn't right for her brother to dangle that over her head, no matter how much he was grieving.

She placed a hand on her brother's shoulder. "You don't mean that," she whispered. "She needs you. You're her *familye.*"

"*Nee,*" he said angrily. "*Mei familye* is gone. *Mei fraa* is dead, and the *boppli* is Hannah's. She will have to raise her alone, because I'm not marrying her the way I promised Lydia."

Tears pooled in his eyes, and he fled from the room, leaving Hannah holding his child.

Chapter 3

Eli rose from the edge of the bed, having ignored the desperate knocks at the door from his sister, knowing it was time for the funeral.

Nothing could prepare him for this, and even his prayers were too weak to comfort him. He'd slept for the past two days, not thinking about his child. He'd overheard his *mamm* and sister telling Hannah they would return with a couple of bottles so she could give the infant goat's milk. After he'd snatched a few things from the room he no longer shared with Lydia, he'd taken them out to the *dawdi haus,* where he'd remained for the past two days. He hadn't wanted to face what was before him, and now, as Ellie knocked at the door relentlessly, he would have to.

His tongue stuck to the roof of his mouth as he tried to tell her to leave him alone, but she continued to knock and call out to him. His head ached as he stumbled to the door and opened it just a crack, his eyes squinting against the bright morning sun that streamed in through the opening.

Ellie stood there, clad in a black mourning dress and bonnet.

He couldn't look at her.

She stared at her brother's disheveled clothing that he'd likely slept in for the past two days, his auburn hair standing on end on one side. She felt sorry for him, and wanted to pull him into her arms and make the pain go away, but she couldn't imagine being in his place. She could see the torment in his blank stare, his posture speaking volumes of his pain.

"Hannah and *Mira* are waiting in the buggy with *Mamm* and Jonas. We'll wait for you to dress."

She'd spoken his child's name so softly; he'd barely heard her.

He didn't want to hear it; he simply nodded and closed the door.

His thoughts slammed against his brain; he didn't want to think anymore. He was a father; it was what he and Lydia had wanted so much, and now she was gone trying to give that to him. His arms were empty, and his heart was broken beyond repair. How could he go and bury his wife the way his family expected him to? He knew the community would frown if he was not there, and he also knew they would frown if the child was not there, but he couldn't deal with her right now. He had to get through the funeral and the meal afterward that he would be expected to attend.

He felt as if someone had knocked the wind out of him, and he hadn't the strength or the will to draw in a breath.

Had his *mamm* felt this way when she'd buried his *daed?*

One would never have known; she'd handled herself with grace and a quiet dignity. He couldn't do that; he wasn't as strong as she was.

He combed through his hair and looked at himself in the mirror, tugging on the long whiskers along his jaw. He'd grown the beard as an outward sign he was married, but now he was not.

He no longer had a wife.

I should have no beard, he thought to himself as he stared at his reflection.

Picking up a pair of scissors, he pulled a section of his beard and began to cut away at it angrily. His throat constricted as he remembered all the times Lydia would rake her fingers through it when they would cuddle. But as he looked in the mirror, watching himself lop off his beard, he was compelled to erase all remembrance of her, hoping it would take away the hurt he felt deep in the pit of his stomach.

When he'd cut as much as he could, he picked up his razor and shaved his chin thoughtfully, every stroke of the blade just as intentional as the one before it. He didn't stop until his chin was smooth.

He could be shunned for such an act of rebellion, but he didn't care. If it would keep him from having to attend Lydia's …

He closed his eyes against the thought of her funeral. He wasn't ready to say goodbye or let her go.

He dressed and shuffled his feet toward the door, wishing he didn't have to go through with this.

If he could bury his head in his pillow until the pain left him, he would. Sleep was the only way to keep his mind quiet of the thoughts that hurt so deeply.

Opening the door, he didn't expect Ellie to still be standing there waiting on him. She drew a hand to her mouth to stifle the gasp, but the look in her eyes spoke volumes of her shock at seeing his clean-shaven face.

"Not a word," he grumbled under his breath as he made his way to the waiting buggy.

His mother shared his sister's reaction, but she didn't say a word as he climbed in the open seat next to his brother-in-law. When they neared the graveyard, Eli choked up at seeing the entire community of buggies lined along the road. They had all gathered to pay their respects the same way they had when his father had passed on. His mother put a hand on his shoulder from behind him, but he was too inconsolable for it to comfort him.

Hannah felt awkward holding his child in his presence. He'd glanced at her briefly before climbing into the buggy, and she wondered if it was intentional. Had he wanted her to notice his clean-shaven face? She tried not to read too much into it, but had to wonder if he intended to follow through with the promise he'd made to Lydia. His mother had asked her to stay and care for the infant, and she'd agreed only for the child's sake. He was in no shape to take care of her, and from the way he reacted to her just now, it might be a permanent situation with her, and she would accept that.

In the two days that she'd cared for Mira, she admittedly had grown attached to her, despite every effort to guard her heart. She knew that if Eli didn't take over the care of his child soon, it would only be that much more difficult for her to separate herself from little Mira if he refused to honor his promise. Being the closest thing she'd likely ever get to having a *boppli* of her own, she considered offering to stay on as nanny to the child if that was all he would offer, and despite how tough it would be if she had to let go, she'd prayed for God's will.

Jonas parked the buggy, and hopped down to help the women out. Eli stared at the ground, allowing Ellie to take hold of Mira so Hannah could get out. She extended the child toward her brother, but he shook his head, his mouth forming a deep frown as he continued to keep his eyes cast down.

She sighed heavily, showing disapproval of her brother's reaction, but decided to let it go for now. Rather than say something she might regret, she prayed he'd bond with the child before she became too attached to Hannah, and she to the child.

She handed the baby back to Hannah, and urged her to walk beside her brother. It was proper for him to have his child at his side during the service, but she wasn't so sure about Hannah's presence—especially given her brother's clean-shaven face. She imagined the Bishop would take that as a sign he was willing to accept Hannah as a wife, and would likely expect him to marry her. Still, he should have waited to shave until a respectable amount of time had passed.

It was too late for all of that now.

Chapter 4

"I think you should marry Hannah the way you promised Lydia."

The Bishop's statement was more than mere suggestion, and Eli knew it.

The *only* reason he would even consider such a thing would be to make sure she continued to take care of the child. She would have to understand that he would never be a husband to her, but he doubted she would ever agree to it.

He would ask her just the same.

He knew the Bishop would not accept her continuing to live on his property without a marriage between them, even though he would stay in the *dawdi haus,* but he needed her to take care of the *boppli.* She would be nothing more to him than a nanny, and someone to cook for him and wash his clothes.

He put down the plate of food he had no intention of eating now. He couldn't believe he was even entertaining such thoughts when he'd just put his wife to rest less than an hour ago, but he had no other option if he wanted Hannah to stay on to take care of the child.

How could he honor such a promise when his heart would never be in it. He and Hannah had a history, and she'd want a regular marriage. As his friend, she deserved nothing less than that, but he wasn't the one to give her that.

The Bishop had strictly warned him they would have to be married immediately, or she would have to leave his home. Could he let her take the child—Lydia's child?

No; that was out of the question.

But so was a marriage for anything other than convenience. He would never betray Lydia's place in his heart by opening up to another woman in her stead, and he could never be anything more than friends with Hannah.

He glanced at her from the other side of the living-room of the Hochstetler's home where they'd gathered for the post-funeral meal. They weren't Lydia's family, but they were the closest thing she had to a real family; she'd come to stay with the older couple when she'd moved to the community. *Frau* Hochstetler had been friends with Lydia's *mamm,* and so when the woman passed away, she'd moved here with them. It had been Eli's luck, or so he thought.

Now, all he could think about was wishing he'd never met her so he wouldn't have to endure the pain of losing her. Was it right to wish for such a selfish thing? His jaw clenched as he looked away from the woman, who was not his wife, holding his child. He was supposed to share that child with the love of his life. Now all he felt was empty and broken. His faith was weak, and his heart ached with a deep sadness he hadn't even felt when his own father had passed away.

Though he knew he was obligated to marry Hannah, he felt nothing short of pure terror at the thought of it.

"I'll make all the arrangements," the Bishop was saying.

What? Had he missed an entire conversation just now?

He looked at Bishop Troyer blankly.

"I'm sure the Hochstetler's will be more than happy to accommodate the wedding. They cared for Lydia a great deal, and would want to make certain you and her *boppli* were well-cared for. Hannah will make an excellent *fraa*. In time, you'll heal, and be able to love her."

Eli put a hand to his mouth to cover the bile he thought was sure would escape him if he didn't stifle it.

Breathe, just breathe, he said to himself.

"My suggestion is that we *handle* it before the end of the week," he continued, despite Eli's apparent aversion to the subject. "Any longer than that and you'll have to either move from your farm, or move her off the property. It won't be considered proper after that, except that we know you're staying in the *dawdi haus.*"

How? Did either Ellie or Hannah tell you my business?

Either way, he wasn't ready to think about getting married in front of the entire community. He'd just buried his wife, and already the Bishop was deciding and planning for his future wedding. He knew it was the way of the *Ordnung,* but that didn't mean he had to accept it, did it?

He supposed it did if he intended to remain in the community.

The real question weighing on his mind was; did he want to remain in the community?

He supposed he did if he wanted to have a mother for the child Lydia had left behind.

Chapter 5

Eli felt numb as he tried to react appropriately as the entire community either hugged him or shook his hand, offering condolences and raving about what a beautiful gift Lydia had left behind in Mira.

Guilt tugged at his heart every time a comment was made about the child. He hadn't set eyes on her since the moment she was born. He'd been too preoccupied with Lydia's passing to notice too much about the infant, but he had heard her all day at the funeral. She'd cried and cooed, and slept soundly, though he was very aware of her soft breathing even from across the room.

Was that his only connection to her? Lydia would likely have called it intuition, but to him, it only served as a grim reminder of his loss.

He knew what was expected of him, and he wasn't sure if he could go through with it.

When everyone had left, his *mamm* approached him and pulled him into an awkward hug. He feared really hugging her back because he knew it would cause him to breakdown, and he wasn't ready to face the emotions that had plagued him since his *fraa* had taken her last breath.

"I know this is a difficult time for you," she said quietly. "But you need to think of the *boppli* now. She's not Hannah's responsibility—unless you do what's right and marry her. I understand your reluctance to bond with Mira, because I imagine she reminds you too much of Lydia, but that's not fair to the wee one."

She knew him well; he couldn't deny that.

He wanted to collapse in her arms and cry like a child, but he clenched his jaw instead, stifling his emotions that begged to be let loose. It tortured him, despite his attempts to get past his obligations. He longed for the end of the day when he could collapse onto the bed in the *dawdi haus* when he could sleep away his grief.

"Do you want me to talk to her for you?" his *mamm* asked.

"I can't be a husband to her the way she deserves," he confessed, feeling a large weight lift from him.

"I know," she whispered. "You can't do it on your own, but *Gott* will help you."

"I *can't,*" he said weakly.

"Each day will get easier. You and I have something in common now, and I understand your heart is breaking. I had the luxury of being able to grieve, but you have to think of Lydia's *boppli: your boppli.* She loved that *boppli,* and that was her gift she left behind for you. When the breaking in your heart begins to lift, you'll be able to hold her and protect her the way your *fraa* made you promise. You *must* do this for her; it was her last wish for you and her *kinner.*"

He understood what his *mamm* was trying to say; it made sense to him, but his heart would not cooperate. He could feel the emotion rising up in him, trying to escape. The tears filled his eyes and his throat constricted, his breath hitched and he clenched his jaw to stop it, but it was too late. Tears poured from his eyes despite every attempt to stifle them. He evened out his breathing trying his best to keep the others in the room from knowing what they could not see with his back turned to them. His mother had a way about her that continued to bring it out. She wept as she held him close, and he was comforted by her sobs that covered up his own sorrowful tears that continued to spill uncontrollably.

For some minutes, he wept alongside his mother, letting her embrace beget more tears from him than he ever thought he had in him. Before he could break free, Ellie had covered the two of them

132

with her arms, and soon Jonas was among them, praying quietly. Bishop Troyer laid his hands on them and prayed, while he encouraged Hannah to join them, but she shook her head and cast her eyes to the ground.

She would wait for Eli to come to her on his own terms, whatever they may be. She would not take advantage of his grief. She'd made that mistake once and it had almost cost her the friends that now stood by Eli's side comforting him. She didn't belong there—not yet anyway. Her turn would come, but today was not that day. Eli needed time to recover his loss, and she would wait on him and the Lord to make her decision. If Mira was to be her child, she would wait on the Lord for a sure sign.

Though she felt a prompting from the Lord to be patient and wait on him, she was tempted to bolt from the house. Her nerves had been spent, and her heart was near-breaking. Her faith made her stay; she would stay until God told her to go, but she prayed faithfully that he would not make her. She loved Mira already, and she would love Eli if the Lord told her to do so, and she would marry him, even if it was only a marriage of convenience. She had been willing to marry Jonas for lesser reasons, but Eli and Mira were a whole different story. They needed her just as much as she needed them, and for that reason, she would wait. She would wait on God, and she would wait on Eli, no matter how long he asked her to.

Lord, speed his healing, and mend his heart. Give him a heart for his dochder, and for me, if it be your will. Bless me with the strength to wait until you give me your blessing, and the grace to accept if your answer is no.

Her prayer surprised her; she hadn't expected it, and when she opened her eyes, Eli was standing before her.

Had he heard her whisper of a prayer?

She waited for him to hold out his arms to his child, but he wouldn't even look at her tiny sleeping form resting her head on Hannah's shoulder.

"I'd like to talk to you in private," was all he said and then walked toward the front door.

Was she supposed to follow him?

Before she could make up her mind, Ellie was extending her arms to relieve her of the *boppli*. Her throat tightened and she kissed the top of her head, breathing her in as if it was the last time she might hold her.

With shaky hands she turned over the child to Ellie and reluctantly went to meet Eli to discover the fate of her future.

Chapter 6

Eli pulled in a deep breath, and paced the width of the driveway while he waited for Hannah to join him. He had no idea what he was going to say to her, or how he would go about convincing her that his plan was to her benefit. He'd seen in her eyes how attached she was to his daughter, and he prayed that would be enough to convince her to accept his proposal on his terms. He knew that it wasn't fair to ask such a thing, and that it could destroy their friendship, but his only concern at the moment was to provide for the child by giving her a mother. He was not prepared to take care of the child, and he had no idea if he would ever develop a fatherly instinct for her the way that Lydia had hoped.

Guilt tugged at his heart, as he realized he was letting Lydia down. She had wanted a real family for her child, and that was why she'd made him promise to marry Hannah in the first place. He swallowed hard as he realized she'd walked up behind him and was waiting for him to speak his peace.

Right away, he noticed that she'd left the child inside the house with his family. He was grateful for that, knowing it would be easier on him if he didn't have to see her. He already felt guilty enough for not being the father that his wife had wanted him to be.

He looked Hannah in the eye, pausing as he searched for the right words; even though he had no idea what he was going to say to her, but at least he was able to concentrate better without the distraction of the child.

He opened his mouth to speak, but the words would not come. He didn't want to marry Hannah for too many reasons; the biggest of these being that he'd just buried his wife. But the truth of the matter was, Mira needed a mother, and he knew he was not up to the task. Was it right to use his child as a lure for a marriage of convenience? He knew Hannah's desire to have a child of her own, and he felt he was taking advantage of her, but having a chance to be a mother was all he could offer her.

Hannah shifted from one foot to the other, wondering if she should just let Eli off the hook. "I'd like to offer my services as a nanny," she began.

"Nee," he interrupted her. "The Bishop will not allow you to remain on my property overnight to care for the *boppli* unless…"

He couldn't finish the sentence.

"You don't have to marry me, Eli," she said gently. "I know this must be painful for you. I wish I could make this easy for you."

He cleared his throat, hoping it would steady his voice, but his stomach clenched, resisting the words he had to get out before he lost his nerve.

"There is a way. You can accept a marriage of *convenience* with me in order to be the *boppli's mamm.*"

"*Jah,*" she said softly. "I can do that."

It wasn't exactly what she wanted for her future, but she didn't dare delay her answer for fear he would change his mind. If it meant she would be a *mamm,* she would be content with what she could get. Having a marriage of convenience and a *boppli* was better than being a childless spinster.

"I value your friendship, Hannah, and so did *Lydia,*" he said with a catch to his voice. "I know how difficult this is for you, but I need you to understand I won't be able to be a *husband* to you, and I won't be able to give you any *kinner* of your own."

His words were final. It was a reality she'd faced when she stepped aside for Ellie to marry Jonas, and now she was faced with it once again. But this time was different; this time, the offer came with a *boppli* but no real husband attached to it. Could she really accept such a thing and be happy? She thought of how empty her arms already felt without little Mira in them, and decided it would have to do.

"I understand," she said softly.

"I'll continue to live in the *dawdi haus*," he said. "You can move your things into the main bedroom so you'll be across the hall from the *boppli*."

He was going to let her stay in his bedroom? What if he changed his mind later and wanted to move back in his house? She supposed she could move into one of the other rooms in the house, but she didn't understand why he didn't want her to stay where she was, except that it was now Mira's room. He'd moved the cradle into that room between the queen-size bed and the full-size crib, making the room even more crowded, but she supposed if he was moving her into the main bedroom—the room he'd shared with his wife, she would have plenty of room to put the cradle in there. Hannah didn't understand his reasoning for moving her, other than the fact he might not understand the immediate need to have the baby sleeping close in the cradle for the first couple of weeks. She wasn't about to argue with him or tell him how to handle his own home.

At this point, she felt blessed to have a home, a *boppli*, and a husband—even if in name only.

Chapter 7

Eli tried his best to be quiet as he packed up his bedroom to make it ready for Hannah. If it were up to him, he'd seal up the room and never deal with the memory of losing his wife here, but he knew that wasn't exactly being realistic. He didn't want to be in the room, and he didn't want to move Lydia's things, but they were of no use to her now, and seeing them would only be a reminder she was gone. He intended to pack them away quickly in the attic, and never see them again. He would be married in the morning to Hannah, and he would make her as comfortable as possible in his home. It was the least he could do for her, given the burden of a loveless marriage he had contracted with her.

She would never be his *bride,* only the caretaker for the child he could not be a father to.

He wasn't exactly sure what it was that made the situation so difficult, but he could only deal with one problem at a time, and that was to somehow get over his wife's death. Perhaps once his heart healed, there would be room for the child, but right now he didn't feel there was.

He'd prayed hard that first night; he'd prayed until he'd fallen asleep from sheer exhaustion, but he never felt the peace that he sought. Sadly, even now, he was not able to set his gaze upon the child, for fear he would break down. His heart ached, and his soul felt empty. He didn't think he would ever be the same again, and now he understood his own *mamm's* feelings of despair since his *daed's* death. She had tried to tell him that each day would get easier, and it wouldn't always be this way, but right at the moment he wasn't sure he believed that.

After haphazardly packing up everything he could get his hands on, and stuffing it into the cedar trunk he'd brought down from the attic, Eli thoughtfully lifted his wife's nightgown from the peg on the wall where she'd left it the night before she'd died. He drew it to his face, burying his nose in it, and breathing in her scent that still lingered on the garment. Perhaps this piece, he would set aside and keep with him for a time. He closed his eyes, trying to fool himself into believing she was still with him, but he just couldn't make it so. Emotion drew up in his throat, and before he realized, he was sobbing into her white linen nightgown. Uncontrollable sobs forced him to the floor, where he began to pray for deliverance of the pain and emptiness that now consumed him.

From across the hall, in Mira's room, Hannah could hear Eli sobbing, and wondered if he was trying to say goodbye to Lydia. She knew that letting go of his emotions would help him heal, but it brought tears to her eyes to listen to him. She felt bad, and wanted to go to him, but she didn't want to interfere or overwhelm him. She knew that marrying her was the last thing he wanted to do, but she respected him for honoring Lydia's dying wish for Mira.

Dropping to her knees beside the cradle, she placed a hand on the sleeping baby and began to pray.

Danki, dear Lord for finally blessing me with a boppli. Help me to be a good fraa to Eli, and give him the strength to overcome his loss. Bless him with a love for his boppli so she can grow up knowing her vadder. Give me the strength to be patient with him in this unsure time, and to step aside if need-be to allow him time with Mira.

Wiping fresh tears from her eyes, a deafening crash from the other room startled her from her prayer. The raucous continued, followed by low

141

grumbling, but she couldn't quite make out his muffled words.

He was angry.

As a midwife, she was familiar with the stages of grief, and he was certainly exercising his discontent with his wife's death. Thankfully, Mira slept soundly, oblivious to the turmoil in her home.

Another crash rent the quiet night; she had her work cut out for her if he didn't clean up the messes he was now making. The noises moved to the hall, where it sounded as if he was dragging the furniture from the room. She didn't dare poke her head out into the hallway to see for herself, but she could only imagine that he was clearing the room of anything that would remotely remind him of his wife. When he'd offered the room to her, she wanted to tell him she was content to remain where she was, but she didn't want to start off her marriage by undermining whatever efforts he would make to accommodate her in his home.

More noise and another loud crash woke Mira. Hannah tried to pick her up before she let out a scream, but she wasn't successful. She rocked her and whispered to her it was alright, holding her close, hoping it would console her, but it would seem she was ready for another bottle. She would give anything if she didn't have to go out into the hall and face Eli in his state of grief, but it seemed inevitable.

Before she reached the door, he knocked lightly and let himself in. "I heard the crying," he began with downcast eyes. "I would like to move the furniture—perhaps while you feed her."

She didn't want to question him, so she simply nodded and walked past him to go down to the kitchen. She hadn't missed his puffy, red eyes that he'd tried to hide. Her heart ached for him, but she was powerless to help him. She would be supportive, but he would have to walk this journey alone for the most part. Though she wished she could relieve him from all of his hurt, he would have to feel it and work his way through it, while she supported him in the background—perhaps without his knowledge. She would never overstep her boundaries with him, but she would do everything she could to make his life easier.

As she reached the landing at the bottom of the stairs, she could hear him dragging what sounded like the bed from Mira's room across the hall to his bedroom. She felt funny taking the room from him, but she supposed he had no desire to sleep in there anymore. She only wished he wasn't determined to live in the *dawdi haus* even after their *wedding.*

She knew it wasn't a real marriage, or that he would want to share a room with her, but she would feel safer if he was in the main house. It had been too quiet the last few nights, except for the soft breaths from Mira in the cradle next to her. If not for that,

143

she'd have been full of anxiety, she was certain. She wasn't used to being alone in a house, but she was prepared to get used to it. She wouldn't back out of the agreement now with Eli—not just because she didn't want to live alone. She'd chosen to be Mira's mother, and it was a sacrifice she would make for her.

Hannah hummed to Mira while she heated the goat's milk on the stove for her bottle. Upstairs, Eli continued to make noise, and she was determined not to go back up there until he came down. She felt terrible about what he was doing; she knew he was only trying to accommodate her, and it made her feel like she was putting him out. The last thing she wanted was for him to feel uncomfortable in his own home, but he'd made the decision to move into the *dawdi haus*. He'd also made the decision to marry her, and there would be no turning back now. The two of them would be the only ones who had to know it was a marriage of convenience only, and she would do her best not to let the situation be known to anyone else for fear it could compromise his standing in the community. She would honor him as if she was a real wife, even if it could never be.

Chapter 8

Eli wrung his hands as he cringed through the two-hour ceremony that now tied him to Hannah for the rest of his life. He thought about that for a moment, and wondered if he could endure being a widower again. He hadn't thought it would happen to him and Lydia, but here he was, marrying another woman just three days after her death. He regretted making the promise to her, wondering if he hadn't, if she would still be alive. Had she given up because she was content that he and the child would be taken care of in her absence? Had it been his promise that had caused her to let go of this life?

Hannah glanced over at Eli, ignoring the words being spoken by the Bishop, and wondering how other couples managed to stand through the lengthy ceremony. Were they all so in love that the time flew by? For her, it dragged on relentlessly as she worried with each sour expression from Eli that he was about to speak up and put an end to their wedding vows.

If he changed his mind before the Bishop finished, it would humiliate her beyond all reason, and she would lose her only chance at being a mother. She would never be able to live in the community and watch Mira grow up without being able to be her *mamm*.

She lifted her eyes and ran a prayer through her mind, continuing to drown out the Bishop's words that didn't really apply to her since she wasn't really going to be married after all was said and done—at least not in the biblical sense.

Danki Lydia for trusting me to be a mamm to your boppli, she prayed silently. *Please give your husband the strength to go through with this marriage to me. I'll do my best to take care of him and your wee one the same way you would, and I promise I'll make you proud…if you just keep me from being humiliated right now. Whisper in his ear that it's alright to marry me…whisper to him from Heaven…*

Her thoughts drifted back to the Bishop as he finished the ceremony, uniting the two of them until death parted them. She let out a sigh of relief that he was bound to her now, and that she would indeed be Mira's *mamm*. Tears welled up in her throat as the reality of it hit her.

She was a *mamm*.

Never mind that she was also a *fraa,* because she knew it could never be more than a marriage of necessity.

Eli excused himself immediately after the Bishop announced them, leaving Hannah to deal with the sympathetic stares that would surely be followed by a lot of gossip. She ignored the watchful eyes of the single women in the community, feeling awkward at best, but her main concern was Mira, who could be heard crying, and she thought for a moment Eli might go to her, but he walked past her and his family as he disappeared into the *dawdi haus.* He'd insisted that the wedding take place at his home, and now she understood why. She supposed he deserved his solace; after all, he'd had to force himself to marry her, and she knew that. It didn't make her feel any better about the situation, but surely the community had some understanding for him and his time of grief. She was simply going to be grateful he went through with the ceremony, and not worry about him. She would give him all the space he needed, and she would concentrate on taking care of Mira. After all, that's the only reason he married her.

Hannah went to the baby, and her new mother-in-law handed the baby over to her and kissed her on the cheek. "*Wilkum* to the *familye,*" she said to Hannah. "I know the circumstances aren't the best, but in time, Eli will open his heart to you."

147

She hadn't thought of that. Would he *eventually* expect her to be a proper wife in every way to him? She'd been willing to accept that when she planned to marry Jonas, but she'd had time to court him and was close enough friends with him to consider it. With Eli, they hadn't had many dates before Lydia came along and stole his affections away from her. The thought of it pricked her heart; had she loved him more than she'd allowed herself to admit?

Holding fast to Mira, she made her way into the kitchen to warm up some milk for a bottle, her mother-in-law on her heels. Thinking back on the times she'd spent with the woman after Ellie had left for her *rumspringa*, was it possible she'd felt cheated that Eli had recently married Lydia? A strange feeling welled up in her, and she pushed it down.

Frau Yoder put a hand on Hannah's shoulder, startling her from her reverie. "You seem suddenly troubled. Did I say the wrong thing out there in the yard?"

Hannah waited for some of the ladies to gather their dishes of food from the oven and go outside to the tables that were set up for the wedding meal.

"*Nee,*" she said quietly. "I believe I was just thinking about everything and I got a little overwhelmed."

She could not confide in Eli's mother that she'd just realized she loved him, and had been suppressing it for almost two years. Or perhaps she'd felt the rush of love when he'd whooshed by her after their vows had been spoken? Whichever it was, it didn't matter. She loved Eli—her new husband, and she would wait patiently for him to return that love.

Chapter 9

Eli walked into the kitchen in the midst of all the women guests for the wedding dinner feeling as awkward as he could be. He heard whispers, but ignored them despite the strong urge to make them leave his home. The last thing he wanted was to be the subject of gossip among the women in the community. He knew they expected him to stay close to Hannah's side, but he wanted to go back to the *dawdi haus* and hide until the day was over and everyone went home. But that was not what was expected of him, and he knew he had to at least go through the motions. Surely he could get through one day. After that, he could go back to the solitude of the *dawdi haus* where his heart was safe from breaking. He glanced at Hannah, who managed a weak smile, but he couldn't return it.

His *mamm* pulled him into a hug and drew him into the other room, while Hannah stayed behind, trying desperately not to cry in front of her guests. Thankfully, her younger sister, Rachel, stayed close to her the entire day—mostly because she was so enamored with Mira.

"Now that you're a *mamm,* are you going to let me come over and help you with the *boppli?"*

"Jah," Hannah replied. "You know you're always *wilkum* here."

She handed the sleeping baby over to her sister so she could remove the rolls from the oven. She felt awkward, even though this was her house and her kitchen now, but she could feel the eyes on her backside of women she used to count as friends. Some of them were jealous because Eli had been for two days the most eligible catch in the community in a while. Some were simply nosy, busy-bodies who loved nothing more than to have something to talk about to spice up their own dull lives.

"Can you please excuse me?" Rachel said to them. "I need a private moment with *mei schweschder."*

Hannah felt a spark of relief as she kept her back to the women while they filed out through the kitchen door and out into the yard. She watched them from the kitchen window, their expressions unhappy, as they seemed to be voicing their dislike for being ushered out of the house by a teen.

She turned around and suppressed a giggle.

"*Danki* for rescuing me from that awkwardness," she whispered to Rachel. "I couldn't take their stares or their whispering for another minute!"

"Your marriage is none of their business. It's between you and Eli. I heard some of the stuff they were saying. Is it true you're only married to him to take care of the *boppli?*"

Hannah searched for the best words to explain to her little sister. "For now," she said. "Until his heart heals."

"I heard them saying he won't go anywhere near his own *boppli.*"

"He's grieving right now, Rachel. Sometimes, when adults are grieving, they need time to get over that hurt before they can spend too much time with others. He loves Mira, or he wouldn't have married me so she could have a *mamm.* It was a great sacrifice for him to marry me when he's still grieving the way he is, but he did what was best for her."

"So you're not really his *fraa?*"

"*Nee,*" Hannah said sadly. "At least not the way I would be if he was in love with me."

"But you love him, don't you?" she asked.

She cast her eyes down, hiding the blush at her naïve sister's comment.

"Does he know that you love him?"

"*Nee*," Hannah said quietly. "He isn't ready to know that yet."

Ellie walked into the kitchen just then with little Katie who was fussing. "I hope I'm not banned from the house like Naomi and her friends," she said with a chuckle.

"Is that what they said?" Rachel asked. "*Busybodies*!"

"Rachel would you mind taking Katie up to Mira's room with you and putting her down for a nap?"

She rolled her eyes. "I can take a hint."

"*Danki*," Hannah called after her as she left the room.

Ellie pulled Hannah into a hug. "We are sisters now."

Hannah began to weep quietly onto her friend's shoulder. "*Ach,* it wasn't supposed to happen this way."

"I know, and I'm sorry, but I know how much you love my brother. I never really got to know Lydia since I was gone right after their wedding, but you, I do know, and I know what a big heart you have. If anyone can help Eli get his heart back and be a father to Mira, I know you can."

"*Danki,* that means a lot to me."

Ellie pulled away and smiled. "Don't cry anymore; it's your wedding day."

She sniffled. "It wasn't a *real* wedding."

Ellie scrunched her brow. "Of course it was. You'll see, my brother will come to love you just as soon as he's had time to process everything. He'll appreciate you being here for him and for his *dochder*—for your *dochder* now. You and I are sisters now and we are both *mamms,* and Katie has a new cousin. Be happy. It will all work out; God has a plan for you and your new family."

Hannah wiped her tears and forced a smile, just as Eli and his *mamm* entered the room.

He held a shaky hand out to her. "Let's go out and eat with our guests."

Hannah placed her hand in his, the warmth of his skin making her flesh tingle well past her elbow. She followed him out into the yard, where it was evident by their expressions that she was the envy of all the single women in the community.

Chapter 10

Eli stepped into the kitchen with a fresh pail of goat's milk for the *boppli*. He intended to milk the goat for Hannah to keep her out of the barn as much as possible, in order to avoid having to make small talk with her that felt forced and uncomfortable. She stood at the stove dishing up scrambled eggs and bacon onto a plate, and turned when he entered the room.

He paused, feeling awkward when she handed him the food.

She was being kind to him—being a wife— and he didn't like it. It only made him feel even more guilty that he could not be a husband to her the way she deserved. He cared for her, but he would not allow himself to love her, for fear it would betray his wife's memory.

It was only a meal, and she'd made it for him willingly. He owed her nothing for it. After all, he was providing her with a home, and had basically given his child to her. He grumbled a *Danki* under his breath, and took the plate of food out to the *dawdi haus* to eat it. He hated seeming rude and ungrateful, but he was not up for socializing with her.

She'd not said a word to stop him from leaving the house, and he preferred it that way. Having to keep up appearances yesterday at the wedding meal had exhausted him to the point he almost couldn't get out of bed this morning, but he knew that keeping himself busy on his farm would also keep his mind too busy to dwell on his grief.

With Eli out of the house, Hannah sat at the kitchen table alone and choked down the meal around the lump in her throat. She knew he hadn't meant to hurt her feelings, and so she forgave him, but that didn't mean it didn't hurt anyway. If it was possible, she almost felt more lonely married than she had when she was single.

She rose from the table and went to the sink with her dishes. Looking out at the *dawdi haus,* she knew she'd have to go in there after he returned to the barn to resume his chores to get his dirty dishes and clothes. She would continue to cook and clean for him, and take care of his child, hoping that someday he would return her love. If he didn't, she prayed God would remove the love in her heart for him to keep her heart from breaking. She feared her love would continue to grow for him and he would never let himself love her back.

After running water in the sink, she heard Mira crying in her cradle in the other room. Hannah had brought it downstairs so she could cook, not wanting to be out of earshot of the infant. She wondered how new mothers managed to get anything done; so far, she had a lot of things started, but nothing finished—unless she counted the morning meal, but that was nothing short of a disaster.

She went to her child and changed her diaper, then held her close and kissed her, feeling ashamed for complaining the least little bit about her husband. Though he might not ever be ready to be a husband in the traditional sense, he'd given her the best gift a man could give a woman; he'd given her a child to care for and love, and that was a far better life than she would have had if Eli hadn't rescued her from becoming a spinster.

As she prepared Mira's bottle, she reflected on a prayer she'd prayed not too long ago asking God to bless her with a husband. He'd not only blessed her with a husband, but a child too. But was it all part of God's plan for Lydia to have to pass away in order for her to get what she wanted in life? Tears welled up in her eyes as she thought about it.

Dear Lord, did my prayers bring Lydia's death? Forgive me if my prayers were selfish.

Deep down, she knew better, and she was determined she wouldn't waste even a day of the blessing God bestowed on her by dwelling on how it was He blessed her.

She feared if she gave in to such foolish notions it would increase the guilt that already weighed her down.

Chapter 11

Hannah fashioned a sling from a bed-sheet, wrapping Mira in it, and tying it close to her so she wouldn't have to lug around the laundry basket while trying to balance the *boppli* in her arms. With the wee one tucked against her heart, she pulled the ends of the sheet over both arms and crossed it over her shoulders, tying it at her waist. She prayed that hearing her heart, Mira would be soothed by it and get used to hearing it. It was a mother's heartbeat that soothed a fussy infant, and she hoped Mira would be comforted by it, and come to know it as her own *mamm*.

Though it was Saturday, Hannah was determined to get ahead of the laundry that had piled up for the past week, hoping to be finished by the end of the day on Monday. It was beginning to get a little chilly, being the second week of November, and so she placed a bonnet on Mira's head, assuming Lydia had crocheted it.

Heading out to the *dawdi haus,* her first stop would be to gather Eli's things. She worried he would think she was overstepping her boundaries, and so she prayed he wouldn't cross her path while she was in there.

He'd spent most of the day tinkering with something. All she knew was the constant sound of a hammer, and wondered what he could be building. Perhaps it was a new stall for the horse that was about to foal. With winter coming, it would need space inside the barn.

She had noticed that Lydia had not finished canning all of her vegetables, and she hoped Eli would not be upset if she finished the chore. She'd come across the unfinished task in the root cellar when she was searching for staples to prepare for the week's meals. She thought perhaps he wouldn't even notice, since he'd been avoiding her as much as possible.

With him spending so much time in the barn and living in the *dawdi haus*, it almost seemed comical to her that she felt more like a single mom than a married woman. She hoped that time would heal his wounds, and that he would begin to spend time with his daughter. Even if he didn't want to see her or be a husband to her in any way, she prayed that he would begin to be a father to Mira.

Setting down the basket on the floor of the bedroom in the *dawdi haus*, Hannah began to strip the bed so she could change the linens. She almost missed the nightgown that was tucked under his pillow, and realized it belonged to Lydia. Her heart ached at the thought of him pining over a dead woman, but she supposed it would take some time for him to recover from his loss. She couldn't imagine the sort of hurt he was feeling from losing someone so dear to him, but it wasn't because she hadn't experienced loss in her own life. Still, losing a spouse had to be much different than the loss of a parent or extended family such as a cousin.

She retrieved the nightgown from the laundry basket, and folded it neatly, placing it back under the pillow. Then, she proceeded to pick up his laundry from the hamper in the bathroom. Once she gathered all his things, she retrieved his dirty dishes from the sink in the kitchen and place them on top of the laundry in the basket. She hoisted the basket up onto her hip, and the dishes clanked, startling Mira, but she quickly relaxed again and didn't wake Fully.

Relieved, Hannah was careful to be quieter as she exited the *dawdi haus* out into the cold November air. She tucked the small knitted blanket over the baby's head and hands that stuck outside the sling to keep the cool air from giving her a chill. Hannah knew it wasn't too chilly for her, but babies were much more sensitive to the cold than adults were, and she aimed to guard her from the gusts of wind that threatened to bring snow from the Northern sky.

Once inside the main house, she went to the modern laundry room where she'd washed her clothes for the past couple of weeks that she'd stayed as a guest. Eli had done well for himself by installing a windmill and solar panels on the roof of the main house, the *dawdi haus*, and the barn. Those things provided enough electricity to run the home efficiently. And though she had a modern gas-powered dryer, she preferred to hang the wash outside, even in the cold crisp air of late autumn. She'd used the clothesline several times already, and had familiarized herself enough with where everything was in the home. Since she'd taken care of Lydia in her last days of her pregnancy, she was grateful she'd had that time to acclimate herself with the home. It made the transition easier now that she was the woman of the house.

Stopping in the kitchen to drop off the dishes in the sink, she took the time to run some hot water so they could soak. Eli had left them there since the previous morning, and he had not returned for another meal that day. After missing the noon meal, however, Hannah had slipped into the *dawdi haus* and put a plate of food in the refrigerator for him to have for dinner. She was happy to see that he'd used the dishes and he'd eaten the meal that she'd left for him. She knew that keeping up his strength was important right now. If she could help it, she would not allow him to become run-down. She would feed him well and continue to pray for him that strength and peace would get him through this tough time. She didn't enjoy invading his privacy, but it was necessary in order to keep him from wasting away and wallowing in his grief.

Eli took a break from building the stall in the barn, and decided to get himself a drink of water, and he needed to use the bathroom. As he entered the *dawdi haus*, he noticed that things had been moved. Hannah had been in here again, and left him feeling a bit invaded. When he walked into the bedroom, panic filled him when he saw the bare mattress. He rushed to the bed and dropped to his knees grabbing his pillow and pulling it to him. Then he noticed that Lydia's nightgown was still there. It was folded neatly, and had been replaced back under the pillow. Hannah had respected him enough to put it back where she'd found it, and that meant everything to him right now.

He breathed a sigh of relief as he pulled the garment toward him and buried his face in it, breathing a prayer that God would relieve him from his grief and to make him the sort of man Hannah could be proud to call a husband, and Mira could be proud to call him *vadder*.

Chapter 12

Hannah hadn't expected to run into Eli when she returned to the *dawdi haus* to change the bedding. With Mira still strapped to the front of her, and fresh linens in both arms, she hadn't thought about the need to knock on the door.

Taking him by surprise, Eli scrambled to his feet, trying to hide his embarrassment by wadding up the nightgown and stuffing it into the dresser drawer. He'd been so engrossed in prayer that he hadn't heard her approach. He didn't quite know why it mattered that she knew he had ahold of the garment, especially since she already knew it was there.

She immediately tried to excuse herself and back out of the room, but he was already awkwardly moving past her to get out of the house. As he brushed by her, he glanced down at the *boppli* laying against her, his expression quickly fell, his eyes cast down toward the floor.

Her arm tingled from the warmth of his bare forearm brushing against hers, and she was glad he'd left the room so he couldn't see her blushing now. She prayed he wasn't angry with her for barging in on him. she'd tried to apologize, but he didn't seem interested in hearing it; he seemed to preoccupied with getting away from her and Mira.

She swallowed the lump in her throat and asked God to keep her from taking it personally. She was certain the tufts of blond curls on Mira's head painfully reminded him of Lydia. She could see the pain in his eyes when he looked at the child.

Hannah set to work quickly to make the bed so she didn't have to invade his space any more than she had to. As for the nightgown; she would leave it in the drawer where he left it.

When she finished, Mira began to wake up, and she went back to the main house to get a bottle ready. Again, she ran into Eli, who had brought in a fresh pail of goat's milk for Mira.

"*Danki,*" she said softly.

He nodded, taking a long look at the infant before exiting the house.

At least he was able to really look at her this time, Hannah thought happily. *Danki, Lord, for small miracles.*

A knock at the door made her wonder if he'd forgotten something, but she didn't think he would knock on his own door, would he?

She hollered "*Kume,*" while she poured the milk into Mira's bottle.

The door opened behind her, and she turned to see who it was. Hannah fell back against the counter, dropping the bottle of milk when she caught herself from falling to the floor. Her heart sank as she gazed upon the *Englisch* woman.

"You must be Hannah," she said.

Lydia!

Hannah couldn't find her voice.

"I'm here for my sister's baby," she said, looking at Mira. "This must be her."

"*What?*" Hannah said.

Did she just say she was here for the boppli—as in to take her away? Did she say she was Lydia's schweschder?

Hannah was having a hard time looking past the identical resemblance to Lydia.

"My Mennonite cousins called me only yesterday, or I'd have been here sooner," she said, reaching for Mira.

Before she realized, the woman had managed to lift Mira from the bunting she'd had tied to her.

Hannah looked at her and quickly surveyed the door, wondering if the woman intended to really *take* Mira. Surely Eli would stop her, wouldn't he?

The woman looked at her and frowned. "I'm guessing you didn't know Lydia had a twin? I'm Alana. I've been shunned because I left after taking the baptism. The community wouldn't even let me attend my parent's funerals with the rest of the family. I wasn't allowed to attend my own sister's wedding, and now I've missed *her* funeral too, but they won't keep me from her baby!"

"I can't speak for *mei mann,* Eli," Hannah said, feeling suddenly vulnerable and threatened.

"Yes, I was told my sister's husband remarried two days ago!" she said, her lip curling up at the sight of Hannah. "What kind of man remarries so soon after his wife dies?"

"Your *schweschder* made him promise to marry me shortly after giving birth…so that Mira would have a *mamm,"* Hannah said defensively.

"*Mira?"* Alana asked. "Whose decision was it to name that child after my mother?"

"Lydia named the child. I was the midwife in attendance."

"So it's *your* fault my sister is dead!"

Tears welled up in Hannah's eyes. "*Nee,* Mira was breech, and Lydia was bleeding too much. By

167

the time the ambulance arrived, she was already gone."

"Who called for the ambulance?" Alana asked.

"Eli and I *both* insisted, even though Lydia was against it."

"I was also told that Eli won't even have anything to do with my sister's baby," Alana continued.

Was she *looking* to find fault in order to give her a reason to take the child away?

"He's grieving," Hannah said, defending him.

"The child clearly needs a mother!"

Hannah pulled the fresh bottle of milk from the pan of hot water on the stove and tested the warmth against her wrist. Mira had begun to cry, and she held her arms out to take the child.

Alana snatched the bottle from her. "I'm perfectly capable of feeding my sister's baby!"

Hannah didn't say a word, but stayed close in case she didn't calm down in the stranger's arms.

She sat in a chair at the kitchen table and placed the bottle in Mira's mouth. She began to gulp it down.

"When's the last time you fed her?" Alana asked. "She's acting like she's starving!"

"She had a bottle a little over two hours ago," Hannah answered calmly.

Alana leaned down and kissed Mira's head, closing her eyes and smelling her head. "I should be the logical one to raise my sister's child—not a *stranger.*"

Mira looked content in Alana's arms, and it brought tears to Hannah's eyes. Was she going to attempt to take her away?

"I'm guessing since my sister's husband is living in the *dawdi haus,* the two of you haven't *consummated* your marriage."

Hannah hung her head out of embarrassment at the woman's forward statement.

"I didn't think so," Alana said. "In that case, I can go to the Bishop and have your marriage annulled."

Panic rose up in Hannah. Could she do that?

"I'll marry Eli and raise my sister's baby. After a lengthy confession, I'll be welcomed back into the community, and when I marry him, I won't be shunned anymore."

Just then, Eli walked into the door. He'd not wanted to enter the house and run into Hannah again, but he needed to find out who owned the car that was blocking him from leaving his driveway to go into town.

There in front of him was his child in the arms of…

His heart drummed against his ribs, and his breath caught in his throat. His legs felt suddenly wobbly as he stumbled forward, knocking over the chair in his path.

Lydia?

Chapter 13

Alana looked at the man in front of her, wondering about his clean-shaven face. Was this her sister's husband? If so, why had he dishonored his wife by shaving his beard? Was it because Hannah hadn't become his wife in the biblical sense?

Eli looked to Hannah, who looked just as befuddled as he was by the mysterious woman's presence. It was obvious to him that she was the twin sister his wife had mentioned a time or two during their short-lived courtship and marriage.

"Are you Alana?" he asked.

"Yes I am," she answered. "I'm guessing by your reaction to me that you must be Eli."

"Jah," he replied.

"We have a lot to talk about," she said. "Will you take me out to visit my sister's grave?"

He looked to Hannah. "Can you be ready to go so I can take her to the graveside?"

"I'd like to go with just you," Alana said.

"It wouldn't be proper to go without an escort," Eli said.

"Then we'll take Mira with us."

Hannah's heart sank. Was this woman about to take her whole world away from her?

"*Nee,*" he replied. "She's *mei fraa.*"

"That's exactly what I want to talk to you about," she said as she set Mira's bottle down and lifted her onto her shoulder to burp her.

Again, Eli looked to Hannah. "Are you ready to go?"

She would not argue with the man, but it was obvious Alana didn't want her to go. She nodded to him, deciding to obey her husband.

Grabbing Mira's knitted bonnet and sweater, she tried to coax the infant out from Alana's arms, but she merely held her hand out to take the knitted things. Hannah picked up the thick quilt and handed it to the woman while she put on her black cloak and bonnet.

"Maybe I should warm an extra bottle," she said, hoping to stall a little for time.

She didn't know why, but perhaps she hoped Eli would make her go alone once she left the room to make the bottle. Alana followed her, so that plan backfired on her.

"You'll need to move your car," he said to Alana.

"Why don't we just take my car?"

Hannah looked to Eli to give a quick excuse, and he didn't disappoint her.

"We don't have a car-seat for the *boppli,*" he said calmly.

She smiled. "I've got one! It'll be much faster if we take my car."

Hannah nodded slightly to him. She was all for getting this trip over with quickly and getting rid of Alana so she could be rid of her.

"I'll get my things out of the car while you put the horse and buggy away."

"Your *things?*" Hannah asked.

Alana looked around her. "Surely this house has an extra room that I could stay in."

Hannah kept quiet hoping Eli would tell her to leave, but this time he disappointed her.

"You're more than *wilkum* to stay here during your visit."

Then he disappeared to put away his horse.

She knew it was their way not to turn a relative away, but she was a shunned woman. Surely he wasn't going to let her stay on for an extended period of time—except that he wasn't there during that part of the conversation and didn't know what she'd said to her.

Surely he *had* to know, didn't he?

She would not be able to say anything now, and so she kept her mouth shut and went along with Alana pushing her around. It made her angry, but she would let it go until Eli fixed it.

With Eli and Alana both outside, she prayed that the woman would not come between her and her husband and child.

But then she had a thought.

Was it selfish of her to keep Mira away from her blood relative? Was it really better for Lydia's sister to raise her? Surely Lydia would have mentioned her with her dying breath and make Eli promise to marry Alana instead of her if she trusted her, wouldn't she? Perhaps she didn't trust her estranged sister, and for that reason, Hannah would keep a close eye on her.

Let your will be done, Lord, she prayed.

Chapter 14

Alana brought her suitcases into the house and dropped them on the floor beside the kitchen door. Then, she extended her arms out to Mira. "I'll put her in the car-seat."

Hannah let her take the baby from her. She reasoned that she was, after all, Mira's *aenti.* So she let it go—for now. Since Alana seemed a bit bossy, she had to wonder why it was that Lydia had not warned Eli about her. Had she forgotten about her when she was taking her last breath, or had she not thought her own sister would pose a threat to her daughter's future? Either way, Hannah had made a promise to Lydia that she would be a *mamm* to her *boppli,* and she was determined to protect her at all cost—even from her own *aenti.*

Eli took his time putting *Moose* in the barn, hoping by stalling, he could come up with a way to get Alana out of his mind. When he'd set his eyes on her, she'd taken his breath away. She looked so much like Lydia, it was tough for him to suppress the urge to pull her into his arms and make himself forget his wife was gone. But could he really fool himself like that for more than a few minutes?

Realizing what he was thinking, he dropped to his knees beside a large bale of hay. *Lord, forgive me for thinking about holding Alana when I'm married to Hannah. Help me to pull myself together and face Lydia's death before I destroy my future and the future of Hannah and Mira. Help me to figure a way out of the mess I'm in, and show me your plan for my life. Let your will be done, Lord.*

Once Mira was all strapped in, Eli came out of the barn, his expression heavy. Hannah climbed in next to the baby in the back seat, and Eli surprised her by getting in beside her.

"Wouldn't you feel more comfortable up front with me, Eli?" Alana asked. "It would give us a chance to talk."

"Nee," he said politely. "I can hear you just fine from back here, and I prefer to sit with *mei familye."*

He felt Hannah relax beside him, and her closeness sent a strange shiver through him. the warmth of her thigh that touched his made it tough for him to concentrate on anything else.

What was happening to him?

His emotions were all over the place.

He reasoned that it was because they were about to go to the graveside of his beloved Lydia, and he was simply still in shock from her death.

But it was more than that, and he knew it.

He was certain Hannah could sense it too.

Resting his elbow against the window, he leaned his chin on his palm and stared out the window as they passed farm after farm.

His neighbors.

The trees were nearly bare, and the miles of farmland was littered with colorful leaves. Winter would be upon them within days, and the snow would close them in for the season. Would he be able to bear the cold of the *dawdi haus?* It wasn't that the house lacked a fireplace, because it had a nice stone hearth. It was the lack of love and family that the place represented. He didn't like being all alone out there, and it would get even lonelier with a long winter separating him from his only child.

He let his gaze wander to Mira. She was truly a beautiful baby. Her curly blond hair reminded him of Lydia, and her blue eyes mirrored his own. He reached across Hannah and touched Mira's small hand. Her milky skin was warm enough to melt his heart.

He removed his hand, glancing at Hannah. Tears filled her eyes, and she smiled warmly at him. He forced a smile, but it wasn't as tough as he thought it was going to be.

Alana pulled into the cemetery with a loud sigh. "Which way?"

Eli pointed and told her the section marking to look for. She pulled into the lot beside the row of graves where Lydia was laid to rest. Turning around in her seat, she asked Eli to take her to the grave.

He placed a hand on Hannah's arm.

There was that strange shiver again.

"*Kume,*" he said to his wife.

She unbuckled Mira and lifted her into her arms, and slid across the seat to exit the car. She walked beside her husband as they made their way to the gravesite. It was an emotional setting that made Hannah feel uncomfortable.

Alana fell to the ground and began to weep, repeatedly apologizing to Lydia for not being there for her, while Eli worked his jaw to keep it clenched against the tears that would surely fall if he didn't keep his emotions in check.

Strong frigid winds brought dark clouds swiftly overhead, and Hannah worried icy rain would soon be upon them.

"Perhaps I should take the *boppli* back to the car out of the wind," Hannah said, interrupting Alana's confession to her sister.

Alana jumped up from the grave and wiped her eyes and looked at Eli. "I should go with her to help protect my sister's baby. I'll give you some time here, Eli."

He nodded and the two women headed toward the car. When they were nearly there, Alana stopped and handed Hannah the keys.

"You know, I forgot to leave a memento at my sister's grave. You get the baby in the car, and I'll be right back."

Hannah accepted the keys, though she was certain it was an excuse for Alana to converse with her husband about going to the Bishop regarding their marriage. After strapping Mira in the car-seat, she turned around and watched as the woman seemed to be deep in the middle of a long lecture with Eli.

After a few minutes, however, Eli nodded to her and began to walk away, and it appeared to anger Alana, who followed closely on his heels, apparently chattering about her plans to get her way.

Hannah felt a sharp pain at her ribcage, heartburn souring her stomach over the woman's actions. It seemed she was determined to have her cause heard, and she didn't seem like the type to back down. Worry turned to fear in Hannah's stomach, but Eli's expression remained calm as he slid into the back seat of Alana's car next to her. She looked to her husband for comfort, and he gave it to her with a simple gesture.

He placed his hand on top of hers, tapping lightly only twice before removing it, but it was enough to let her know he was not going to stand for Lydia's sister getting in the way of her last wishes for her family.

Chapter 15

They rode back to the house in silence, and Hannah's heart beat faster the closer they came to the farm she wasn't sure she'd be calling *home* very much longer if Alana had any say in it.

Eli unexpectedly took Mira from Hannah and walked into the house with the two of them, and then handed her back once they got inside the kitchen. Reaching down, he picked up Alana's bags and began to walk outside with them.

"Where are you taking my things?" she asked impatiently. "I plan on staying here."

He turned and looked her in the eye. "You can stay in the *dawdi haus.*"

She twisted up her face and planted her hands on her hips in a huff. "I'm not living out there with you. We aren't married yet!"

"We aren't going to be married because I'm already married—to Hannah. And I won't be living out there either; I'm moving *mei* things back in the main *haus* with *mei familye.*"

Hannah's heart thumped harder at the thought of Eli being in the house with her. Surely he intended to sleep in one of the four bedrooms upstairs—unless he decided he wanted to move her out of his own room so he could return to it. Either way, she would accommodate him; after all, it was *his* house.

"That isn't going to stop me from going to see the Bishop in the morning!" she called after him.

Eli kept walking with her bags, set them inside the door and haphazardly tossed his few things on top of the bed, wrapped it up in his quilt, and grabbed his pillow with his other hand.

"I'll send Hannah out with some clean linens and towels for you," he said as he took his things from the bathroom. Luckily, he hadn't moved his things fully into the small cottage, or it would have been much too time-consuming to gather his things, and he intended not to make another trip out to the *dawdi haus*. He wouldn't step foot back in the place until Alana was long-gone, and he hoped that would be soon.

It wasn't that he intended to keep her from seeing her niece, but if she meant trouble for his wife or child, he would have no other choice but to make her leave. A sudden rush of responsibility washed over him, leaving him feeling strange about his change of heart where Hannah and Mira were concerned. He knew deep down it was his duty to protect them. He felt compelled to in such a strong way—a way that almost made him think he loved them both.

He entered the main house, his arms full. Walking past Hannah, he went up the stairs and hesitated before going into the room he shared with Lydia. It seemed like an entire lifetime ago that he was in that room with her holding her hand as she slipped away from him, but now, as he entered the room; he didn't recognize any of it.

Everything was different.

In the corner, Mira's cradle rested on a braided rug he didn't recognize. Doilies and late-blooming wild flowers propped in Mason jars rested on both lamp tables, fancy oil lamps in place of the copper ones that were there before. In general, the room looked *feminine,* but he set his things on top of the yellow and white wedding-ring quilt he figured Hannah must have sewn for her dowry. All in all, the room was fresh and sunny in appearance, the yellows adding a cheerfulness to the room. It looked so different; he thought he might just be able to be comfortable in the room again.

Hannah entered the room just then with Mira asleep on her shoulder.

He looked at her holding his child and suddenly remembered what made him begin courting her at a time that seemed like a whole other lifetime ago. It was her big heart that appealed to him.

She set the baby in the cradle without a word to him, and then eyed his things on the bed. Immediately, she went to the dresser and began to remove her things from the drawer. "I'll have *mei* things packed quickly, but I'll need to have you move the cradle across the hall for me."

He walked over to her and placed a hand on hers, stopping her from packing. "I want you to stay."

Her breath hitched, and she bit her bottom lip. Surely he didn't mean what he said.

Chapter 16

Hannah wrung her hands nervously when Eli asked her to sit beside him on the bed. She knew he was her husband, and she didn't fear him, but she'd not been in this situation, and he'd been married before already.

"I know I said I would not be a husband to you in any way, but it seems Alana is challenging that. I hate to even ask to place such a burden on you, but I'm afraid until she leaves, we are going to have to make it *appear* that we are married in every sense of the way—if you understand my meaning."

He was being kind and she understood, but it made her nervous to put on pretenses. She nodded nonetheless.

"I'll need to stay in the room with you and Mira at night—but I'll sleep on the floor."

"That won't be necessary," she said. "I trust you."

He cleared his throat nervously. It was evident he wasn't through talking about the problem.

"She didn't just threaten to go to the Bishop; she mentioned talking to a lawyer. If you and I are not married in the traditional sense, she could pursue action to annul our marriage. At least that's what she claims. I don't think we need to consult a lawyer because she can't force me to marry her if I don't want to. I want you to know I'm dedicated to this marriage—even though it's only for convenience. I've watched you with Mira, and I believe Lydia made a wise choice when she asked you to be her *mamm.*"

His voice broke a little, and she knew it wasn't easy for him to talk about any of this.

"Danki," Hannah said softly.

"I need to know if it's alright with you if I act *affectionately* toward you around Alana so she gets the idea we are a *real couple.*"

"Jah, but do you really think that'll be necessary?"

He stood up and began to put his things away in the empty dresser that he was used to using before.

"I'm afraid Alana has become even more *Englisch* than Lydia described to me, and she isn't going to take our word for it. She's going to want to see for herself that she can't break up our *familye.*"

"*Ach,* I have a tough time understanding how she thinks she can come here and take over."

"Lydia was the last of her *familye,* and they were very close when they were *kinner* in the same *haus,* but Alana wanted to separate herself from her twin and be her own person. Lydia told me she always felt like she was her shadow, and she wanted the world to see *her* and not the two of them as one. It's not easy for me to understand either because Ellie and I are not identical twins. The only thing I do understand is the bond between twins, and I imagine it must be greater if the person is a clone of you. She believes because she is an identical replica of Lydia that she's the logical *replacement* for her, and that Mira will automatically bond with her because of it. I don't agree with that because they don't share the same heart."

He hung his head.

Hannah knew this was all too much too soon for him; it was for her too. Still, she would trust that he knew what was best—especially if it helped her to remain Mira's *mamm.*

Chapter 17

Hannah was happy to see Rachel when she showed up to help with the evening meal. Having finished her chores at home, she'd taken the extra time to lend a hand where it was greatly needed. Not to mention the fact she knew she would feel less intimidated by Alana with her sister around. Rachel was, after all, far more outgoing than Hannah was herself, and if Alana spoke out of turn, Rachel would be the one to put her in her place. She'd always been a little mouthy that way, but she supposed it was more because of the cousins she was always hanging around. That, and her young age.

Lately, she and her cousins had talked non-stop about taking their *rumspringa*, and Hannah dreaded the thought of it for her younger sister, whom she worried would not return if she got a taste of *Englisch* freedom, as she referred to her upcoming right-of-passage. With her birthday just around the corner, Hannah hoped that spending extra time with her and Mira would make her crave a future as an Amish wife rather than the wild and rule-free life of the *Englisch.*

"Whose car is that outside?" she asked as she bound in the door and went straight to the infant seat to pick up the baby.

"It belongs to Alana—Lydia's twin sister. She's here to cause trouble for me, so I'm glad you're here. I don't trust her."

Hannah handed her sister the baby's bottle so she could feed Mira while she finished putting her pie in the oven.

"What sort of trouble?" Rachel asked.

She wiped her hands on her apron and sat across from Rachel at the kitchen table.

"She caused Eli to move his things back in the *haus,* and he has to stay with me until she leaves."

Rachel giggled. "You're blushing!"

"We have to sleep in the same room!" Hannah said in a high pitch.

"Isn't that what married couples are supposed to do?" Rachel asked, rolling her eyes.

Hannah sighed and jumped up from her chair, crossing to the window and looking out at Alana, who was coming toward the house.

"Under normal circumstances, that would be correct," she said hastily. "But you know he isn't ready to be a husband to me, and he might never be, but she threatened to go to the Bishop and have our marriage annulled. So now we have to make it look like we are a regular married couple so she'll leave us alone! She thinks she is better-suited to be Mira's *mamm* than me. Promise me you won't say anything to her!"

"Why would I tell her?" she said. "No one is better-suited to be her *mamm* than you. Besides, it's none of her business, but I hope you know what you're getting yourself into."

"Ach, me too!"

Alana let herself into the house and reached to take the baby from Rachel, but she stopped her with a look. "I'm not finished feeding her!"

Alana whipped her head around to Hannah. "Who is she holding onto my sister's baby? Is this your nanny?"

"Nee, I'm her *schweschder,* Mira's *aenti*—the same as you!" Rachel said boldly.

"No!" Alana said through gritted teeth. "You're not the same at all. I'm blood-related and should be raising her instead of your sister, who is involved in a marriage of lies."

"It isn't lies," Rachel snapped before Hannah could say a word. "Eli needed some time to heal from his loss."

"It's only been a few days!" Alana shot back. "That's all my sister meant to him? She doesn't even get a proper mourning period from her husband?"

"It seems to me that *you* intend to take that mourning period from him—that *you* should marry him instead. Should he be a proper husband to *you* if he marries you? Or should he *grow* to love his new *fraa?*"

"Seems to me he wasted no time—or maybe he's only trying to make me *think* he has so I'll be on my way. I'm not going anywhere!"

Hannah's heart did a somersault behind her ribcage. Would nothing make this woman leave them alone?

Just then, Eli came in with some wild, yellow daisies from the meadow and handed them to Hannah, kissing her lightly on the cheek. "I thought these might look nice on the table for dinner; I know how much you like wildflowers."

"Wouldn't those be better for my sister's grave?" Alana asked, her eyes narrowed on Eli. "I noticed there aren't any flowers at her grave-side, and that's shameful, given the so-called support she has from this community."

"I believe flowers are for the living," Eli said sternly. "Your *schweschder* was not shallow like that or selfish. She would be happy knowing I've brought flowers into the house to share with *mei familye.* She also liked having fresh-picked flowers in the *haus,* and I'm going to continue to bring them—to Hannah and Mira now."

Alana marched toward the door. "I *love* how every one of you has forgotten my sister so quickly."

"It seems to me that *you* forgot her while she was still alive, and now you want to come in here and convince us you loved her so much that you want to take over everything in her life now that she's gone? Where were you when she was here with us, missing you? You could have come back home and been a guest at our wedding, and a part of her life, and even been there when she took her last breath, but you weren't. Don't come into this *haus* and try to make anyone here believe you were a *gut schweschder.* The time for that was when she was still alive."

Eli hadn't meant to be so harsh, but she'd pushed her limits with him.

Alana rushed from the house and slammed the door behind her. Hannah, who was still standing at the sink, watched her run into the *dawdi haus* with her hand over her mouth.

She was crying, and Hannah felt compelled to go to her and comfort her.

Chapter 18

"She what?" Hannah asked loudly.

"She offered me a job at her advertisement agency answering the phone and filing papers," Rachel said excitedly. "She's going to teach me how to use the computer."

"Why would you want to be around Alana?" Hannah asked. "She's selfish and worldly."

She looked at her little sister with her day-dreamy eyes, and realized that was *exactly* Alana's appeal to her. She could offer her a life she'd been craving for far too long; she and her band of wild cousins that hang out in town constantly. If her *mamm* were still alive, she knew Rachel wouldn't be so out of control. She'd tried her best to fill her *mamm's* shoes and take care of her sister, but she had a wild streak in her that just couldn't be tamed, no matter how much punishment their *daed* threatened her with.

The only good news in Rachel's statement was that it made it sound as if Alana was thinking of leaving.

She regretted letting Rachel go to comfort her instead of going herself, but she hadn't shown up for the evening meal, and with Mira being fussy, Hannah agreed to let her sister take a plate of food to her. She hadn't paid too much attention to the time, thinking the girl had come back in the house and was washing the dishes. But once she'd put Mira down to sleep, she came back downstairs to a messy kitchen, completely devoid of her sister.

Now, she ran some dishwater in the sink and watched the girl with a farther-off look in her eyes than usual, and asked her to help with a task that held no meaning to her. She didn't want to be Amish any more than Hannah wanted to be an *Englischer*.

"*Daed* will not let you go!"

Rachel shook her head. "He told me as long as I go with the cousins, I can go, and he agreed to help me with a little money to get an apartment. But now since I have a job waiting for me, he's sure to let me go."

Hannah sighed, knowing her *daed* didn't know what to do with Rachel any more than she did. Perhaps she'd been too caught up in her own whirlwind life to notice Rachel had grown away from her. She really thought that having her help with her new home and baby would help settle her down a bit, but it would seem it had only had the opposite effect on her. she knew there would be no stopping her if she had permission from their *daed,* and so supporting her decision would be the only thing that would keep communication open between them.

"Promise me you won't just run off without telling me goodbye," Hannah said.

Her expression fell. "I'm not even sure I'm going."

Hannah's ears perked up, though she feigned sympathy for her younger sister. "What do you mean?"

"She said several times *if* she returns. But she did say that if she doesn't, she has a friend who can take her business over and I can work for her!"

"Seems a little like an unstable promise to me," Hannah said as she sank her hands into the warm, sudsy dishwater, flinging some bubbles at Rachel with a giggle. "Alana is just a little too wishy-washy, so promise me you won't come back here being like that."

Handing a dry towel to her sister, she turned and noticed Alana behind her. She hadn't heard the kitchen door, and wondered just how long Alana had been standing there holding her dirty dishes in her hands.

Chapter 19

Hannah rolled over to a gurgling baby beside her, and wondered how she'd gotten there. She panicked thinking she could have gotten up and put the infant in bed with her without so much as waking up. Was she really that exhausted?

When the bedroom door opened, she turned and saw Eli enter the room with a bottle for the baby. He must have put Mira in bed with her, but had she been sleeping so soundly that she hadn't heard her cry? Then she remembered finding Eli asleep in the oversized chair beside the bed, with his feet propped up on the ottoman. She'd draped a quilt over him before getting into bed. Though she was grateful he was sleeping in the chair, she felt guilty for taking the bed when he surely had to be uncomfortable sleeping there.

She sat up and held her hand out for the bottle, but he set it down on the bedside table between the bed and the chair, then lifted his daughter from beside Hannah and sat down in the chair with her. He tucked a burp-cloth under her chin and held the bottle for her, smiling at her.

"I'm your *daed*," he said softly. "I'm going to help take care of you, and I'm going to protect you and teach you what you need to know to grow up and be just as special as *both* your *mamms*."

Hannah could hear the shakiness of his voice, and it brought tears to her eyes that he would include her as Mira's mother. She watched him in the pale moonlight that filtered in through the sheer curtains on the windows. He was truly a handsome and loving man, and she was lucky to have him.

If it was possible, she fell even more in love with him right then and there as she continued to watch him care for his infant daughter. It was an answer to many prayers, but she still had one unanswered—that Eli would someday be able to return that love to her.

He held Mira up on his shoulder to burp her.

"How am I doing?" he asked. "I've watched you, and it seems this is what you do."

She giggled lightly. "You're doing everything right. You're going to be a *gut daed* to her."

"*Danki,*" he said. "I don't know what I was so afraid of. Loving her, I suppose. I think I was so afraid of losing her that I didn't want to get too close to her."

"That's understandable," Hannah said, propping herself up on her elbow to face him. "After *mei mamm* died, I would go to visit your *mamm* and cook with her because I needed a *mamm* so badly that I convinced myself she was the perfect replacement. But after a while, I stopped going because I was afraid she would leave me too. I suppose that helps me to be a little sympathetic for Alana."

"I suppose we should keep her in our prayers," he said as he rocked Mira.

Hannah flopped back down on her pillow and yawned, which caused Eli to yawn.

"How long before she's going to wake back up again wanting another bottle?" he asked.

She giggled. "In a couple of hours!"

"Then I better get her back in the cradle and get to sleep myself," he said. "This farm wakes up at the same time every morning no matter how much sleep I get."

She giggled softly in agreement as she watched him place the sleeping baby gently back in her cradle.

He went to the chair and picked up the quilt, and then pivoted toward the bed where Hannah was.

Without a word, she pulled open the covers on that side of the bed inviting him in.

He slipped in the bed facing her and reached up to push back a stray hair from her face. His touch sent a fluttering desire through her, but she suppressed it.

He surprised her by pulling her close and kissing her full on the mouth. She deepened the kiss, but only for a moment, not wanting things to go too far too fast. He kissed her forehead and tucked her under his arm with her head resting on his shoulder. She was content to cuddle with him while she listened to his soft breath in the quiet night that mixed with the equally-beautiful sound of Mira's.

Chapter 20

Hannah bolted upright in a half-sleep state when she first heard the creaking of the floorboards. Forcing her eyes open; she first glanced at the sleeping baby in the cradle, as she felt the empty spot next to her in the bed. Daylight had not quite reached the room, but it was enough to see that it was Eli, fully-dressed, toting *two* cups of coffee, who was in the room.

She flopped back down to the mattress, relieved that her instincts were wrong for a change, and there was no reason for her to get up.

Eli sat on the edge of the bed and handed her a cup of coffee with cream—surprisingly, just the way she liked it. She took a sip, wondering if he expected her to help him with chores in the mornings. She wasn't opposed to helping with gathering the eggs and milking Greta, but she was certainly used to doing much more.

"Did I oversleep?" she asked, taking a sip of the coffee. She could get used to him bringing her coffee.

He climbed in next to her, his shoes already off, and she assumed he left them in the mudroom. She sat up next to him and he opened his arm to her, pulling her close enough to rest her head on his shoulder. This was something she could get used to.

"I was wondering if you'd like to take a sleigh ride with me later."

"A sleigh ride?" she asked jumping from the bed and peering out the window at the thick blanket of snow that had fallen overnight.

She looked back at him. "There must be at least three inches of snow!" she whispered.

"It's more like four," he said. "I had to shovel the walkway for you."

"*Danki.*"

"Will you ask Rachel to watch Mira for about an hour so I can take you for that sleigh ride?"

"Do you think that's a *gut* idea to leave her here alone with Mira when Alana is lurking around?"

"She's gone!" he said, pulling an envelope from his shirt pocket with a smile. "She left a note. Read it for yourself."

Daylight was beginning to seep into the room, and it was just enough light to read the note by. She ran through it quickly, getting to the part where Alana said it was best if she left.

"This is wonderful news," she said loudly, and then hushed herself.

Mira stretched and yawned, causing her parents to smile at one another.

"So what do you say?" he asked. "Will you do me the honor of allowing me to court you properly by going for a sleigh ride with me later?"

"Courting?" she asked. "Are you sure?"

He kissed her lightly on her cheek and then smiled over at Mira and nodded.

"*Jah,* I'm sure!"

THE END

Amish Weddings
Rachel's Secret
Book Three

Samantha Bayarr

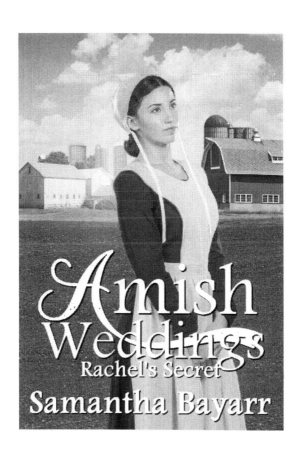

Amish
Weddings
Rachel's Secret
Samantha Bayarr

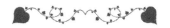

A note from the Author:

While this novel is set against the backdrop of an Amish community, the characters and the names of the community are fictional. There is no intended resemblance between the characters in this book or the setting, and any real members of any Amish or Mennonite community. As with any work of fiction, I've taken license in some areas of research as a means of creating the necessary circumstances for my characters and setting. It is completely impossible to be accurate in details and descriptions, since every community differs, and such a setting would destroy the fictional quality of entertainment this book serves to present. Any inaccuracies in the Amish and Mennonite lifestyles portrayed in this book are completely due to fictional license. Please keep in mind that this book is meant for fictional, entertainment purposes only, and is not written as a text book on the Amish.

Happy Reading

Chapter 1

Hannah shivered when her feet hit the wood floor, as she made her way downstairs in a half-sleep state to make a pot of coffee for her husband. The wind, coupled with a familiar banging noise had startled her from a deep sleep.

The screen door banged against the frame.

Rachel was the only one who never latched the kitchen door. Eli had come in from the barn after his evening chores, and her sister had already gone home after the evening meal. So how was it that the door was flopping around on its hinges now? Were the late-winter storms strong enough to jar it loose; or had it finally broken from the sheer force of the wind?

Curious, Hannah went to the kitchen door and opened it so she could latch the screen, when a note wedged in the frame dropped to the floor. Snow swirled around her bare feet as she bent to pick up the envelope.

She looked at it, noticing right away that it had her sister's handwriting on the front. Her heart pounded; it was the letter she'd been expecting for more than two years.

Christmas and the new year had passed, and the upcoming spring season was full of possibilities for the eighteen-year-old, who had the notion that since she was officially an adult, she was fully prepared to face the *Englisch* world and all its temptations.

She wasn't surprised by the note; she'd been expecting it.

She'd been dreading it ever since her sister's birthday.

Why hadn't she shared with Rachel the news of her *boppli* yesterday when they'd visited? The answer to that was simple; she'd been too cowardly even to tell Eli, for fear he would not be happy about it. He'd confided in her his fears of having another child after what had happened to Lydia, and she had to admit, it frightened her a little too. But they couldn't live their lives in fear of what *might* happen, because that simply wasn't living in faith. Still, she'd chickened out every time she'd tried to tell him, and she certainly couldn't tell Rachel her news before telling her own husband.

Thinking about it now, she wished she had.

It likely wouldn't have mattered to the anxious girl who was full of dreamy notions regarding her future, but she hoped her news would keep her home at least another year—to give her more time to grow up a little more before embarking on such an adult adventure.

Rachel was determined to grow up way too fast, and her cousins were of no help to her in that department. They were all too eager to prance around in the *Englisch* world where they didn't belong—at least not until they were old enough to handle it. At only eighteen, Rachel was already wise beyond her years, given the hardship they'd suffered when their *mamm* had died, but even that could not prepare her for what she would encounter in the unfamiliar and fascinating *Englisch* world.

Hannah held the letter close to her heart, collapsed onto the kitchen chair and began to weep; she missed her little sister already. Worst of all, she mentioned corresponding with Alana, and how she'd agreed to take the job with the woman, and that made Hannah worry even more about her. The young girl had no idea what she was getting herself into with the troublesome Alana. She prayed because it was the only thing she could do at this point; she knew it was out of her hands.

Herr Gott, please turn this situation around for your greater gut, and keep your light shining in mei schweschder so she will be a beacon of truth to Alana. Guard Rachel from the bad influences that could change her heart and turn her away from her familye; put a hedge of protection around her to keep her from making mistakes that might ruin her future. I understand she has her own free will, Lord, but bless her with an extra measure of wisdom to make the right choices and resist the temptations that are lurking around every corner. Bless mei daed with gut health and strength, and keep him busy so he won't be lonely in his empty haus. Please keep me from getting too caught up in mei own life that I neglect him. Danki, Amen.

She dried her eyes and lifted her bone-weary frame, shuffling toward the sink to make coffee for her husband, and a bottle for her daughter. The sun had not yet risen fully, but as she gazed out the kitchen window at the deep blanket of snow, she saw a twinkle of twilight that filled her with peace.

Chapter 2

Rachel pulled her thick scarf over her face as she cowered behind a tree and watched Hannah open the door to find the note she'd left for her. She knew leaving the screen door to bang around would bring her sister to the door. She hated leaving this way, but if she'd tried to tell her sister goodbye, she would have had to endure a lecture and countless hours of begging her not to go. No, it was better this way; better for both of them.

Six months would fly by quickly, and she would return and settle down while she was still young enough to court. She wanted the best of both worlds; she craved the excitement that only the *Englisch* world could provide, but she also wanted to follow in her sister's example and find a good man and have a family.

She had learned from her sister's mistakes that waiting too long to have a family could be disastrous. It was true that God had blessed her sister with abundance, but she nearly ended up a spinster, and Rachel was determined it wouldn't happen to her.

She didn't want to leave Hannah or Mira, who had just learned to say her name, but she knew life changed every day, and time was too short on this earth to do the things you feel compelled to do. Seeing the world from the other side of the fence was one of those things for Rachel. It was a craving that could only be quieted by going exactly where her heart led her to go. She knew getting help from Alana would put a thorn in her sister's side, but she prayed in time, Hannah would forgive her for doing what she felt she needed to do before settling down in the community and taking the baptism.

Her desire to live out her life as an Amish woman in the community hadn't changed; her heritage was here, and so was her family, and she would sooner perish than to be shunned like Alana. She could see the coldness in the woman's eyes, and she had prayed many a night that she would not be influenced by it. In the midst of her prayers, she almost felt that her presence could somehow bring peace to the woman, and for that reason alone, she could not ignore the prompting she felt right down to her very soul.

She shivered in the pre-dawn hour, the wind blowing snow against her cheeks. She stood there with a lump in her throat as she watched her sister close the door. Through the sheer curtains, she could see by her sister's silhouette she was crying, and it almost caused Rachel to run to her and tell her it was just a silly prank and she would stay. She would miss her niece growing up; she'd surely miss out on witnessing a lot of *firsts* for the toddler by the time she returned from her adventures.

Not to mention, Hannah, whom she suspected was trying to tell her something all week. She'd been sick, and her cheeks had filled out a little. Rachel had noticed her holding her stomach a time or two, and she knew that could only mean one thing; Hannah was pregnant. It had caused Rachel to make her decision hastily.

She now knew she could only stay away for six months; any longer than that and she would miss out on the most important milestone of her sister's life, and she would not be that selfish as to let Hannah down. But now, this was her time, and her life, and she was going to seize the opportunity so she wouldn't live with regret; always wondering what might have been out there for her to explore. She would get it out of her system and return fully ready to follow in the good example of her sister's life.

Hannah rose from the table and out of Rachel's sight. At the end of the long driveway, her cousin and her friend waited in a warm car for her, but she was determined to remain in the cold just a few minutes longer—until she was fully ready to leave her sister and niece behind.

Chapter 3

Rachel tucked her chin down, narrowing her eyes against the wind and sleet that assaulted her as she forced her feet to take her down the driveway and away from her family. If she wasn't brave now, she would never leave, and she figured she would regret that for the rest of her life. She wanted to take the baptism at the end of her journey with no regrets, and this was the only way. Already, she missed her sister and her niece, but she was certain once she got to the city, the six months would fly by all too quickly, and it would be time to return home.

She breathed in deeply as she reached for the handle to the car door, the icy air stinging her lungs. She looked up one last time at the house that she could barely see through the thick snow and the wooded area that lined the long driveway.

"I'll miss you, my dear sister," Rachel whispered, lifting her eyes. "Lord, take *gut* care of *mei schweschder's familye*, and take care of that *boppli* I'm certain she's carrying. Please keep *mei schweschder,* her *kinner,* and her *mann* safe until I return, and help Hannah to understand why I had to go. Put forgiveness and understanding in her heart for me at this time."

Rachel opened the car door and slid into the front seat without saying a word to her cousin, Lucy, or her friend, Amber. They had each had their sorrowful times of bidding their families goodbye, but she'd had to go through it twice; once when she said goodbye to her *daed* and now for her *schweschder* and her *familye*, the latter of the two being the hardest.

She looked at Amber and Lucy, and forced a smile.

"I'm ready; let's go!"

They drove away, and Rachel resisted the urge to look back.

All three girls remained silent, except for the occasional direction being given when Amber missed a road sign. They were lucky that her brother, Seth, had given her the car when he returned recently from his *rumspringa*. Rachel was surprised at how well she drove in the icy snow. She had trouble controlling a buggy in the snow and couldn't imagine trying to maneuver a car in the slippery stuff.

Still, they all wore their seatbelts; they weren't taking any chances—even though she passed her driving test with a score of one hundred percent. She and Lucy had each read the short booklet that contained all the rules of the road and took turns quizzing Amber. If not for the actual driving part, Rachel could have likely passed the written part at least. They'd quizzed her relentlessly, making sure nothing would stand in the way of them leaving, and failing the driver's license test would certainly have done that.

Lucy leaned up from the back seat and flipped on the radio, and they all started singing to an old song that had become sort of their motto.

Girls just wanna have fu-un, oh-oh girls just wanna have fun…

When it was over, Rachel turned it down. "We're gonna have fun, right?" she asked. "You don't think we should have waited do you?"

"You'll see when we get to the great apartment Seth left for us—it's going to be great!"

"Do you have the address?"

"*Jah,* but we have to go to the landlord's office first to sign the lease that Seth signed over to us."

"I'm just happy we each have to pay only a hundred dollars a month. That's going to leave a lot of spare change to do some fun things. Lucky for us no one else rented it for the past three months."

"How close are we?" Lucy asked.

Rachel turned around and showed her the map, putting her finger on the street they needed to be on. It was only a few more blocks, but it was frustrating not knowing where they were; it certainly added to the length of their trip. She knew they would learn their way around before long, but for now, they would keep the map close.

Amber turned down the main street and pulled in front of a nice building where their new landlord worked. They all got out and stretched their legs while Amber looked for loose change in the center console to put in the parking meter.

They all smiled, excited to start their life in the city. Inside the lobby, a young woman not much older than they were answered a phone and stared at a computer screen.

Without looking up, she tapped on a sign-in sheet on the counter in front of her window. Amber filled in all three names, and then the girl shooed her toward the lobby seating where Lucy and Rachel had already made themselves comfortable on the button-backed leather settees.

Before long, an older man in a suit opened the door between the lobby and the office, and introduced himself.

"I'm Mr. Baker," he said with a friendly smile. "You young ladies must be related to Seth Mast; I can tell by the way you're dressed." He chuckled to himself, but the girls merely smiled their annoyance.

"He's *mei bruder*—brother," Amber spoke up.

He beckoned them in to the back of the office. They each rose and followed him single-file down the long corridor. At the end of the hall, he led them into a nice boardroom with a large table and swivel leather chairs with high backs. They sank into the oversized chairs at the man's prompt.

He helped himself to a bottled water from a mini-fridge in the corner near a coffee pot, and offered the girls a bottle. They each nodded, and he doled out three bottles to them. With his own water, he took a seat at the head of the table.

"I'm sorry you came all this way," he finally said. "But I'm afraid I can't rent you that apartment Seth was in."

Rachel gasped, wondering if she'd gone through all of this, just to end up back home in the community after less than a day away.

Chapter 4

Rachel wrung her hands while Amber tried desperately to convince Mr. Baker just how much they needed that apartment, and how they had nowhere else to go.

"I can't rent that apartment to a group of young ladies; it's not fit for you!"

"But we were counting on the rent being so low, and it's close to town," Amber argued. "Seth said you keep *gut* security in the building, so we'd be alright."

"I don't consider having fake cameras in the lobby good security," he chuckled. "Nowadays, they can tell the fake ones a mile away!"

Lucy and Rachel had remained silent the entire time, knowing it was Amber's brother who had put them in the predicament by promising something that wasn't in his authority to offer them.

"When your brother asked if he could sublet his lease to family, I agreed; I never thought it would be to his sister. If one of you has a brother or a male cousin that will stay there with you, then I'll lease you the apartment, but I can't, in good conscience, let you rent that apartment. When I bought the building, I thought I could turn things around for it, but I have a lot of once-homeless men in the building who now work for me, and I don't have any women in the building at all. It's just sort of worked out that way because of the neighborhood it's in."

Amber slumped back in the chair and looked at the other two. "Now what are we going to do?"

Mr. Baker leaned back in his seat and sipped from his water bottle. "Do you young ladies have jobs?"

"I'm the only one who has a job lined up," Rachel said. "And it's only part time—three days a week."

"I can let you have an apartment in this building for the same rent, as long as you work part time for me here. The young lady I have working the desk now isn't working out; she ignores the clients, and she talks on the phone with her friends constantly."

They had noticed that.

"I need someone for the building next door too," he said. "It's only four hours every morning, so you'd have the rest of your day free. Is that workable for the three of you?"

Lucy and Amber agreed to each take a building.

"I can come and help on Tuesdays and Thursdays, if that's alright?"

"Excellent," Mr. Baker said. "I'll get the key and show you the apartment myself, and if it's to your liking, we can come back down and sign the papers. How long will you be staying?"

"Six months; maybe longer if things work out here," Amber answered.

"I'll just put you on a month-to-month lease. That way, if things change, you won't be obligated one way or the other."

Rachel liked that idea—especially if she had to leave early for Hannah's delivery. It wasn't something she would miss, and babies didn't always come along on schedule.

They followed Mr. Baker to a third-floor apartment. "My wife decorated this one with a *country* motif, so you little gals might like it. Personally, I like everything modern."

He turned the key and let them in, and it was almost like home. Country yellows and reds filled the room with a sort of home-like quality; Rachel thought she could settle here for a long time. They all smiled at one another, giggles abounding.

"It's fully-furnished, as you can see; it also comes with a complete set of dishes and pots and pans. I think I can tell by the looks on your faces, this is the right place for you."

Amber collapsed onto the country red sofa and smiled. "You couldn't have picked a more perfect place for us!"

"It's a two-bedroom unit, so you'll have to share."

"We'll take it," Amber said.

Rachel breathed a sigh of relief. For the next six months, this would be their *home*.

Chapter 5

Hannah braved the walk that it took to get to the mailbox while Mira slept soundly in her crib. She'd hoped for a letter from Rachel by now, and it greatly disturbed her that she'd been gone for almost two weeks without any word from her.

Relief washed over her as she lifted the hand-written envelope from the box, holding it close to her and whispering a sincere *danki* toward the heavens. She'd been so worried, and even now, her stomach soured with anticipation for what the letter might say. Snow alighted on her cheeks as she made her way back to the house, and she hoped it would be the last snow for the season. On the slippery walk, she felt almost unable to wait that long before reading the letter. She didn't dare hurry, even though Eli had carefully and meticulously shoveled the icy path for her.

He'd walked with her nearly every day, knowing how anxious she'd been to get a letter, and even though he would have rather gotten the mail for her each day, than to risk her slipping, he kept the path clear, knowing how important it was for her to go for herself. He knew she needed that, and he wouldn't deny her of it, but that wouldn't stop him from assuring her safety. She felt fussed-over, and she suspected he knew she was expecting a baby, but she still hadn't worked up the nerve to tell him the news.

Once she reached the kitchen door, she went inside and immediately sat at the kitchen table without even removing her coat or her boots. She would mop up the puddle of melted ice later; for now, all she cared about was tearing into the letter and hearing her sister's news.

My dear sister, Hannah,

I'm sorry it has taken me so long to write to you, but as you can see by the return address, there was a change of plans when we got here. The apartment that Seth had leased was not fit for us, and the landlord refused to rent it to us. We were able to negotiate a better deal with him for a much nicer apartment that is in a safer community. The only condition is that we must work for him at his offices, and that has taken up a lot of my time. Also, we have a really nice apartment to live in, we don't spend much time here, because we are all working, and on our time off we are enjoying some of the winter activities here such as ice skating and sledding before it all melts. Spring is upon us!

I'm hoping that by now you have forgiven me for not saying goodbye to you, but I feared you had some news for me, and I knew it would keep me at home with you instead of where I am now. I know this is nothing more than a taste of freedom on my own, but I needed this time before I devoted myself to you and your family. I know that in six month's time you will need me to help you, and then I would never want to leave with a brand new niece or nephew to help care for. If I'm wrong then forgive me, but I suspect you didn't tell me because you haven't yet told your mann.

Tell him; I have a feeling he knows anyway!

When I return, we will have plenty to talk about and I will have plenty of stories for you along the way. I promise I will write to you every week until

I'm home with you again. Please write me at the address listed below just in case the snow smudged my writing on the front of the envelope. I love you dear sister. Take care of yourself and the new boppli, and give Mira a kiss for me. I'll be home before you know it. In the meantime, please write to me and tell me that I am correct in my assumption of your condition.

With love, Rachel

Tears filled her eyes as she read the letter over again. How had Rachel known she was pregnant? Was she correct in believing that Eli knows as well? Perhaps because it was her first pregnancy, she didn't quite know how to conceal it. It wasn't that she was trying to be sneaky, but she feared her husband's reaction. She knew that he would fuss over her and worry; and she hoped to spare him of that as long as possible.

It wouldn't be long before he would be able to see for himself regardless.

She giggled at Rachel's letter. She knew her little sister was wise beyond her years, and it was good advice, but she still wasn't quite ready to tell Eli. Every time she went to tell him, the words just would not come. She knew it was important to be truthful with him; after all, he trusted her.

Eli startled her when he walked in through the kitchen door. He pulled his boots off in the mudroom just off to the side of the kitchen, and stuffed his feet into his warm slippers.

He met her with a kiss. She desperately tried to dry her eyes, trying to hide the tears, but he'd already seen.

"Did you get a letter from Rachel?" He asked.

"*Jah*," she said. "Would you like some *kaffi*?"

She jumped up from the table and he slipped his hands in hers to stop her.

"First," he said with a smile. "I want to talk to you about something."

She began to shake as she looked in his eyes knowing that he must know her secret. "*Jah*, I'm expecting a *boppli*," she blurted out.

A smile rose on his lips, and he pulled her into a hug. Even though he already suspected, it was a relief to hear her finally say it. He wept as he chuckled. He couldn't be happier. He didn't dare tell her that he already knew, because then it would ruin the fact that she finally told him. He'd been waiting for weeks to hear the words he already knew, and now it was out there in the open, and it brought him relief.

"I've been putting off telling you because I was afraid you would be upset."

He pulled her away and looked her in the eye.

"Why would I be upset?" He asked.

She shrugged.

She wasn't about to answer that question. The last thing she wanted was to bring up hurtful memories for him and cause him to worry about her.

"Do you suppose we'll have a boy?" He asked.

"I don't know," she said, crying and giggling at the same time. "But it would be nice for Mira to have a little bruder."

"*Jah*, and it would be nice to have a *sohn* to teach him how to work the farm, and I could sure use the help."

She looked at him curiously hoping he wasn't putting up a brave front for her sake. She truly wanted this child; but more than that, she needed him to be happy about it.

"I'm so happy you told me finally," he said, letting it slip that he already knew.

She merely smiled at him and he held her for several more minutes while they both laughed, making plans for their future child.

"The reason I came in here, was because I spoke to Jacob Yoder yesterday, and he's decided he's getting too old to work the back forty between our farms, and he offered it to me for sale. It would mean I would have to hire some help for the spring planting, and it would bite into our budget just a little bit, but it would pay off at harvest time. It seems our *familye* is growing and could use the extra income an extra forty acres could provide."

"*Jah*, I think that is a *gut* idea. How many do you think you'll need to hire?"

"I was thinking two maybe, and I could put them up in the *dawdi haus*."

"Did you have anyone in mind?"

"*Yeah* I was thinking of your cousin Zack, and his friend Seth."

"*Seth* is the one who has always been sweet on Rachel, but she would never give him the time of day." she said, giggling. "I sure hope she can handle having him here when she comes back here to help me with the new *boppli*."

"I wouldn't worry about that. He won't have time to bother her since he'll be working, and I suspect she won't have much time to be bothered by him either if she's going to be helping you with our new *sohn*."

Hannah giggled. "I hope you're not counting on the *sohn*, because Mira could end up with a little *schweschder*."

They both laughed and hugged happily. For now, anyway, the worries over the new baby had been put aside, and it looked as if Eli would not suffer any ill effects from the past. It would seem that the past two years and her love had healed him, and right now she couldn't be happier. With spring on the way in just a few weeks, there would be new hope in this home and that's exactly what it needed.

Chapter 6

Rachel very sleepily answered the door buzzer, thinking Lucy had locked herself out of the apartment again getting the newspaper from downstairs.

She flung the door open, surprised to see…

"Seth! What are you doing here?" she asked, pulling her robe around her and smoothing her hair down. Her face must have turned about ten shades of red. She wasn't sure why she cared what she looked like, except that she knew how much he liked her.

He cleared his throat and smiled at her fidgeting. "*Mei schweschder* lives here, you know! I had a few days free before I begin a new job with *your schweschder's mann,* and so I thought I might come to the city and hang out for a few days."

She shook her head, trying to wake up. "How did you get here so early?"

Was that all she really wanted to say to him? For now, she was annoyed he'd woken her when she could have slept at least another half-hour. She'd gotten the letter from Hannah telling her Seth would be working with Eli, and she was never so happy that she was in the city away from him. But here he was, invading her sleep—maybe it was just a nightmare! The thought of dreaming of Seth set her teeth on edge—almost as much as having to deal with him now in person.

He watched her put on a pot of coffee, delighted he was getting under her skin. "Zach dropped me off on his way to see his cousins. *Ach,* I can't believe you got such a nice apartment. When Amber wrote to me and told her how Mr. Baker had treated you, I was happy. He and his *fraa* are a few of the really *gut Englischers* I met while I was here for the past year."

It was the quietest year of mei life, Rachel thought.

"They even gave Amber and Lucy jobs so we could stay here. I help them on my days off from Alana's office."

"Why are you working for her? Wasn't she trying to steal your *schweschder's boppli?*"

Rachel shook her head at him and sighed. "She was worried about her own *schweschder's boppli,* but when she saw how *gut* Hannah was with her, and the love Eli had for them, Alana bowed out and left them alone. I've gotten to know her in the past few weeks, and she's really a kind person. She's lonely though, and has been talking a lot lately about wanting to settle down in our community to be near her niece. I think it would be *gut* for both of them honestly. But that is for *mei schweschder* to decide. I know Hannah, though, she will *wilkum* her for Mira's sake."

"I guess I shouldn't rely too much on the rumors in the community, ain't so?" he asked.

She leered at him as she poured two cups of coffee from the pot. *"Jah,* leave the gossiping to the trouble-makers," she reprimanded him as she handed him the cup of coffee.

"Danki for the *kaffi,"* he said with a wink.

"Don't read too much into it," she groaned, still half-asleep. "I'm sure I'm having a nightmare, and perhaps the *kaffi* will make it—and you go away!"

He chuckled. "I don't know why you resist my attention so much. You know I've always adored you."

She sat down across from him and really looked at him, unable to come up with a significant answer to his statement. He'd certainly grown up in the past year; he'd gotten taller, and his muscles had filled out. His blue eyes sparkled under the bright lights of the kitchen, and his smile was certainly nice.

No matter how handsome and sweet he was, the fact remained, he was Amber's older brother, and she'd only ever seen him as an annoying older brother who loved to tease them relentlessly their entire growing up years. She knew he'd always joked about marrying her someday, but she'd always discouraged him. Now, as she really looked at him, she had to wonder what it would be like to be held by his strong arms, and kiss his full lips.

"Rachel!" he said. "Why are you staring at me? Did I spill *kaffi* down the front of me?"

She jumped up from the table, embarrassed that he'd caught her swooning over him. Imagine; her swooning over Amber's brother! It was too ridiculous to even think about. It would never work, and she had better get the thought as far from her mind as she could before it got her into trouble she might not be able to get out of. If she gave him even the slightest bit of encouragement, he'd have them married with two *kinner* before she was able to blink.

"I wasn't staring at you, so don't get so full of yourself!" she said. "I was just thinking how I'd be late for work if I didn't wake up and get moving."

"If Amber and Lucy are working here today, I can drive you so you won't have to take the bus. My car is still here, isn't it?"

She whipped her head around after dropping her coffee cup in the sink. "How do you know I have to take the bus?"

"Amber wrote to me and told me," he said, winking at her again. "Will you let me drive you to work, even though you don't like me?"

He pushed out his lower lip, causing her to think about kissing him.

"You're staring again!" he said with a chuckle.

Her lips formed a narrow line. "I was not. I told you…"

"I know; you're not awake yet!" he interrupted.

She sighed and went to her room to change, leaving him in the kitchen alone.

When she finished dressing, she brushed her teeth and combed out her long, auburn hair and returned to the kitchen, hoping to get another cup of coffee before she had to catch the bus. She found Seth lounging on the sofa, his suitcase sitting by the door.

"You can't stay here!" she said to him.

He looked back at her and smiled. "Where else am I going to stay?"

"Not here!" she squealed.

"Why not?" he said, pouting out his lower lip again.

Why does he have to do that? Probably because he knows what it's doing to me!

"It wouldn't be proper," she finally said.

"You can trust *me!* Or is it yourself you don't trust?" he asked with another wink.

"Stop that!"

She hadn't meant to say it out loud.

"Stop what?" he chuckled. "I'm not doing anything."

She narrowed her eyes. "You know *exactly* what you're doing," she said. "It's what you always do; get under my skin."

"Well it must be working or else you wouldn't be getting so mad at me."

She was fuming; she turned around to snap at him, when she noticed the clock on the stove. "Now you've made me miss my bus and I'm going to be late for work!"

"I told you I'd be happy to drive..." he stopped mid-sentence as he sat up from the sofa to face her.

"What's wrong?" she asked, still annoyed with him.

He allowed his gaze to travel over the lines of the short dress she was wearing, and back up to her long hair that hung over her shoulders in waves.

She'd never looked lovelier to him.

Chapter 7

Seth stood there with his mouth hanging open, unable to process the overwhelming attraction to Rachel.

"*Ach,* I've never seen you dressed as an *Englischer* before."

She didn't like his comment, and she certainly didn't like the way he was staring at her.

"Put your eyes back in your head, *bruder,*" Amber reprimanded him as she came into the kitchen. "Who invited you here, anyway?"

"*Ach*, you invited me! You said I should see the great apartment you got," he said. "Is that anyway to greet your favorite *bruder?*"

She hugged him. "That was a figure of speech—it was not an invitation, and you're *mei* only *bruder,* so how can you be my favorite?"

"By default!" he said, chuckling.

She looked up at Rachel who was wearing annoyance all over her face and her posture. "What are you still doing here? Aren't you going to miss your bus?"

"I already missed it!"

"Give me the keys to *mei* car," Seth said. "I'm going to drive her."

"That car belongs to me now! You gave it to me!"

He turned and winked at Rachel, but she was getting more annoyed by the minute.

"Then can I have the keys to *your* car so I can take Rachel to work?"

She smiled at Rachel, but she wasn't going to get a return smile from the girl, and she knew it. "*Jah,* the keys are over there on the hook by the door. Take your girlfriend to work so she'll get that mad look off her face."

"I'm not his girlfriend, Amber; and for the record, I'm annoyed that your *bruder* made me late for work!"

She turned to Seth. "How did you make her late for work?"

He chuckled. "I didn't ask her to make me *kaffi,* she just did it."

Amber's eyes widened. "You made him *kaffi?* This keeps getting more interesting by the minute."

Rachel narrowed her eyes at Seth. "Can we go, please before your *schweschder* has us married?"

Amber laughed. "*Ach,* you know we're only teasing. We wouldn't have so much fun with it if you wouldn't pretend to be so mad!"

"Pft, who's pretending?" she shot back.

Seth looped his arm in Rachel's and steered her toward the door. "Let's go before you two turn this into a cat-fight."

She was so distracted; she didn't realize he had his arm around her until they were at the elevator. Her flesh was heated where she felt the warmth of his embrace. She looked up at his six-foot frame, wondering when he'd gotten so tall. She fidgeted with the ribbon at her waist, feeling as if the elevator was taking forever.

With a sudden jolt, the elevator stopped, sending Rachel into a state of panic. Seth put a hand on her shoulder as he went to the control panel to see if he could get the elevator moving again.

"Don't get upset," he said calmly. "This used to happen in my building too. Usually within a few minutes, it restarts and everything is fine. This sort of thing happens in older buildings."

She stood close behind him, leaning over his shoulder as he pushed the buttons with no results, and then opened the phone box. He picked up the receiver and held it to his ear.

The look on his face said it all. The line was dead. "I'm sorry, Rachel; I think we're stuck in here until someone tries to use the elevator."

Tears filled her eyes, and she became very rigid. He pulled her into his arms and held her as she nervously sobbed. "Shh, everything is going to be alright; you'll see. We won't be in here more than a few minutes."

She collapsed into the strength of his frame. She was truly afraid, and if they couldn't get out of here fast, she might embarrass herself by hyperventilating.

"Shh," he soothed her, as he kissed her hair. He breathed her in; she smelled like flowers and sunshine. He loved her; oh how he loved her. He held her close and began to sweep his lips over her forehead and her cheeks until he reached her mouth; he just couldn't help himself.

Rachel melted into Seth's sturdy frame feeling the closeness of his solid physique. She guarded herself, trying not to feel anything for him, but his kindness and gentleness was wearing her down. She could sense how much he loved her; she could feel it in his touch. When his lips found hers, she deepened the kiss with a passion for him she never knew she had.

The door to the elevator suddenly swung open, and luckily, there was no one on the other side of the door to witness their scandalous embrace.

Chapter 8

Seth felt Rachel slip from his embrace when the door swung open, and he felt his heart go with her as she exited the elevator. Was she angry? How could she just walk away from him so swiftly, after what the two of them had just experienced? Was it possible that she was embarrassed, or did she really truly not like him? Whatever the reason, he felt his heart sink to his shoes.

"*Ach,* slow down, Rachel," he called after her. "What's your hurry?

"I'm late for work!" she called from over her shoulder.

Is that all? I can deal with that better than rejection.

He followed her close on her heels to get to the car in the parking lot behind the building. After opening her door for her, he hopped in the other side and started the car.

Rachel felt strange; he was being such a gentleman, and she was fretful about the very passionate kiss they'd just shared, and had to think about what happened before he spoke to her about it. She sat beside him in silence as he drove her to her job with nothing more than an address. She'd never been in a car with a man before, and she had to admit she kind of liked it.

He pulled the car up to Alana's building and he hopped out while she was busy unbuckling the seatbelt she still wasn't used to wearing. He opened her car door and walked with her and opened the office door for her, then surprised her by placing a fast kiss on her cheek.

"What time do you get out of here? I'd like to pick you up," he offered.

"Ach, you don't need to do that," she said. "I can take the bus."

He smiled, making her legs feel wobbly. "I was hoping you'd let me take you out to dinner somewhere after work."

"You mean like a *date?*" she whispered, aware that Alana was just inside the office.

He could see the fear in her eyes and realized it might be too soon to ask for a date.

"*Nee,*" he fibbed. "As friends."

"*Ach,* I supposed that would be alright," she said, feeling a little confused. "I finish at five o'clock."

He seemed to be running hot and cold with his feelings, and she wasn't sure how she felt either, so it was probably best if she didn't read too much into it.

He put up a hand and waved. "I'll be here at five."

He turned and walked back to the car, and her confusion increased. Had she wanted him to kiss her once more before he left?

If only the elevator door hadn't opened when it did; maybe then she would know the answer to her question. She'd enjoyed the kissing, and that confused her greatly. She hadn't ever thought she could be attracted to him. He was Amber's annoying older brother, and that was all; wasn't it?

She walked inside Alana's office, feeling the woman's eyes burning a hole in her thoughts.

"I'm sorry I was late, but I got stuck in the elevator of my building," she said, realizing how ridiculous the excuse sounded even to her.

Alana laughed. "With that handsome guy? Is he your boyfriend?"

She shrugged. "He's not my boyfriend; I've known him all my life. He asked me out on a date—I think, but I'm not sure I want to go."

Her eyes widened. "I'd like a date with that cute guy; if you don't want to go out with him, I'll be happy to go in your place!"

"You will not!" Rachel surprised herself by saying. "He's *my* boyfriend!"

Chapter 9

Rachel wasn't sure she liked the idea of Alana's interest in Seth. Truthfully, she wasn't even sure if she, herself, had any interest in him beyond friendship. Maybe it was the excitement of seeing his familiar face from home; or perhaps it was simply that she'd never thought of him in that way.

That kiss in the elevator had changed everything.

"You might as well not even be here today," Alana said as she walked by the front desk where Rachel sat daydreaming about that kiss.

She looked up at her boss. "I'm sorry. I'll tuck away my thoughts for later and get to work on those files."

"You'll do no such thing," Alana said. "I'm taking you shopping for the perfect dress for your dinner date tonight."

"When I asked him if it was a date, he suddenly backed down and called it just dinner between two friends. Besides, I don't have money for a new dress."

Alana waved a hand at her. "He told you that because of the way you reacted to his kiss. I bet he felt rejected. For the record, the dress is my treat. You've been a life-saver the past couple of weeks, and saved me countless hours of work with your great ideas for keeping this office organized."

Her face lit up, but then quickly dulled.

"Do you think it's a *gut* idea to get a new dress? He might think I'm taking this too seriously."

Alana giggled. "Men like it when a woman dresses up for them. Besides, you don't want to let him go, do you? He's too cute to throw back in the pond—you've got a great catch with that one!"

"I suppose," she said. "But what if he really does just want to be friends?"

"How good was his kiss?"

"Who says I kissed him?" Rachel asked defensively.

"That dreamy look in your eyes is giving you away!" Alana said with a smirk.

"You twisted my arm." Rachel said with a smile. "Let's go shopping!"

****

All the way back to his sister's apartment, Seth wondered what it was he could have done so wrong with Rachel. She'd kissed him back in the elevator, he was sure of it, but had she thought he'd taken advantage of her vulnerable state when they were trapped in there? She'd kissed him back with an equal amount of passion that matched his own.

So what was the problem?

He drove past a section of town where they'd built a connecting freeway, and his eye caught billboard after billboard of couples in their same age group modeling clothing for a new store. Was it the way he was dressed?

She'd converted to *Englisch* clothes so quickly, yet the entire time he'd spent among the *Englisch,* he'd stayed true to his Amish upbringing, and had never tried any other clothing. It hadn't even crossed his mind until he saw Rachel in that dress. She looked so different, and he liked it.

Was it possible since she was dressed as an *Englischer* that she didn't want to be seen in public with him as an Amish man? He would gladly change for her if he thought it would make her happy. But would changing his clothes be enough to make a difference?

Pulling the car into the parking lot of the shopping plaza, Seth made up his mind he was going to get a new shirt and a new hairstyle that was more befitting an *Englischer*.

He was determined to shock Rachel with his new look in the same way he was shocked by hers.

Chapter 10

Rachel looked at herself in the dressing room mirror, delighted by her reflection. Was she sure about such drastic changes for a date—with Seth?

He was still very Amish, and she was ready to live as an *Englischer,* but she could see he'd settled back into the Amish community, and their strict rules regarding his clothing. Was she really going to let that bother her?

Perhaps going through all this trouble was not worth it considering she was going out with an Amish man who would not be the least bit impressed by her new *Englisch* way of life—at least for the next six months.

Truth was, he'd admired her very much in the dress she'd picked out with her first week of pay. But did she really want to date an Amish man— especially the very man she'd tried so hard to get away from in her community? She had intention of dating *Englischers* while she was here in the city. Alana had offered to introduce her to several young men, but she'd constantly made excuses. Was it possible she was simply too afraid of dating an *Englischer,* and dating Seth was *safe?*

Now that she'd kissed him, he suddenly didn't feel quite as safe as before. It would be too easy for her to fall in love with him; the kiss had nearly put her there. It had shocked her to the point of being speechless. She'd reacted badly when the elevator doors opened, and because of this, Seth had acted aloof. Was it possible he'd thought it was a mistake to kiss her? Or perhaps he'd kissed her to calm her down. Either way, she would not allow her emotions to rule her; she would stay casual with Seth, and guard her heart from being toyed with.

He was definitely going to like this dress; it was much more feminine and frilly than the one she'd worn to work. She'd never felt such silky material next to her skin. The light pink, flowery sheer overlay came with a solid pink slip, and lace at the fluttery sleeves that draped down past her elbows.

Cinching at the waist, it complimented her slender figure, and the fluttery material would flow nicely in the cool spring breeze. The leather flats she wore matched the dress perfectly, so they wouldn't need to make a trip to the shoe store.

She exited the dressing room to show Alana the dress she'd finally decided on after trying on practically every dress in the store. It wasn't that the store didn't have nice dresses; she was waiting for that one dress to speak out to her, and this one did just that.

Alana's expression as she exited the dressing room said the rest.

"Now we *have* to go to the hair salon to get your hair done!" she said.

Rachel had to admit, she liked being pampered, but she was capable of doing her hair. "What's wrong with *mei* hair?"

Alana smiled. "Nothing is *wrong* with it, but this is your first date with the guy, and I think you only get one chance to make a lasting impression."

"It's *not* a date!"

"Then why are you blushing?" Alana asked.

Rachel sighed; she had no answer. She could feel her cheeks heating, and wondered if she'd be this much of a mess during dinner.

She went back into the dressing room to change, and Alana stopped her. "Leave the dress on. We'll go pay for it and have the sales-girl cut the tags for us so you can wear it out of the store. That way if Seth is there at the office waiting on you when we get back, you won't have to change."

"I didn't really think about that."

They made their purchases and left the store. At the far end of the mall, they found a hair salon, and again, Alana offered it to be *her treat.*

"I can't let you do that!"

"I have a project that is going to require some extra time that I could use your help with. We'll consider this a bonus for the hours you'll be putting in. How long is he staying to visit?"

Rachel hadn't thought about his length of stay until that moment. Reality hit her hard right then. She couldn't go out on a date with him; he'd be going back to the community in three days, and the thought of it already broke her heart.

Chapter 11

Rachel stared blankly into the salon mirror while the woman styled her hair like she'd seen in the magazines her cousins hid under their beds. She'd looped pale pink ribbon and silk flowers in her hair—almost into a crown, leaving the rest of it cascading down her back. She was so elegant—almost like an *Englisch* bride.

She sighed, willing the thoughts from her mind. She would not think about marriage to Seth except that he'd asked her so many times. But that wasn't something she could even consider—especially since he'd acted so strangely after their kiss. It was almost as if he regretted it.

She certainly regretted it, but likely not for the same reasons he might. He was probably feeling *buyer's remorse,* whereas, she was thinking how much her heart would break if he was truly teasing her all these years, and never had intention of marrying her.

The woman trimming the edges off the bottom of Alana's hair finished, twirled her around to face the mirror, but her eyes traveled to Rachel.

"He is going to fall so in love with you, Rachel!"

"That's what I'm afraid of!"

"You're afraid of him falling in love with you? Why?"

Rachel bit her bottom lip to suppress tears that threatened. "I'm afraid if he falls in love with me, and I'm afraid if he won't. I guess that kiss sort of hit me harder than I thought. I think I've loved him all my life and I'm just now realizing it. I've not been able to get that kiss out of my mind all day. What will I do if he rejects me?"

Alana looked at her and smiled. "He won't reject you; you're not just beautiful on the outside, your kind heart shows your inner beauty."

The tears flowed freely with her comment, and Alana rushed to grab a tissue from the box on the counter in front of the mirror.

"Don't start crying; you'll have puffy, red eyes, and that won't do for your first date. He'll think you hate him for sure!"

Rachel laughed half-heartedly. "Maybe that would be for the best."

"No!" Alana said. "Falling in love is a beautiful thing. If it's God's will for you to be together, it will happen naturally."

She cast her eyes downward. "I pray you're right."

Alana put a hand under Rachel's chin and lifted gently. "There'll be none of that. I want to see a smile on that pretty face. You're about to go on your first date with the man of your dreams!"

"It's not a date, remember?"

"It is if you want it to be!"

Rachel looked at the confident smile on Alana's face, but she wasn't convinced. Only time and a lot of prayer would reveal the outcome.

Chapter 12

Rachel stepped onto the sidewalk where Alana had parked her car at the curb in front of her office. She'd purposely parked the car behind Seth's, hoping he would see them, and at least come and greet his date for the evening.

Maybe she was right after all, and it indeed wasn't a date at all.

Seth positioned himself in a casual lean, up against the front counter of Alana's office where Rachel answered the phones, his left leg crossed over the right at his ankle. When he saw them pull in behind his car, his heart began to race, and he prayed he hadn't overdone it by trying to fit into her new world—a world he discovered after a year he didn't belong.

When his attention turned to Rachel, who was getting out of Alana's car, her beauty nearly took his breath away. He leaned up from his elbow and straightened himself, while still trying to act casual; all the while, his heart was beating so hard and fast, he feared it would break free from his ribcage.

Rachel opened the door, and immediately, her gaze found Seth, who stood by the counter dressed as an *Englischer*. His dark blonde hair was cut short, and had some sort of product in it to make it lay every-which way in a messy—organized style.

It suited him.

Gone, was his black, felt hat, and his baby-blue button-up dress shirt was cuffed at his forearms, the tail un-tucked over a pair of new blue-jeans, his feet clad in a pair of brown loafers. His dimpled smile completed the look, and Rachel didn't think he could be more appealing than he was at this moment.

"You look lovely," he said to her, breaking the vanity rule, and probably the humility rule too. He smiled widely, and she feared if she wasn't careful, he might tempt her to break a lot more rules tonight.

She couldn't help but think how handsome he looked too, but she wasn't about to embarrass herself by saying it, so she simply smiled. *"Danki."*

He held out his arm for her, and she looped her arm in the fold of his elbow, looking back at Alana as they walked out the door.

Alana winked at her and told her she'd see her on Monday morning. Rachel hadn't heard a word; her heart was pounding in her ears. If not for her arm holding onto Seth's sturdy frame, her wobbly legs might just buckle under her. He escorted her to his car and paused before opening the car door for her. He paused again, leaning in and kissing her slowly and thoughtfully on the cheek. Her skin tingled, and her eyes drifted closed while his lips lingered on her cheek.

There it was; the love for him she had bottled up in her heart. It all came gushing forth all at once, filling her with hope that he returned her feelings.

She breathed him in, noticing he must have been wearing some sort of aftershave; it smelled very masculine, and she liked it.

He let her in the car and then slid in beside her behind the wheel. "I'd like to take you to my favorite little bistro, if that's alright."

She nodded, feeling elated he wanted to take her somewhere that was special to him.

It was a good sign.

The place he was talking about was only a few blocks away, and immediately, she recognized it as a place she'd already discovered; it was a favorite of hers too.

"I love this place!" she said excitedly. "They have the best…"

"Biscuits and gravy," they said in unison.

"*Ach,* they taste Amish-made," he added. "That, and their mashed potatoes alone kept me from getting homesick for *mei mamm's* cooking while I was here in the city."

"*Jah,* I've only been here a few weeks, and I've eaten here twice a week since. This will make it three for this week!"

"I'm so happy we can share this," he said, pulling her hand in his and lifting it to his lips, placing a gentle kiss on the back.

Her arm tingled at his touch, and she craved another kiss like the one they'd shared in the elevator.

He smiled. "I want tonight to be special. Even if you never want to see me again, at least I'll have this night with you at the start of the spring season, and I'll never forget how lovely you are."

What did he mean by that? She wasn't about to ask him, but it seemed like a strange thing to say. Was he setting himself up for rejection—or her?

Chapter 13

Rachel shushed herself as she and Seth walked in the door of her apartment. They'd been laughing all evening, and it was late. She found the light-switch in the quiet apartment, remembering her roommates had a long week, and were likely asleep; she would probably not see them until late the next morning. They'd already gotten into the habit of sleeping in on weekend mornings, and she knew that was one of the things that would be difficult to break once she returned home.

Though she'd had a wonderful time, he hadn't tried to kiss her again, which left her feeling a little disappointed. Now that they were back, she felt a little awkward, wondering if she would get a goodnight kiss.

"Hey, I noticed you don't have a TV in the living room," he said. "I was kind of hoping I could watch a little while I was visiting. Once I go back, I'll have to give all that up!"

Rachel wondered if she should offer to let him watch hers.

"I have one in my room," she said. "But it's only a small one. Amber and Lucy took the bigger bedroom—it's almost twice the size of mine, and it has a bigger TV."

"Any size TV is better than none at all," he said with a chuckle. "Is it okay if we watch a little TV in there before I try to get some sleep on that stiff sofa? That thing was not meant for sleeping; I think it's more for looks than anything." He was rambling, and he knew it, but he wanted to give her time to process what he'd asked of her. It was probably risky, given his feelings for her, but most likely not too much since she clearly didn't seem equally interested in him beyond friendship.

"*Jah,*" she said, wondering if she could trust herself to be alone with him in such a setting. She loved him, but she could be careful—especially since it seemed he'd changed his mind after that kiss in the elevator.

Was it possible he'd felt nothing for her when they'd kissed?

He followed her into her room and closed the door behind them. "Don't want *mei schweschder* seeing me in here and getting the wrong idea."

She nodded.

He went straight over to her bed and sat on the edge and removed his shoes, and then reclined back onto her pillow, patting the other side of the bed beside him, inviting her to cuddle up next to him.

Her heart beat double time while she reached for the remote and flipped on the TV. She sat on the edge of the bed and removed her shoes, wondering if she should change from her dress into a pair of sleep pants.

Seth held his arm out to her, and she cuddled up under his arm. It was nice there—comfortable, and he smelled so good she wasn't sure she could trust herself after all.

He reached up and grabbed the quilt that was folded at the end of the bed and pulled it up over them, while Rachel turned on the Western movie that was in the DVD player.

Once she was settled, he kissed her hair; mumbling something about what a nice time he'd had with her this evening. She tipped her head and looked up at his smiling eyes, allowing him to kiss her lightly at first.

She deepened the kiss, leaning into his solid frame, allowing his mouth to slide from her lips, to her neck, and then down to her shoulders. She reached down and unbuttoned his shirt, feeling his warm skin on her hands. It ignited a passion in her that was an unstoppable force.

He pulled her closer, his kisses intensifying.

She was powerless to stop herself from wanting more from him, or to resist his passion for her, but she didn't want to.

Chapter 14

Rachel stirred from a deep sleep, wondering where she was. Her hand rested on Seth's bare, washboard stomach, and she quickly withdrew her hand. She opened her eyes only a tiny slit, noticing he was still asleep. If she moved her head from his shoulder, she might wake him up, and she wasn't sure she was ready for that; her dress was somewhere on the floor, she thought. The only thing she was sure of was that it wasn't on her.

Somehow, she didn't think this was *Gott's wille.*

Truth was, she loved him even more now, though she wished they would have waited until they were married.

Was last night a mistake? It hadn't felt like it when they were in the throes of passion.

Panic and guilt mixed with the love she knew she had for him, but it was obvious they would have to get married now, and that hadn't fit into her plan—a plan she would now have to change.

Filled with mixed emotions, she was glad he wasn't up yet so she could sort through what had happened. Neither of them had expected things to go that far, but now that they had, how would they handle it? They'd broken every rule that flashed through her agitated mind, and many more than that she was certain.

She remained quiet next to him, waiting for him to wake up; she would have to rely on him to give the answers to her questions.

****

Seth had been awake for some hours, waiting for Rachel to wake up so they could talk about what happened. He knew he would dishonor her further if he didn't ask for her hand in marriage immediately. He intended to; it was what he wanted, but he still feared her answer would be no. She'd turned him down so many times over the years, but they were older now. They were both adults, and after what happened between them only a few hours ago, well, things had changed. He feared she would think he allowed it to happen to trap her into marrying him, but he loved her too much for that.

Perhaps some donuts and coffee would help to lighten the mood when she woke up—which would likely be soon. He could see through the curtain that the sun was beginning to start the day.

He slid his arm from under her as slowly as he could, and quickly dressed, and then tip-toed out of the room. He was slightly in fear of what had happened between them, and he still needed time to think of how he would ask her to marry him without scaring her off. This would be the real one, and funny, but he was suddenly nervous about it. Since this would be the one that counted, he feared rejection more than ever.

Since he'd always done his best thinking when he took a walk, he decided to go to the donut shop he knew was just around the corner. He'd pick up a dozen donuts and be back before she woke up.

****

Rachel tried her best not to choke on her tears as she rose from her bed, shaking and feeling as if she couldn't get enough air. He'd slithered out of the room, and she'd heard him leave the apartment. Had she been nothing more in his eyes than someone to use for his own pleasure, only to be tossed aside when he was through?

Why hadn't she stopped herself from giving in to him?

She'd gotten too caught up in the love she'd allowed herself to feel for him, and stupidly thought there was a future for the two of them.

But now, as she lay in the bed all alone and naked, it was obvious he'd left her and didn't intend on returning.

She sprang from the bed, anger and fear consuming her as she scrambled for her clothes. One thing was for certain; she could not stay in this apartment any longer. Amber would surely know her shame, and she could never face her; she wasn't even sure how she would face herself.

She grabbed her suitcase from under the bed and began to pull the few things she'd purchased from the dresser and the closet. She hadn't been there long enough to personalize the room with anything other than her quilt, which she also folded hastily and stuffed it into the matching handled bag she'd made to travel here with. She'd brought it from home—taken it from her dowry she'd been putting together since she'd turned fifteen. Now, it only served as a reminder that she'd tainted it and she could not use it on her marriage bed—if she ever got married. No man in the community would marry her after she'd sinned with Seth.

Had he told her he loved her just to get what he wanted? No. Seth wasn't that type of man. The only explanation was he must have changed his mind, but even that felt so wrong.

She choked down her tears, trying her best not to wake Amber or Lucy. There was no way she could face them now. She would have to put some distance between them. She couldn't go home; Hannah would know immediately that something was wrong, and she'd have to confess.

The only place she could go was to Alana's condo; only a short bus-ride from this side of town.

****

Seth paid for the donuts, feeling light on his feet. Surely the sweets and hot coffee would be the perfect segue to his marriage proposal. When he exited the donut shop, he could see Rachel leaving the apartment with her suitcase and another bag slung over her shoulder. She was too far away to be within shouting distance, and the tray of hot coffee he held would not permit him to run to her.

He stood there for a moment, dumbfounded at what he was seeing. There was no denying she had packed her bag—likely the minute he'd left the apartment, because he hadn't been gone that long.

She was leaving him.

How could she after the night they'd shared together? Had it meant nothing to her?

Suddenly, the thought of drinking the coffee and eating the donuts sickened him. A lump formed in his throat as he watched her walk down the street in the opposite direction.

As he neared the apartment, she continued on, but was walking slower than he was, and he'd closed the distance between them a little. He called after her, but she continued on without turning around. How could she leave him? Didn't she love him like she'd said she did?

Tears welled up in his eyes and he dumped his purchase from the donut shop in the trash bin beside the bench that was just outside her building. He collapsed onto the bench and watched her continue to walk down the street.

If he went after her, would it matter? He had to reason that if she had her mind set on leaving him, trying to stop her might work for a time, but it would only put off the inevitable. If she was this determined to get away from him that she would move out of her own apartment, there was no sense in trying to stop her.

He wiped his eyes and sniffled, knowing he didn't want to be near his sister, who would have tons of questions he wasn't willing to answer. All she would have to do was to take one look at him and see he was not himself. If he knew her as well as he thought, she would have likely come out to the kitchen in the middle of the night and noticed he wasn't sleeping on the sofa.

He went up the elevator and crept into the apartment and grabbed his suitcase from the closet in the hall. His few things he'd brought to stay the weekend were in there, with the exception of his shaving bag that he'd left in the bathroom, which he grabbed as quietly as he could. He hoped what Rachel had told him about the two of them sleeping in on weekends would keep him from running into either of them now.

He hated having to take the bus back instead of waiting on Zach to swing back and pick him up tomorrow night, but under the circumstances, he wouldn't be able to stay here; surely they would ask him where Rachel was, and he would have no explanation for it.

He walked toward the door with a heavy heart, when he noticed the note Rachel had left on the kitchen table.

He picked it up and read it;

Amber & Lucy,

I'm sorry for leaving this way, but I knew if I didn't, you'd try to talk me into staying. I've become homesick, and decided to take an early bus home this weekend. I've been worried about Hannah and her new pregnancy, so I feel it's my duty to help her.

I pray you understand. I will write to you once I settle in back home.

Rachel

He tossed the note back onto the table and grabbed the keys to his car. He'd have to leave a note for his sister so she wouldn't think it was stolen. He knew he had to hurry if he wanted to catch up to Rachel. If he drove her home, the long ride would give them time to talk this over.

He prayed silently that she would listen to him and give him a chance as he penned a quick note to Amber about the car. He would have to return it to her at the end of the week, but she would understand him taking Rachel home instead of letting her take a bus.

Lord, please let me catch up to her if it's your will. Please forgive me for the mistake I made, and give me the chance to make it right. I love her, and I pray she loves me too.

He grabbed his things and ran from the apartment. Hopping in his car, he started it quickly and headed down the street in the direction Rachel had gone, hoping to catch her before she reached the bus station.

Chapter 15

Rachel suppressed the tears while she waited for Alana to open her door. The minute the door swung open, the water-works began.

"What happened?" Alana asked, pulling her into a hug and noticing she was still wearing the same outfit she was wearing for her date last night, and her hair was a mess, the ribbons and flowers standing on end. Was Rachel even aware of the condition she was in physically?

Alana couldn't even be sure she knew what condition she was in mentally.

"He walked out on me!" Rachel sobbed. "I gave into him and let him take my—my—virtue, and he left early when he thought I was still asleep. He stayed overnight with me, but then he left just before the sun came up."

Alana was shocked. Did Rachel know what she was implying? Surely the girl hadn't gone *that* far on her date with Seth—not on a first date! She was aware of the history between them, and that they'd known each other their entire lives, but it was still their first official date. She struggled for the words to say to the young girl, but she couldn't be sure they were talking about the same thing.

"Maybe he didn't want to get caught in your room by his sister," she said, trying to offer comfort in an awkward situation.

"*Nee,* he left the apartment," she continued to sob. "I heard the door, and when I went out there, he was gone."

"Oh, Honey, I'm so sorry," Alana said.

"Are you going to go home now?" she asked, eyeing Rachel's suitcase.

"*Nee,* I can't go home; Seth took a job working for Eli at the farm and he's planning on living on the property—in the *dawdi haus.* I certainly can't stay at my apartment, because Amber will know something is wrong, and I won't be able to hide what I've done with her *bruder*. We've known each other too long; she'll know."

"That does sort of pose a problem, doesn't it? Well, no worries; you can stay here with me until we figure this out. I have a spare room, and you're welcome to it as long as you need it."

"Danki," she said with a sniffle.

"Do you want me to take you over there to talk to him to make sure this isn't some sort of misunderstanding?"

Rachel took the tissues Alana offered her. "What is there to misunderstand? He left; he doesn't really love me."

"Then make him face you and tell you himself!" Alana suggested.

She wiped her eyes and jutted out her chin.

"You're right! He owes me an explanation, and I aim to get it from him!"

****

Seth drove up and down all the roads leading to the bus station, wondering how she could have gotten there so quickly. It was much too far away for her to have gotten there already, but he would never have thought she could pack her things fast enough to get out of the apartment before he returned with her surprise breakfast.

On the last leg of the trip, he pulled into the bus station and parked his car. Outside the station, a bus was loading with passengers, and he pushed by them, weaving in and out of the crowd gathering on the bus. Pushing past them, he hopped up the stairs, calling out to Rachel with no answer. He spoke to her as the authority over her to answer him, but she was not on the bus.

All eyes seemed to be on him, and his erratic behavior. He realized his appearance conflicted with his speech, but he didn't care. If Rachel was within a mile of that bus station, he aimed to find her.

Excusing himself from the bus after the driver threatened to throw him off the bus, he ran into the building, calling out her name and looking at every face to be sure he wasn't overlooking her if she should happen to be ignoring him.

He was met with several scowls, and a few sorrowful looks, but no one offered him any hope that they'd seen her.

Rushing to the ticket counter, Seth begged the man at the window to tell him if there were any earlier busses that had left within the last few minutes. The answer let him down further. So he stood in the middle of the waiting room and waited—just in case she might be in the bathroom.

****

Rachel didn't feel like talking about what had happened, and Alana had sensed that when they'd pulled up in front of her apartment building and had managed to keep quiet the entire trip.

"Let's go clear up this misunderstanding so you lovebirds can work things out."

Rachel scowled at her comment, but went inside the building, noticing that Seth's car was missing from the spot. Happy that both Amber and Lucy were not there made it easier to go up there to face the ghosts that already haunted her.

Letting herself into the apartment with the key they kept in the potted plant outside their door, Rachel was relieved that the apartment was quiet. Walking over to the sofa, she noted the bedding still folded the way it was the previous night where it lay unused. The next place she checked was the closet.

"His suitcase is gone!" she said, whipping her head around to face Alana.

Her voice was shaky as she noticed the note Alana held up.

"It's a note from Seth," she said. "I think you should read it."

She crossed the room and took the note from Alana, reading it repeatedly, tears dripping onto the page.

Amber,

Something has come up, and I need to take my car and go home. I'll have to get someone to bring the car back to you since I'll be starting my new job with Eli, and won't have time to break away.

I'm sorry we couldn't spend more time together, but I had to go.

Seth

"I suppose that's my explanation; he took his car and went back home, but he won't be at his own *haus;* he'll be at *mei schweschder's haus.* How can I go home with him there?"

She left the apartment, it dawning on her that Amber and Lucy were likely still asleep, and she would much rather avoid them if she could.

She was silent through the elevator ride, tears pooling in her eyes as she remembered the kiss they'd shared when the elevator had stopped between floors.

When she got to the car, it began to register what had happened, and the shock began to wear off.

"I can never go home," she sobbed.

Chapter 16

Rachel ran to the bathroom, hoping the contents of her stomach would stay there until she reached her destination.

She barely made it in time.

Now, as she hugged the commode, she leaned her head on her arm and cried. It was just this sort of thing that she missed the most about being home. Hannah had always held her head and her stomach whenever she was sick, and she'd provided an endless supply of cool washcloths for her face and neck. Now, as she sat collapsed on the bathroom floor alone, she craved home more than ever.

She'd been sick for more than a week, and she suspected that working so many long hours with Alana had caused her to become so run-down she'd caught a bad flu. Mid-summer was not the usual time to catch the flu, but she knew germs didn't live by the clock—they lived in people who were vulnerable to it.

Right now, that would describe her.

She'd barely been able to keep up with her work all week, and had tried to hide it from Alana, not wanting to let her down after all she'd done to help her in the past few months. She'd given her a project to keep her busy so she wouldn't think about Seth, and it had worked for the most-part. The hurt was still there, but the pain from it was no longer like an open wound.

From behind her, Alana handed her a tissue, and soaked a washcloth in cool water and handed it to her, as if she'd read her mind. She'd not taken the time to close the bathroom door, and now she wasn't sure if she regretted it, or was grateful she was no longer alone.

"Danki," Rachel whispered.

"Don't thank me yet," Alana said. "I have one more thing for you."

Rachel struggled to turn so she could take the box Alana had handed to her. "What is this?"

She didn't have to wait for the answer; the front of the box contained the word *pregnancy test* written in bold lettering.

"What do I need this for?" she asked.

"I know you're young, and possibly a little naïve, and there's nothing wrong with that," Alana said in her defense. "But since we live in pretty close quarters, I've noticed you haven't had a cycle in the nearly three months you've been here. You're moody, and sick, and your appetite has changed."

Rachel had tried to put her encounter with Seth out of her mind all this time, and now it was all flooding back into her mind like a breech in a beaver dam.

She began to cry and held her head over the commode for round two. Alana rubbed her back lightly, shushing her gently, and praying for her. Rachel had become like a little sister to her, and now she felt helpless. She'd let her own sister down when she'd needed her most, and here she was doing whatever she could for Rachel, hoping it would serve as restitution.

When she was finished, Alana handed her a fresh washcloth and ducked out of the room. "I'll give you some privacy so you can take the test. Make sure you read all the instructions; I'll be in the kitchen if you need any help, or if you want me to wait for the results with you."

"*Danki,*" Rachel said, her nose stuffy from crying.

Once Alana left the bathroom, she closed the door behind her, and opened the box with a shaky hand. It hadn't even occurred to her that she could have become pregnant from that night. Maybe Alana was right; she was naïve.

As she tried to read the instructions, her mind kept drifting to that night. She'd been so happy and in love with a man she'd never even considered for a husband, until she'd foolishly given herself to him. Never for a second would she have thought she'd be facing pregnancy as an unwed mother. How could she go home and face her family with such shame on her head? Her *daed* would shun her, but would Hannah?

After following the instructions on the box, Rachel went out to the kitchen. "Would you wait with me?" she asked meekly. "I don't know if I'm prepared for what it will probably say."

Alana walked back to the bathroom with her, and the two stared at the stick, waiting for the results. It didn't take long for the word *pregnant* to appear in the little window, and Rachel stared at it with unbelieving eyes.

Her breath caught in her throat. "I have to go home," she whispered around the lump in her throat.

Chapter 17

Rachel tried to act casual as she greeted Hannah and Mira. It felt so good to be home; the three months that she'd stayed with Alana had greatly disturbed her sister, but she made excuses that it was easier for her job to be there.

Rachel lifted her head from Hannah's shoulder and pulled away from her sister's embrace. "What is *he* doing here?"

Hannah studied her younger sibling's over-reaction to seeing Seth. "He's working here. I wrote to you and told you about Eli needing his help."

"I don't want to see him!"

"Don't you think you're being a little harsh and unreasonable?" Hannah asked.

Her sister had never had such a strong reaction to Seth. There had been a measure of teasing on his part, but her sudden intolerance for him was unusual.

"Did something happen between you two when hc went to visit?" she asked. "Did he finally take his teasing too far? If he's done something to hurt you, Eli will put him off the property and take him straight to the Bishop to be dealt with if he expects to take the baptism, as I suspect he does."

He'd hurt her plenty, but Rachel was not ready to reveal her secret.

She didn't want to have to confess her own shame, let alone, Seth's, and so decided she would let the matter drop. "I need to know if you'll let me stay here for a little while. I'm not ready to go home yet, and from the confirmation in your letter, it seems that you need my help."

She patted Hannah's swollen belly, hoping it would distract her even for a moment.

"*Jah,* you're always *wilkum* to stay here, but don't you think you should go by the *haus* and at least see *daed* to let him know you're home?"

"*Nee,* I'm not ready to see him or talk to him—or anyone, for that matter. Maybe later in the week."

She couldn't see him without shaking and wondering if he'd shun her for the shameful secret she would not be able to conceal for too much longer. But for as long as she could, she would stay with Hannah and hope that she would take pity on her and let her stay since she hadn't yet taken the baptism. Alana had offered to take her back with her if Hannah shunned her, but she prayed that would not have to be an option. It wasn't that she hadn't become close with Alana; she wasn't exactly family, and that made all the difference in the world to Rachel right now in her vulnerable state.

"As long as you go see him at some point," Hannah said. "He misses you."

Rachel hoped Hannah would let the matter drop so she wouldn't have to discuss it with her sister anymore. She feared breaking down and spilling her guts, and that could only lead to her being marched over to the Bishop for a confession that she also was not ready for.

"I see Alana dropped you off," Hannah said. "Didn't she want to see Mira?"

"*Nee,*" she said, trying to keep her composure. "She said she wanted to give us a chance to visit first."

"You have your suitcase with you," Hannah said. "Does this mean you intend to stay?"

"*Jah,* I'll be staying—at least for now, that's my plan."

Hannah put a finger under her sister's chin and lifted until their eyes met. "Your eyes are red and puffy like you've been crying. Is something wrong?"

Tears pooled in her eyes. "I didn't have an easy time while I was away; it wasn't as *gut* of an adventure as I thought it would be, but I don't really want to talk about it."

"I wish you'd tell me why you won't see Amber or Lucy, and why you've been staying with Alana for the past few months. Has she influenced you and changed you?"

"*Nee,* she's a *gut* person, and if not for her, I wouldn't have had the courage to come home now. Maybe I need a friend right now more than I need you to be *mei schweschder.*"

"*Ach,* you know I'll do anything for you. I'll pray that you work this out—whatever it is, and find your way back home."

She hugged her sister, allowing her to finally break down and cry. It broke Hannah's heart that her little sister had encountered something in the *Englisch* world that had affected her in such a negative way. She prayed for healing over her, and that she would trust her enough to let her help.

Chapter 18

Rachel tried her best to be quiet when she'd tried to tip-toe to the bathroom in the middle of the night, but if she didn't hurry, she would have an awful mess to clean up in the hallway of her sister's house.

Hannah poked her head out of her bedroom door and listened to her sister getting sick in the bathroom for the third night in a row. She'd noticed other changes in her, and suspected Seth might have something to do with all of it. But how would she confirm her suspicions? She couldn't just outright accuse her little sister of being pregnant, any more than she could accuse Seth of fathering the child. He'd acted funny since Rachel had returned, and she'd noticed him watching her. He hadn't approached her even once, and that wasn't like him; they'd known each other their whole lives.

Rachel had been very emotional having Seth at their farm with her. Neither of them were acting like themselves, and they both spent a lot of time wondering where the other one was, but never spoke.

Alone in the bathroom, Rachel cried, just as she'd cried herself to sleep every night since she'd returned home. Her heart ached for Seth, but he hadn't gone near her or attempted to talk to her. She'd been there several days already, and she didn't understand his aloof behavior. It would seem that she would have to go through a pregnancy alone, and she would live in shame for having to raise her child without a husband.

Rachel heard a light knock at the door, but before she could react, Hannah was inside the bathroom soaking a washcloth, and then placed it on her head. She'd missed her sister's care for her, but she was no longer a child. She was a grown woman who would have to grow up even more now that she was about to have a child of her own.

Hannah kissed the top of her head lightly, whispering a prayer for her younger sister, whom she suspected to be pregnant. But until Rachel was ready to confide in her, she would not try to pry it out of her. It would seem that her sister was more in need of care than she, herself, was. Funny that Rachel had come home to care for her during her pregnancy, but it would likely be Hannah who would be seeing Rachel through hers.

****

Seth walked toward the main house after hearing Hannah ring the large bell at the end of the front porch. The bell served as an alert when they were in the field where they worked to keep the crop healthy for harvest time—a time that would be upon them before they realized. He began to walk into the kitchen when he noticed Rachel sitting on the porch staring out into the field at nothing. She didn't look happy; had he hurt her more than she'd hurt him by what they'd done? If only she hadn't left him. He stood at the end of the porch and watched her, wanting so badly to go to her and pull her into his arms. He still loved her so much, even if she didn't return that love.

Confused as to why she wouldn't just talk to him, shame filled his heart at what he'd done. He'd acted selfishly, not stopping to think of the consequences of his actions; he'd unintentionally dishonored her, when all he'd wanted to do was love her and marry her. He walked slowly toward her, not wanting to startle her from the thoughts she seemed deep into. He feared her becoming angry and lashing out at him. The last thing he needed was to cause a scene with her and lose his job. But that wasn't what was most important to him at the moment; Rachel was.

He knew marrying her was the right thing to do under the circumstances, if she would only give him a chance to ask, but he didn't think she wanted anything to do with him.

He approached her cautiously. "May I sit with you?" he asked timidly.

She turned to face him, seemingly staring right through him, but she didn't say a word either way. He took that as giving consent, and slid onto the porch swing next to her. He heard her breath catch, and he felt helpless to comfort her for fear she would break down right here under the watchful eyes of her family.

He sat there with her for several minutes without saying a word, as he pushed at the porch floor, gently rocking the swing. Finally, she leaned her head on his shoulder, and he tucked his arm around her. His love for her rushed into his heart with a force that took his breath away and left a lump in his throat. He closed his eyes and leaned his head against hers wanting to marry her right then and there.

Without a word, Rachel suddenly put a foot down to stop the swing, stood up, and then went in the front door, leaving Seth on the swing alone and feeling like the wind had been knocked out of him. Tears filled his eyes as he cried out to God.

Lord, forgive me for hurting the woman I love. Please grant me an opportunity to ask her to marry me so I can make this right with her. Fill her heart with forgiveness for me so we can be married.

****

Hannah hadn't missed the scene on the porch between her sister and Seth, which only confirmed her suspicions about the two of them. But she had to wonder if either of them was aware of Rachel's pregnancy. Being a midwife, she recognized the symptoms in her sister almost immediately. That, coupled with the strange attitude toward Seth. It was obvious to Hannah that something had occurred between them, and that it had affected them in a negative way. For something that should bring a couple together, she knew that the act between an unwed couple could cause too many unforeseen problems, and she felt sorry for both of them.

With Rachel in her room refusing to eat at the same table with Seth, Hannah decided it was time to pay her sister a visit and offer her the pregnancy test she'd gotten for her in town the day before. She'd been slightly amused when the pharmacist had looked at her swelling abdomen and at her purchase of the test, looking as if he wondered if she really didn't know if she was pregnant. She didn't bother correcting him; she would never shame her sister like that. His opinion of her didn't matter, and so she quietly made her purchase and left the pharmacy.

Once she was upstairs, she retrieved the pregnancy test kit from her top dresser drawer and knocked lightly on Rachel's door.

She held up the kit when her sister answered the door. "I bought this for you, but if there is no possible way you could be pregnant, then I apologize for coming to that conclusion."

"You don't need to apologize," Rachel said, tears welling up in her eyes. "I already took a test with Alana, and it was positive."

Hannah pulled her younger sister into her arms and allowed her to cry, pushing back a wave of envy that she'd shared that moment with Alana instead of her own sister.

"Is Seth the *vadder?*" she asked.

"*Jah,*" she answered over her sobs.

"Does he know?"

"*Nee,* he left me the morning afterward when he thought I was asleep, and he returned home as if nothing had happened between us. I thought he loved me."

"From the pain I see in his eyes when he looks at you, I'd have to say he *does* love you."

"Then why did he leave me?" she sobbed.

"I don't know," Hannah tried comforting her. "Maybe he panicked and needed some time to think. Now that he's had that time, maybe you should talk to him and find out what happened. From what I saw from the two of you on the porch earlier, I'd say you both love each other, and there is probably a *gut* explanation for all of this. Don't be so willing to throw your love away on a misunderstanding."

"I'll talk to him," she agreed. "But not today; I don't feel like talking to anyone right now."

Hannah didn't like being pushed aside, but she was grateful she got as much out of her sister as she had. For now, she would give her some space to figure things out with Seth, and she prayed he would do the right thing by her sister.

****

Seth waited for a new opportunity when he could speak to Rachel again. His heart and his arms ached to be near her. He could not believe he'd let so much time go by without attempting to make things right with her.

That opportunity came along that evening when he found her sitting on the porch swing staring out at the stars.

Once again, he approached her cautiously.

"May I sit with you?"

Unlike earlier, this time she nodded.

Rachel could feel her heart speed up as Seth sat close to her on the swing and boldly put his arm around her, resting it on the back edge of the swing. Once again, he sat silent for a time, pushing the swing gently with one foot, simply enjoying being near her.

"I want you to know," he blurted out suddenly. "I think we should get married."

"Should?" she asked. "What do you mean by that?"

He cleared his throat, realizing his delivery was not exactly tactful, but he didn't know what she wanted to hear from him.

"I just think that under the *circumstances,* we should be married."

"What circumstances?" she said louder than she'd meant to. "Did *mei schweschder* put you up to this *proposal?"*

"Nee," he said defensively. "It was my idea to marry you."

"If that's your idea of a proposal, the answer is no!"

She rose from the swing and scurried into the house before he had a chance to process what had just happened.

Chapter 19

Rachel finished putting Mira down for a nap for worn-out Hannah, realizing that taking care of a toddler was more work than she'd realized. How was she ever to get through this alone? So far, Hannah had not turned her away after learning the news of her pregnancy, but she hadn't thought about how she would break the news to her father.

She went downstairs and outside, the wind picking up. She looked to the sky, realizing a storm was fast approaching. Wanting to feed the barn cats and bring in the eggs before the rain prevented it, she walked out to the barn to handle the little chores she'd taken over for Hannah.

Seth was coming in from the field, intending to put away the team of horses before the storm hit, while Zach and Eli went up to the main house to get washed for the afternoon meal. He'd seen Rachel go into the barn, and had offered to put the team away alone, hoping he would have a few minutes with Rachel.

Before he made it to the barn, it began to pour, causing him to unhitch the team hastily, aware of the lightning.

Rachel sat in the corner of the barn cowering and shaking every time thunder shook the rafters over her head. The doors swung open and she jumped to her feet, seeing Seth urging the horses into their stalls. He plucked his hat off and hung it on a post, and then unbuttoned his shirt and wrung it out. She watched him from the shadows, remembering that night, and longing to place her hands on his warm skin once more.

He looked up and saw her staring at him, and smiled. She smiled back, and that was all it took for him to rush to her side. He pulled her into his arms and into a kiss before she could catch her breath. Running her hands through his wet hair, she kept him there kissing her until he broke free from her and looked her in the eye.

"I love you so much," he said, desperation in his tone.

His mouth found hers again, his love consuming her.

"I love you too, Seth."

He stopped kissing her and held her close. "If you love me then why did you run away from me? I went to the bus station looking for you, and drove up and down the roads looking for you for hours, after I went back to your apartment and found the note you left for Amber. I was so hurt, I left thinking I could forget you, but I couldn't."

"I didn't know you went looking for me," she admitted. "But why did you leave when I was still sleeping? I wasn't asleep, you know. At first I thought you were only getting up to use the bathroom, but when I heard the apartment door, I went out there to look for you, and you were gone."

He chuckled.

"Why do you find that so funny?" she asked, annoyance in her tone.

"Because I went to the corner donut shop to get us coffee and donuts. I was going to propose to you when I returned, but I saw you walking down the street with your suitcase. That's when I found your note and decided to look for you. I was devastated when I didn't find you, and even more hurt when I found out you'd stayed in the city with Alana."

"You were really going to propose to me over coffee and donuts," she asked, giggling.

He smiled. "What's wrong with that?"

"Nothing," she said. "I can't think of a single thing."

"I'm sorry for the misunderstanding, and for jumping to conclusions," he said. "This whole thing could have been avoided if we had only talked about it first. I've loved you all my life, and I should have known you weren't that kind of person."

"I love you too," she said as he pressed his lips to hers again and giving her a quick kiss

"Does this mean you'll marry me?' he asked excitedly.

"I don't want you to marry me just because of the *boppli*," she said.

He pulled away from her. "*Boppli*? You mean you're pregnant?"

She smiled. "You really didn't know?"

He pulled her close and began to kiss her, picking her up off her feet and twirling her. "We're going to have a *boppli.*"

She giggled. "Put me down!"

He set her down gently and lowered himself on one knee in front of her, pulling her hand into his and looking seriously into her eyes. "I love you, Rachel; will you marry me?"

Tears filled her eyes. "I love you too, Seth; and I will be honored to marry you."

The corners of his mouth formed a sincere smile, and she thought the twinkle in his eye might just resemble a tear.

Chapter 20

Rachel readied herself in the dress she'd worn on her first date with Seth; they'd decided to get married in the garden with only a few guests to witness because they had planned to get married as *Englischers*. They thought it was best if they married immediately to avoid any talk among the community about her condition. Alana fussed with last minute details, trying her best to recreate her same hairdo she'd worn that night, and as Rachel watched her new friend and *sister,* she couldn't help but think she was doing an almost perfect likeness.

Seth stood at the makeshift altar waiting for his bride, feeling like the luckiest man in the community. It would be both a privilege and an honor to marry the woman he'd loved his entire life. With the added blessing of the baby, he eagerly waited for her to approach and consent to be his wife so they could begin their life together.

After working the back forty, Eli had decided it would be too much work for him to continue to work without help, and had given it to Seth in exchange for the pay he owed him so Hannah would have her sister close to her.

Rachel took a deep breath, trying to calm her giddiness. She'd never been so sure about anything in her life as she was to be marrying Seth. He was her best friend, the father of her child, and would now be her husband.

She walked out the kitchen door and toward the garden trellis to meet Seth in front of the Magistrate, who'd agreed to come and perform the ceremony for them. It wasn't a church wedding like she'd always thought she'd have, but it was the man she was marrying that was more important.

As she approached the garden altar, she locked her gaze on Seth, who was wearing the baby-blue button up shirt, his new jeans, and the brown leather loafers, the same as he had on their first date. How handsome he looked as he stood there wearing the best thing of all—a smile, that was just for her.

THE END

Amish Weddings
Alana's Wish
Book Four

Samantha Bayarr

Amish
Weddings
Alana's Wish
Samantha Bayarr

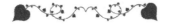

A note from the Author:

While this novel is set against the backdrop of an Amish community, the characters and the names of the community are fictional. There is no intended resemblance between the characters in this book or the setting, and any real members of any Amish or Mennonite community. As with any work of fiction, I've taken license in some areas of research as a means of creating the necessary circumstances for my characters and setting. It is completely impossible to be accurate in details and descriptions, since every community differs, and such a setting would destroy the fictional quality of entertainment this book serves to present. Any inaccuracies in the Amish and Mennonite lifestyles portrayed in this book are completely due to fictional license. Please keep in mind that this book is meant for fictional, entertainment purposes only, and is not written as a text book on the Amish.

Happy Reading

Chapter 1

Alana scattered feed for the chickens while Mira and Katie chased the hens around the yard. She giggled at her little niece's antics, but the toddler was curious about everything.

Hannah watched from the wooden glider under the large oak tree in the yard, a hand resting over her enlarged abdomen. Beside her, Ellie sat in a chair, a little too queasy in her early stages of pregnancy to tolerate the motion of the swing.

The screen door banged against its frame as Rachel brought out a tray of lemonade. It was a sweltering last day of October, and the women were almost ready for the cooler days of autumn to begin.

Alana set the feed pail down and rushed to greet Rachel. "Let me take that for you," she said, taking it from her. "You need to be more careful on the porch steps."

Rachel patted her slightly swollen abdomen. "I'm not as far along as Hannah or Ellie, but I am feeling a little clumsier these days. *Danki.*"

She went over and sat next to her sister on the wooden swing and leaned back, enjoying the slight breeze that rustled the leaves on the branches above them that had already begun to change color.

Setting the snack tray on the little table next to the swing, Alana served up the lemonade. Then she gathered Mira on her lap and let her sip from a cup. The wee one made a face and then smiled, showing that she enjoyed the tartness.

Alana couldn't help but be a little envious of this lifestyle as she let her gaze fall upon the three pregnant women in front of her. She never thought she'd want to live in the community again, but since she'd come back with Rachel, she wasn't sure if she wanted to return to the city.

She'd talked with her business partner about selling her half, and building a little house here in the community. After all, she didn't want to stay in the *dawdi haus* on her sister's property for too long. She considered staying on to help out with Mira after Hannah had her baby, but then she'd be stuck until after winter probably.

With the baby coming along any day now, Alana worried she would be too attached to Mira to want to leave. In some ways, being with little Mira was almost like having a little bit of her sister back with her. She missed Lydia dearly, but she had come to love Hannah, Rachel, and Ellie, as if they were her sisters. She felt blessed that they had welcomed her not only into the community, but into their family life.

Eli, Jonas, and Seth came up to them, along with Josiah and Noah Bontrager; they were looking for some refreshment from the hot day. Alana, feeling embarrassed, jumped up and offered to refill the pitcher of lemonade for the men. They thanked her as they lowered themselves onto the grass under the tree to relax while they waited. Rachel jumped up and went into the house, following her closely.

"Have you noticed the way that Josiah looks at you?" Rachel asked.

"Don't start that, young lady." Alana reprimanded her.

"But I know you want to be married and have a *familye*," Rachel encouraged her. "And he's a *gut mann*."

"I'm sure he is," Alana agreed. "But he's got to be at least two years younger than I am."

"As a matter of fact, Josiah is exactly your age—maybe even a few months older, and a fine catch, if I do say so myself."

"Isn't he courting Becca King?"

Rachel laughed. "Becca follows him around, but she's about five years too young for him. But you would make a good match for him. He seems very interested in you; I see the way he looks at you."

"I've seen it too," Ellie whispered with a giggle as she entered in through the screen door of the kitchen.

Alana watched Josiah and Noah from the kitchen window while Rachel sliced lemons for the lemonade. Was it possible that she could have a normal life and live in an Amish community again? She had lived as an *Englischer* for so many years, and now, she worried she was too old to begin a new life with a husband and *kinner*. Still, she had admired the man from afar, but had never given consideration to him as a possible husband. He was kind, and a hard worker, and certainly very handsome, but for some reason, she just wasn't attracted to him beyond his looks.

"He's a nice-looking man, *jah*?" Rachel asked with the snicker.

"I think if it were up to the three of you, you'd have me married off by the end of the week!"

Alana sighed, wondering if it was indeed possible for her, but she would not reveal that it was Noah whom she had her eye on instead of Josiah.

Chapter 2

Alana checked on her pie for the third time, making sure that the crust did not brown too much; she wanted it just a little golden brown. It was her *mamm's* recipe for apple crumble pie, and she was making it for the harvest community gathering, hoping that Noah would bid on it and she would be able to spend the afternoon with him at the harvest picnic.

She'd had her eye on Noah since she'd come back to the community, and she'd been happy to see him every day that he'd been helping Eli and Seth with the new corral for the new foals. He was interested in the *Englisch* world, and for that reason alone, they had made a connection, and Alana had thought he was her destiny.

The goal for the pie bids and other activities was to raise enough money to purchase materials for a community barn where they could hold meetings, church services, and even barn dances and Sunday night singings. The only thing Alana cared about was making sure that her pie was bid on by the one she intended.

Unfortunately, she'd been dropping hints all week to him while he worked closely with Eli and Josiah, but she was certain her hints had gone unnoticed. Not only had she described her pie, but also her pie dish that was just like the pink-flowered pie-pan that had belonged to her *mamm*. She talked about it right down to the little blue flowers around the edges of the glass dish. She even talked about the linen doily, which she would use to cover the pie to keep the flies away until it was her turn to be bid on. She'd boasted about the little blue corn-flowers that she'd embroidered on the edges herself. She supposed now it was up to him if he wanted to bid on her pie or not, and if he didn't, she would know he wasn't interested, and hadn't paid any attention to all the hints that she'd dropped.

Alana peeked inside the oven, realizing that it was a perfect golden brown and ready to be removed so that it could cool. Grabbing the thermal hand mitts, she reached inside the oven and lifted the dish, pivoting to set it on the counter, when it slipped from her hands and crashed to the floor. Not only did the dish break into a million pieces, but the pie was ruined for sure and for certain. Not only did she barely have time to bake another pie, but now it would not be presented in the correct pie dish. She crouched on the floor on her haunches, cleaning up the mess, while grumbling under her breath about how clumsy she was.

She supposed it was possible that Noah would not remember about the blue, flowered dish, and therefore she could keep it covered with the white linen doily until it was time for the bidding. Hopefully he would at least notice that and bid on her pie so he could spend the day with her at the harvest picnic.

After cleaning up all the mess, she looked at the time, and was happy that she would have enough time to bake another pie in time to go. It wouldn't begin until just before the noon meal, and so she would have to hurry. She set to work quickly, and placed the crust and the ingredients into a plain white pie dish. She thought perhaps the color alone would fool him, knowing it was the same milk-glass as her other pie dish with the flowers.

She had no idea why she was so nervous, other than the fact that she knew there were plenty of single women still in the community that could possibly catch Noah's eye. Truth was, she couldn't even be sure that she was completely interested in him, except for the fact that the thought of him spending the afternoon with another female set her teeth on edge; especially if that woman turned out to be more conservative than she was. It had been so long since she'd been in the community, and she was a little clumsy at wearing her *kapp,* and adjusting her dress length appropriately.

Shortly after her return to the community, she'd gone to the Bishop and given a full confession, and he'd honored her baptism and welcomed her into their community. For her, that gave her the opportunity to marry, and to be a working part of her family's lives. Being an *aenti* to Mira was the most important thing to her, but she had to admit she suddenly found herself wanting a *boppli* of her own.

After placing the fresh pie into the oven, Alana went to get herself ready for the harvest picnic.

Chapter 3

Alana waited for Eli and Hannah to get ready for the harvest gathering. She wrapped her pie in the doily, hoping that Noah would remember what she'd said about it. Thinking back on it, she'd gone on too long about it, and had likely made a nuisance of herself. She went over it in her head again, hoping she hadn't been overheard by anyone else, for fear they would consider her actions brash.

With the familiar sound of buggy wheels grinding in the driveway, she knew Eli had the buggy ready and waiting for her to go. She gathered up her pie, and after double-checking she'd turned off the oven, she went outside the *dawdi haus* to meet them. Tucking her pie under the front seat of the buggy, she took Mira from Hannah and sat in the back with her.

Eli had advised his wife they should stay home due to the closeness of her impending delivery, but she had insisted she hadn't felt even the slightest twinge of labor, and in fact, had more energy than she'd had most of the pregnancy. He'd reluctantly agreed to let her have her way, and Alana couldn't have been more delighted to tag along—especially since it gave her another excuse to help with Mira.

Once they arrived at the five-acre plot of land that had been dedicated for the site of the community barn, Alana climbed out and rested Mira on her hip, while balancing her pie in her other hand. She took it straight over to the table where the bidding would begin, feeling confident that she would have a delightful afternoon with the object of her affections. She'd packed a colorful quilt to lay out in the grass, and she'd included a batch of her tart lemonade in a large Mason jar for them to share with their meal.

As she stood in front of the bidding table waiting for the event to begin, she looked around for Noah, but didn't see him. She balanced Mira on her hip, trying to keep her attention away from the balloons and cotton candy maker behind them.

Meanwhile, Becca King walked up to the table and pushed her pie plate in front of Alana's in line for bidding. A closer look caused Alana to gasp when she saw the exact pie plate she was supposed to present her pie in if it hadn't broken. Now, not only was hers in front of Alana's for bidding, it was in the very pie dish that she had hinted to Noah would be her pie.

As soon as Zeke Yoder began beckoning the single *menner* to gather around the bidding table, Alana backed up, suddenly feeling nervous about the whole thing. She suddenly wished she hadn't let Rachel and Hannah encourage her to participate in such a foolish game. Just when she thought things couldn't get any worse for her luck today, a swift breeze tossed her embroidered doily over onto Becca's pie.

When Zeke opened up the bidding for Becca's pie, Noah pushed his way to the front, and Alana wanted to tug on his sleeve and tell him it wasn't her pie, but Josiah distracted her by moving toward the front of the small crowd. It didn't take long for the two of them to get into a bidding war over that pie. Meanwhile, Becca stood off to the side, giggling the entire time. It made Alana want to stomp her feet like a little child, but what sort of example would that be for Mira?

Instead, she lifted her eyes toward the heavens and whispered a prayer. *Lord, let your will be done.*

It was Noah who finally won the bidding, having out-bid Josiah by an extra twenty dollars. Alana didn't miss the look of confusion on his face when Becca came forward to claim the pie. Josiah, however, looked back at Alana and simply smiled, a look of relief on his face.

Becca picked up her pie, and pulled the doily off the top where it had blown, and placed it back on Alana's pie. "This belongs on this pie," she said, snickering. "The wind tossed it over, but I supposed it was my luck that it did."

She smiled a satisfied look as she looped her arm in Noah's, making sure Alana noticed.

She didn't care. She was over the whole thing.

She wished she could take back her pie— especially when Josiah was the only one who bid on it, but he even bid against himself since the crowd had dwindled after Becca's pie had been claimed. After paying a total of twenty-five dollars for her pie, Alana decided she would be a good sport for the benefit of the cause. After all, having a community barn was a good cause, and who was she not to play along after she'd willingly entered the bidding contest.

Alana sighed, realizing it was over for her as far as getting to spend the afternoon with Noah.

She handed Mira over to Eli, who had come to claim her after trying his hand at the tug-of-war against the team of horses. From the look of his mud-covered pants, his team had lost.

Now, sadly, without Mira to distract her, she would have to put away her envy of Becca, and make the best of an awkward afternoon in Josiah's company.

Chapter 4

Alana spread out the colorful quilt she'd borrowed from Hannah, and retrieved the Mason jar of lemonade she'd made to share with Noah, and served up a glass to Josiah. She felt awkward, wondering how they would fill the entire afternoon with conversation, until he let out a hearty chuckle.

Annoyed, she sipped from her lemonade, trying to keep her thoughts to herself.

"You know, when Noah outbid me for that pie, I was so disappointed he would get to spend the afternoon with the woman I've had my eye on," he said. "But you have no idea how relieved I was that I lost when I saw it was Becca King's pie I was bidding on."

Alana practically choked on her lemonade.

"What?" she asked, trying not to cough.

"I heard you hinting around about the pie dish and the blue and white cloth that would cover it, but imagine my surprise when I saw it was Becca's pie. I almost wondered if you'd tricked me into bidding on her pie, until I glanced over and saw the expression on your face. When she replaced your cloth over your pie, I knew then it was an accident. But lucky for me it was, or I wouldn't be here with you now enjoying this refreshing autumn day."

Alana looked at Josiah—really looked at him. He was certainly handsome, and older than Noah, who suddenly seemed immature by comparison, and she wondered if this man was always so content with his life.

"Would you like to stand in line to get a plate of food?" he asked. "Or if you'd like, you can stay put and I can go get us each a little of everything."

She didn't exactly want him to pay the dollar for her plate, because then she feared he might take it as a date, and she wasn't sure she was willing to consent to that at this time. With Noah spending the day with Becca, she supposed anything could happen there. She'd seen two people fall in love over smaller things than being forced to spend a day together. She hoped Josiah didn't have his expectations set too high for the day they would spend together, and letting him pay for her meal might just set the stage for a misunderstanding.

"I can pay for my own meal," she protested.

"Nee," he said. "I would feel like a heel making you pay for your meal after you baked that wonderful pie I get to enjoy."

"But you paid for that pie!"

"I paid a contribution toward the building fund, but I couldn't begin to repay you for the trouble you went through in making that pie."

You have no idea just how much trouble it was.

"Danki," she said, as she remained on the quilt. "Make sure you get me a lot of that fried chicken *Frau* Yoder made. I hear it's the best in the community."

"In that case," he said with a chuckle. "I better get in line before it's all gone. Even though she usually brings a whole buggy load to all the events, there never seems to be enough to go around."

She let him go and pay for her meal, reasoning with herself that the money was going for a good cause. She supposed it would be another thing if they were at the diner in town and he agreed to pay, but for a community meal that normally comes without a cost, she decided this one time would be acceptable.

When Josiah returned, he'd gotten three plates for them to share. She thought it was way too much food, but she wasn't about to say anything, especially not after seeing the look on his face. He was proud of his choices.

"I got one plate full of chicken, one with all the potatoes and casseroles, and one with healthy stuff so we wouldn't have to feel guilty for eating all the rest of it."

"Is that how it works?" she asked with a smile.

"*Jah,*" he said proudly. "I hope that someday when I find a *fraa* she feeds me this way."

So there it was; he was looking to get married.

She had to wonder why he hadn't married yet. It wasn't that he wasn't a handsome man, or lacking of land. He had one of the biggest dairy farms in the community. Perhaps he was too busy running his farm to spend time courting.

She'd done the same thing in a way; she'd thrown herself into her work in the city, and never took the time to date. She supposed the lack of acceptable dates in the city was the main reason she was back in the community, considering courting an Amish man.

"Here," Josiah said, handing her one of the extra plates he'd tucked under the food plates.

"You thought of everything, didn't you?"

She smiled, thinking how considerate he was. Perhaps the day spent with him would be filled with a few more good surprises.

Chapter 5

Becca brushed past Alana's quilt, her tantrum kicking up grass. Knowing she'd likely regret going after the girl to find out what happened, Alana stood up and reluctantly excused herself to Josiah.

"Wait a minute, Becca," Alana called after her.

She didn't catch up to her until they reached the lumberjack event, and Alana thought the slip of a girl might just grab an ax and chop down a whole tree with all the pent-up anger she was holding in. Alana finally caught up to her at the entrance to the covered bridge near where all the buggies had parked. She leaned over the railing and began to sob.

Alana put a hand on her shoulder, and Becca shrugged it off.

"You're the *last* person I want to see right now!"

What did I do? Alana asked herself.

She cleared her throat, unsure of what to say in response. "I know we're not exactly friends, but I'd like to help if I could. Did Noah *do* something to offend you?"

She whipped her head around and swiped at a tear from her cheek. "*Jah,* he said he bid on my pie because he thought it was...because—oh, it's too embarrassing to even say out loud!"

"It can't be all that bad, can it?"

"It's worse than bad—it's downright horrible!"

"You might as well tell me what happened, because I'm not leaving you alone until you tell me."

Becca sniffled. "Noah said he only bid on my pie because he thought it was *your* pie!"

She began to sob all over again.

Alana tried not to smile. Imagine; Noah wanting to spend the afternoon with her after all.

Only problem was, since she'd spent a nice afternoon with Josiah, she'd agreed to take a buggy ride with him later. Though it suddenly crossed her mind, she knew it wouldn't be proper to try and get out of it now. Any excuse would fill her with guilt, and it wouldn't be fair to him. She had to admit, he'd been fun to be around—a refreshing change from what she thought she wanted. She already knew Noah was immature and rebellious, while Josiah was more responsible—almost to the point of boredom. Could she live with comfortable and responsible, or did she want edge-of-your-seat excitement like the kind she imagined she'd get with Noah?

Being polar-opposites, both men had their good qualities and their not-so-good. It was only a question of which of the two brothers she was more attracted to. Before spending the afternoon with Josiah, she would have said Noah hands-down, but now she wasn't so sure anymore. The bit of information Becca handed to her didn't come with its own set of problems. Knowing Noah would have rather spent the day with her than with Becca, seemed suddenly like a strange concept.

Alana was certainly faced with a big dilemma—one she didn't trust herself to make a decision on alone. She *knew* how she'd handle it if she left her decision to herself alone; she'd give a long list of excuses to Josiah, and then go for a buggy ride with

Noah. Trouble was, that was her former, impulsive side—a side she was trying very hard to get away from.

No, she knew now that to seek the counsel of Hannah and Rachel—both married women, would be the best course of action; that, and likely a lot of prayer.

Noah approached them and Becca started to back away from him.

"You stay away from me," she said. "Haven't you embarrassed me enough?"

Becca turned swiftly and lost her footing, bumping into the low railing and toppling over its edge. Alana tried to grab her arm, but the girl fell the couple of feet into the rain-swelled creek below with a little splash.

Noah jumped over the rail and into the water, dragging her to shore, all the while, she was kicking and sputtering, and yelling at him to leave her alone.

Once they were up on the bank of the creek, Noah sat in the grass and laughed heartily while she angrily pulled weeds and muck from her hair that had come undone from her prayer *kapp*.

"Ach, I don't see what is so funny about me falling into the creek, Noah Bontrager!"

By this time Alana had rushed down to the edge of the creek to help her. "Noah, you should be ashamed of yourself for saying the things you did to her!"

He stood up and looked around for his hat. "I saved her life just now!" he said defensively. "Don't I get any credit for that?"

"It's probably best if you leave her alone for now," Alana said to him.

Josiah came up to see what the ruckus was all about, and when he saw Becca struggling, he rushed to her and took her arm in his. "Are you alright?" he asked kindly.

"Your *bruder* got me so upset, I fell in the creek."

He took off his jacket and put it around her shaking shoulders. "Why don't I give you a ride home? Noah, We'll talk later!"

"It ain't like I pushed her in!" he said. "I tried to help her—even *after* she was so rude to me."

Josiah scowled at his brother and then looked over at Alana. "Do you mind if I cut our afternoon short?" he asked. "I should take her home before she catches a cold. I'll have to get a raincheck on that buggy ride this evening."

Alana nodded, suddenly feeling disappointed.

Chapter 6

Alana watched Josiah walk away with Becca, feeling suddenly angrier with the girl. But why; she just couldn't figure that out. Here she was, standing alone with Noah, the man she thought she wanted, but now as she watched Josiah leaving with Becca, she felt suddenly confused.

Wasn't this what she wanted?

"I can't believe you were going to take a buggy ride with *mei bruder,*" he said in a teasing way. "Don't you know all he wants is a *fraa?*"

She sighed and walked back toward the picnic lunch that was spread out for her and Josiah, figuring she'd just as soon clean up the mess and go home; the walk alone might cool her off a bit. Did it bother her that he'd taken Becca home, or the comment that Noah made about him wanting to be married?

She had to wonder if that's what she wanted too.

"Hey," Noah said. "Don't throw away that food; I'll take it home with me! It'd be a shame for it to go to waste—especially since *mei mamm* is no longer with us, we don't get to eat like this too often. Besides, maybe it'll smooth things over with *mei bruder* after that Mouthy-Becca finishes talking his ear off about how awful I am!"

She handed him the plates of food and began to gather her things. "I don't think Josiah will take her side. But he's doing what you should have done— which is take her home."

Whose side am I on?

"I'd rather give *you* a ride home; it's the least I can do since you gave me all this food. That, and *mei bruder* did sort of leave you stranded."

"Not really," she said in his defense. "I came here with Hannah and Eli."

"*Jah,* but doesn't that make you feel like a *third-wheel?*"

I hadn't thought about it that way until now!

She nodded, thinking her day couldn't possibly get any stranger. Perhaps with Noah taking her home, it would end the way she'd imagined it would after all.

"Let me walk over and let Hannah and Rachel know I'm leaving," she said to him.

He walked with her, and when she approached the women, they smiled.

"I'm going home," she said, ignoring the looks she was getting. "Where's Mira?"

"Eli took her over there to feed the ducks," Hannah said, pointing.

They looked as if they were having some important bonding time, so she decided not to disturb them.

"She looks like she's having a great time; she'll certainly sleep soundly tonight."

"Eli, too, I pray," Hannah said patting her large belly. "He hasn't been sleeping very well for the past week or so, worrying about the delivery."

Alana felt bad for her, having the cloud of worry that must be over their heads right now.

"You'll do just fine," Alana tried to reassure her. "I'll see you at home."

They walked back to Noah's buggy, and he took his time assisting her up. He patted his horse and hopped in the other side of the open buggy, sliding a little closer to Alana than she expected him to.

He picked up the reins and let them fall gently on his horse, and then turned to her once the buggy was in motion. "You and I are a lot alike, you know," he said.

"How do you figure?" she asked, playing along.

"I'd have to say we're both quite *worldly— Englisch,*" he said with a smile.

"You're well-past the age of beginning your *rumspringa,* Noah," she remarked.

"I missed my time because of *mei mamm's* passing, but it's been a reasonable amount of time now, and I think it's time I went before it's too late!"

"It isn't as glamorous as you think it is," she said.

"Don't you want to return to the city once Hannah has her *boppli?* That *is* what you're waiting for, isn't it?"

"I came back to the community to stay, and I had to give a full confession to lift the ban. Being shunned isn't fun—not when you have family that stays behind."

He steered the buggy into the driveway and pulled up to the *dawdi haus.* "Why did you leave in the first place?"

"Because I thought I was living in the shadow of a perfect sibling."

He sighed. "I know what that's like! Josiah has always been the responsible one. He took over the dairy farm after *daed* died, and kept it up; he even took *gut* care of our *mamm* until she passed a year ago. Everyone around here thinks he's so much more mature than I am; we're only ten months apart!"

"My sister and I were twins, and everyone thought she was better than me; turns out, they were right about her."

Alana reflected sadly, still mourning the loss of Lydia.

"I didn't know her very well, but I'd say you're just as nice as she was," he said, offering her comfort.

"I'm glad you thought she was nice; but the truth is, I didn't know her very well either, and she was my own sister."

He stopped the horse and turned to her with a smile. "I feel as if I just grew up a few extra years!"

She returned his smile. "Me too!"

He cleared his throat. "Since *mei bruder* won't take you for a buggy ride tonight, is it alright if I take you instead?"

She looked at his hopeful blue eyes and hesitated, but she couldn't figure out why. Wasn't this what she'd wanted all along?

Suddenly, she just wasn't sure anymore.

"I have a strange feeling I should just stay home tonight."

It wasn't the answer he wanted; judging by his fallen expression, but it was the only one she could give.

Chapter 7

Hannah's screams rent the air, causing Alana's hair to stand on end. If this was how painful childbirth was, she wanted no part of marriage and having babies. She wrung her hands, not knowing exactly what to do. Was this how scary it had been the night Lydia had died?

"Maybe we should take her to the hospital," she whispered to Rachel from the corner of the room while she readied everything for the impending birth. "How long before the doctor gets here?"

"He'll be here," she reassured Alana. "But the best thing you can do is remain calm. It won't do Eli or Hannah any *gut* with you pacing and sweating like you're waiting for something bad to happen. She's got another hour or two before she gives birth."

"I think I want to go check on Mira," she said. I'm sure all this noise is keeping her awake.

"Wait!" Rachel cautioned her. "First go over and let Hannah know you're going out to take care of Mira, or she'll worry, and I need *her* to stay calm right now."

Alana did as she was advised, but she couldn't be certain Hannah had heard her over her own bawling and breathing. Eli, however, nodded, and she took that as a sign he would let her know if Hannah inquired about her; somehow, Alana didn't think she'd be too worried about her whereabouts at the moment, judging from her cries.

Once she was outside of the room, she doubled over for a minute, breathing heavily, and wondering how it was that women had managed to survive childbirth since the dawn of time. It baffled her that women actually *wanted* to be pregnant and have families—for this kind of pain?

I'll opt out of that self-torture!

Feeling relieved that for the time-being she was single, and that she was able to use Hannah's delivery as an excuse to get out of the buggy ride with Noah, she decided perhaps it was time she revisited her sudden change of heart to get married. Frankly, the whole thing scared the daylight out of her.

Maybe it's time I thought about returning to the city and my career. Maybe I was right for leaving in the first place; the Amish community is no place for me. I just don't think I want the same things and I don't fit in.

After checking on Mira, who was sound asleep, despite the cries from her mother, Alana busied herself in the kitchen taking care of the supper dishes that had been neglected because of Hannah's present labor. Now, she was thankful for the distraction.

Outside the kitchen window, the wind howled, announcing an early winter storm. She shivered a bit despite being elbow-deep in hot dish-water, knowing they'd likely have a little icy rain. It seemed such a shame, given the reasonably warm day they'd had for the harvest picnic earlier in the day. She looked at the wall-clock, realizing it was now nearly five in the morning, and yesterday's conversations had long-since been put away.

With the break of the new day, Hannah would bring another child into the world, and it would continue to go on as always. It was times like this when she thought of Lydia the most. She wished she could have done things differently then, and wondered if her sister watched her from Heaven, and was pleased with her for being part of her only child's life.

She rinsed the plates and stacked them on a clean towel on the counter as she thought about how many times Lydia must have stood at this very sink. Surely she thought of her a time or two while she washed the same dishes Alana washed now.

Forgive me, Lord, she whispered around the lump in her throat. *Lydia I pray you can forgive me for not coming back while you were still alive. You'd be so proud of the way Mira has turned out; she reminds me so much of you. She has the kindness and the gentleness that you always had. I know you'll be pleased to know that you could not have picked a better mamm for her than Hannah.*

Lord, watch over Hannah and that wee one she's trying to bring into this world. Please spare her life so she can go on taking care of Mira and the new boppli. Give me the strength to stay here and help where I'm needed, and to stop being such a coward for this lifestyle. If it is your will, I'll stay and become whatever it is you'll bless me with.

Danki

A tear ran down her cheek, her prayer surprising her. Not half an hour before, she was ready to leave all of this behind. God had truly blessed her with a new sister, who happened to come with a younger sister. And then there was Eli, who was truly everything a brother should be. Best of all, she was about to become an *aenti* again, and for some reason even she couldn't explain, she just couldn't wait for it.

Chapter 8

Alana dropped the utensils back into the dishwater and scrambled to wipe her hands when the sound of a baby crying reached her ears.

She stood outside the door where Hannah was laboring and listened—fearful of something gone wrong. But then, the sound of laughter filled her ears and her heart with joy, the weight of the fear lifted away.

Knocking at the bedroom door, she was greeted with a multi-voice invitation to enter the room. A weak stream of sunlight shone through the curtains, illuminating it just enough to see Hannah smiling adoringly at her infant, who wriggled and kicked and cried.

Her breath caught in her throat at the sight of him flailing around while Rachel tried to cover him with a blanket.

Hannah looked up at Alana with a welcoming smile. "*Kume,* meet *mei* new *sohn,* Adam."

She lifted her eyes toward Heaven, whispering a sincere thank-you before she walked toward the bed where the family—her family, surrounded Hannah and the baby.

Leaning down, she gave Hannah a big hug. "I was praying for you—I was so worried," she sobbed, not meaning for her emotions to escape all at once.

Then she laughed, tears falling unchecked as she wrapped her hand around Adam's little foot. "He's so beautiful—I know I'm not supposed to say that, but I can't help it. The wee ones are truly God's beauty filling the world with such joy."

She was rambling and blubbering, but she didn't care. She was just so happy everything turned out alright. Part of her wished Lydia could see her little one had a new baby brother. Her sister had always wanted to be nothing but a *fraa* and a *mamm*. Alana, however, had been her polar-opposite in every way.

Perhaps taking after her sister, and learning her ways was not such a bad idea after all. As she held Adam's little foot, she determined right then to make Lydia proud to call her *schweschder*.

Rachel had finished swaddling him, and offered Alana the chance to hold him.

She looked to Hannah. "Is it alright?"

"Of course it is," she said with a smile. "You're his *aenti.*"

I like the sound of that.

She held out her arms and drew the infant close to her, and she had to admit, it was something she could get used to.

Chapter 9

Josiah and Noah showed up bright and early to help Eli finish the corral, but when Alana answered the door; she let them know the news of baby Adam. She invited them in, feeling a little unsure of the awkwardness at having both brothers in the same place—especially knowing they both vied for her attention. The baby was crying, which gave her a bit of a distraction, but when he stopped fussing, she had to assume he was finished with his bath and happily resting at his *mamm's* breast.

"He sure has a healthy set of lungs on him," Josiah said with a smile. "He'll make a *gut* strong hand on the farm soon enough for Eli."

"What if he doesn't want to be a farmer?" Noah challenged him.

"You mean like you, little *bruder?*" Josiah shot back. "Then I pray that Eli has a strong back that can carry the load alone, and the patience to wait for his son to come to his senses and embrace what he was born to be."

"I wasn't *born* to be a farmer the way you were," Noah complained. "I want to see the world outside of this community."

Alana listened intently as she brought coffee to the table to serve the men.

"You'd go back with me, wouldn't you, Alana?" he asked as she poured a cup in front of him. "You'd show me around and show me how to be an *Englischer.*"

She thought she would only days ago, but hearing the sounds from the other rooms in the house—the sounds of her family—now, she wasn't so sure.

"I'd have to give that some serious thought," she said quietly. "I came back here to be close to Mira, my sister's child, and I don't want to miss any more of her life than I already have. That would be a tough decision to make right now."

She hadn't given up her business yet, but she thought now more than ever that she could. She wanted the kind of life her friends and family had. They were the only family she had left now that Lydia was gone. And even though they weren't her *real* family, with the exception of Mira, they had taken her in and welcomed her as if she was. For that reason alone, she owed it to them and to herself to see just what the family life was all about. When she'd left the community, she'd been far too young to understand the value of family. Now, it seemed the hard lessons from that decision had left her wise beyond her years in too many ways.

Noah had called her *worldly,* and suddenly, that description didn't sit well with her. She looked down at the plain dress she was wearing. It didn't feel as foreign as it had the first time she'd worn the plain clothing after returning. To an outsider, and even her friends back in the city, they would think she was Amish, but was she only playing a part?

Was she capable of settling into this lifestyle as an adult, or would she be happier out there with Noah, with the open invitation to visit little Mira any time she wanted?

That was no life for her. Noah, as immature as he was, would never make her a good husband in the *Englisch* world, and likely not the Amish one either. But Josiah—he was a force to be reckoned with. He'd made his feelings known to her and so had Noah, but then he'd seemingly taken them back the minute Becca King acted up.

Had he merely been fixing his younger sibling's mistake with the girl, or had he changed his mind about the attention she was giving him?

Only time would tell, and Alana wanted no part of the drama Becca was bringing to the situation.

Chapter 10

Alana continued to listen to Noah and Josiah as she began to cook breakfast for everyone that had stayed awake all night waiting for Adam's safe arrival. She busied herself, acting as if she wasn't eavesdropping while they discussed what needed to be done to finish the corral alone, so that Eli could stay with Hannah and his new son. There were certainly differences between the two brothers that she hadn't noticed until now.

Josiah, who'd taken over the dairy farm after his father's death, had held his family together, while Noah acted just as foolishly as she had when she'd left. The only difference was; she'd left the community when she was much younger than Noah is now. Being just between the two of them in age;

either was a choice for a suitable husband, but age alone could not sway her decision.

Noah seemed determined to leave the community, and for that reason alone, she would not even consider him right now, even though, truthfully, she thought him to be her first choice. Was it his sense of adventure and his wild ways and rebellion she was attracted to? Those were the very things she was trying to get away from, wasn't she?

She cracked eggs into a bowl and began to whisk them with a touch of cream. She daydreamed for a minute about cooking in her own kitchen for a husband and possibly children of her own. The thought terrified and excited her, and she wasn't certain which one outweighed the other. Glancing over at the men at the table, her heart skipped a beat when her gaze met Josiah's.

He smiled, and she practically spilled the egg mixture onto the counter. She smiled nervously back at him, and though she didn't think he noticed her nervousness, if he did, he didn't show it.

Rising to his full height of six feet, he moved his muscular frame to the sink and deposited his coffee cup into the dishwater.

"*Danki* for the *kaffi*," he said sniffing the air. "Do I smell cinnamon bread warming in the oven?"

She nodded. "Would you like a piece?"

He smiled and nodded as she grabbed for the oven mitt.

Noah moved to the counter just then. "Hey don't get any sweet ideas about Alana," he said to his brother, who towered over him by at least four inches. "I've got a rain-check for a buggy ride later with her."

Alana wished she could sink back into the dishwater at that moment. The look on Josiah's face made her cringe.

She cleared her throat to speak, but couldn't find her voice.

"I think I'll take a *rain-check* on that cinnamon bread," he said, eyeing his brother. "Let's get to work so we can get back to our own farm and get the rest of our chores finished."

She didn't miss the eye-roll from Noah, thinking he was too old for such an act of rebellion.

What was happening to her?

Had she really matured that much in the last twenty-four hours?

Chapter 11

Alana swallowed nervously the bite of cold eggs she'd been pushing around her plate the entire meal. While Noah had tried to chat her ear off, Josiah hadn't said a word—despite the fact she'd made it a point to turn down his invitation to take a buggy ride.

Josiah had kept his nose in his plate and gobbled his food quickly, asking to be excused to finish the job he'd offered to help Eli with. He'd grabbed his younger brother by the scruff of his shirt and urged him to come with him.

"I ain't even finished my breakfast yet," he complained.

"Well you might have had the time if you hadn't been so busy trying to make a date with a woman you're too dense to see was trying to let you down easy!"

"Can't you see she and I are alike—almost as if we're soulmates!" he argued.

"*Jah,*" Josiah agreed. "Until the next pretty girl comes along. You shouldn't be so prideful, Noah."

Alana looked up from her plate of cold eggs as Josiah ushered his brother out the kitchen door.

Had he just called her *pretty?*

She looked around the large table, realizing she was the only one left at the table. Eli had taken his meal in to share with Hannah, while Rachel had offered to change Mira since she'd made breakfast.

Even out in the yard, she could hear them arguing—over *her!*

Did she want to be argued over—like she had no say in the matter? What if she chose neither of them? it would serve them right—wouldn't it?

On second thought, maybe she should see how things panned out. So far, Josiah had not made another move toward asking her for a buggy ride, and it made her heart sink as she watched them in the yard gathering lumber from the back of the buggy.

They'd had such a wonderful time at the harvest picnic—until Noah and his childish antics had spoiled the day and interrupted their time together.

Alana admired Josiah from the kitchen window as he picked up several boards while Noah goofed off, kicking at rocks in the driveway and making excuses to his brother. Josiah was certainly the more responsible of the two, but was he so responsible that he didn't know how to have a little fun in life?

Josiah had been so different with her yesterday than he was with his brother now. Truthfully, she might not have had as much patience with Noah if he was *her* younger sibling. Then it dawned on her; had Lydia been the same way with *her?*

Lydia had always been the responsible one; always doing what she was told, and learning everything she could about being a good Amish woman. Because of her faith and perseverance, she'd brought a delightful baby girl into the world, and brought unselfish happiness to her husband and friend—even in her death.

Alana had no idea what it was like to be that unselfish. She'd never put anyone else's needs before her own, and had no idea what that was like. Lydia had always put her first, and she'd repaid her by running away from her and hadn't even been there to share the most important events in her life with her. She'd not attended her wedding, or even been there the day she'd given birth, and died. Would she have chosen her to marry her Eli if she'd been there? Perhaps it was for the best that she wasn't, because Hannah was clearly the best choice for him.

The real question was if *she* was the right choice for anyone. She'd like to think so, but she supposed she better leave it up to God to do the choosing for her. As she watched the two brothers outside the kitchen window, she knew she couldn't trust herself to make the right decision.

Perhaps a talk with Hannah or Rachel might be a good idea as well.

Chapter 12

Alana stood at Lydia's graveside, the cold, November wind whipping through her, chilling her straight to her bones. She shivered, perhaps some from the unease she felt in being at the grave of the twin she'd separated herself from. She'd been so wrapped up in gaining her own identity, that she'd lost the one person in this world she could really connect to.

She felt so much regret.

She'd lost out on sharing her sister's best years with her. Her *daed* would have called her prideful because he wouldn't have understood, but she knew it was more than that. It had been a sort of restlessness that even she couldn't explain.

Kneeling down, she began to weep, begging her sister's forgiveness. As if floating on the wind, she heard her sister's angelic voice, telling her in her sensible way that she loved her no matter what.

"You'd be so proud of Mira," Alana sobbed. "She laughs like you do. I pray she grows up to have a kind heart and a quiet spirit just like you."

She yanked a wayward weed from the edge of the primitive headstone. "I wish I could be more like you," she whispered.

Hearing a crunch in the dry leaves behind her, she turned around, startled to see Josiah.

He crouched down on his haunches and pulled at the weeds that grew around Lydia's grave-marker. "She was a kind woman," he said gently. "I see a lot of her in you; especially when you take care of her wee one."

"That's very kind of you to say," she said, wiping at her tears. "But I could never be as good of a person as my sister was."

"After *mei daed* passed on, I used to come here and have these long, tortured talks at his graveside," he said sadly. "I wanted to be just like him; to be strong for *mei familye,* and to be the kind of person he was. After many months of pushing myself on the farm and trying to remember just how he did everything, and chiding myself every time I'd make a mistake, I realized a valuable lesson."

She looked up at him as he stared off in the distance, reflecting for a moment.

"I realized that I could never fill *mei vadder's* shoes, and I should stop trying because the only person's shoes I could fill were my own. I didn't have to be as *gut* or better than *mei vadder;* all I had to do was to be the best version of myself."

She looked into his wise eyes. He'd grown up too fast just like she had, but for different reasons. He'd taken the responsible road, while she'd been nothing but a coward, running away from all responsibility. While he'd stayed and faced the things that scared him the most, she'd run from them. In the end, they'd caught up with him just the same as they had for her.

"I know *mei bruder* is tempting you to return to the city and remain an *Englischer,* but I pray you'll stay and give me a chance to get to know you better," he said kindly.

She looked into his eyes again, seeing a softness there she hadn't noticed before. He'd just poured out his soul to her, and she couldn't help but wonder if the sincerity she saw there was an answer to the prayer she'd been asking for.

He stood, reaching for her hand, and she slowly placed her hand in his, feeling the warmth and strength of it. Assisting her to her feet, she dusted the grass and dry leaves from her black apron, and followed him along the path in the graveyard, her cold hand still cupped in his warm one.

It sent a warm shiver through her as they walked in silence, the wind dying down to a gentle rustling in the colorful leaves still clinging to the branches overhead. She felt a peaceful sort of quietness just then as she looked up into the beams of sunlight filtering through the trees. They flickered in her heart to bring a warmth there she'd never known could feel so liberating.

Chapter 13

Alana bounced Mira lightly trying to console her, but she was fighting a much-needed nap.

"My, but you do have a bit of stubbornness in you just like your *mamm,*" *she said with a smile.*

Turning around at a noise, she saw Hannah in the doorway holding Adam on her shoulder.

Mira looked up and saw her, wriggling from Alana's arms and running to Hannah, wrapping her tiny arms around her legs.

"*Mamm,*" she cried.

Alana's heart thumped, realizing what she'd just said. "I'm sorry; I didn't mean…" she stammered.

Hannah handed the baby to Alana and picked up Mira, soothing her, as she laid her head on her shoulder, a ragged, half-yawn, half-cry escaping her.

"It's alright, Alana," she whispered, trying not to disturb Mira, who was already falling asleep. "I knew what you meant. She's a lucky one; she has two *mamm's* and an *aenti* who can show her all the things her birth *mamm* isn't able to show her."

Alana looked at the peaceful look on Mira's face as she settled down, realizing Hannah was a good mother to her, and the wee one loved her very much.

"I don't know what I can show her," Alana said. "Except how to be rebellious, and clumsy at being Amish."

"That's not true," Hannah said as she slowly and gently placed the sleeping toddler in her crib.

"Lydia told me that you were the only one who could make her *mamm's* sugar crème pie."

That was true.

"She told me that while she felt clumsy at being an Amish *fraa,* you would have made the perfect one because you could always outdo her on wash day, and you had an easy time in the kitchen cooking and canning, while she struggled with these things."

Alana handed Adam back to Hannah and they walked out of Mira's room.

"She told you all that?" Alana asked, surprise in her voice. "I didn't think I could ever fill my sister's shoes as a wife, mother, or even a part of the community."

"*Ach,* you shouldn't try to fill your *schweschder's* shoes. The only person's shoes you should fill are your own, and I think you fill them nicely.

She smirked. "You know, you're the second person to tell me that today."

Hannah smiled. "It's *gut* advice. It sounds as if it's a sign from *Gott.*"

"*Danki,*" Alana said awkwardly.

"You're a *gut aenti,* and a *gut* working part of this community. You should hold your head up and move forward. Each day is a new day, full of possibilities. Embrace what *Gott* has in store for you. I have a feeling you won't be disappointed."

Alana thought about her time with Josiah earlier that afternoon, realizing that she just might have found the answers to her prayers. They'd been right in front of her the entire time.

Chapter 14

Alana readied herself for her buggy ride with Josiah, saying a quick prayer that she was making the right decision. They'd made such a connection in the graveyard the day before, and she realized they had more in common than she'd thought. Not to mention the way his hand in hers had made her tingle all the way to her toes.

Yes, she was certainly attracted to him, but there was more to it than that. He had a way about him that made her feel she could spend a lifetime with him. He was strong, and stable-minded; but most of all, he was kind. She felt almost giddy as she checked herself in the mirror, suddenly realizing he wouldn't be so concerned with her outward appearance as he would be with what was in her heart—even if he *had* said she was pretty.

Hearing buggy wheels in the driveway, her heart did a flip-flop. She took in a deep breath and let it out with a whoosh. To her, this was more than a buggy ride; it was the possible start to her future, and what could be the deciding factor in her staying in the community.

A quick tap on the front door of the *dawdi haus* let her know he was probably just as anxious as she was for this evening. She looked one last time at the dark purple dress that Eli had given her, stating it had been her sister's favorite.

Wish me luck, dear schweschder, she said with a smile as she smoothed out the dress.

She walked to the front door and swung it open, only to see…

"Noah! What are you doing here?"

"At the risk of making a fool of myself, I'd like another chance to take you for a buggy ride before *mei bruder* makes you his *fraa* and you regret it for the rest of your boring life!"

Her breath caught in her throat at the thought of being Josiah's wife. Was marriage really on his mind where she was concerned?

She looked into Noah's hopeful, but immature eyes, hating that she had to let him down, but it was his presence here that let her know she was making the right decision by taking the buggy ride with Josiah.

She cleared her throat. "I'm sorry you put yourself out there the way you have, but I'm afraid you're wasting your time being here. I'm prepared to have what future God wants for me, and I'm afraid you're not the right one for me."

She hated the look that fell across his face, but she couldn't let him go on thinking there was a chance between the two of them. It would be cruel for her to avoid the truth just to keep from seeing the look of hurt on his face. If he'd asked her a week ago, she would have gone off with him to the city, and it would have ended in disaster.

"I suspect the reason you're so interested in me is because I came from a place you want to be more than ever right now. You don't need me to hold your hand in your adventures. If you feel you must go, make certain you're going for the right reasons. Your *bruder* needs you right now."

"What do you know?" he asked harshly. "You left that all behind, and I think you'll regret giving up your freedom to stay here and be stifled in this community. I want to be free, and nothing is going to stop me—not even *you!*"

She sighed as she watched him jump into his buggy and steer the horse quickly out of the driveway. She stood there for a few minutes, thinking how he reminded her of herself at a time in her life when she didn't want anyone stopping her either. She, too, had felt stifled.

Now, as she waited for Josiah, she felt it in her heart that she'd been wrong.

****

When Josiah pulled up into the driveway, Alana was still standing in the doorway of the *dawdi haus,* still deep in thought.

He hopped down from the open courting buggy and approached her. "I like that you're ready and waiting for me!"

She looked up at him, wondering how he could have gotten more handsome between yesterday and today, but somehow he had. His genuine smile and dimples made her swoon unexpectedly, her heart fluttering.

Snapping out of her reverie, she wondered if she should tell him why she was really standing there, and decided it was probably best if she did.

"I certainly am ready, but I'm standing out here because Noah was just here, making one last attempt at trying to steal me away for a buggy ride tonight."

He shook his head and sighed. "I'm afraid that boy is going to find the exact trouble he's looking for. He's determined to run off to the city and *find himself;* whatever that means."

Alana knew what he meant, but she couldn't explain it to Josiah in a way he would understand unless the same craving drove him, and it seemed it didn't.

"Didn't you ever have the desire to just get away and leave this all behind?"

She knew she was risking a lot asking him the question, but she hoped to get him to understand.

He lowered his head. "I did actually leave for a day," he said. "Right after *mei daed's* funeral. I never said anything because I realized I didn't belong there; my place was here with *mei familye. Ach,* it was a foolish thing I did, but I had to know if staying here was what was really in *mei* heart; turns out, it was."

He did understand!

"*Danki* for sharing that with me," she said quietly, letting him know his secret could be trusted with her.

"You shared with me yesterday, so I figured I owed you."

He held his arm out for her and she took it, the warmth of his hand on her arm sending shivers right through her. Assisting her into the buggy, he offered her the lap-quilt, tucking it around her, and making her feel like she could melt into his arms and stay there for a lifetime.

Chapter 15

Josiah put his arm around Alana, tucking her close to shield her from the wind. Having her there beside him felt like the most natural thing in the world, and he thought he could certainly stand to have her there for a lifetime. A small part of him worried about getting too closely involved with her, wondering if she would ever return to the city.

He supposed only time would prove such a thing, and since she'd turned down Noah's offer, he figured he was as safe as any man of the same concerns. He tilted his head against hers, determined not to worry tonight. He would let it go the direction it was going to go and let God take care of the rest.

Alana never thought she could be content in the arms of a man—especially an Amish man. It wasn't that she had anything against the Amish—it was who she was. But since she'd spent most of her life running from what she was, she never thought she could be happy in the very spot she was now. His strong arm around her made her feel the safest she'd remembered feeling. She giggled inwardly, thinking that if Lydia could see her now, she wouldn't believe it—even after seeing it with her own eyes.

Leaning back, she enjoyed the quiet banter between them as if they were an old married couple already. He shared with her his thoughts about the new shelves he'd put in the cellar as if they were all ready for her, and she offered what she would can from his large kitchen garden that would feed them for the winter—as if they were an old married couple. It was almost as if they were making plans for their future without really making them. It was almost as if things were already decided between them.

Were they?

When he finally parked the buggy in front of a place he'd called Goose Pond, he shared story after story of catching frogs and fish as a young boy there, and how his *daed* had taught him and Noah to skip rocks across the glassy surface, and how it was his *mamm* who'd taught the two of them to ice skate on that pond in the winter.

At the far end of the pond, he pointed out the B&B that was owned by the King family—Becca's family. "She tried to use her *familye's* wealth to get my attention, but I have no desire to keep her company, much less to run a B&B. she's a restless youth who is going to get *mei bruder* into a lot of trouble if he isn't careful around her."

"I don't think he has any real interest in her. I think they both have a desire to grow up too fast, and to go off on their *rumspringa,* but I don't see them going together."

"She's certainly a troublesome one, that girl is; she tried to get me to kiss her when I took her home!" he said with a chuckle. "She thought that was a courting ride I took her on."

Alana giggled. "I would have put her out of the buggy and made her walk home!"

He chuckled. "I was tempted, but Noah had upset her, and her *grossmammi* and *grosspappi,* Bess and Jessup King have been friends of our *familye* for as long as I can remember. I suppose when she came out here to stay with them since her *daed* passed on, she thought she had some sort of future arrangement with me or something."

"Some families do still arrange the marriages in the communities, but only to a certain point. I suppose that's why she's always following you around."

He sighed. "She's going to have to stop following me around now that I'm courting you," he said.

Alana's breath caught in her throat. She hadn't expected him to be so blunt about it, but she supposed they had an understanding since they were sitting in the cool moonlight in a courting buggy. Somehow, him saying it out loud made it official, and she accepted that.

"Look!" he said, pointing up into the night sky. "A shooting star. Make a wish!"

I wish Josiah would kiss me!

He pulled her into his arms unexpectedly and pressed his lips against hers, his warm breath keeping her teeth from chattering as she deepened the kiss. All the love she feared she would never have for a man came rushing forth in that kiss, leaving her almost breathless.

"*Danki* for the wish!" he said, smiling and exposing his dimples.

"What wish?" she asked, feeling embarrassed.

"You wished I'd kiss you, didn't you?" he asked. "If not, then *my* wish wouldn't have come true."

"And what wish was that?" she asked, smiling back at him.

"My wish was that *you* would wish for me to kiss you, so it worked."

She giggled. "You don't have to wait for another shooting star," she said with a smile. "You can kiss me again if you want to."

He smiled. There were those dimples she would be happy to see every day for the rest of her life.

He pulled her close, lifting his eyes to the sky.

"I hope our future will be filled with shooting stars, just so I can have an excuse to kiss you any time I want to."

Pressing his lips against hers, she looked up into the sky, and watched another shooting star fly across the heavens.

Chapter 16

Alana bolted upright in her temporary bed in her temporary home; she was to be married at the end of the week. How had this happened so quickly? It was almost as if it was *pre-planned.*

Had it been? Josiah had said the entire community had teased him relentlessly for planting a large crop of celery in faith that he would be married this wedding season. Was she his answer to prayer, or was she the only one who was willing to marry him?

No. He certainly had other prospects. Becca King was evident of his popularity. So why had he picked *her?* Lydia had always told her that her indecisiveness and insecurities would some day be the ruin of her if she didn't get them under control. Was she overthinking this to point of self-sabotage?

She flung back the heavy quilt and shivered before she pulled on her robe and went to the window. Barely twilight, Alana could see the light dusting of snow that had decorated the ground overnight. She shivered again, not yet ready to embrace another cold winter, until she remembered the talk she'd had with Josiah the night before while he'd parked his buggy on the bank of Goose Pond.

Ice skating was something she and Lydia had looked forward to every year when they were younger, and *daed* had taken them sledding a time or two on a rolling hill that had not seemed so scary once she'd grown older. Were these things she would someday do with her own children? The thought of having children with Josiah made her heart skip a beat. She leaned her head against the window and watched light snow flutter around whimsically, daydreaming of the kisses they'd shared for hours.

A smile tugged at the corners of her mouth. It suddenly no longer mattered if Josiah was thought of as *narrish* among his peers for having faith that *she* would be his bride this season; she had happily put that to rest when she'd confided in him that she'd returned because she, too, had faith that she would be married. She hadn't told another soul, for fear that she'd be ridiculed, but that hadn't seemed to bother Josiah, who'd boasted about his faith.

Yes, it would seem that their meeting and marriage had been pre-planned, but by God, and not them. She wasn't used to having such obedience. She had always been the one who would make rash decisions and refuse to think things through carefully. But this; this had been thought of with too much care.

She lifted her eyes toward the heavens and whispered a prayer.

Danki, Lord, for helping me to have the faith I needed, and the courage to listen to you for a change instead of my own wants. Help me to be the kind of fraa that mei schweschder was to Eli, and the same kind of humble and willing servant to mei husband as I am to you.

Her stomach filled with butterflies at the thought of living in the large house with Josiah. But then it hit her; how was she going to live with having Noah around all the time? Would he give up his quest for her once the two of them were married? Josiah had assured her that Noah would be perfectly happy living in the *dawdi haus* in back of the property, but somehow, she just didn't see him as being anything other than a restless nuisance if he stayed there. Was it possible that Josiah would consider leaving his family's home and starting over somewhere else?

Suddenly, her stomach was in knots again, and the only thing she wanted to do was to talk to Lydia; she was the only one who understood her restless heart. How could she possibly be so conflicted now? She was about to be married, and if she didn't sort out her fears soon, she would not be able to marry him.

Dressing quickly, she prayed that Eli would harness a buggy for her so she could travel the few blocks to the cemetery, rather than walk the distance in the slippery, first snow-fall. Tucking her arms into her heavy, wool cloak, she pulled a knitted shawl over her head and went out to the barn.

When she opened the barn door, she surprisingly found Josiah. Not expecting to see him there since the corral had been finished the day before, Alana approached him cautiously, wondering if they were the only two in the barn.

He held up the lantern, his warm breath making a puff of icy air roll from his mouth when he spoke to her. "*Ach,* you should be in the *haus* where it's warm."

"What are you doing here?" she asked, suddenly forgetting she was about to flee to the graveyard to have a one-sided conversation with her sister.

Seeing him had put aside all her doubts and fears, his confident eyes giving her the strength she needed at that very moment—almost as if he knew.

But how could he have?

"I left my tools here yesterday and I needed them to repair the hinge on the barn door at my place, and I knew Eli wouldn't mind if I came over to get them. What are you doing out here so early?"

Could she tell him her foolish doubts she'd had only a few minutes before? It was probably best not to since having him here was the answer to her prayer.

"I was going to make a trip to the cemetery to *tell* Lydia of our plans to marry. I know it sounds foolish, but I needed to have a talk with her."

Had she said too much? The look in his eyes would say not.

"I stopped by there on my way here and told *mei mamm* and *daed* about you, and our plans to marry, but I can see in your eyes, it might be more than that for you. If I had to guess, I would say you have concerns about Noah and his living on the farm with us."

How did he know? Was he able to look inside her and *see* what she was thinking?

She nodded, feeling suddenly guilty that she'd not wanted his brother to be so close when they started their life together. She wanted time with him alone, to be like other married couples. Was that so much to ask?

"Not to worry," he assured her. "When I told him last night of our plans to marry, he packed his things and said he'd been offered a room over the bakery in town at the Miller's, and a job too, but he'd not wanted to take it because he was worried about what I would think of such a thing. After *mei mamm* passed on, he's been doing all the cooking, and I never thought much of his desire to bake like our *mamm* did. She didn't have any *dochders,* and so I would often find Noah in the kitchen with her baking pies when I needed him to help with things around the farm, but there he would be, tied up in apron strings *baking.*"

This was good news, wasn't it?

She had to giggle at the thought of Noah, who put up a tough front—baking pies!

Josiah laughed. "I have to admit; I'm relieved that he won't be there. This way, he gets to go into the *city* and work and live among the *Englisch,* without being too far away. I wasn't going to ask him to leave our *familye* homestead, but now I can have my bride all to myself, and we can start a *familye* of our own."

He pulled her into his arms, and suddenly, everything in her world was set in her mind and in her heart. She would never be alone again, and he understood her. God had certainly sent her the right man to marry, that she was certain of.

Chapter 17

Becca peered into the window at the bakery as she walked by, wondering why Noah was behind the counter with Mr. Miller, who seemed to be showing him where everything went.

"Noah." She mouthed the word as she waved to get his attention.

He scowled at her.

She persisted, waving again.

He excused himself and went out to greet her, annoyance clearly showing in his expression. Poking his head out the door, his warm breath mixed with the cold air, the rush of cold causing him to shiver. "Why don't you come inside where it's warm?"

"I didn't want to interrupt you," she said. "Are you working here?"

"*Jah*, I just started. Why?"

"What happened?" she asked. "Are you having financial problems with the farm?'

"*Nee*, I don't want to live there once *mei bruder* marries Alana."

He didn't miss the look of anger twisting up her face. "Married?" she practically screeched. "He proposed to *me* when he took me home from the harvest picnic!"

Noah raised an eyebrow. "Why would he do a *narrish* thing like that? Maybe you misunderstood him."

"I suppose I misunderstood his kiss, too!" she said angrily.

Noah laughed. "Josiah—kissed *you?*"

"Ach, I don't see what's so hard to imagine about that. He isn't going to marry that *Englischer,* Alana; I'm going to talk to the Bishop about this!"

"Whoa!" Noah said, ushering her out of the bakery and out into the cold street. "Josiah would never ask you to marry him, and then turn around and propose to Alana. They went for a buggy ride and got engaged; they'll be married on Thursday."

"Not if I have anything to say about it!" she said, storming off.

"Wait," Noah called after her.

Mr. Miller was waving him back into the bakery. They had customers, and he couldn't worry himself over the drama Becca was creating as usual. With Alana moving in to his home in just a few days, Noah couldn't afford to lose his job or the roof over his head. He would have to worry about Becca when his shift was over; right now, all he could worry about was his own predicament.

Chapter 18

"Think, Josiah!" Noah demanded. "What did you say to that mixed-up girl?"

"I don't remember; I was too busy thinking about Alana. I could have said anything to her!"

"Did you *kiss* her?" he asked cautiously.

Josiah looked off in the distance for a moment.

"Did she *say* I kissed her?"

Noah grabbed his older brother by the shoulders and gave him a swift jolt. "You mean you don't know?"

"I was so mesmerized by my picnic lunch with Alana that I could have said or did almost anything without recollection, I suppose," he admitted.

"Well, you better start thinking because she's on her way to see the Bishop right now to make you marry her!"

Josiah paced. "There's only one thing to do; I'll have to go see the Bishop myself and get this cleared up."

"He isn't going to take kindly to you making unintentional proposals to that girl."

"I didn't propose to her—intentionally or unintentionally; she's *stretching the truth.*"

On the drive to the Bishop's house, Josiah tried his best to remember their conversations, replaying the ride home in his head. He was certain they had not even discussed marriage, but then his mind was on Alana the entire time.

"Alana!" he said aloud. "What is she going to say when she finds out about this?"

"Wait!" Noah cautioned him. "No use in telling her unless it's a problem. No sense in getting her all upset for nothing. I'm sure the Bishop is going to straighten this whole thing out."

"I pray you're right," Josiah said as he pulled his buggy into the Bishop's driveway.

"Look!" Noah said pointing near the barn. "The buggy for the B&B. That means Becca has already had a chance to tell him her lies!"

"Let's not jump to conclusions," Josiah tried to convince himself more than anything. "Maybe he's talking some sense into her. Maybe it won't be as bad as we think."

"Well, she ain't in there inviting them for Sunday supper!" Noah said.

Josiah scowled at his brother as he hopped down from the buggy, his hand shaky and his palms sweaty.

What had he gotten himself into?

When they walked up to the door, Josiah remembered some of their conversation finally, trying to keep it straight in his head.

Bishop Troyer let them in, and they could hear Becca crying in the kitchen with *Frau* Troyer.

"You poor dear," she was saying.

Bishop Troyer pointed to the door. "Perhaps it's best if we talk out on the porch."

Josiah pushed in front of his brother, eager to get out of the house. It didn't matter one bit that it was cold out, he'd take that over whatever was going on in the kitchen between Becca and *Frau* Troyer.

He offered them a place to sit on the wicker furniture on the wraparound porch. They'd had the best porch in the community, outside of the one at the B&B, which was four times the size of the Bishop's.

"Why don't I start by letting you know that Becca is still very distraught, as she feels she's been *tricked* out of a proposal that was offered to her first."

Josiah had always been one to think before speaking, but he *had* to interrupt the Bishop and put a stop to all of this misunderstanding.

"I didn't offer to marry her," he said. "She was trying to put words in my mouth the entire trip to her *haus*. She said she wasn't happy that I'd spent so much time with Alana at the picnic, and asked me if I thought she was worthy of marrying. I didn't want to hurt her feelings, so naturally, I told her that she was. The whole thing started when Noah bid on her pie at the picnic. We both thought it was Alana's pie, so we were bidding against each other, but it turned out that pie was Becca's and Noah won the bidding—and the afternoon with Becca."

"She thought because we both tried to outbid one another for her pie that we were both interested in *her,*" Noah said.

"If not Becca," Bishop said. "Then I'm assuming you were both vying for Alana. I'm also assuming since you plan to marry Alana, that the two of you have your differences worked out where she's concerned?"

"Absolutely," Josiah was quick to answer.

"I'm certainly glad to hear that, however, there is still the issue with your commitment or lack of commitment to Becca."

"Why are you taking her word for it?" Noah demanded. "What about Josiah's word?"

"There is also the matter of the kiss between you," the Bishop said. "What can you tell me about that?"

"The way she tells the story, I declared love for her and bent down on one knee!" Josiah complained. "I answered a trick question from a tricky girl, and she asked for a kiss on her forehead for the bump she got when she fell in the creek."

"That seems to explain most of it, but it's not the same story she gives."

"I didn't propose marriage to her, and I didn't kiss her in any way that was inappropriate; I pecked her forehead the same way I would if she was *mei* little *schweschder;* honestly, that's how it all happened," Josiah insisted.

"I believe you," Bishop Troyer said, patting his shoulder, hoping to comfort him. "But she's saying you did, and unless you can come up with a witness who heard otherwise, or she admits she was mistaken, I can't marry you and Alana on Thursday."

He sighed. What was he going to tell Alana?

"I understand," he said, hanging his head. "I suppose I better go over and talk to Alana about all of this, and pray she doesn't break off our engagement."

They bid the Bishop goodbye, and went back to their farm, all the while, an idea was hatching in Noah's head that was just too perfect to fail. He'd gotten his brother into the mess with Becca, and he was determined to get him out of it.

Chapter 19

Alana tried her best to be patient with Noah, who seemed to have all the answers all of a sudden, but she wasn't altogether sure he wasn't just grasping at straws.

"Trust me when I tell you I know what that girl is made of," he said. "And when *mei bruder* gets here in the morning to tell you everything, don't let on that I already told you. I was too afraid of your reaction to all of this, and afraid you'd break his heart, to let it go to chance when he spoke to you in the morning. I convinced him to wait until then to break the news to you, hoping I could fix things in the meantime."

"You really think it's wise to invite her into your home?" Alana asked.

She was skeptical to say the least.

"The Kings' are getting up in age, and she's bragged a lot about taking over the B&B for them. When her *daed* passed away, he was their only child, and that makes Becca their only heir to the place. Trust me when I tell you; she can't do anything for that place beyond bossing around a bunch of employees. That pie she brought to the picnic came from the bakery where I got a job. She can't cook, or clean or do any of the things she needs to do in order to be a farmer's *fraa*. Any man who marries her will have to give up his life to run the B&B for her, because if it's left to her, she'll run it into the ground. She told me herself she can't take the place over until she gets married; that's why she's trying to trick Josiah. I'm sure she thinks that if she traps him in this marriage he'll have to help her with the B&B. She likes that place too much; she said it gives her the best of both the Amish and *Englisch* worlds, and she likes the prestige. She won't want to give it up to marry *mei bruder*."

Alana sighed as he hopped back in his buggy to leave. "I'll say a prayer that your plan works, but I don't like the idea of her being over there even for a minute. What are you going to do if your plan backfires on you and she goes back with you? She'll be there from sun up to sun down every day; can you handle that?"

"If she agrees to the conditions, I'll be so busy keeping her busy, she won't have time to even look at Josiah, much less try to carry on anything with him. I'll let her have run of the main *haus* all by herself— but only until I can think of a new plan if this one fails. But I'm confident she'll be so overwhelmed she'll not likely be there more than the amount of time it takes for it to dawn on her that she'd be more like one of her own employees rather than a *fraa.*"

Alana could do nothing more than shake her head at Noah.

"If you ask me, you're going to be spinning your buggy wheels trying to get rid of her, and once she gets a foot in the door, you won't be able to pry her out!"

"When she sees how much work is involved in running a small dairy farm, she'll change her mind real fast, and she'll have no choice but to admit she misunderstood Josiah's intentions, because we both know she'll never admit she outright lied about the entire thing."

"Do you have a *plan B?*"

He shook his head and shrugged. He had one, but he wasn't about to tell Alana, for fear she'd try to talk him out of it.

Chapter 20

"I don't think it's proper or wise for you to be here with me since I'm about to marry your *bruder*," Becca said to Noah, who'd gone to the B&B to find her.

"Well that's just it," he said, trying to keep a straight face. "Josiah sent me to fetch you."

"For what?" she asked. "Is something wrong?"

"Nee, I'm here to bring you back to the farm with us—to get to know your place there. He needs you to learn how to cook and clean and gather the eggs, and a whole other list of things, but he needs you to get started now."

"Noah Bontrager, you're not funny. I can't be there unescorted all day with two *menner* I'm not married to."

"Don't worry about that!" he said with a smile. "Alana agreed to help teach you to do the cooking and such, since I know that you don't do any of that here at the B&B. I know that you can't bake, or you wouldn't buy your pies from the bakery in town and try to pass them off as your own. But Alana can teach you all that."

She pursed her lips. "I do not buy pies from the bakery, Noah!"

"Did you forget I work there now? Mr. Miller showed me your weekly order!"

"Why would Alana want to teach me to be a *fraa* to the *mann* she was supposed to marry?"

"You're doing her a favor by marrying *mei bruder*. He's only taking a *fraa* for the extra help around the farm. When Alana found that out, she said she'd be more than happy to help you marry him."

"I get to take over the B&B once I'm married," she said. "Surely *you* can take over your *familye* farm so that Josiah and I can live *here* once we're married."

"I moved into town and took a job at the bakery; I can't run that farm—only Josiah can, and he's not about to fail our *daed* and all the hard work he put into that farm his whole life. That farm is Josiah's birthright; I don't know how to run a dairy farm. All I ever did was take orders from *mei bruder*. If he left me to take over that farm, I'd have it run into the ground inside of a few days!"

"But I don't want to be the *fraa* of a farmer!" she said.

"You should have thought of that when you accepted *mei bruder's* proposal of marriage," Noah said, hoping he wasn't pushing his limits.

"What proposal?" she asked, giggling nervously. "I don't remember Josiah proposing—at least not to me!"

That's what I thought you'd say!

Noah let it go at that, breathing a sigh of relief as he steered his horse away from the B&B, realizing just how close he'd come to offering to take his brother's place and marry Becca.

Now, he wouldn't have to.

Chapter 21

"I don't know how you did it, Noah, but I'm glad you did!" Josiah said as he readied himself for his wedding to Alana.

Noah chuckled. "Maybe I'll tell you about it some day."

"As long as you didn't threaten her or anything like that," Josiah said jokingly.

"Only with a lot of hard work!" he said. "She's too lazy to be a farmer's *fraa*. She likes having things handed to her, and doesn't appreciate the value of working for what you have."

"She isn't going to stop the wedding, is she?"

Noah smiled. "Not a chance! The Kings' told me she went to stay with a friend in Indianapolis until Christmas. That should give you and Alana a *gut* start to your lives before you have to run into her again."

A knock door at the interrupted them, but when Alana poked her head in the door, Noah excused himself so the two of them could visit for a moment before the ceremony.

Josiah looked at his bride, thinking to himself how lucky he was to have such a beautiful woman with a kind heart to be joining his life. He pulled her into his arms and held her close.

"I've wanted to talk to you for the past couple of days; I've been trying to build up enough courage to talk to you about something."

Here it was; she'd been waiting for him to tell her about Becca, but did any of it really need to be said? Noah had told her the outcome of his talk with the girl and how she'd changed her mind so fast it was like night and day.

"As long as you're not about to call off our wedding, I don't need to hear it," she said, letting him off the hook.

"You don't have to worry about me calling it off, Alana; I love you and I want to spend the rest of my life making you happy."

"You don't have to try very hard," she said, smiling. "Just being *you* makes me happy. I love you too."

All at once, she thought about the many wishes she'd made recently, feeling overwhelmed at how many of them had already been granted. They were her prayers, and God had answered them.

Josiah dipped his head down and pressed his lips to Alana's.

A hasty knock at the door startled them.

Noah poked his head in the door. "The Bishop is waiting!"

Josiah smiled at his bride. "Are you ready to go get married?"

"*Jah,* I'm ready to become a farmer's *fraa.*"

She smiled; she was more than ready.

THE END

Amish Weddings
Becca's Return
Book Five

Samantha Bayarr

Amish
Weddings
Becca's Return

Samantha Bayarr

A note from the Author:

While this novel is set against the backdrop of an Amish community, the characters and the names of the community are fictional. There is no intended resemblance between the characters in this book or the setting, and any real members of any Amish or Mennonite community. As with any work of fiction, I've taken license in some areas of research as a means of creating the necessary circumstances for my characters and setting. It is completely impossible to be accurate in details and descriptions, since every community differs, and such a setting would destroy the fictional quality of entertainment this book serves to present. Any inaccuracies in the Amish and Mennonite lifestyles portrayed in this book are completely due to fictional license. Please keep in mind that this book is meant for fictional, entertainment purposes only, and is not written as a textbook on the Amish.

Happy Reading

Amish Weddings
Becca's Return
Book Five

Chapter 1

Becca paced outside the bakery, dancing slightly to keep warm while she waited for Noah to get a break from his customers and notice she was out there waiting on him. Slush formed on the sidewalk under her feet where she wore a clean path through the fresh snowfall. Her breath came out in icy puffs, and if not for her nervous stomach, she might have been able to enjoy the twinkly lights and Christmas decorations that smothered the downtown square in holiday cheer.

The slightest hint of warm gingerbread mixed with the aroma of freshly-cut pine trees from the tree-lot taking up residence in the vacant lot next to the bakery. Normally, they were two of her favorite scents, but her stomach was such a jumbled ball of nerves, she worried she might lose her breakfast if she didn't get that talk over with Noah before she changed her mind and chickened out.

All her life she'd wondered what life would be like outside the community, and now that she'd found out, she wished she could rethink that decision. She hadn't been home since the day before Josiah's wedding to Alana, thinking she could make things right for herself in the *Englisch* world, but she'd made such a mess of things for herself in both worlds, she didn't know where else to turn—except to Noah.

With only ten days left before Christmas, she was running out of time to claim her inheritance at the B&B. Her grandparents had put strict conditions on the terms with which she could claim the B&B as her own, and so far; she hadn't complied with any of the terms. Truth was, if they were to discover the secrets she'd been hiding from them, they would likely send her packing back to the *Englisch* world. Only problem was, she knew she didn't fit in there anymore than she did in the community. Unfortunately, she was stuck trying to stay in the community, and Noah was her last hope to do so.

Noah finished boxing up Mrs. Smith's white Christmas pies, and then assembled a tray with wedges of peppermint bark and two cups of hot cocoa, figuring the half-frozen Becca would be more than happy to join him inside at one of the bistro tables. Since he hadn't seen her in over five weeks, he wondered what she was doing outside the bakery now. If not for the fact that he knew she stood to inherit the B&B, he wouldn't have expected to see her back in the community after the humiliation she had suffered from Josiah's rejection. Still, he was curious to find out what she wanted with him, even though he had a strong hunch he already knew.

By the time he finally beckoned her inside the warm bakery, her cheeks and nose were pink, and her lips were practically blue. But there was something really different about the way she looked. If he wasn't mistaken, he'd almost say she looked— humble.

Pulling the white shawl from her head, static crackled, and she pushed down flyaway blond strands.

He noticed right away she wasn't wearing a prayer *kapp,* though her hair was pulled back. Had she rejected the baptism and forsaken the ways of the Amish? She removed her coat, and he was shocked to see the plain, pastel dress that looked Mennonite rather than the ones approved by their Bishop. Had she converted?

She sat at the little round table without a word, immediately sipping from the hot cocoa he offered her, cupping her hands around the large mug to warm them. Her teeth chattered, but she calmed them with another sip.

Lifting her eyes, her gaze met his finally, a look of desperation filling her eyes, making Noah feel a little uneasy.

"I need your help," she finally said. "If you decline my offer, I'm afraid I'll have to leave the community *permanently."*

"Ach, it can't be all that bad, can it?" he asked.

"I'm afraid *mei* entire future depends on your answer."

He looked at her, desperation in her eyes, making him sweat.

"If you're here to get me to marry you so you can inherit the B&B, you can forget it," he said firmly.

She sat quietly across from him, her gaze fixed on the mug of hot cocoa nestled between her hands, her lower lip quivering.

Was she crying?

He hadn't meant to upset her; he just didn't want to marry her. She was one of the prettiest young women in the community, and she certainly seemed to be calmer and *nicer* than the last time he'd dealt with her. But that didn't mean marrying her was an option.

No matter what the circumstances, or whatever she was offering in return; he couldn't marry her.

He didn't believe he was capable of loving her.

Truthfully, he didn't even *like* her very much.

Chapter 2

Becca sniffled. "You're *mei* last hope, Noah Bontrager."

"But you're the Kings' logical heir since Jessup's other *kinner* showed no interest in the property or moving back to the area; they'll give it to you without you having to resort to marrying someone you don't love."

"*Grosspappi* Jessup says he'll sell it to Melvin Bender; the man has been pestering *mei pappi* about it for more than a year. *Pappi* says he's getting too old, and *Mammi* Bess is having trouble getting up and down the stairs; they can't do for the place like they used to. The only reason she agreed to let me stay with *mei* cousins for the past few weeks is due to the fact they had no reservations. But this week, they'll be full-up."

"*Jah,* I heard Jessup say at the church meeting that they will be all filled day after tomorrow. A couple of us went over and helped them put up the lights around the porch and the Christmas trees; you know how those *Englischers* love their Christmas decorations."

Yes, she knew all too well; after all, it was one of the reasons the B&B appealed to her so much. Owning it would be almost like having the best of both worlds.

She stared into her cup. "About my offer…"

He sighed. "Becca, even *if* I was interested in marrying you, ten days is not enough time to be baptized and get all the preparations done for a wedding. Everyone will be too busy with their own plans for the season. Not this close to Christmas—not even in this community!"

"I wasn't planning on being baptized; it wasn't one of the conditions," she said, her gaze still fixed in her mug of cocoa.

"You don't want to be baptized?" he asked, though his tone showed more surprise than he felt.

"I've been attending the Mennonite church with *mei* cousins, and I have to admit, I enjoy it better. At least I understand it more."

"*Jah,* I've been to a few myself, and I liked it too. But that doesn't mean I want to abandon everything here; I'm going to be an *onkel,* and *mei bruder* and I are getting along for the first time in years. I moved back to the *dawdi haus* while you were gone."

She looked up at him briefly, her eyes pink and misty.

"Surely you don't want to work at this bakery for the rest of your life knowing the Millers won't let you take this place over; they have two sons who will be in line for it before you will," she tried reasoning with him.

She was right about that; there was no future in this job, and no possibility for promotion. He didn't even earn enough money to live in town, and had had to move back into the *dawdi haus* on Josiah's farm. Mr. Miller's eldest son had needed to move into the loft apartment above the bakery after the pipes had broken in his house and flooded the basement. Not only had their son taken over the apartment, he was also now working at the bakery, which cut Noah's hours at a time when he needed the money most.

Truthfully, Becca's offer would be very appealing if it didn't involve the permanency of being married to her. He allowed himself to imagine, only for a moment, what it would feel like to own a B&B—until he remembered he'd be *half-owner* with Becca.

"I can't marry you for the sake of owning *mei* own business, no matter how appealing it is," he said.

"Think of the marriage as a contract—a business deal," she pleaded.

"That would prevent me from being married for real reasons and starting a *familye* some day."

Her heart sank at the thought of it.

"Come to work for me there for the next few days, and then make your decision," she practically begged him.

"We are only ten days away from Christmas, and you're supposed to be married by Christmas Eve?" he asked skeptically. "How can you expect me to know in less than ten days if I want to be permanently married to you? It's impossible, and *mei* answer has to stay at *nee—no!*"

She looked up at him, tears filling her eyes; he had no idea how desperate she was.

"Don't look at me like that!" he scolded her. "You have no shortage of *menner* in this community who would marry you for the sake of having an instant business to run. And they wouldn't care if they had to marry you in name only just to get it."

"Think about that for a minute, and then perhaps you'll realize why I asked *you* instead of one of them. You have morals and standards, and that is exactly why I want you to consider this."

Noah looked at the cup of cold cocoa in front of him that he hadn't even touched. "*Mei morals* and *standards* are *exactly* the reason I *can't* marry you, Becca. I'm sorry, but the answer is still no."

She was embarrassing herself more than the stunt she'd pulled with Josiah only a few weeks ago. It was obvious she wasn't going to convince Noah, but her time was running out for more reasons than she could admit.

His rejection was not her biggest problem at the moment; she couldn't even go home now.

Chapter 3

Noah woke up early, not able to sleep after his disturbing conversation with Becca the day before. He'd been quiet at dinner, and Alana had noticed and mentioned his mood, but he'd shrugged it off as being overtired from working overtime at the bakery while keeping up with his chores at the farm.

With winter in full-swing, chores were twice as tough, and took twice as long to complete. Not to mention, he'd carried a double load with working part time in town at the bakery. He enjoyed his work there; it reminded him of the days he'd worked side-by-side in the kitchen with his *mamm* creating one delectable dessert after another. She had a big imagination, and a creative side he seemed to inherit, or perhaps the time spent with her had rubbed off on him, and he'd managed to mimic her skills in the kitchen.

Here on the farm, he took his meals with Josiah and Alana now, not wanting to overstep his boundaries with kitchen duties. As tough as it was for him, he had to allow *mamm's* kitchen to belong to Alana now, and give her the courtesy of finding her place there. His *mamm* would have been happy to have Alana in the kitchen with her, and certainly would have approved of Josiah's choice in her as his *fraa.*

Walking into the barn, Noah stomped the snow from his boots and shivered. It wasn't much warmer in the barn, but at least it was a shelter from the wind and snow. The horses nickered and the milk-cow bellowed from her stall. He knew if he didn't get to the milking, she would be bawling before he got through mucking up the stalls for the horses. She always had to come first that way, but he didn't mind, he knew Alana would need the milk for breakfast. He suspected she was already in the family way, but since his brother hadn't mentioned it yet, he would continue to provide the milk for the morning meal the way she'd asked him to.

A rustling noise from the loft caused him to turn his head in time to see a sprinkling of hay flutter to the floor of the barn. He hoped that it wasn't a wild critter, such as a raccoon, but could only assume that one of the barn cats had made its way up to the loft for the night. When he heard a tiny little groan, his ears perked up wondering what, if not a human, could possibly have made that noise.

If he wasn't mistaken, it almost sounded like a woman; but who? Was it possible some of the younger kids in the community had found their way in the loft of his barn when they were out later than they should have been? The way he figured, as long as they weren't up there drinking, or doing immoral things, he would leave well enough alone. He'd been young once, and had had his share of sleepovers in his cousin's barn when they were out too late to come in at a decent hour.

He paused for a moment and chuckled to himself, wondering when he'd grown up so much. He wasn't so old that he'd forgotten what it was like to run around the community prior to *rumspringa*. Although his experience with his own *rumspringa* had only consisted of living on his own for three weeks, he'd still maintained his job at the bakery, and therefore, had gained a sense of independence from his brother.

Noah patted Brownie's side as he sat on the milking stool preparing to milk her as part of his morning chores. "I've got a real tough one for you today, Brownie," he said, as though the cow could understand every word he was saying. "It's about Becca King."

Chapter 4

Becca stirred slightly at a noise, pulling the wool horse blankets around her shivering frame; she hadn't meant to fall asleep, but she had been too emotionally and physically exhausted to stay awake a moment longer. Now, she shivered, and was desperately in need of making her way to the out-house.

Noah stood in the way of that at the moment.

She let out a little gasp when she heard her name being spoken by Noah down in the main part of the barn.

Was he talking to the cow?

If she let her presence be known in the loft of the barn, she'd have to give him an explanation for why she was there, and she'd hoped to avoid such a thing. If only she hadn't spent her last bit of money on the bus ride home, she would have had the cash to stay at a motel in town. As it was, she didn't even have the money to get back to her cousin's house, and she was stuck in a place that her lies and her sins had gotten herself into.

She continued to listen, hoping he might say something significant; something that would indicate he would accept her proposal. If not, she would have to find a way to leave the community and go back to her cousin's house because it was the only place she had left to go if Noah continued to reject her.

Despite the howling wind rattling the rafters of the barn, she could hear the milk squirting into the large stainless steel pail.

"You have no idea how badly I wanted to rescue Becca from her troubles," Noah said to Brownie, continuing his conversation where he left off. "And I wanted to kiss that pouty mouth of hers, right there in the bakery. I know it's not right to accept her proposal when I'm not sure if I love her like a man should love his *fraa*, but I wanted so much to help her. I felt sorry for her. The truth is, I never liked her very much, but there was something different about her yesterday at the bakery; something almost bearable. She's changed, and I wonder if I should give her offer some thought."

Noah heard a gasp behind him; he'd forgotten that he'd heard a noise already once before and wondered who was listening to him. He had always had talks with Brownie while he milked her, and today should be no different; except it was obvious someone was listening to his very private conversation.

He stood, wondering if he should grab a stick or something before confronting whoever was up in the loft. When he reached the ladder, he looked up but didn't see anyone.

"Show yourself," he said boldly. "Whoever you are, come on down. You know it's not polite to eavesdrop on other people's conversations."

Becca reluctantly moved to the edge of the loft, shaking and shivering, some from nerves and some from the cold. He looked up at her, a scowl spread across his face.

"Come down from there this instant," he scolded her. "What on earth are you doing up there so early in the morning? What if I hadn't come out here? You might have frozen to death!"

Truth be told, she shivered, thinking she might just be halfway there. She tried to speak, but her teeth chattered too uncontrollably for her to get even one word out. She tried to work her way down the ladder, but lost her footing. Noah rushed beneath her, catching her before she fell to the barn floor. Scooping up her tiny frame in his arms, he nestled her against his broad frame, and carried her out of the barn and into the *dawdi haus*. He knew he needed to get her warmed up, or she might suffer hypothermia. Barely conscious, she did not protest him taking control. Once inside the *dawdi haus*, he sat her down on the sofa in front of the fireplace and stirred the coals, adding several wedges of freshly-cut wood to bring about a rousing fire. She lay on the sofa, eyes closed, her beauty and innocence reflecting in the glow of the flames.

He stared at her for a moment, watching the gentle rise and fall of her breath, thinking how vulnerable she looked at that moment—and how beautiful. Despite the high flames from the roaring fire warming the room, she continued to shiver. He tried to rouse her, but she simply groaned, keeping her eyes closed.

The poor thing must be exhausted.

Noah sat on the sofa and pulled her into his arms, pulling a heavy quilt over the both of them, hoping his body heat would warm her enough to save her from hypothermia. It was quite possible that the only thing that might have saved her was the fact that she'd been wrapped in several wool horse blankets. After several minutes, her shaking quelled, and she began to relax; her breathing more even.

Pulling out his cell phone he'd gotten while in town, he called the doctor and asked him to make a house call. Josiah knew he'd gotten the phone, and had not reprimanded him for it, knowing how many other things he'd given up to help him with the farm, and it wasn't like he'd taken the baptism yet, so he wasn't risking anything other than reprimand from the Bishop for putting off his baptism repeatedly. Up until now, having Becca in his arms, he hadn't any reason to want to take the baptism. Now, he could see himself as her husband, sheltering her from all harm, and loving her the way a *mann* loves his *fraa*.

What had I been thinking, rejecting her the way I had?

If he was being truthful with himself at all, he would have reminded himself of the feelings he had for her ever since that feisty picnic with her and her pie. It had angered him that she'd tried to trick his brother into marriage after they've had such a great time during their picnic.

Their turning point had been when he told her he thought he was bidding on Alana's pie instead of hers. He was only trying to be truthful with her since he cared about her and wanted to start the relationship with her on a good note. But everything had gone downhill since that moment, and he hadn't been able to recover from it since. That was all behind them now; he would make things right with her and let go of the grudge he'd been holding against her for what she did, how she'd reacted to him, and the things he'd said that had hurt her deeply.

He kissed the top of her head, breathing in the smell of fresh hay on her, thinking it was a right-fine smell for his *fraa* to have.

Chapter 5

Noah wriggled out from under Becca to answer the door.

"Doctor Davis, *kume,*" he said. "She's over there on the sofa. I was trying to warm her up with the fire and quilts."

He didn't offer that he'd used his body heat to bring her temperature back to what he thought was pretty close to being normal.

He went into the kitchen to put on the tea kettle, thinking some warm herbal tea would do her some good. That, and he wanted the doctor to be able to assess her without him hovering nervously. Keeping himself busy so he wouldn't worry about her was best for him at the moment.

He was eager for her to wake up, so he could give her the news that he would agree to her offer of marriage. He couldn't wait to tell her that he would do it for her, and not for the sake of the B&B.

After several minutes, the doctor met him out in the kitchen and asked if he could sit down while Noah offered him some tea. Dr. Davis had been with the community for so many years, and was married to one of the prominent Amish women in the community, and they had all considered him an honorary Amish.

"She's going to need lots of fluids, and…"

A groan from the other room interrupted the doctor's instructions, and Noah heard Becca calling his name. He rose from his chair, letting the doctor know he would go to her. When he reached her, her eyes fluttered open and shut a few times, but he knelt before her where she laid on the sofa.

"I'm here," he said to her gently. "And I accept your offer, but you must preserve your strength and get better. You gave me quite a scare. I don't want *mei fraa* to be a frozen icicle."

She smiled weakly and then closed her eyes. He kissed her soft warm cheek, thinking he couldn't wait for her to get well so he could kiss her properly and seal the deal.

Once he was back in the kitchen, he offered the doctor a warm muffin.

"I wish I had time. They smell wonderful, but I've got to get moving."

"How long do you suppose she'll be groggy and sleepy like that? Do you have any special instructions for me to take care of her?"

"She should rest and stay off her feet at least for the next two days. I suspect she collapsed from the cold and from exhaustion, and she seems to be a little dehydrated which could be dangerous for the baby. But don't worry. Keep fluids in her, and she and the baby will be all right. I'm sure she'll be able to carry the baby full-term. I'll come back to check on her tomorrow afternoon."

Noah hadn't heard a single word after the word, *baby*. His expression blank, he nodded automatically, as he let the doctor out into the cold and snow.

After closing the door, Noah collapsed onto the kitchen chair and stared into his teacup and wondered just how far along Becca was in her pregnancy.

Suddenly, it dawned on him that her pregnancy could have had something to do with the reason she was searching so desperately for a husband.

Had she only asked him to marry her to avoid being shunned? No, since she hadn't taken the baptism yet, she would not be shunned, but it was probable that Jessup and Bess would not give her the B&B if they found out. He could only assume that since he found her in his loft that she had not gone home and had not told Bess about her dilemma or her condition.

He had declared his love for her, and could not take it back now. It was obvious she needed him now more than ever, but was he strong enough to honor his commitment to her after learning of her pregnancy?

Chapter 6

Noah offered Becca some warm tea, feeling anxious to talk to her about her condition. Was it possible she had no idea that he knew? How was it that he could address such an awkward subject without causing another misunderstanding like they'd had the day of the picnic? He would do anything to avoid hurting her, but he was unsure of how to deal with her situation tactfully.

Was it possible that even she didn't know that she was carrying a child? No, that would be foolish; surely she had to know. If Becca herself knew, he wondered who else knew. Was the father of the child aware of her condition, and if so, why hadn't he claimed her or the child? Was it possible he'd abandoned her?

Noah was caught between feeling sorry for her, and suppressing the anger that tried to rise up and influence him about the situation. He wished that she had trusted him with her news, but she hadn't, and now it had to be dealt with. He wondered if he should just keep quiet about it and wait for her to tell him on her own, but would he be able to go through the motions until she revealed the truth to him? He supposed for her sake he had to, but what would his brother think when he found out? Would his brother accuse him of fathering the child?

He stoked the fire, and then sat down on the sofa, pulling her close to him to keep her warm. She stirred and looked at him curiously. "I need to talk to you Noah," she said.

He shushed her. "We'll have plenty of time to talk later. Right now I need you to rest. That's what the doctor ordered; plenty of rest and fluids."

Her lashes fluttered and her speech was broken, but she continued to protest until sleep claimed her.

Whatever trouble she had found herself in, he would protect her even if that meant saving her from herself. She seemed to be her own worst enemy, but that did not mean that she and her baby deserved to suffer ridicule and shunning. He would do whatever it took to convince her grandparents of her stability as an heir to the B&B, even if it meant he had to claim the child as his own. He realized that would open him up for a lot of reprimand and possibly a visit to the bishop, but he was prepared to face all of it for her sake and the sake of her child.

Feeling thankful that today was not a work day at the bakery, Noah rested back on the sofa with Becca in his arms, intending to stay right there with her the entire night. He'd had a long day with her, trying to keep her warm and trying to get her to eat hot soup and drink plenty of herbal tea and water.

He hadn't seen his brother all day, and he was grateful for that as well, because he just wasn't ready to give an explanation as to Becca's presence with him in the *dawdi haus*. He would make that announcement later when he revealed his plans to marry her, but for now, he would take care of her in the solace of his temporary home.

After today, it would seem that he would be part owner of the B&B, and he wasn't certain how he felt about that just yet.

After several hours, Becca woke up in Noah's arms. Was it possible she had dreamt of him telling her he would marry her? No she had heard it, even though she had been groggy. She remembered Dr. Davis being there, and questions he had for her. Had he told Noah she was pregnant? She had to assume he hadn't, or he would not likely be cuddled up to her now. She hated to lose this, because she really cared for him. But she had cared for Lance, and he'd done nothing but lie and hurt her. Noah was nothing like Lance, which is exactly why she prayed that he would not back down on his promise to her. She knew he was a good, honorable, and morally upstanding man, and because of this, she prayed that God would bless her with Noah for her husband.

Hours later, she woke back up again, and Noah was no longer there with her. Had she dreamed the whole thing? She prayed that she had not, but it appeared that she was still in the *dawdi haus*.

A noise from the other room would indicate that she was not alone in the house. Footfalls brought Noah into the room, and his smile warmed her heart as he sat on the edge of the sofa and handed her a cup of hot tea.

"The color is back in your cheeks, and your eyes look a lot brighter than they did yesterday. Are you feeling up to a trip to the B&B? I'm sure Bess and Jessup are worried sick about you."

She knew it was time to come clean about her pregnancy, but she was terrified he would reject her all over again. She knew it wasn't right to continue to keep it from him, but perhaps if she could get her foot in the door with *Mammi* Bess, then perhaps the woman would take pity on her, and she would not have to leave the community, and Noah wouldn't feel forced to marry her.

She nodded, feeling a little uneasy about the situation, but she was prepared to take whatever may come.

Chapter 7

Becca tensed up when Noah pulled his buggy into the overflowing parking area behind the B&B. *Mammi* Bess had not exaggerated in her desperate letter begging Becca to return home from her visit with her cousins to help with the Christmas guests.

Noah sensed her tension and patted her gloved hand. "Don't be nervous, I'll be right by your side," he reassured her. "Bess and Jessup have always liked me, and I think they'll be pleased that I'm becoming part of the family."

She smirked. "They'll be pleased with the extra help for the Christmas season."

Bess had not been strict with Becca, and it was times like these that she wished the woman had. It wasn't that she was placing any blame on *Mammi* Bess for the condition she was in, but her naïve nature didn't help matters when Lance lied to her about the two of them being married. And now because of that, she would be stuck raising a child on her own if Noah backed out of their agreement once he discovered her condition.

Luckily for her, she hadn't invested too much of her heart into Lance, or it would now be broken. She'd been merely infatuated with him and his *Englisch* lifestyle, and she'd allowed that to open the gateway for him to lie to her. None of that mattered now, because he was married to another woman.

Noah patted her hand once more. "Are you ready to go in there and tell them the news of our engagement?"

"Are you sure you really want to do this?" She asked him.

"*Jah*," he said. "That's what we agreed upon. Let's go get you the B&B; it's what you wanted, am I right?"

She simply nodded and allowed him to assist her out of the buggy. When her feet reached the ground, his hold on her lingered, bringing a new warmth to her that was unexpected. A strange feeling came over her, almost as if it was an outpouring of love from her heart toward him. His touch caused her to swoon, and that confused her further. Was she beginning to have feelings for him?

Although she had to wonder if he changed his mind for the simple fact of being part owner of the B&B, she prayed that he would have feelings toward her as well. The last thing she wanted was for him to see her as a soiled mess, rather than the victim of someone else's lies. It wasn't that she sought his pity, but she would almost prefer that over him losing respect for her because of a misunderstanding of her condition. As far as she knew, she had been a married woman when her child was conceived, and it saddened her that her child would be born out of wedlock unless Noah stayed true to his commitment.

Noah slipped his hand in Becca's, and led her up the steps to the large wraparound porch of the B&B. He took a deep breath and squeezed her hand lightly. "Are you ready?"

She nodded, though her insides were battling fear, regret, and anxiety.

Luckily, once they were inside the front door, she was met with a brief hug and an apron, along with an urgent invitation to help in the kitchen. The rich aroma of all her favorite holiday foods filled her with a sense of *home.*

"*Kume,*" Bess said. "There is much to be done for our guests. I was so worried you wouldn't get my letter on time."

"I wouldn't miss the Christmas season," Becca said with a bit of hesitation.

Noah followed closely on her heels, and could hear the uneasiness in her voice, and hoped her *mammi* would not detect it. The woman seemed so preoccupied, that she hadn't even yet asked why Noah was even there. He had asked to take a leave from the bakery, and Mr. Miller had accepted since his son was still there to help.

Noah had his own family to help now, at least as long as Becca didn't reject his offer. He'd seen a change in her, and he had to wonder if her conscience was bothering her just enough to prevent him from rescuing her. Really, he'd be rescuing her from herself, since she seemed determined to be so self-destructive. He prayed she would get over that, and realize she needed him, if for no other reason than for the child she was carrying.

"Can I put you to work?" Bess surprised him by asking.

"*Jah,*" he said. "That's why I'm here."

"Well, in that case," Bess said, snatching the apron from Becca and handing it to Noah. "I'll need *you* in the kitchen with me since you know your way around a pie; as for you, Becca, we have little guests who want to learn to ice skate."

Noah didn't miss the look of worry that spread across Becca's face, and it was up to him to provide an excuse for her.

He handed the apron back to Becca. "Actually, she got a chill two days ago when she stayed out too long, and the doctor recommended she stay indoors for a few days to keep her temperature up."

Bess flashed her a look of concern, but Becca forced a smile, and he could see in her eyes he'd said a little too much. He wasn't about to lie to the woman, and Becca admired him for being truthful, a quality she admired in him. But that didn't mean she wanted her *mammi* to know what had happened either.

"It was silly, really," she said, with a pasted-on smile. "Just a miscommunication that had me waiting out in the cold."

"She was waiting on me, and I didn't get to her on time since I was held up with chores," he chimed in, rescuing her.

The woman smiled and continued to spout off orders to her staff, while going back to the chore of kneading bread dough. "Get washed up so you can help me, Becca."

She turned her attention to Noah and tipped her head to the side. Nothing got past that woman, and he would have to listen to her lecture him for something later, but thankfully, she didn't have the time now. "You'll find the list of signups for ice skating on the podium in the front hall. I think you'll have four young students. Make certain the permission slips are signed by the parents before you take them out there. I wouldn't let them stay out more than an hour. We'll have hot cocoa ready for them when you return with them, so bring them in through the service door."

He smiled and nodded.

"*Danki,*" Bess said. "*Wilkum* to the *familye.*"

He walked away smiling.

How did she know?

Chapter 8

Noah walked through the kitchen with four children ranging in age from five to ten, joking and laughing, while Becca admired his interaction with them. She continued to watch from the large kitchen window above the sink as he walked them down to the pond where he would teach them to skate.

Skating was something that she and Noah had in common; they had both been taught by their *mamms*. It was a bond they shared in common, among other things that helped them to understand each other better.

"You love him, *jah?*" Bess asked Becca.

Feeling embarrassed, Becca returned to the task of washing dishes. She nodded and smiled as she continued to sneak peeks at Noah from the kitchen window. She had to admit that her feelings for Noah were much different than they had been for Lance. Now that a little bit of time had gone by since she'd last seen him, and after the way he'd treated her, she felt fortunate that her heart was not breaking the way it might have if she had really loved Lance.

No, things were definitely different with Noah. They had an understanding, and a similar upbringing, and for that reason, she felt confident that even if they rushed into this marriage, they could grow together and love each other the way it was supposed to happen.

"I know you think it's harsh that Jessup and I want you to marry in order to take over the B&B," Bess said to her. "But I think you picked the perfect one to marry and help you with the B&B. Noah will make a *gut* addition to this *haus*. He has çooking skills and all the skills needed to run this place successfully, and he can teach you the things you need to know. We don't want to see it fail, and we don't want *you* to fail either. You know we want what's best for you, and your *vadder* would want it this way."

She knew what her *mammi* was saying was true, but her *mammi* had no idea the torment whirling around inside her at the moment. Looking at the clock, and judging by the lack of activity down at the pond with the children, she knew it was time to put a pan of milk on the stove for the hot cocoa; the children would need it once they came in. She shivered lightly remembering how cold she'd gotten when she'd slept in Noah's barn loft, and didn't envy those children being down there at the pond in the cold. As children though, they were far more resilient than she was in her condition.

Becca watched snow fall lightly, but her heart warmed when she realized Noah had saved her from having to go out into the cold by offering to *mammi* Bess that he would give the children the skating lesson.

Was he protecting her out of love for her, or was there more to it than that? She had to wonder from the looks he'd been giving her if he didn't already know about the *boppli* she carried. It would be just like him to remain quiet about it until she was ready to tell him. She knew it was time, and she prayed for an opportunity to tell him later today. She needed to tell him before things went any further; she owed him that much.

No sooner did the milk begin to steam on the surface, then she heard the kitchen door swing open and four children rushing in from the cold and stomping their snowy boots all over the floor in the mudroom. The sound of children's laughter warmed her heart, but the thought of Noah being the one making them laugh put a tickle in her own heart. He was definitely good with children, and that was important to her, considering the wee one she carried would not be his own. If he was this good with other people's children, then surely he would be that good with one he raised that was not his own. At least, that was her prayer for her *boppli*.

Noah ushered the children to the service table in the corner of the large kitchen, and then went to the stove to help Becca prepare the cocoa.

"Is there any chance we could risk spoiling our appetites with a few of those Christmas cookies and a taste of that fudge on the tray?" he asked *Mammi* Bess.

She smiled and nodded, and then turned her attention to Becca. "Your *kinner* are going to be spoiled with that one for a *vadder*."

Her comment caused Becca's breath to hitch, and Noah hadn't missed her reaction to her *mammi's* comment. Was it possible that Becca had already thought of him as the father of her child? Or perhaps she hadn't thought about it until just now when her *mammi* mentioned it, but they would be married in a few days, and he would raise the child as his own. He prayed Becca could accept that.

Chapter 9

Becca eagerly worked through her day, while she and Noah exchanged glances several times throughout their workday. Was this how things would be once they took over the B&B for themselves? Would their lives be so consumed with work all day for others, or would there be time to spend with just each other?

She longed for the time when the guests would turn in for the night so she could have some private time alone with Noah, before she had to return to the servant's quarters out back of the B&B. The medium-sized guesthouse on the back of the property had been given to her by *Mammi* Bess, with the promise that she and her new husband would live there after they were married. She never dreamed a year ago that it would be Noah that she would be sharing that little house with. She'd made the mistake of confiding in Lance that she would inherit the B&B once they were married, and she felt it was that inheritance that prompted him to pretend they were married.

At last all of the residents had turned in for the evening, and Becca entered the oversized sitting room where Noah was stoking the fire. Evergreens decorated the mantle, along with brightly-colored glass balls scattered among the branches. It was truly a romantic and magical setting. To the other side of the hearth, a twelve-foot Christmas tree.

She stood next to him and held her hands out toward the fire to warm them; she had gotten a chill again and had not wanted to tell him. He put his hand on hers and then put the fire poker down, and pulled her into his arms.

"Let me warm you up," he said.

She did not try to resist him. Instead, she rested her head against his chest and listened to his heartbeat. She watched the flames lick at the freshly-cut logs he'd placed in the hearth, and thought how wonderful it would be if their evenings together could all be like this one. Unfortunately, she knew it wouldn't be possible as long as they had her condition standing between the two of them. It was now or never that she tell him, before she lost her nerve.

She lifted her gaze to meet his, but he dipped his head and pressed his lips to hers. Oh how she wanted to deepen the kiss, but she feared getting lost in him and his passion for her, and it would cloud her judgment of telling him the truth.

"Wait," she said in between kisses. She was barely able to concentrate, but she knew she must tell him before things went any further between them. "I have to tell you something."

"Not now," he said deepening his kisses.

When he felt her become slightly rigid, he continued to kiss her but spoke softly to reassure her. "I already know what you have to say," he said, still kissing her. "I know about the *boppli*, but it doesn't matter. It doesn't influence my decision. When you're ready to tell me, I'll listen, but until then, I still intend to marry you."

Happy tears welled up in her eyes, and a lump form in her throat, but she swallowed it down to keep it from constricting her ability to kiss him back. She loved him; she'd known it all along, but she needed him to understand the circumstances in which she'd become pregnant. She needed him to understand that she still held fast to her morals, and was worthy of being his wife.

She pulled away from him gently. "Please, Noah, I really need to tell you the circumstances."

He sat down on the sofa and beckoned her to cuddle up underneath his arm. She went to him eagerly, knowing she was safe there.

"I know it may be hard to believe, but I thought that I was married to the *boppli's vadder* at the time that it was conceived."

He looked at her curiously, but was open to her explanation.

"I had been seeing Lance, an *Englischer*, for about three months. While I was staying with my cousins, I met him in town. He seemed very kind, and very honest, but I was wrong about that. I was naïve and careless with him, and told him far too much about myself; things he ended up using against me."

"Did you love him?"

"I thought I did," she said. "But it turns out I was merely mesmerized by his way of life in the *Englisch* world. I was infatuated with him for the differences between us, and the chance to escape the strict rules of the *Ordnung*. When I confided in him my need to be married in order to inherit the B&B, that's when he saw the opportunity to swindle it out from under me. In the end, he realized he would actually have to be married to me in order to be part owner of the B&B."

"I'm confused," Noah said. "Were you married to him or not?"

"We got an actual marriage license from the courthouse, but it was his friend whom he claimed was ordained online, who performed the ceremony. He had no intention of running the B&B with me; he only wanted to sell it for his own benefit. When I told him about the *boppli*, he backed out of his commitment to me, claiming he wanted to sell the B&B and travel, and didn't want to be tied down to any *kinner* just yet. That's when I found out that he had not filed the marriage certificate, and therefore we were not legally married. Because of this, he ran off and married another woman. So here I was left pregnant and unmarried, and yes that's why I tried to trick your *bruder* into marrying me. I'm so sorry I did that. I was panicked and afraid. I left the community and went to Lance one last time, but that's when I discovered he had married someone else. I knew then my only hope was to return to the community and try to win your heart, or at the very least, convince you to run the B&B with me."

Noah pulled her close and kissed the top of her head. "I'm so sorry you had to endure all of that. It's never fun when someone lies to you. If you would have told me all of this the day of the picnic, I would have asked you to marry me that day. I was smitten with you, and it was funny that I set off at the beginning of the day thinking I wanted to share my day with Alana, but it was not *Gott's* will for that to happen; it was in *Gott's* plan for you and I to be together, and I know that now. I want you to be *mei fraa*, and not as a business deal for the B&B, but because I love you."

"I'm curious," she said. "How did you know about the *boppli?*"

"Doctor Davis let it slip," he admitted. "He might have assumed I was the *vadder*. But how did *he* know about it? You aren't even showing."

"I am underneath this baggy dress!" she said with a chuckle. "But I had gone to see him when I returned to the community the first time—almost four months ago. So when he came to see me at the *dawdi haus* the other day, he brought a battery-operated machine to listen for the *boppli's* heartbeat. He let me listen through the earphones, but I was so exhausted from not sleeping for more than two days that I could hardly think of anything past sleeping once I knew the *boppli* was not in danger. I know it was *narrish* to stay in the loft of your barn, but I was desperate, and had no money to return to the city with *mei* cousins, and I feared returning to the B&B, worried *mei Mammi* Bess would know I was pregnant and would turn me away. I couldn't stand to endure any more rejection."

"Well now you won't have to," he said. "That is, if you'll consent to be *mei fraa.*"

She turned to him, noting the sincere look in his eyes, and the gentleness of his embrace. She could feel the genuine love emanating from him, and she could hardly resist him. She loved him too, and wondered how it had sneaked up on them so quickly. She supposed she knew it all along, and perhaps he had too, the way he claimed.

"*Jah,* I'll marry you, but I need you to teach me to cook and the things I need to be a true partner to you in this business, so that one day we can pass it on to our own *kinner.*"

He kissed her gently. He liked the sound of that. At one time, he'd found her to be selfish and spoiled, but she had grown up in the blink of an eye, and he liked the changes.

"It's a deal," he said. "I love you, Becca."

"I love you too, Noah," she said, leaning in for another kiss, the warmth of his love warming her far better than the roaring fire in the hearth.

Chapter 10

Becca could hardly wait to tell her *mammi* the *real* news of her engagement to Noah. She hadn't slept much, despite doctor's order that she get as much rest as possible. The main house would likely be filled with activity and noises soon, and she wanted the chance to talk with her grandmother alone before the day became too busy.

Dressing quickly, she left the guesthouse without getting any coffee, knowing there would likely be a large pot already brewed in the main house in anticipation of the guests needing it. She probably would need the coffee to get through her day, but she knew she had to limit her caffeine consumption for the sake of the baby.

Stepping outside the doorway of her home, she was grateful to see the path had already been cleared and there was a fresh sprinkling of salt down on the ground to keep her from slipping. Looking up, she saw Noah hard at work shoveling the rest of the walkways. He waved to her and blew her a kiss, which made her giggle.

Walking into the main house with a smile on her face, she was greeted by her *mammi* and the smell of fresh coffee. She was never happier to get both.

"Gudemariye," her *mammi* said cheerfully, dusting the tops of the coffee cakes with fresh cinnamon. Becca pulled off her coat and grabbed an apron from the peg by the door, ready to jump in and help prepare the first makings of breakfast for their full house of guests.

Mammi Bess ushered her into a chair and set a slice of coffee cake in front of her. "I know you came straight over here without getting anything to eat," the woman reprimanded her. "You sit and get some nourishment into your skinny little frame, and then you can help. You won't be much *gut* to me if you collapse from hunger."

She busied herself bringing a glass of milk to the table and set it in front of Becca. Then she brought her a little sip of coffee in the bottom of a teacup and set that in front of her.

Becca looked into the nearly-empty cup. "Did the guests drink all the *kaffi* already?"

The older woman smiled. "That's all you'll be getting from me unless the doctor tells me you can have more!"

"*Ach,* you don't need to fuss over me, *Mammi.*"

"*Jah* I do!" she insisted. "If I'm not mistaken, you need to limit yourself with the *kaffi*—for the sake of the *boppli.*"

Becca nearly choked on her milk. She wiped her mouth with the napkin in front of her and stared into her grandmother's eyes.

"Did you think I didn't know?" she asked.

Becca nodded.

"I've been around you your entire life, and I've been around long enough to recognize a pregnant woman when I see one."

"I'm sorry I didn't tell you, *Mammi,*" Becca said. "I was afraid you would turn me away."

Bess crossed the room and pulled Becca into her arms and cradled her, rocking her back and forth. "I would never turn you away; you're *familye,* and I love you, dear girl. I want you to be happy, and that is the *only* reason we put that condition on your inheritance of the B&B. we didn't do it to hurt you, but to make you grow up a little. I'm sorry we put so much pressure on you. If I'd known the condition would cause you this much grief, I would have made it easier on you."

Becca sobbed in the shelter of her grandmother's arms. "I wouldn't have wanted you to make it easy for me; you're right, I needed to grow up. I can hardly take back my mistakes or that would take back *mei boppli,* and I could never do that. I'll be alright, and so will the *boppli.* We have *familye* that loves us, and we will never be alone."

"Is Noah the *vadder* of your *boppli?"* she asked.

"*Nee,* but he will be!"

"He's agreed to marry you, then?"

Becca smiled. "*Jah, Mammi,* he's a *gut mann."*

"*Ach,* you don't have to tell me that. You've made a wise choice. Now I won't have to take back any of the wedding invitations I sent out."

"Invitations?" Becca asked with a gasp. "How did you know I would be married? Did you know I would marry Noah?"

"I didn't," she admitted. "That's why I sent out generic invitations. I didn't say who was getting married. You know we usually have a wedding here on Christmas Eve with one or more of our guests, and the community looks forward to them. Now they will be surprised when they see it is one of our own who will be married. And it just so happens that we don't have a wedding for a guest this year, so you and Noah will have the ceremony all to yourselves. Of course since it's to be performed by a Mennonite preacher, you don't have to worry about the baptism unless you want to take it later after you're married and have settled into the community."

Becca giggled at her grandmother's silly planning that seemed to work out in her favor. She had thought of everything, even if she had accidentally planned it that way.

"Do you have time to sit with me for a minute so I can tell you everything?" she asked her *mammi.* "I want you to know the whole story."

Bess motioned for the staff to take over in her stead while she sat at the table in the corner with her granddaughter so the two could have a long-awaited talk, hoping it would lift the burden from Becca's shoulders once and for all.

Chapter 11

Becca woke with a jolt of excitement; it was Christmas eve, and her wedding day. All the guests would be arriving in just a few hours, and she had a ton of stuff to do, but she wanted to take the time to offer a prayer of thanks for the many blessings she thought she would never have.

Not only was she about to marry a handsome man whom she loved dearly and respected greatly, but she was now the proud co-owner of the B&B, and she would be a *mamm* in the spring. She wished her *mamm* and *daed* could have been here to share her special day, but she was gaining an entire family on Noah's side, and the women in the community had welcomed her home, and helped her prepare for today, her special day.

Though a lot of the weddings at the B&B took place in the gazebo—even at Christmas, their wedding would take place in the assembly room, even though she suspected there would be so many in attendance they would likely fill the entire house.

Already, she could feel how exciting the day would be for her. She and Noah had spent the past few days making their rounds among the community to let friends and family know of their nuptials, and they had already been showered with many gifts to begin their life together. Among those gifts had been the handcrafted cradle her *daed* had made for her when she was born. Little did she know that her grandmother had kept it for her in the attic of the B&B all this time.

She was excited over her Christmas Eve wedding, and all the love and support the community had blessed them with even though their wedding would not be performed by the Bishop.

Although *Mammi* Bess had told her not to work today, she still had some work to do on the light blue wedding dress that Hannah, Alana, and Rachel had helped her sew at the last minute. She'd waited to cinch the waist since her pregnancy girth had begun to expand every day from her grandmother's holiday cooking. The woman had promised to put some meat on her bones, claiming her too thin, and she had to admit, she'd been unable to resist some of the sweets Noah had taught her to make for the guests. She'd tried to argue with him that taste-testing too many of those treats to be sure the guests would like them was going to render her unable to fit into her wedding dress, but he'd told her he didn't care.

A knock at the front door startled her from her busy thoughts, and she rose from the bed and pulled her robe around her to see who it was. She was certain it was her *mammi* with a tray of goodies to start her day. The woman was spoiling her, and she was enjoying every minute of it. Before long, she would be taking over, but her grandmother assured her she would always be close-by.

A letter carrier stood on her doorstep, and she wondered why he hadn't stopped at the main house rather than the guesthouse.

"Are you Miss Becca King?" the man asked.

She nodded, and he handed her a letter, asking her to sign for it, and then disappeared as she stood there in shock at the return address.

It was from Lance.

She collapsed onto the nearest chair and held the envelope with a shaky hand, unable to open it.

Noah rushed into the house, asking her why she'd left the door open, but she couldn't answer. She just sat there, staring at the letter.

Pulling her into his arms, Noah held her close, trying his best to calm her shaking shoulders as she began to sob.

"I got a certified letter form Lance. It's bad news, I just know it," she bawled.

"Shhh, let's open it and see," he said with a calming tone.

"I can't open it, I'm too afraid. I don't want him to ruin our day."

"He can't ruin it if we don't let him. Whatever the letter says, we'll deal with it together."

She relinquished the letter to Noah and he opened it, reading it aloud.

My dear Becca,

When I heard the news of your upcoming wedding to Noah, I was filled with mixed emotions;

grief, because of losing a woman with such a good heart; anger with myself for taking advantage of that big heart, and relief that you found someone who could appreciate that quality in you. I'm happy you've found someone who will truly love you and take care of you and our baby the way you both deserve. I'm not mature enough to be a parent, and I'm not sure I'll ever grow up.

Tell Noah what a lucky man he is, and how much I appreciate him stepping in and taking over for me as a husband and father, because I just am not able to.

I'm sorry for the way I treated you. I know I must have put you in a bad position, and risked you being shunned. I don't understand that practice, but I know how important it is to you. I'm enclosing a copy of our marriage certificate which I never filed, so your Bishop can see for himself you were under the assumption that we were married—if it will keep you from being shunned.

Thank you for understanding. I know the two of you will have a happy life together. You belong in the Amish community, not in my English world. I wish I could have loved you the way you deserved, but I'm glad you found someone who can.

Yours Truly,

Lance

Noah looked at the marriage license enclosed in the envelope, and looked at Becca. "None of this matters to me," he said. "I believed you. It's sad that he lives in a world where a person's word means little more than the paper this is written on. I'm glad he officially let you go so we can start our life together without anything holding us back."

He kissed her, thinking he would never tire of her pouty-mouth. "Let's go get married and start our life free from the past."

She wiped her tears and smiled at Noah's strength. Her prayers had been answered, and she truly believed God had made the right choice for her and her *boppli.*

Noah and Becca bid a good night to the last wedding guest and he walked her back to the guest house out back of the B&B—their new home. When they reached the door, he scooped her up in his arms and carried her into the home, while she giggled, thinking it was quite an *Englisch* thing to do. He took her straight back to the bedroom and deposited her onto the freshly-made bed, and then pulled an envelope from his jacket pocket and handed it to her.

"What's this?" she asked, her face flushing. "Please tell me it's not more bad news."

He smiled. "Open it!"

She opened the flap carefully and slowly, not taking her eyes off Noah, who seemed to be eager for her to see the contents of the envelope.

Unfolding a document, she looked up at him as he smiled.

"There must be some mistake!" she said.

His brow furrowed. "Mistake?"

He glanced at the document in her hand and shook his head. "*Nee,* there's no mistake."

Her mouth hung open. "But my name is the only name on the deed to the B&B. We *are* married, aren't we?"

He chuckled. "Of course we're married. I asked Jessup to put only your name on the deed to the B&B

because I needed you to know without a doubt that I married you because I love you, not because of your inheritance."

She threw her arms around him and began to kiss him passionately. "I believed you, just like you believed in me. I love you too, Noah Bontrager!"

He kissed her deeply. "I love you more, *Mrs. Bontrager!*"

THE END

Amish Weddings
A Christmas Wedding
Book Six
Samantha Bayarr

A note from the Author:

While this novel is set against the backdrop of an Amish community, the characters and the names of the community are fictional. There is no intended resemblance between the characters in this book or the setting, and any real members of any Amish or Mennonite community. As with any work of fiction, I've taken license in some areas of research as a means of creating the necessary circumstances for my characters and setting. It is completely impossible to be accurate in details and descriptions, since every community differs, and such a setting would destroy the fictional quality of entertainment this book serves to present. Any inaccuracies in the Amish and Mennonite lifestyles portrayed in this book are completely due to fictional license. Please keep in mind that this book is meant for fictional, entertainment purposes only, and is not written as a text book on the Amish.

Happy Reading

Amish Weddings
A Christmas Wedding
Book Six

Chapter 1

Rachel busied herself making one pie after another, waiting for Amber to return from the city for a long Christmas weekend at home. Amber had written to Rachel and asked her to keep the news from Seth, and she'd reluctantly agreed, hoping to surprise him. Truthfully, she hoped that by keeping the unexpected visit from her husband, it would assure that she could keep him from disappointment in case his sister didn't show up.

They hadn't seen Amber since their wedding just over a year ago, and though Rachel couldn't understand the sudden urgency to return from the city, she hoped that while she was visiting, she would at least take the time to see Elijah, so the poor man could move on from his heartbreak over their breakup, and marry once and for all. She would enjoy seeing her best friend and sister-in-law marry her lonesome cousin she'd left behind to stay in the city, but it would be good for him to get the closure he needed if she didn't intend to stay.

Then a thought occurred to her; what if Amber was using this visit as a way to come back home? The thought of it made her almost giddy. She'd missed her best friend and sister-in-law, and would welcome her in every way she could. Was it possible that Amber was ready to come home and settle back into her life within the Amish community?

Rachel hoped it was so.

She took frequent breaks from baking; the weight of her infant son slowing her down only a little. She'd wrapped him snuggly against her in the sling she'd fashioned from a couple of yards of stretchy material she'd gotten from the flea market in Shipshewana. She'd seen a similar thing for sale in an *Englisch* store, and decided she could make one of her own for no more than the cost of a few yards of material. It had worked out beautifully.

Thankful that her husband had not questioned her furious baking, Rachel continued to work, realizing she'd made enough pies to feed at least half of the community. Perhaps she could extend an invitation to their closest friends and family, including Elijah, to welcome Amber home.

Amber watched miles of farmland roll by in a blur from the window of the car, as she wondered if this visit was a big mistake. Even though Elijah had convinced her to come, she wasn't convinced that he wouldn't turn her away once she got there.

Surely her brother Seth would have compassion for her after his own mistakes that he'd made with Rachel. Still, she was a little unsure of the welcome she would receive from her family, that is if she would get one at all. She hoped Rachel would smooth the way between her and her brother. She'd been gone far too long and far longer than planned, and she'd become very distant from him in the past year.

Watching the thick snow from the window, she pressed her nose to the glass, her breath fogging up the window just a bit. At least they would have a white Christmas; that always put Seth in a good mood. Dread filled her at the thought of spending Christmas alone, and she prayed her brother would welcome her, knowing it would be less stressing on her to spend the holiday with family. She swallowed down the lump in her throat, knowing she wasn't ready to come home yet, but she couldn't bear the thought of being alone for the holidays.

Besides, she'd promised Elijah a visit, and she'd promised him an answer.

Chapter 2

"Get in this *haus* before your *bruder* sees you!" Rachel, said practically dragging Amber by the arm.

She'd looked as pale as the snow when she'd first opened the door, but after a moment of pure stupor, she'd come to her senses and urged her sister-in-law into the house before her husband heard the car full of *Englischers* pulling out of the driveway. Rachel had waved at the car mindlessly as if to thank them for driving Amber, her focus only on her sister-in-law.

Once Amber set her bag down, the two estranged women stared at each other for some moments before the slightest little gurgle from Rachel's baby interrupted the silence.

"You're pregnant!" Rachel blurted out. "*Very* pregnant!"

Amber pulled off her coat that no longer reached around the front of her swelled abdomen, feeling that the gesture would give her a moment to respond without rolling her eyes and making a snide remark to hide the awkward feeling that tried to bring insecurity with it.

"Why didn't you tell me about this in your letter?" Rachel asked, tears welling up in her throat when she remembered how she felt when she first learned of her own pregnancy.

"Who is the *vadder?*" she continued, not giving Amber a chance to answer the first question, let alone, the ones that followed. She had several more, but she could see she'd overwhelmed her friend, and that was the last thing she wanted.

"Sit down," Rachel said, scrambling to clear some of the baking mess from the table. "Tell me everything."

She sat slowly, their gaze meeting, tears pooling in Amber's eyes. "I don't want you to judge me."

Rachel slacked her lower jaw dramatically as she pointed to baby Jesse, who slept peacefully, snuggled against her in the sling she'd wrapped him in. "I have *no* right to judge you, and I wouldn't; you're my oldest and dearest friend—and now we're *schweschders.*"

Amber nodded, wiping a tear.

Rachel jumped up suddenly, feeling the need to busy herself while she listened to Amber's story.

"Let me get you some hot tea; you must be freezing."

Amber nodded. "*Danki.*"

After she put the tea kettle on the stove, she looked at her friend, who still hadn't said a word. She had been through the same thing only a year ago, and remembered how tough it was for her to bring her secret to the community.

"Are you alone?" she asked. "Or will the *boppli's vadder* be joining us?"

She pulled off her mittens and laid them on the table in front of her; that's when Rachel noticed the ring on her finger. It sparkled, drawing her attention to it like a moth to a flame.

She snaked her fingers up underneath Amber's hand, lifting the ringed finger to more closely examine it. "You're married?"

Amber's lower lip quivered. "I *was,*" she whispered.

Rachel stifled her questions that entered her mind one-by-one, too afraid to even ask what happened to her husband; instead, she wrapped her arms around her friend as if to guard her from the hurt threatening to harm her. Letting her guard down, Amber let loose the sobs she'd been holding back for some time. Rachel smoothed Amber's hair as she leaned against her, sobbing, and amazingly enough, not disturbing Jesse even a little. She imagined the worst for her friend and sister, but she had to know how she managed to get herself in such a spot and hadn't turned to her family before now.

Crossing to the sink, she brought back a clean dishtowel and handed it to Amber so she could dry her eyes, but she'd taken a moment to glance out the window toward the barn, feeling fortunate that she hadn't seen any sign of Seth. She and Amber needed some *girl-time,* without Seth's stern nature where his sister was concerned, so the two of them could sort out the problem, and possibly come up with a solution.

Amber sniffled. "I was married to an *Englischer,*" she began. "You remember Jake, our landlord's son?"

Rachel's face twisted up. "*Jake* did this to you? I always thought he was such a kind person—sort of a loner, but I thought he was having health problems too…"

The words seemed to spark more tears from Amber.

"He was never a very strong person; they found out he had leukemia, and they tried something called a stem-cell transplant or something like that I think, hoping it would save him, but instead…"

More sobs.

The only thing Rachel knew about Jake after only meeting him once briefly, was that his health seemed to be failing, and he'd been traveling the country with some friends. It never made sense to her then, but it had begun to make more sense now.

Rachel's heart sank at the thought of what Mr. and Mrs. Baker must have gone through when their son had died—what *Amber must have gone through*...

"Did his body reject the transplant?"

"*Nee,* he was handling it really well, and he came home, but then he got pneumonia, and his kidneys couldn't handle the stress of being sick…"

"When did you marry him?"

"We married in secret the same weekend you left to come home…"

"I'm sorry I was so involved with my own problems to notice, but why would you marry him knowing he had so many health problems?"

"When he was first diagnosed, he didn't think he was going to make it, and so he made this—*bucket list,"* she said, still sniffling.

"You married him even though he was *not well?* What's a *bucket list?"*

She nodded again, not looking at Rachel.

"A bucket list is almost like the list of things we want to do during *rumspringa* before we take the baptism and join the church, except his was a list of things he wanted to do before he *died*…"

More sobs as she ran a hand over her swelling abdomen, as if to protect the child from what she was saying.

Rachel pulled her closer, quieting her sobs. "I'm so sorry you had to go through this—to be a *widow* at such a young age."

"I only married him to help him with the final item on his bucket-list—getting married, but I didn't think losing him would affect me this way. I really did care for him."

"I suppose it has to do with the *boppli* you're carrying. How are the Baker's doing? Are they supportive of you?"

She nodded. "This *boppli* is all they have left of their only *sohn.* But they know I didn't love Jake the way a *fraa* should. Honestly, I think I love him more now since he's been gone—or perhaps I'm scared of being alone. He's been gone six months, and I don't want to do this alone. That's why I'm here."

Rachel kissed the top of her head and went to the stove to refill her teacup. "You'll have the support of me and your *bruder,* for sure and for certain, but you know marrying an *Englischer* won't sit well with the rest of the community—and I can't speak for your *mamm,* but I'm sure she'll *wilkum* new *grosskinner* to the *familye."*

"It's not *mei mamm* I'm worried about—it's *mei daed.* He's always been so strict, you know that; he didn't want me to go for *rumspringa,* but I suppose this is why he didn't want me to go," she said, running a hand along her bursting belly.

"I thought I recognized the car that pulled in, but I was so shocked to see you this way, I didn't realize it was the Bakers' who dropped you off. Are they alright with you coming home to birth your *boppli?"*

"They're getting a room at the B&B; they're staying for the wedding, and then they'll return home."

"Whose wedding?" Rachel asked.

Amber looked at her soberly. "Mine," she whispered.

Chapter 3

Seth walked into the kitchen just then, Elijah behind him.

Your timing couldn't be worse, derr husband.

"Look who I found coming up the driveway." He said toward his sister and wife "Looks to me like..."

He stopped mid-sentence when his gaze fell upon his sister's enlarged abdomen, swollen with child.

Amber started to greet her brother, but he hesitated. "Hello Seth; hello Elijah," she said."

Seth watched his sister's gaze travel to Elijah, and wondered if she had been expecting him. The two exchanged a glance, ignoring him momentarily. An odd feeling crept over him, putting suspicion in his mind about his best friend's involvement in his sister's condition. Perhaps the child belonged to Elijah and he had somehow overlooked a connection between his sister and his best friend. Surely he would've known if his own friend had been seeing his sister behind his back. He ran a hand through his thick hair, trying to imagine the absurdity that such a thing could go on right under his nose. But he had to know the truth; he was curious. An underlying promise from Elijah to marry Amber always remained in the back of his mind; however, now he had to wonder if that promise had been broken.

He looked soberly at Amber's blotchy face and red-rimmed eyes. The private conversation he'd interrupted between his wife and his sister seemed to be far from over, and he wished he could exit the room without being seen, but that window slammed shut the moment he'd noticed the unspoken banter that he wasn't a part of.

He looked at his sister sternly, biting his lower lip to keep his emotions at bay. A thousand thoughts whirled in his head, and the possibilities of what his parents would say when they saw her in her condition. Surely there had to be a good explanation for this, but judging by the sparkly ring on her finger, he would have to say there wasn't one. At least not one that would be accepted by his parents or the community.

Unsure of what to say, he waited as Elijah took her hands in his and asked her outside for a private talk. Seth just stood there, unable to say a word. It was obvious Amber was expecting Elijah, and his friend had been keeping something from him. How long had it been since his sister had been gone anyway? He would have to guess that it had been well over a year, since he and Rachel had recently celebrated their first anniversary.

Amber looked back at her brother while Elijah was leading her out the door. He grabbed his coat and put it around her and all she could do was stare at her brother. Her eyes cast downward but then lifted again. "We'll talk when I return."

He wanted to stop them, but instead, nodded to his sister. Once she was out the door, he looked to his wife for the answers, but he could see by the look in her eyes she felt obligated to keep Amber's confidence.

Still, he felt compelled to try, and so he asked her gently. "Do I really have to wait until she returns from the barn and her *talk* with my best friend?"

"*Jah,*" she said as she kissed her husband, but gave him a sobering look. "I'm afraid it would probably be best coming from her. She's had a long hard journey making her way back home, and I don't think that we should do anything except have compassion for her situation. You interrupted our conversation, so she didn't finish telling me everything."

His eyes widened. "Do you mean there's more?"

"I'm afraid there is, and now I'm certain that it has to do with Elijah, but it could be *gut* news." She smiled at her husband and then offered him a cup of coffee, which he dearly needed. He'd suffered a bone-weary chill from working in the barn too long without taking a needed break; coffee would hit the spot.

He sat down at the kitchen table and let out a heavy sigh. "The only reason I let her go with Elijah is because he's my best friend and I trust him, but I don't like thinking that he's been keeping something from me. He obviously knew she'd planned to arrive for a visit today; did you?"

She paused, hoping he would forgive her. "*Jah,* I knew she would be here, and I'm sorry I kept it from you; she wrote to me and told me, but her pregnancy surprised me just as much as it did you. I had no idea; not until I opened the door just now."

"She married an *Englischer*, *jah*?"

Rachel nodded. She didn't want to say any more, knowing that the conversation had to be between her husband and his sister.

"I'm sorry I kept it from you, but I honestly thought her visit would be a *gut* surprise for Christmas. I just had no idea how much of a surprise her visit would be for all of us—except for Elijah, I suppose."

Rachel knew what the conversation involved between Elijah and Amber out in the barn, but she didn't dare speak the words, for fear of upsetting her husband even more.

Chapter 4

Elijah felt awkward taking a very pregnant Amber into the barn for *the talk.* Though he'd anticipated this talk most of their lives, he never imagined he'd be proposing to the love of his life when the child she carried belonged to another man. He knew the circumstances, and had made an agreement with her, knowing he'd rather have her as his *fraa* this way than not at all.

Amber followed him into the barn, seemingly feeling awkward herself. She'd been quiet the entire trek through the fresh snow, even though he held her hand and the small of her back to keep her from slipping on the icy patches. His care for her well-being had felt foreign and familiar at the same time—confusing her further.

Though she'd anticipated this talk with him most of her life, she never imagined it would be like this, under these circumstances. Her entire lifetime could not prepare her for this. She'd put him off for six months already, and now, with the baby due any day, she'd run out of time to stall him. Giving birth out of wedlock would shame her at the very least. When the community discovered her condition and the circumstances behind it, being banned from them would be inevitable, and she prayed Elijah had taken that into consideration when he'd proposed.

Though she knew what he intended to say, an awkwardness consumed her. She fidgeted with the tassels on her scarf, waiting, anticipating the words that suddenly felt as if they shouldn't be said. They both knew why they were there; did he really have to be so formal and go through the motions? Being a widow, his proposal filled her with unexpected guilt. She forced a smile, even though inwardly she felt only guilt. Jake had given her his blessing before he'd passed away, but that didn't matter now; what mattered to her couldn't be described any other way except the strange feeling that consumed her—a good strange, that for some reason, made her feel *bad*.

She'd always loved Elijah and always dreamed of marrying him, and wondered why she had agreed to such a foolish thing with Jake. Taking into consideration his poor health, she knew going into the marriage with Jake that it would be doomed from the very start, but she'd felt sorry for him. She never dreamed she would give in to him the way she had as a married woman. That one night with her husband had left her pregnant and a widow, and very much in need of changing her circumstances. She hadn't been fair to Elijah, who'd waited patiently for her back home in the community, yet she felt rebellious enough to marry Jake on a whim—just because he'd asked her.

Trying not to think about Jake in his grave, she forced another smile, wondering if he could be watching her from Heaven. Would his memory haunt her forever? Or perhaps guilt caused her to wonder if his spirit still lingered? She looked around the barn, sunlight filtering in through the windows. Outside, the wind howled and swirled, bringing a Christmas snow that would normally fill her with the holiday spirit. Right now, she wondered if there were other spirits wandering about.

Elijah fidgeted with his scarf, but bravely looked Amber in the eye. She never looked so beautiful to him—even carrying another man's child.

"I've always loved you, Amber, and I know you care for me too," he began. "I think I'd like to officially ask you…"

Her breath caught in her throat just before Elijah finished his sentence—the sentence she'd longed for most of her life, but she couldn't let him finish it because if he did, she'd have to agree to it.

"I'm sorry," she blurted out. "I can't do this."

She walked swiftly away from him, bursting through the barn door and out into the cold air. The icy air filled her lungs, as her chest heaved with fresh sobs. Guilt consumed her as she made her way up the slippery path alone toward the house.

When she reached the kitchen door, her brother and Rachel still sat at the table sipping coffee. She froze in her tracks for a moment before bursting into tears.

Seth jumped from his chair. "What did he say to make you cry?"

She looked at her brother, fearing she would faint. She had to get out of there, but he wasn't going to let her go without an answer.

"Tell me what he said to you!"

"He asked me to marry him!"

Seth opened his mouth to speak, but words caught in his throat; his face turning pale.

She broke from her brother's grasp and waddled down the hallway to the guestroom she knew would be waiting for her. She closed the door behind her, feeling safe from his prying eyes. Collapsing onto the bed, she let go of all the tears she'd been suppressing for almost a year.

Chapter 5

Elijah felt the bottom drop out of his plans as the woman he loved rejected him for the second time. Why had she come back here if she had no intention of accepting his proposal? He paced the barn floor for several minutes, talking to himself, trying to reason with himself to explain her rejection.

Hadn't her betrayal been enough?

Funny, but he hadn't felt betrayed—until now.

Feeling completely discouraged, he waited for her to go in the house and then walked toward his buggy. Snow pelted his warm cheeks, stinging him, but it almost felt numb compared to the pain from his broken heart.

He heard the screen door of the house slam shut against the frame and looked back, his heart skipping a beat as he hoped just for a second that Amber had come to her senses and changed her mind.

No such luck.

Seth held up a hand to him as he hopped in his buggy and picked up the reins, his horse lifting his front hooves impatiently. Elijah didn't want to stay there any longer, and Seth holding him back from leaving felt like an intrusion on his emotions. He wanted to go home and bury his head and his shame and embarrassment. She'd done it to him again. She'd rejected him all over again, and this time he wasn't sure he could get over it.

Seth stood there for a moment looking at his best friend, and wondering what he could've been thinking by asking his pregnant sister to marry him. He refused to believe Elijah had fathered her child, but he had to know the truth.

"What happened here?" Seth asked. He kept his tone even, and suppressed the primal urged to challenge his friend to a fight for his sister's honor.

Elijah just sat there staring straight ahead and shrugged. "I have no idea what just happened here," he said. "I asked your *schweschder* to marry me, and she turned me down."

Seth looked at Elijah, confusion filling him. "Why?" He asked. "Why would you ask her to marry you unless the *boppli* she's carrying is yours? Is there something I need to know that you've been holding back from me or keeping from me?"

Elijah shook his head. "I'm not the *boppli's vadder*," he said. "But you know I've always loved your *schweschder*."

"I'm sure this is none of my business," Seth said. "Or my own sister or my best friend would have told me long before shocking me with this news. I'd like to know what's going on, but if you think I should wait to hear it from Amber then I understand."

Elijah pulled off his black felt hat and swiped his hand through his thick hair. "I'm in the middle of this mess, and I don't understand it myself. I don't know how I can explain it to you any better than she could. I thought that our future was set and that we had come to an agreement, but now that it's a reality I'm not so sure."

Seth put a hand on his friends arm and patted his shoulder. "You know you've always been like a

Bruder to me, and I've always been ready to welcome you into *mei familye*, but maybe you need to give her some space to sort things out. There's obviously more involved from what I'm seeing and hearing from the two of you, and perhaps once we sort this out it'll all work out."

"I pray that you're right, Seth." He said. "Will you tell her that I'll be here after the evening meal to take her for that sleigh ride I promised her."

Seth patted him again. "I'll let her know."

Elijah slapped the reins against his horse and set him off riding down the long lane that went away from his friend's house. He tried not to let discouragement cloud his judgment, but he just couldn't help but wonder what he had been thinking by entering into such an agreement with Amber.

Did he dare to change his mind at the eleventh hour, even if it meant he'd likely be looked upon as a traitor of his friendship with Seth?

Chapter 6

Elijah drove his sleigh across the snowy fields to get to Seth's house to pick up Amber as promised. His stomach roiled, and he felt the burn of acid trying to force its way up. Aware that his nerves teetered on the brink, he decided not to push her for an answer. He'd spend a nice evening with her and see how things progressed before making another attempt to bring up the proposal. He knew that preparations were already being made at the B&B for the wedding on Christmas Eve, but he would be the one left looking like the fool if she changed her mind. He knew the Bakers had offered to take care of her and the baby, but Amber didn't want to be without a husband, and she wanted her child to have a father.

He'd proven his worth to her; his willingness to be everything she needed him to be, but he feared being made a fool of a second time by her. When she'd left for her *rumspringa,* he'd wanted to go too, but feared he'd push her further away if he did. He'd put off his own baptism, waiting for her to return, and it turned out his instinct paid off, or he would be shunned for marrying her. Though his family wasn't happy he hadn't joined the church, they were happy that he would finally be marrying the woman he'd loved since they were children.

Amber walked cautiously through the house, hoping she wouldn't run into Seth before she left for her sleigh ride with Elijah. They'd had an awkward dinner after she explained her situation to her overprotective brother. He'd warned her that she would need to face their parents tomorrow, and they would expect to be invited to her wedding to Elijah—that is if she went through with it.

She knew deep in her heart that marrying Elijah would make her happy, and provide security for her and the baby, but she had to be sure that she still loved him—she'd loved him all her life, but she'd not taken him into consideration when she'd gone off and married Jake Baker. For that, she felt unworthy of his kindness toward her. And although she hadn't really loved Jake the way a wife should, she still wished he could be there to help raise their child. It felt strange that she would be raising the child with Elijah.

She yawned as she looked out at the snow swirling around; she'd tried to take a nap before dinner, but she'd felt too anxious. Now she felt almost too tired, she wished she could call off the sleigh ride, but she knew she needed time to talk to Elijah about the wedding. She'd hurt his feelings earlier when she'd panicked about his proposal, but now that she'd had a talk with her very logical brother, he'd set her straight on the importance of having her family around to help. She wouldn't be as close to them if she returned to the city with the Bakers.

It would seem there were a lot of reasons she *should* marry Elijah, but the biggest needed to be that she still loved him—truly loved him. She'd already had one loveless marriage, and didn't want another. They had a strong friendship, but in the end, it wouldn't have been enough to last forever, and though it lasted until death parted them, it might not have had the strength needed to survive a lifetime commitment. Her marriage to Elijah had that potential, but she needed to be certain.

When the sound of jingling bells reached her ears, she looked at the clock on the kitchen wall, noting Elijah had arrived almost twenty minutes late; that wasn't like him.

Had he been late because he'd considered changing his mind?

She couldn't bear the thought of it.

Chapter 7

Elijah took Amber's hand and led her safely to his sleigh. He made nervous small-talk about the snow, carefully avoiding anything that might upset her. He knew from talks with Seth about Rachel's pregnancy that women in that condition could be very emotional, and jumping into a conversation about marriage again would likely escalate those emotions tonight. He doted on her, making her his main focus, creating an atmosphere pleasant enough to rekindle their friendship.

Tucking the heavy lap-quilts around her, Elijah urged his team of horses forward, causing the jingling of the bells to set the romantic mood for their sleigh ride. Intermittent moonlight illuminated the path just enough to light the way through the fields of snow.

Amber leaned into Elijah and he put his arm around her, feeling a spark of hope rise up in him.

"I'd forgotten how romantic sleigh rides could be," she said, surprising him.

He agreed with her, but he mostly kept silent. He'd decided to let her do the leading for the night, and they would move at *her* pace. With only five days until the wedding, he felt pressured to secure an answer from her, but he kept quiet about the subject. Instead, he rattled on about the weather, and his delight over sharing her company, knowing her willingness to be out with him would have to serve as her answer—for now.

"*Jah,*" he said. "I brought hot *kaffi* in a thermos; it's under the seat if you want some."

"Perhaps when we stop to give the horses a break," she said. "Right now, all I want to do is enjoy the snowflakes and the sound of the jingle bells."

She leaned into him a little more, putting a smile on his face. It would seem that he had reason to hope all would work out, and she would be his wife in only a few days, and soon after that, he'd be a father.

Though he wanted children of his own, he'd made a vow to her and to God that he would raise her child as his own.

Amber sat upright suddenly. "Oh!" she said.

He looked at her as her hand went to her abdomen.

He slowed the team. "Am I going to fast? I'm not hurting you, am I? This won't cause you to go into labor, will it?"

She giggled. "Stop worrying, silly!" she said. "It seems the *boppli* likes the jingle bells, at least the sudden kicks I'm feeling would suggest it."

He looked at her with wide eyes. "The *boppli* can hear the bells jingling?"

Amber let out another giggle, her hand still on her belly. "Of course she can—or *he!*"

"*Ach,* do you think it would be alright if I felt the kicking?"

She smiled, grabbing his hand and setting it on the top of her enlarged abdomen where the kicks were poking at her ribs.

Elijah stopped the team at the edge of Goose Pond and turned to Amber, his hand still on her belly, his full concentration on the kicking baby.

"He sure active, isn't he?"

Amber pursed her lips. "What makes you so sure this *boppli* is a boy?" she asked.

"I'm not," he said. "Just hoping, that's all. If it were up to me, we'd have a dozen boys."

Amber gasped. "A dozen! You expect me to carry eleven more *bopplin,* and all boys? What if I want a girl?"

Elijah smiled. "You can have one after we have all the boys."

She narrowed her eyes. "After all that? I'll be too tired!"

"We can space them out so you can rest in between, but it would be nice if humans were like cats, because then you could have a whole litter at once."

Amber burst into tears. "You want me have a *litter* of *boppli's?"*

"Nee, I didn't mean it like that!"

She scooted away from him. "Please take me back to *mei bruder's haus.*"

"Did I say something wrong?"

She wouldn't answer him; she wouldn't even look at him.

Apparently, he had!

Chapter 8

Amber sat silent beside Elijah, her chin jutted out, while he steered the sleigh toward her brother's farm. His mind reeled with possible excuses to keep her out longer with him, but she'd stirred up a fire in him that brought heat to his cheeks. He took a mental inventory of how many days he had left to get her to agree to marry him, and it didn't look promising. If he wanted to marry her by the week's end, he'd better figure out a way to keep his foot from getting in the way when he spoke to her. Right now, he felt as if that foot had wedged itself in his mouth so tightly, there would be no getting it out of there.

Should he even bother to tell her he didn't *have* to have a dozen boys? It wasn't like he'd made it a deal-breaker or anything. The only trouble with that;

he'd already said it, and things like that had a way of sticking with you once they were said, and could not be un-said.

And so he remained quiet.

The wind gusts and whirlwind of snowflakes caused her to burrow under the heavy lap-quilts while Elijah urged his team through the winter storm to take her home as she'd requested.

Another failed attempt at getting close to her.

Would he ever get the chance to make things right with Amber? It had been so easy when they were young, but everything changed when she'd left for her *rumspringa*. The bottom had dropped out of his world that day, and to look at her, he would have to say the same thing for her.

If only she hadn't gone. But if she hadn't, would he be getting ready to marry her now? Perhaps things had to work out this way in order for them to get to where they were now; but where exactly was that?

He looked over at her shivering frame and reached an arm around her, tucking her close. Though her silence bothered him, he would fulfill his obligation to protect her. The moon had hidden itself behind a thick band of clouds, and the fury of snowflakes assaulted them with an icy chill that mirrored the mood between them.

"I'm sorry," he finally said, breaking the silence between them.

One of them had to say it, and he figured he ought to be man enough to admit he'd pushed her too far. He loved her, and he wanted to marry her, but the answer to that question would be up to her, without any pressure from him.

She kept her face forward, but didn't say a word.

"The silent treatment might have worked when we were children, but we're about to be parents ourselves, and I think it's time we talked this through. I love you and I want to marry you, and I'm trying to put myself in your shoes. I have no idea how I would feel being pressured to marry before a proper mourning period had passed, but sometimes, when you're a grownup, you have to do things that might feel wrong, but in your heart you know it's right."

He didn't wait for an answer from her; he hopped down from the sleigh and took her hand to assist her, and then walked her to her brother's door.

He prayed her silence came from being deep in thought and prayer herself about their future, and tried to shrug it off. A lump formed in his throat, but he swallowed it down.

He'd planned his whole life around her, and now his future rested in her hands.

He had no other choice but to trust her, and his faith.

Chapter 9

Amber tried on one dress after another, trying to find one that didn't show off her protruding belly as much, but it was no use; her father would take one look at her and pass judgment before she had a chance to open her mouth to explain. If she could get through dinner without crying her eyes out, it would be a miracle. On top of her already jangled nerves, she'd foolishly invited Elijah to join them, hoping it would cushion the blow with her parents, but she still hadn't given him an answer, and she felt that had the makings for a stressful evening.

She fanned her fingers, holding her left hand out so she could admire the ring Jake had given her. All these months without him, the ring had served to comfort her. Women in public had admired the ring and commented on it, and having it on her finger had somehow made her feel less conspicuous—less widowed. Reaching with her right hand, she wiggled it off her finger, pausing before pulling it away. She felt funny without it—empty in a way.

She wrapped it in a swatch of blue fabric she'd snatched from the top of Rachel's sewing box and tucked it in the small bureau drawer. Fanning her fingers, she felt unprotected, but her *daed* would frown upon such an *Englisch* trinket. She knew what the ring represented in the *Englisch* world, and for that reason alone, it made her feel less abandoned in her time of confinement. That ring had given her cause to hold her head up when people stared at her—always alone, and always vulnerable. When asked about her husband and his excitement over the impending birth, she was able to tell them with her head held high that she was a widow; sympathy would quickly follow her admission, in which case, filled her with a temporary comfort.

Her father would call that prideful, but she would call it survival.

Whether she could admit it or not, Jake's death had traumatized her in some ways, perhaps the very reason she had put off answering Elijah. The possibility of becoming a widow again sent shivers through her. What if Elijah's health failed? She couldn't go through that again, especially not with a husband she loved as much as she loved Elijah.

Glancing up in the mirror, her large abdomen became her focal point. If not for the child she carried and the promise she'd made to Jake and Elijah, she'd run back to the city and hide. Truth be told, she wanted to be married. She felt too vulnerable without a husband, but getting married again didn't come without risk.

A knock at the door startled her, but her gaze did not leave her own reflection. She wished she could collapse into herself and hide from her family. Her brother had been an easy one to face in comparison to what her stern father would have to say when he saw her condition.

The doorknob slowly turned, and she couldn't find her voice to prevent entry from the unwelcome intrusion.

Rachel poked her head through the breech in the door. "Your *mamm* and *daed* are here and they're anxious to see you."

Amber smoothed her hands over her enlarged belly, showing it off and turning to the side to glance in the mirror at the enormity of it. "They won't be so anxious to see me when they see this." She pointed to her stomach, tears filling her eyes.

Rachel took her hands and led her to the bed and sat opposite her on the freshly-made quilt.

"*Nee,* they know about the *boppli,* and they're happy to *wilkum* new *grandkinner* to the *familye.* "

"*Ach,* how do they know?" Amber could feel the blood draining from her face, her breath catching as she strangled the cries threatening to escape her constricted throat.

"Elijah went to them and told them about Jake; then he asked your *vadder* permission to marry you. He knew you dreaded facing them, and he knows how vulnerable you feel being a widow; he had a long talk with Seth, and this was the result. He paved the way for you with your *familye* so you could relax and enjoy this time with them."

Amber wiped a tear that clung to her cheek. "He did that for me?"

He'd always done the same thing when they were young and they'd found themselves in a little bit of trouble. He'd taken the blame for many messes she'd gotten herself into as a young girl; and now, he had willingly taken the burden from her again and made things right with her *daed*.

How would she ever be able to thank him for such a selfless gift? She supposed an answer to his proposal would do it.

She smiled, and Rachel hugged her.

"Let's go visit with *mei familye* and *mei* fiancé," Amber said.

Rachel returned the smile and walked out to greet the family with her sister and friend.

Chapter 10

Elijah greeted them in the hall and asked to speak to Amber in private before they went out to meet up with the family. She nodded, and Rachel smiled before leaving them alone in the hallway.

She knew he intended to propose, and this time she felt confident she could listen to him without rejecting his offer of marriage.

He waited for Rachel to walk into the kitchen so they could have a private moment before joining the family for what would turn out to be a noisy and chaotic dinner, but enjoyable, nonetheless.

Taking her hands in his, Elijah lifted them to his cheek and held them there, his eyes closed as if he needed a moment to gather his thoughts.

Amber's heart thumped heavily behind her ribcage, and although it was quite chilly in the house, she felt a warmth wash over her, cloaking her with a familiar love.

He paused, searching her hazel eyes for any sign that she might still reject him. He sucked in a deep breath, holding it there momentarily, preparing himself for the worst.

She smiled softly, realizing how hard it must be for him to deal with an emotional pregnant woman. She wanted so much to put an end to this torture and tell him yes, but she could see by the look on his face that he needed to ask her.

He cleared his throat. "You know I love you, Amber," he said, taking another deep breath as if to brace himself for rejection. "I've loved you since we were *kinner*. I've wanted to marry you almost my entire life. I'd like to raise your *boppli* as my own flesh and blood, no matter if it's a boy or a girl, I'll still love it. Will you and your *boppli* become *mei familye*? Will you marry me?"

She smiled at his endearing proposal, feeling more ready than ever to marry Elijah once and for all. "*Jah*, I'll marry you; we both will." She patted her belly and smiled as he pulled her into his arms and placed a gentle kiss on her lips.

Despite their long history together, he had never kissed her before, and she hadn't expected it to be so electrifying. She deepened the kiss, allowing him to envelop her in his love, a love that she returned easily.

After a few minutes of being lost in kisses that she never knew could be so wonderful, he pulled away from her gently, and smiled proudly.

"Our *familye* will be wondering what has happened to us."

"I don't care," she said, collapsing against him and burying her head against his chest. She needed to listen to his heart beating, needed to know that he was alive and well. That he wouldn't leave her. She pushed down fear as his arms enveloped her, holding her close to his heart.

He indulged her for several minutes, realizing she needed a moment to rid herself of a year's worth of fear that had built up in her like a stone wall around her heart. Her heart had hardened by her circumstances, but now he could feel her relaxing in his arms. When her breathing calmed, he kissed the top of her head and urged her out toward the kitchen where her family eagerly waited to see her.

Amber tucked her arm into Elijah's, and the two of them walked out into the kitchen where family members stopped every conversation to turn around and look at them as they entered the room. With all eyes on them, most of which immediately traveled to her obvious pregnancy, Amber tensed. Elijah put a hand on the arm she had tucked in his elbow and patted it protectively.

"She agreed to marry me!" he burst out to the crowd.

Pitying looks quickly turned to smiles, and the roar of laughter and multiple voices ringing out *congratulations* to them filled the room with a lighter feeling. Thankful for the distraction, Amber allowed a smile to creep along her lips, and she breathed in a sigh of relief. Her mother practically threw herself into Amber's arms and began to sob.

"Mei boppli is having a boppli." She cried and laughed at the same time.

Before she realized, her father joined them in one big hug, and Amber began to cry happy tears too, surprised by, and grateful for all the family and community support she had.

Chapter 11

Elijah assisted Amber into his sleigh so they could try once more for their first official *date*. Even though they would be married in two days, their circumstances were unusual, and the Bishop had allowed them one year to take the baptism without risk of the ban. It would be a very lenient ban, if anything, since neither had taken the baptism yet. They were both delighted they could remain in the community with their family and friends, even if they had to be married by a Mennonite preacher. Amber almost preferred that, if for no other reason than it would mean a shorter ceremony and less time on her swollen feet.

She'd almost forgotten what a kind man Elijah was. She'd forgotten how much she loved him and cared for him her entire life, but now it was all coming back to her, while her emotions urged her to sit up and take notice. Paying attention to every detail, Amber didn't want to miss a single opportunity to admire all the hard work Elijah had put into their date, right down to adding extra jingle bells to the harnesses, making the romantic allure of the sleigh ride even more intense.

She giggled at the magic of the night, her breath crystalizing in front of her in rolling puffs of blue against the full moon. Pulling the large lap quilts up a little closer around her shoulders, Elijah sheltered her from the feather-light snow that swirled around.

"I brought a thermos of hot cocoa," he said, dipping his head near hers and smiling. "I'll get you some when we park the sleigh on the edge of the pond."

"You thought of everything, didn't you?" She giggled.

"I tried," he said with a smile.

She ran her hand along her abdomen, wondering what Jake would think if he could see her now with Elijah. Funny that she would think of him at this moment, but she supposed there would be plenty of other times in the future when she would think about what he might be missing out on with their child. She said a quick prayer in her head, asking God to relieve her of the guilt she felt, and to give her the strength to move on completely; holding back in any way would not be fair to Elijah, who had waited long enough for her to return his love fully.

This time when he stopped the sleigh in front of the pond, she didn't resist his advance on her. He pulled her close; protecting her from a sudden gust of wind. Pressing his lips to her warm neck, she closed her eyes, relishing the desire in her heart for him. She turned her head toward him, burying her face in his neck and breathing him in. The smell of warm hay and hickory smoke reminded her of many winters helping him smoke meat in his family's smoke house.

When he pressed his lips to hers, her whole body felt a surge of excitement as if he'd shocked her with a spark of static electricity when their lips touched. She smiled, thinking how much she liked kissing him. His lips were soft and warm; a welcome contact in the cold night air. Despite the fact they'd planned to marry almost their entire growing years, he'd never tried to kiss her even when they were teens; she had no idea why she'd never kissed him because she certainly did enjoy it.

"I love you, Amber," he said.

She leaned in and kissed him again. "I love you too, Elijah."

She meant it with all her heart.

Chapter 12

Amber had tried all morning to ignore the achy feeling in her back, but now those aches and pains began radiating around her front as well. She'd experienced early contractions several times in her last weeks of pregnancy; the doctor had called them *Braxton-Hicks* contractions.

The contractions she felt now, however, were strong enough to take her breath away. Visions of herself collapsing in front of all the wedding guests filled her with fear. The pains, now time-able, could have the potential to put tears in her eyes. She looked in the mirror practicing the smile she would keep on her face until the end of the wedding. She could fool everyone into believing she was simply tired, couldn't she?

Being Christmas Eve, friends and family members had gathered at the B&B for the wedding. She could hear the low rumblings of conversation and muffled laughter downstairs where they all gathered. Becca had been kind enough to reserve them a room for after the wedding, allowing her access now to ready herself for the ceremony.

From the sound of the voices, she wondered if the entire community had shown up for this day. She crossed to the window and peeked down at the long line of buggies parked along the long driveway that led to the B&B. All the horses had apparently been put up in the large barn, and she was thankful Becca and Noah had thought of everything, right down to the very details of decorating the chapel, where they held weddings, with her holiday favorite; poinsettias. She'd had the pleasure of admiring them earlier last evening when she'd arrived at the B&B to stay in the very room where Elijah would be joining her after the ceremony.

Another sharp pain startled her, but she continued to get ready. She intended to be married before she had this baby, especially since it wasn't due for almost another week. Breathing in and out slowly until the contraction subsided, she wondered if she would be able to fool everyone who'd shown up to witness her marrying Elijah.

A swift knock at the door made her jump, her heart now racing. Quickly dabbing at beads of sweat that had formed on her brow, she drew in a deep breath and let it out slowly as the door opened.

Rachel poked her head in the door, and as she peered in, she paused, noticing Amber's distress.

"Are you alright?" she asked.

Rushing to Amber's side, she leaned into her, allowing her to collapse against her with the next contraction.

"I'm certain it's my nerves putting me into another false labor," Amber said. She was trying to make excuses, but she could tell by the concern on Rachel's face, she wasn't convinced.

"Will you be able to get through the ceremony? We can do this another day when you're feeling more relaxed."

"No!" Amber begged. "Please don't tell Elijah I'm feeling poorly; he'll insist we wait, and I *need* to be married before this *boppli* arrives. Promise me you won't say anything."

Rachel hesitated as Amber winced through another contraction. "They're too close together to be false labor!"

Amber shook her head. "They were this bad last night when I was trying to sleep, but they went away after an hour; I've been like this an hour already, so they ought to stop themselves any moment. Let me rest for a minute and calm down, then I'll be ready."

"If you're certain," Rachel said. She was reluctant to leave her friend, but she had to go out and stall the guests for another few minutes at least.

Once alone again, Amber prayed for a calm spirit so she could go out there and marry Elijah and get through the day without any more of these false pains. She took in a deep breath and rose to her feet just as her father entered the room to escort her to the ceremony.

He bent toward her and kissed her forehead. "I'm proud of you, *dochder*. You're doing the right thing, marrying Elijah. He'll be *gut* to you and the *boppli.*"

A lump formed in her throat, but she would not cry—not even happy tears. It was her wedding day and nothing was going to spoil it now that she knew her father was proud of her. His words comforted her, bringing her the peace she needed to move forward with her life.

Her gaze traveled to the many smiling members of the community; people she'd grown up knowing, who'd come to support her on this special day. The unconditional love among her family and friends could only be matched by the look of pure joy in Elijah's eyes as she took her place beside him in front of the Mennonite preacher.

They joined hands and he smiled at her; a pain nearly caused her to wince, but she forced a smile and faced the preacher, begging him silently to hurry so she could rest. Taking a deep breath, she righted herself, knowing she didn't really want to rush through the ceremony; it was something to be cherished.

Elijah noticed how tense Amber had gotten, and her breathing seemed strained. He feared she might back out of the ceremony, but every time he glanced in her direction, she smiled a reassuring smile at him. Suddenly clenching his arm, he looked over at the furrow in her brow and the bead of sweat that had formed along her hairline. His heart raced at the possibility she would back out before the ceremony ended.

"And do you, Amber, take Elijah to be your lawfully wedded husband, to love and to cherish, to honor and obey in sickness and in health, in good times and bad, for as long as you both shall live?" the preacher asked.

"No! Not now!" Amber squealed.

Elijah felt faint; his heart sped up and his legs wobbled underneath him. *"Why not?"* he barely whispered before looking at her.

Sobs consumed her as she stared at the puddle of water at her feet. She doubled over and cried out. "I need to lie down!"

Elijah snaked his arm around her to hold her up.

"What's wrong?" he asked.

"My water broke, and—I'm—having—the *boppli,"* she groaned through a hard contraction.

Rachel and Hannah rushed to her side, whisking her away toward her rented room with the help of her *mamm,* Elijah on their heels.

"Wait," Amber cried out. "I want to finish the ceremony."

Doctor Davis, who'd been a wedding guest, went out to his buggy to get his medical bag so he could work with Hannah and Rachel, who were the community midwives.

"Wait," Amber said again, against the advice of *mamm* and her husband-to-be. "I don't want to have this *boppli* unless I'm married. Please get the preacher!"

Elijah turned to Rachel. "Will you get him, please?"

She ran back down the stairs and convinced the preacher to finish the ceremony *upstairs* at Amber's bedside before she gave birth.

He smiled and agreed after Rachel made her excuses to the rest of the family and community who'd shown up to witness the nuptials.

When they arrived at the room, the preacher waited until Amber was comfortable in bed, Elijah and her *mamm* at her bedside.

Elijah's face lit up when he saw the preacher out there waiting when Rachel opened the door. He felt just as anxious to get through the ceremony as Amber did, but he would never tell her that. He would agree to marry her in-between contractions if that's what she wanted; he loved her that much.

He held her hand through a tough contraction as Rachel and Hannah began to ready things in the room for the birth that seemed eminent. He smiled, his heart warmed at the thought of sharing such a precious event with her.

She looked up toward the door and saw the preacher. *"Please!"* she begged. "Marry us before the *boppli* gets here!"

He looked to Amber's *mamm* to give him clearance to enter the room.

The woman smirked, holding fast to her daughter's hand the opposite side as Elijah. "If she can still think more about you marrying her than the *boppli* being born, she's got time for you to finish the ceremony, and it's important to her to be married before the wee one arrives."

He entered the room reluctantly, Amber groaning against a painful contraction. He paused at the foot of the bed, not wanting to intrude.

"Please finish the ceremony," Amber's mother urged him. "Elijah is going to have to leave the room if *mei dochder* ain't his *fraa,* and she needs him to be here when the *boppli* arrives."

The preacher nodded. "Very well," he said clearing his throat. "I believe we left off waiting for an answer from Amber; do you take Elijah to be your husband?"

She nodded, wincing and groaning through a contraction. "I do!" she squealed.

He smiled nervously and squirmed. "Well then, by the power vested in me, and before these three witnesses, I pronounce you husband and wife."

He skittered toward the door, and turned his head just slightly. "You may kiss your bride if you'd like to," he said over his shoulder before leaving the room.

Neither of them cared that he rushed through to the end of the ceremony, skipping most of it. He'd said the most important part; he'd pronounced them married.

Elijah pressed his lips to Amber's and she kissed him back only for a moment before pushing him back and letting out a loud groan.

"Breathe with her," her *mamm* suggested to Elijah, demonstrating for him. She knew it was important that her daughter lean on her husband in a time such as this, and she'd been helping her so far, but realized it was time to step back and let her daughter be a wife, and Elijah a husband.

He did as his new mother-in-law suggested, keeping Amber's focus away from the pain. He felt thankful he could do something to help her, not wanting to see her in pain.

Another contraction started almost immediately after the last one, and Elijah sat on the edge of the bed facing Amber while the women and the doctor readied everything, trying to give her as much privacy as possible.

"I have to push," she squealed.

"Go ahead," Doctor Davis said. "Bear down."

Elijah slid onto the bed and propped her up in his arms so she could push. She squeezed his hands and groaned through a long push.

"Hold your breath for just a moment," the doctor warned. "The baby is crowning, and we need to ease the head out slowly, so try not to push."

Amber pulled in a deep breath and held it until the doctor told her she could let out the breath.

She and Elijah smiled at one another after the doctor cleaned the baby's face and nose, clearing the mouth; the half-birthed infant letting out a little cry.

"One more push should give us a baby," he said with a smile.

Amber groaned, pushing with all her might as the baby slipped from her loins.

"It's a boy!" Elijah said with a smile.

Hannah and Rachel quickly wrapped the infant in blankets after the doctor tied and cut the cord. Then, they placed him in Amber's waiting arms.

Elijah touched his new son's cheek and put his finger on his hand, allowing him to grip his extended finger. "What're we going to name him?"

"I've given this a lot of thought," Amber said. "I know we didn't take time to discuss it, but I'd like to name him after *both* of his *vadders*. I was thinking Jacob Elijah sounds nice."

"I think that's a fine name," Elijah said proudly.

"Well, I had a name picked out for a girl, but I had a feeling it was a boy all along; you got your first boy; only eleven more to go, and then I can have my girl!" she said with a smirk.

"I didn't really mean that!" he said with a sigh. "You know that, right?"

"No!" Amber said with a squeal.

Rachel was suddenly at her side, whisking away little Jacob at the doctor's insistence.

Elijah turned around to face him, worry consuming him.

"What's wrong," he asked, while his wife cried out and squeezed his hand.

"We've got another baby crowning," he said calmly. "Don't push!"

Elijah could feel the blood draining from his face. "Another *boppli?*" he asked. "How many are in there?"

"Just one more," the doctor assured him.

He whipped his head around to face Amber.

"You knew and you didn't tell me?"

She pushed through a contraction, feeling weak.

"Doctor Davis thought he heard another heartbeat only yesterday when he examined me, and he only suspected; *mei mamm* and Rachel were the only ones I told because they knew more about these things than I did, and I wanted their advice. I'm sorry, but I didn't want to say anything unless I was sure; I guess I'm sure now!"

He squeezed her hand and smiled. "It doesn't matter; two will make us twice as happy."

She groaned again, birthing her second child—a girl.

Tears filled Elijah's eyes at the sight of her. "I have a *sohn* and a *dochder*. *Danki* for making me a *vadder* and a husband in one day. I feel like the luckiest *mann* in the world."

Amber giggled and cried at the same time. "I'm the luckiest woman!" she said. "*Danki* for sharing this with me. *Danki* for loving me enough to be a husband to me and a *vadder* to *mei kinner.*"

Rachel swaddled the infant and handed her to Amber. "What are you going to name this wee one?" she asked.

Amber looked up at her friend and smiled widely, then turned to her mother. "Her name is Rachel, after the *two* most important women in my life."

Her *mamm's* lower lip quivered as she held out her arms to hold her namesake. Cooing to the wee one, she kissed her. "*Wilkum* to the *familye*," she said to her. "I'm going to spoil you and your *bruder*."

Rachel bent down and hugged her friend, tears welling up in her eyes. "I'm so glad I could be here for you on your special day, and I'm happy Jesse has two new cousins! Our *kinner* will grow up together as cousins, just like we always said so when we were *kinner* ourselves. Ain't it a miracle how *Gott* seems to work everything out?"

Amber smiled as she looked at her family, both old and new, feeling abundantly blessed with more miracles than she ever thought possible.

THE END

ATTENTION:

ALL my future books will be offered SUPER DISCOUNTS for the FIRST few days ONLY! If you would like to be informed of new books published so you can take advantage of this special price, PLEASE sign up HERE for my email list, to take advantage of this SPECIAL OFFER before the book goes to regular price. Thank you!

SEE the next books in this series...

Please enjoy the sneak preview chapter of

Amish Suspense, The Amish Girl: Book One

Collection is now on Kindle HERE

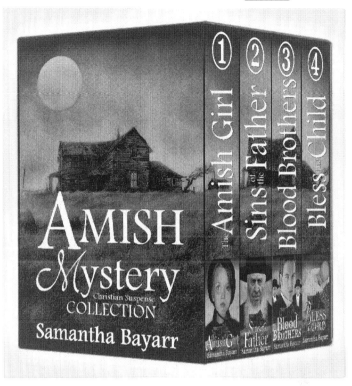

The Amish Girl

Samantha Jillian Bayarr

A note from the Author:

While this novel is set against the backdrop of an Amish community, the characters and the names of the community are fictional. There is no intended resemblance between the characters in this book or the setting, and any real members of any Amish or Mennonite community. As with any work of fiction, I've taken license in some areas of research as a means of creating the necessary circumstances for my characters and setting. It is completely impossible to be accurate in details and descriptions, since every community differs, and such a setting would destroy the fictional quality of entertainment this book serves to present. Any inaccuracies in the Amish and Mennonite lifestyles portrayed in this book are completely due to fictional license. Please keep in mind that this book is meant for fictional, entertainment purposes only, and is not written as a text book on the Amish.

Happy Reading

Chapter 1

Ten-year-old Amelia bolted upright in bed, her heart racing from the crack of lightning that split the air on such a quiet, summer night. The crickets' song had suddenly stopped, and all she could hear was the muffled sound of her own heart beating.

Tilting her head to listen, her eyes bulged in the dark room as she tried to focus. The pale moonlight filtered in through the thin curtains beside her bed, a gentle breeze fluttering the sheers against the sill. Outside her window, the cornstalks in the field swayed, flapping their leaves with a familiar rhythm.

It smelled like rain was on the way.

She sucked in a ragged breath, her exhale catching as if she was out of air. Her heart beat faster still, fear flowing through her veins like ice water. A bead of sweat ran down her back between her shoulder blades, causing her to shiver.

Had she been dreaming?

Scooting to the edge of the bed, her legs felt a little wobbly as she let her feet down easy against the cool, wood floor. It was a comfort on such a warm night, though it increased her risk of wetting her pants.

She reached for the door handle, but pulled her hand away, the hair on the back of her neck prickling a warning. Tip-toeing back to her bed, she climbed in under the quilt, crossing her legs and leaning on her haunches to keep from wetting herself.

An unfamiliar voice carried from the other room, causing her heart to race and her limbs to tremble. It was an angry voice.

Another shot rent the air. It was the same noise that had woken her.

Her mother cried out, calling her father's name.

"*Mamm,*" Amelia whispered into the night air.

Once again, she pushed back the light quilt, her need to see her mother forcing her wobbly legs to support her tiny frame. Moving slowly, she made sure to be quiet, cringing every time the floor planks creaked.

It was unlike her parents to be so loud in the middle of the night, but something was terribly wrong.

Wondering who belonged to the mysterious voice, she listened to him arguing with her mother. Her voice was shaky, like she was crying, and it frightened Amelia.

"We don't have any money," her mother cried. "Please don't do this!"

Where was her father, and where had the other man come from? Who was this man, and why was he upsetting her mother? She peeked around the corner from the hallway, spotting a man dressed in black, with a gun raised and pointed at her mother.

Amelia shook, and her teeth chattered uncontrollably.

A single lantern flickered from the table, her eyes darted around the dimly-lit room, trying to place her father. She pulled in another ragged breath when she spotted him lying on the floor, blood pooling around his head. The noise that had woken her hadn't been in her dreams, it was the gunshot that had killed her father.

Every instinct in her warned her to hide, but her feet seemed unwilling to take her back to her room.

"This is your last chance," the gunman warned. "If you won't give me my money, you lose your life!"

"No!" she screamed. "Please, I don't have it."

"I had to spend the last ten years in jail for nothing," the man said through gritted teeth.

"While the two of you spent *my* money on this nice farmhouse, and all those acres you have out there? You've been enjoying your life all these years with your horses and chickens and such, while I've been locked away with nothing!"

He aimed the gun at her, and she dropped to the floor, crying and pleading with him to spare her life.

He ignored her pleas.

Amelia shook violently, her gasp masked by a second gunshot, killing her mother right before her eyes.

She let out a strangled cry, and the man holding the gun turned toward her, his eyes locking with hers for a moment.

"Well, now, isn't this a nice surprise!" he said, tilting his head back and laughing madly.

His laugh sent chills through her, causing her bladder to empty uncontrollably.

For a moment, Amelia was paralyzed with fear, her feet unmovable in the puddle of urine.

Lightning lit up the room, a crash of thunder bringing her back to her senses.

She forced her feet to propel her forward, heaving them as if they were chained to the floor. Swinging open the back door, she ran toward the cornfield that separated them from the Yoder farm. Glancing over her shoulder, she looked back to see the man was behind her, hobbling as if he had a lame leg.

"Don't run, little Amish girl," he called after her. "I'm not going to hurt you!"

She entered the cornfield, visualizing the path she took on a daily basis when she visited with Caleb, her neighbor and friend. She'd never come through it in the dark, and her mind was too cluttered with fear that ripped at her gut to follow the path. Bile rose in her throat, but she swallowed it down as she ran. Cornstalks whipped at her face and arms, her mind barely aware of the stings that meant they'd drawn blood.

She stumbled, her breath heaving, as she scrambled on her hands and knees long enough to right herself. Her bare feet painfully dug into the rocks and dirt in the field, but her instinct was to stay alive.

The small barn at the back edge of the Yoder property had been a meeting place for her and Caleb. A place where they'd played with the barn cats and their kittens, and washed their horses after a long ride. But most of all, it was a place she knew there was a gun. Caleb had taught her how to shoot it, using tin cans for practice, but she'd never thought to turn it on a human—until now.

The main house was still too far away. Amelia knew her only chance of surviving this man's fury was to surprise him with the unexpected. All she wanted was for him to leave her alone, and she didn't have the physical strength to run any further. Pointing a gun at him the way he'd pointed it at her mother was the only thing on her mind. It drove her to reach the barn before the man who intended to kill her.

All she could think about, as she ran faster than she'd ever run before, was getting her hands on the gun she knew was in the Yoder's barn. The gun would give her power—the power to stop this man from killing her. Neither her *mamm* nor her *daed* had a gun, and now they were dead—both of them. Amelia didn't want to die. It was one of her biggest fears in her short life, and right now, that fear drove her to stay alive at all cost.

She entered the barn out of breath, her eyes struggling to focus. If not for the large window near the tack room filtering in the flashes of lightning, she would not be able to find her way. Crawling under the workbench, Amelia grabbed for the strongbox that housed the gun. The lock on it had long-since been broken, but she shook so much, she struggled to pry open the rusted lid. A flicker of lightning revealed the Derringer inside the metal box, and she snatched it quickly, and cracked the barrel forward. She'd done it a hundred times before when she and Caleb practiced, not knowing she'd ever have to use it to defend herself.

Shoving her shaky hand inside the box of ammunition, she grabbed haphazardly, and then loaded two bullets. Gripping the small handgun, she aimed it toward the door, waiting for her stalker.

"Come out, come out, little Amish girl. I'm not going to hurt you," the man called out to her.

Amelia sucked in a breath and drew the loaded gun out in front of her, darting it back and forth until her eyes focused on her assailant. Lightning blinked him in and out of her sight.

She flinched when he struck a match and lit the lantern hanging up just inside the doorway, turning up the flame until it lit up the room.

Amelia stayed crouched down under the work bench in the tack room, gun extended in front of her. She held her breath when she saw the look in his eyes, and knew he meant to do her harm.

The man spotted Amelia's feet underneath the work bench and smiled widely, but it wasn't a kind smile. "Why are you pointing a gun at me?" he asked. "I'm not going to hurt you!"

Her entire body tensed up, fear making her grip on the gun grow tighter. She stared at him, breathing hard through clenched teeth, her hands shaky.

He laughed at her. "We both know you aren't going to shoot me."

She pulled back the hammer of the gun fast and sure, without taking her eyes off of him.

His hands went up in mock defense, but he laughed nervously. "This isn't funny, Amish girl. I put my gun away, but you better put that gun down before I have to hurt you!"

She raised the gun as he moved slowly toward her, keeping it trained on his heart. Though she only meant to intimidate him the way he was doing to her, she had no intention of pulling the trigger. Her aim was too accurate.

"Put the gun down, little Amish girl," he said through gritted teeth.

Thunder rumbled, making her jump as he lurched toward her.

She let out a scream as she accidentally squeezed the trigger, a single shot discharging with a puff of smoke from the end of the barrel. Her eyes closed against the explosion that rang in her ears like the crack of thunder from the oncoming storm. When the smoke cleared, she could see that the bullet had gone straight through the man's chest, and he'd collapsed to the ground in front of her.

She kept the gun trained on him, staring into his unblinking eyes; her hands shaking and her breath catching, as she strangled the whimpering that intermittently escaped her lips.

She hadn't meant to shoot him; hadn't meant to kill him, but now he was dead—just like her parents.

THE END

This is the end of the free sample chapter.

Remember to get it on sale

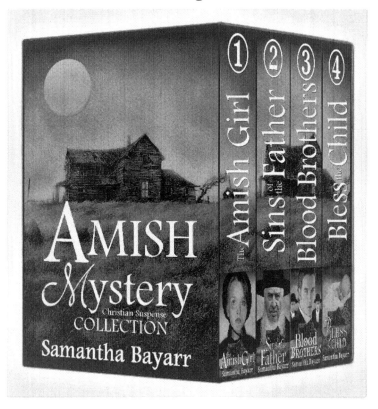

YOU MIGHT ALSO LIKE THESE COLLECTIONS FOR THE SAME LOW PRICE!

573

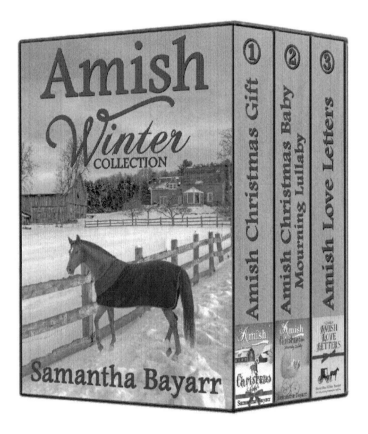

Amish Brides Collection

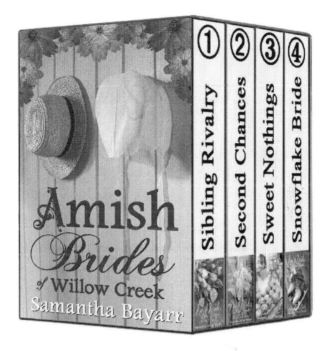

Please LIKE my Facebook Page

ATTENTION:

ALL my future books will be offered SUPER DISCOUNTS for the FIRST few days ONLY! If you would like to be informed of new books published so you can take advantage of this special price, PLEASE sign up for my email list, to take advantage of this SPECIAL OFFER before the book goes to regular price. Thank you!

SEE the next books in this series...

48633662R00353

Made in the USA
San Bernardino, CA
01 May 2017